THE AVON ROMANCE

Kathleen E. Woodiwiss, Johanna Lindsey, Laurie McBain, Shirlee Busbee...these are just a few of the romance superstars that Avon Books has been proud to present in the past.

Since 1982, Avon has been continuing a different sort of romance tradition—a program that has been launching new writers of exceptional promise. Called "The Avon Romance," these books are distinguished by a ribbon motif on the front cover—in fact, you readers quickly discovered them and dubbed them "the ribbon books"!

Month after month, "The Avon Romance" has continued to deliver the best in historical romance, offering sensual, exciting stories by new writers (and some favorite repeats!) *without* the predictable characters and plots of formula romances.

"The Avon Romance." Our promise of superior, unforgettable historical romance...month after dazzling month!

LORI LEIGH

ON THE WINDS OF LOVE

AVON
PUBLISHERS OF BARD, CAMELOT, DISCUS AND FLARE BOOKS

AVON BOOKS
A division of
The Hearst Corporation
1790 Broadway
New York, New York 10019

Copyright © 1986 by Lori Carleton
Published by arrangement with the author
Library of Congress Catalog Card Number: 86-90837
ISBN: 0-380-75072-4

First Avon Printing: August 1986

AVON TRADEMARK REG. U.S. PAT. OFF. AND IN
OTHER COUNTRIES, MARCA REGISTRADA, HECHO
EN U.S.A.

Printed in the U.S.A.

K–R 10 9 8 7 6 5 4 3 2 1

For Joyce and John with love,
with very special thanks to
Laura Ashcroft

ON THE WINDS OF LOVE

Chapter One

In the Year of Grace 1789

The Duchess Lisette de Meret curtsied before the royalty seated on the podium. "I don't intend to stay and watch the exhibition," she whispered to the schoolmistress beside her. Once before she had been naïve enough to sit through an execution. Since then she had decided that never again would she watch a victim climb the stairs to the scaffold, kneel on the pillow, and await the inevitable blow. If it weren't for a dictum from her uncle, King Louis XVI, ordering her to appear at the place de Grève for the execution of a traitor, Lisette would be enjoying a ride on her speckled-gray gelding in the park. But the King expected his niece to honor her position as a duchess and represent the de Meret family—at least she must make an appearance.

"If you leave, it will cause another scandal," the mistress warned in a hushed voice as they rose from the cramped position.

Lisette could imagine the speech the mistress was planning: "On June tenth, the Duchess Lisette de Meret committed the unpardonable sin of ignoring a direct command from the King of France." The girls attending the elegant finishing school would all gasp at the appalling statement.

Vive le Roi, the masses chanted when the King made his entrance. Ignoring the schoolmistress's warning, Lisette slipped into the crowd as the drums rolled to announce the execution would begin. Standing in the center of the square, she had a view of the grand Hôtel de Ville to the north. The windows on the second story were glutted with guests. To the south was the Seine River, where small boats were crowded against the shore as spectators rivaled for the best vantage points. The tower of Notre-Dame was evident against the Paris rooftops, and the bells sounded above the din of hundreds of peasants, tolling in a mournful lament for the man who was about to die.

The King expected her to try to escape, Lisette realized, looking across the plaza. Her uncle was watching her as she crossed the cobbled street to the hôtel. He would scold her at her next visit to the palace, but nevertheless he adored her, and his wrath never lasted long. The King would forgive her for leaving the square, despite what Mistress Prissy said.

Reaching her destination outside the school grounds, Lisette collapsed against the stone wall. With each panting breath the bone stays in her corset bit unmercifully into her ribs. She withdrew an embroidered linen *mouchoir* from her shift pocket and patted the beads of perspiration on her forehead.

Lisette stepped back and surveyed the eight-foot obstacle surrounding the school. She had climbed it often; the cobbled wall held the worn footholds from her previous escapades, which had resulted in many hours in the school's chapel repenting her transgressions. "Thou shalt not climb walls" had become her eleventh commandment.

Hearing the approach of heavy footsteps on the stone walkway, Lisette suddenly sucked in her breath and pressed against the wall. Hidden in the shade of an apple tree, she hoped she wouldn't be seen. What if cranky old Prissy had noticed Lisette had disappeared and sent the executioner after her? Lisette *had* to make it over the crest of the wall and down the branches of the apple tree inside the grounds to elude pursuit.

The climb seemed endless in those dreadful seconds as she heard the footsteps grow louder. She could envision her captor dragging her back to the execution. In her haste, Lisette's foot slipped, and she dangled four feet off the ground.

"Lady Lisette?" came a gentle, familiar voice.

Lisette looked down to see the lopsided grin of her liveryman. "Oh, Patrick! *Mon Dieu,* but you scared me." The strong liveryman gave her a boost to the top of the wall. "I thought you were Charles Sanson and you had come to take me to the scaffold."

Patrick bowed and swept the hat off his graying hair in a gallant gesture. "I am honored to have been of assistance, Duchess de Meret. But what would an executioner want with you?" he teased.

It seemed these days that there wasn't a man, woman, or child who was safe from the executioner's sword. "I don't intend to find out."

Waving to Patrick, Lisette dropped from the tree branch to the neatly manicured lawn of the school grounds. Rows of trimmed hedges hid her from the watchmen hired to protect the young girls from the riots that had recently plagued Paris.

Once in her room, Lisette eased the door shut and sighed in relief as the latch clicked into place. She noticed a white envelope lying on her writing table and hoped the letter was from her handsome fiancé. But the waxed impression held the escutcheon of the Duc de Meret. Disappointed, she broke the seal and withdrew a single page, penned in her father's hand.

My Dearest Missie,

You must come home immediately. Tell no one that you are leaving Paris, no matter how powerful or persuasive.

Philippe de Meret

"Curious," she murmured out loud. "Why the intrigue?" This made no sense at all. Her marriage to Baron Jolbert was only a few weeks away and there didn't seem to be enough time to make all the arrangements. What could the Duc want from her now? Lisette was expected at court to attend the parties that would be given in her honor. She had an appointment on Thursday morning with the court dressmaker to have her wedding gown fitted. The sealed invitations, trimmed in gold, had already been delivered to the best houses in France.

Lisette folded her father's letter and tucked it into her reticule. Perhaps the Baron had had a change of heart and no longer wanted the marriage? No, she assured herself. He wanted it as much as she did. The worn parchments of his few letters were confirmation of his desire to wed her this summer.

Two years had passed since their engagement, and the legend of the Black Baron Jolbert had grown. He had once been a member of the Black Musketeers, she remembered, and had sworn allegiance to the throne of France before the King disbanded them. His loyalty to the King had earned him a soldier's highest honor; he was a *noblesse d'épée,* a feudal baron by military rank who would inherit his father's title of Earl of Normandy.

There were whispers in the court that the Baron

had paid a fortune for Lisette's hand in marriage—
a marriage to the *noblesse de cour,* the royal house.
Prissy never failed to let a day pass without reminding Lisette that she had been purchased, like
a slave at market.

Since her father had sent her to the school, there
had been no love lost between them. The Duc had
used Lisette's betrothal to fill his coffers, and
shortly thereafter, it seemed, he forgot his daughter was alive. He had proposed a number of suitors
to her, among them a bald man nearly fifty years
old, and a stuffy old Austrian duc who never left
his castle and had no teeth. But Lisette's criteria
for a husband were not the same as her father's,
and she shuddered at the thought of being shackled to a toothless old hermit.

Finally, the Duc relented. His daughter's desire
to have a young husband and his own hunger for
money could both be satisfied in a financial settlement with the Jolbert family. The marriage would
end a generations-long feud, bringing peace to the
north shore of France, and would win the Duc the
favor of the King for his diplomatic efforts. And
while her fiancé, the Baron Jean Jolbert, lost a
substantial sum for her hand, he gained a good deal
in social standing and political influence.

Thirty years old at the time of their engagement, the tall, handsome Baron instantly captured Lisette's heart by sending her a bouquet of
white roses on the morning of their first meeting.
The card was signed "Yours faithfully" and struck
a soft spot in Lisette; it would not be difficult to
love, honor, cherish, and obey this man forever.

Finally, after hours of negotiations with her
father, the Baron had taken her away from the
pomp and circumstance of the betrothal, where
both families had turned out in force to honor the
long-awaited treaty. He spoke of his urgent trip to

Spain, and when they were a safe distance away from her chaperon, Jean had drawn her close to him, the feel of hardened muscles against her skin leaving an unforgettable mark on her senses. Lisette had closed her eyes and puckered her lips, waiting for what she was sure would be her first kiss.

Instead, he had laughed, causing the heat of a blush to spread across her fashionably pale cheeks, announcing her chagrin. "You're so very young, *ma chérie.* I feel like an old lecher wanting to make love to you now." The mellow tones of his voice had come from deep within his broad chest as he held her tightly against him.

Lisette had been mortified. "I'm old enough to know what happens in a man's arms."

"I don't believe you, Lisette, and even if I did, I wouldn't touch you now. No, *petite,* I believe you are a spirited virgin."

"Must you be so vulgar?"

" 'Tis no sin to save yourself for your husband. Remember that while I'm away. Someday I will return, and then we shall see how inexperienced you are."

This time Lisette hadn't closed her eyes when his mouth came near. Jean's light kiss had been warm to the touch and tasted of brandy. She had pressed closer to him, the armozine fabric of his black coat slipping through her fingers as she returned his embrace. He was everything she had hoped for in all the wishes made on the crystal rainbows of her boudoir chandelier. This was a man who took what he wanted, and at that moment, Lisette knew that she could give him her heart on a silver tray.

Jean's gentle massage on her shoulders had made her head fall back, and her eyes had closed while a heady feeling swept over her. Nothing else had mattered except to prolong the excitement she found in his arms as the contours of his powerful body awakened her own desires. She had shivered against him, wanting something more and not knowing what it was. As a moan trembled from deep within her throat, Jean had pulled away and looked at her with soft gray eyes. Lisette had known then that her love was sealed. She hadn't expected such tenderness from him, but he had seemed just as reluctant as she to end the magic of the moment.

"Must you go?" she had asked, her voice faltering around the painful lump in her throat.

"Don't forget me, Lisette," he had murmured against her ear. Stepping back, Jean had pinned a brooch on her mantle. It represented the Jolbert crest of a ruby fleury cross against a golden background. Lisette's fingers had traced the smooth gold edge and the brilliant red stone as she realized she was truly a part of his life. *"The Baroness Jolbert,"* she had said over and over to herself, with tear-filled eyes watching him as he walked away. Lisette had prayed for the day Jean would return to her.

That had happened long ago, she sternly reminded herself, mentally shaking the thoughts away. She had matured since then and had a different perspective on her role as his fiancée.

She threw the doors to the armoire open and ruffled through the gowns to find her favorite blue riding habit. Castle Meret was a long day's ride away, and she didn't want to think about the unescorted journey in a time when riots broke out frequently.

Feeling dignified with her chapeau tilted just enough to be fashionable, Lisette opened the oak door to find the headmistress, poised and ready to knock. Trying to look innocent, Lisette stepped back a pace and lowered her gaze to the floor.

"I see that you made it back to your room." She enunciated every word to convey her displeasure.

"*Oui*, Madame. I have been called to court," she lied. Lisette couldn't let this woman, a well-known gossip, know she was leaving Paris, especially without an escort.

"I received no such notice. The King always personally informs me when you are asked to attend him at the palace."

"I have a letter from my father requesting me to meet him at Versailles. I'm certain he simply forgot to notify you. Oh, and there is no need to provide me with an escort. My father has seen to that, also."

Lisette watched the woman's face turn a bright red with suppressed rage. The mistress raised a hand to her eyebrows, in a mock faint. "Lady Lisette, I don't know what to do with you. In the two years that you have been at this school, my patience has been sorely tested. If the charming Baron hadn't come to your rescue and paid the account, I would have tossed you out."

"My father paid the tuition," Lisette protested.

The mistress cocked an eyebrow. "The funds were provided by the charming Baron," she corrected. "Is it true that he paid over a hundred thousand *livres* for the honor of marrying you?"

"That is none of your business."

"You poor little thing." The mistress made a false attempt at offering her sympathies. "You're probably the last person in Paris to know what everyone is talking about. Your father is penniless, and if it weren't for the King's generosity, he'd be in debtors' prison. Why, some say the Duc has designs on the throne."

Lisette closed her eyes for a moment. She wouldn't let Prissy, no more than a *bourgeoise*, get away with mocking her.

"Madame." Lisette enunciated every word. "You forget yourself." How could this woman fancy herself to be Lisette's social peer?

"You . . . you impudent little brat!" the mistress squawked.

"Say one more word," Lisette warned, "and I'll have your head delivered to me in a gilded box."

The woman stood before the young Duchess utterly speechless, her eyes bulging in shock. Prissy gathered her voluminous skirts and stomped down the hall.

Thoughts of the arrogant Prissy were banished as Lisette saw that her speckled-gray thoroughbred was already saddled and waiting to take her home. Patrick always seemed to have a sixth sense when it came to having her horse ready. He handed the reins to her and cupped his hands, helping her to mount. "Will ye ride in the park without an armed escort?"

Her eyes avoided him and he knew better than to ask what new dilemma she was in now. He seemed to know she wouldn't be back.

He led the gelding out of the barn into the warm June afternoon. Patrick gave her a pistol. "Do ye know how to use the weapon, Missie?"

Lisette smiled. She could shoot, but didn't want to take the time to prove it to him, until she saw the mistress waddling across the lawn toward them, yelling, "Halt! Halt! The King will have me on the scaffold if I allow you to leave my school without a proper escort."

Lisette leveled the gun on Prissy. "You can't stop me. Stand aside."

The mistress blocked the gateway to the street with her arms spread wide.

"Desist, or I *will* shoot you," Lisette demanded. To emphasize her threat, Lisette fired a round into the tree near Prissy.

The mistress fainted, dropping to the ground in a lifeless heap.

"Damn!" Lisette whispered. She had wasted the only shot. The pistol would have to be reloaded. Now she would have to take special care not to meet up with the brigands and beggars that roamed the country lanes.

Patrick roared with laughter, and raised a hand in salute as Lisette passed through the gate. "It will take a man with a will of iron to rein that young filly," he said to himself.

Lisette was eager to leave Paris, to discover what urgent matter had prompted her father's mysterious message. But mostly she felt a surge of excitement thinking about how close she was to fulfilling her dream—a dream of spending a lifetime with a tall man with gray eyes.

Chapter Two

Baron Jean Jolbert reined in his black Arabian stallion and scanned the open field for signs of an ambush. The vale presented a peaceful image of milk cows grazing beside a winding brook. Nearby, stonechats nesting in the branches of an apple tree *wheet*ed scoldingly at the invasion of the men on horseback. The untrained eye wouldn't catch the slight stirrings of the Baron's men as they faithfully guarded their leader who awaited the arrival of the Duc de Meret. His private army of a hundred hussars were well seasoned after a two-year campaign of pirating on the high seas; they were fierce in combat, favored patrons of the brothels, but, most important, they accepted Jean's authority with absolute loyalty.

A tall man of six feet three inches, the Baron had a muscular physique honed to perfection by ten years of a nomadic life. His Norman ancestry was apparent in his broad shoulders, but not in his coloring; Jean's hair was as dark as midnight and cut above the shoulders, falling in gentle waves below his earlobes. Pale gray eyes were a gift from his Spanish-bred mother who had died shortly after his birth, leaving her son to a male-dominated household.

Jean had heard a rumor that Lisette had been

betrothed to an English count. If the gossip were true, Jean had been robbed of a fortune and lost the woman he loved. Immediately, the Baron had assembled his hussars and sent a note to Lisette's father, the Duc de Meret, demanding to meet him.

"The Duc *must* answer the summons." His soft whisper was picked up by his friend, Michel, beside him.

"Are you sure you want to meet the Duc before your father returns?" the Marquis asked warily. He removed his tricorn hat and raked his fingers through short, sandy curls in nervous anticipation. "Your papa will want to know if you break the peace treaty and begin the feud between your houses again."

"My *père* will not return for a week yet, maybe two, and I cannot wait that long for his blessing. If the rumors of my broken betrothal to Lady Lisette are true, I must confront the Duc immediately."

"There are other ways of doing these things," Michel continued. "If he won't agree to the ceremony and produce his daughter for your marriage, I could always escort her to your château, and then you can convince her of your honorable intentions. I suspect your charms would be put to much better use with the lady than with her father."

"A gentleman has no need for kidnapping." The low tone in his voice was a warning that the Baron didn't wish to continue the conversation. Jean dreaded this meeting; he feared it would confirm his worst expectations.

"Must you always be so intent on following tradition? This lady doesn't merit a civil war between your families when there are other means of having your way. It isn't worth the trouble, if you ask me."

"I didn't." Jean glared at his friend. He had accepted the hand of a young girl, no more than sixteen years old when the truce was celebrated. And now, several years later, his sources informed him she had become a beautiful young woman, well worth the wait. If only he had been able to see her for himself. He sighed wearily. Family business had kept him in Spain too long while trouble brewed at home; he was sure the Duc de Meret was at the bottom of it.

The worn leather creaked beneath Jean as he fidgeted in his saddle, watching the Duc de Meret approach. Beside the Duc rode a young man with the dark auburn hair typical of the de Merets. This was Darias, a distant cousin to Lisette, who was greedy for the money and prestige of his royal cousins. They would have to be careful of Darias. Jean had been warned that Darias spent a great deal of time whispering into the King's ear and gaining Louis's trust.

Michel picked at his starched lace cuffs. "Shall we slay him right now and save ourselves the trouble of asking what his plans are? You can guess his answer."

The Baron's gray eyes, shadowed beneath the rim of his hat, gave Michel a look which made his blood run cold. "We shall see for ourselves.

"This is a matter of honor and will affect the future control of France. If the Duc is preparing himself for an ascent to the throne when the revolution overtakes the country, then he will need an alliance with England—the only country which could pose a major threat to his rule. The proper marriage arrangements for himself and his daughter would ensure just that, though he doesn't seem to realize there may not be a throne once the peasants reign. The Duc de Meret is as guilty of treason as I am, and I am guilty of far more crimes than the magistrates could ever accuse me of. I must find out for myself if he is the mastermind behind Lisette's impending marriage to an English count. I'm still not certain if my fiancée is in league with her father."

"What if she is?" Michel asked.

"I'll have to dispose of her, also."

Michel shuddered at the thought, certain his friend would do the deed.

The Baron hailed the approaching riders. His horse lifted its head and snorted, sidestepping the oncoming riders in a battle pose.

"Why have you sent for me, Baron Jolbert?" A bitterness sounded in the deep voice of the Duc de Meret. He was outnumbered, and he knew it. The young Baron's arrogance galled him; after all, they were on de Meret land.

"I want to know why you are sending Lady Lisette out of the country." Baron Jean Jolbert barely held his temper.

"To protect her," the Duc answered calmly. "You have been seen conspiring with the revolutionists since your return to France. It is only a matter of time before Louis will issue a *lettre de cachet* and you are arrested. I cannot allow my daughter to marry you under the circumstances. I have betrothed her to another."

Jean knew that anyone who held a *lettre* had total authority over the person named in the document. There was no chance for defense against such a charge, and often the person accused was never seen again. All the Baron wanted was to leave France with his bride and with all of his extremities still intact.

"The revolution is coming regardless of what you or I do. Yet I still believe in upholding the duties and obligations of my class, unlike some of us. My activities are no threat to you or to Lisette."

"But you act against the King, and that is treason, Monsieur Jolbert. My daughter was destined for a greater purpose than to be married to a traitor."

It took every ounce of restraint that Jean possessed not to draw his rapier and run the Duc through.

"You have insulted my honor, sir. The treaty specifically demands your daughter's hand in marriage. You agreed to the pact and accepted payment in full for the marriage contract."

Darias snickered at the demand. "The funds were used for the betterment of your country."

"Be quiet!" the Duc snapped at his nephew, and Darias withheld further comment.

Jean couldn't let the opportunity pass. "Don't you mean the funds were used for your political aspirations, Your Grace?" The Baron's gaze never left the Duc's face as the charge was made.

The Duc de Meret saved his most devastating remark for last. "I would be grateful to be able to walk away with my life, if I were you. Your father hasn't been as fortunate. He was arrested for treason this morning and could face execution."

"You're lying," the Baron imputed. "The King knows the Earl of Normandy is loyal to the aristocracy."

"I didn't need my brother's blessing to have the Earl arrested," the Duc de Meret assured him.

There was a nervous twitch in Jean's jaw. It was common knowledge there were officials not above accepting a bribe to issue a warrant, but a *lettre* required the signature of the King; therefore Louis must have been warned of the Jolberts' gaining power, or else the Duc had secured the warrant without telling Louis for whom it was being issued.

Jean knew his father was an active member of a secretive body of revolutionists called the Committee of Thirty. Its main function was to distrib-

ute pamphlets listing grievances against the
royalty. There was always the risk of being arrested; however, it was nearly impossible to trace
the originators of the pamphlets. After all, was it
really a crime for the Jolberts to strive for the betterment of France? They were striving for honesty
among the nobles, while the royalty viciously executed anyone who opposed them. Someone had
betrayed the Jolberts, Jean reasoned, and he was
probably facing the blackguard at this very moment.

The Duc relaxed in his saddle. A self-assured
smile tugged at the corners of this thin lips. "If you
decide to call this incident to the King's attention,
your *père* will die. Heed my warning, and leave
France before I have enough evidence to have you
imprisoned also."

The Baron masked his volatile emotions with a
calm façade. "If I leave the country without saying
a word, you'll have my father released in a few
short years?"

"Precisely," the Duc answered.

"You must think I'm a fool."

"You don't have any other choice in the matter."

The Baron's hope for a peaceful settlement was
gone. An ancient code of chivalry still existed for a
man born of the aristocracy, although that pact
would soon be lost as the peasants' cries were heard
and the populace strove for a democratically gov-
erned society. The bloody feud must begin again
and the Baron's kinsmen would die to protect the
seacoast the Duc wanted to dominate. Jean
couldn't believe until now the lengths this man—
soon to be his father-in-law—would go to destroy
the Jolbert family.

"I do have another choice," Jean clarified. "To
stay in France and fight against your ascent to the
throne. My father and I are both willing to sacri-

fice our lives for our country. If I leave now, you'll further abuse your power and oppress this nation to the point of civil war."

The Duc's head fell back as he laughed. "You are a stubborn man, Baron Jolbert. Don't tell me the Jolberts haven't desired power. The marriage to my daughter would have put your family within a generation of controlling the throne."

"What has the de Meret family proven in the past?" Jean argued. "Your brother is a bumbling idiot. The Jolberts are proud of this nation, not cowards who hide behind the palace doors, or resort to kidnapping a member of the nobility to threaten murder. I tell you now, I will not accept this betrayal. Eventually, I will find my father. As for Lady Lisette, she is promised to me, and I *will* have her," he seethed between clenched teeth.

"Then we shall meet again." The Duc dismissed the incident and abruptly left the field.

"Your father will be angry," Michel said quietly.

"He won't be angry. He will be furious."

The Baron turned his horse back toward the sea, but Michel didn't follow. Given the Baron's mood, Michel knew his presence wouldn't be missed for at least a week. He had tried to convince his friend there were other ways of getting what he wanted without a fray. While the Baron roamed the seas with his cousins, Michel had stayed in France to further his romantic interests.

Michel had a plan. He would persuade the lady to return to the Baron's château with him so that the marriage pact would be ratified and the war between the two families would be averted. The Baron's father would have petitioned the King in behalf of his son, protesting this outrage. Since that was now impossible, Michel would find a resolution.

He had a feeling Lady Lisette didn't know her father was preparing himself for Louis's fall and the de Meret ascent to the throne. She probably wasn't aware of how much power the Duc was gaining with the people, and how close he was coming to committing treason himself.

It wouldn't be wise to keep her in the country if his plan did work and she became Jean's wife. They would have to escape France, and return to Spain where it was safe to keep a member of the royal family.

"Totally inappropriate," Michel mused. "Unthinkable, for a mademoiselle to be alone with a man of the Baron's reputation." This wasn't going to be easy. He would have to deploy all of his tact to see that Lisette accompanied him to the château. Then it would be up to Jean to win the lady's heart.

Lisette stopped at a stream to water her horse. Out of the corner of her eye, she thought she saw men on horseback, and decided to investigate. Crouching beside a tree to get a better view, she recognized the men engaged in conversation: her father and the Baron Jean Jolbert. She was too far away to overhear the discussion, but a sense of impending danger warned her not to tarry. What were these two doing meeting like this—this was a confrontation.

The meeting seemed to end abruptly as both men turned their horses sharply and galloped away. She would join the Baron and find out for herself what had been said. Lisette didn't trust her father, and she was nervous about riding without an armed guard. Even this close to home, there were too many highwaymen and bandits to prey on unescorted women.

Her thoughts proved only too prophetic. As she

mounted the gelding she saw a man with a black beard coming from the woods on horseback. When he saw her, he leveled a pistol on her.

"Halt!" the rogue ordered.

In the valley, the Baron heard the shout and spurred his stallion to a gallop. If his cousin had managed to capture a de Meret spy, they would deal with the intruder in the old ways of the feud. A life would be forfeited.

Lisette panicked. She had been discovered, and the Baron was too far off to help her. Glancing back at the valley, she saw the Baron heading her way.

Her riding crop snapped against the gelding's flanks, and the horse surged into a gallop. There were shouts all around her. She was soon to be cut off from the only path to the valley below, and the safety of the Baron's arms.

Now there were several men closing in on her as she spun her horse around, trying in vain to find a way to elude them. Lisette was surrounded before she reached the valley. She screamed, making her horse rear, and strained to hang on to the reins as the gelding bolted in fear toward the hill.

Lisette was blinded by hair falling across her face, and all she could see of her captors was a dark-haired man reaching out for her reins. She slashed at him with her riding crop, but the man's powerful arm circled her waist and pulled her from the horse. Certain her ribs would break from his crushing hold, Lisette wiggled until she finally felt herself drop to the ground.

The powerful hands of her captor gripped her shoulders and Lisette stared blankly at his lace cravat until the pressure of his finger under her chin tipped her head up.

It was her Baron.

Jean brushed the auburn hair from the woman's

face and couldn't believe whom he had found. "Lisette?"

"Oui!" She threw herself into his arms. He had come to her rescue after all. Relief was short-lived when she realized Jean wasn't returning the embrace. Instead, he held her at arm's length and gave her an insolent glare.

"Did you come to watch your father break the treaty?" The Baron laughed sardonically. "It seems the Duc doesn't know I'm holding the spoils before the battle has even begun. The odds are even now that the lady has decided to join us."

The wicked emotion flickering across his face made Lisette cringe in fear. How had her knight become her jailer? She realized now that her pursuers weren't highwaymen, but the Baron's guard. The word "battle" sank into her startled mind. The old feud between the Jolberts and the de Merets had resumed again, somehow.

"Let go of me," she demanded.

"I will take my hands off you when I so choose, mademoiselle. We didn't expect to find you here, but then I did promise we would meet again."

Lisette was terrified as his hands slid down her arms to her waist. Held so close to him, she could feel his breath on her cheek. Jean kissed her, bruising her mouth with the force of his lips. The Duchess thought she would suffocate before he finally released her.

She had to get away from him. With a strength normally beyond her, Lisette twisted free of Jean's grip and ran for the thick copse of trees lining the path. But her petticoat caught between her legs, and as she paused to collect the lace folds the Baron caught her. Lisette beat at his chest with clenched fists and sank her teeth in the tanned flesh of his hand.

Surprised by the pain, the Baron released her,

and Lisette bolted toward the hillside. But he was faster than she was and caught a handful of hair, jerking her to an abrupt halt. Jean cursed again as Lisette thrust the heel of her boot into his knee.

"If you kick me again, you will live to regret it." Setting her firmly on his horse, the Baron mounted behind her, holding her tightly to his chest.

"Assemble the men, Paul," Jean ordered his cousin.

With his prize between his arms, Jean issued orders to his men to destroy any evidence of Lisette's dead horse which had to be killed when its leg snapped during Lisette's capture. "If the Duc heard the shot he might send someone to investigate. Make sure there is a welcome ready for him when he returns. I want you to stay with me, Paul. Make sure your brother, Simon, commands the rear guard."

The sun had set on the valley, and Lisette's hopes went with it. Now she understood why she had been called home so unexpectedly. Jolbert was no longer her betrothed, but her adversary. As tears welled up in her eyes, Lisette asked, "Why have you done this to me?"

The hard lines of determination on the Baron's face softened for a moment. But when he didn't answer her question, anger took the place of sadness. How dare he treat her like this, after he had shown her such tenderness!

In coal-black darkness they rode the paths into the hills. It was unknown territory to Lisette and perilous with its sudden deep fissures that she couldn't see until the horse jumped over them. She had to ride sidesaddle with her arms around the Baron's neck to keep from falling off the horse.

But even as they rode over smoother ground, Lisette wouldn't give in to the lull of a false sense of security. She had to know what Jolbert's plans for her were now that the feud was reinstated. And as the Baron slowed the pace and finally stopped Lisette vowed she would find out before he took her farther from her home.

As the men made camp the Baron deposited her beside a tree and ordered Paul to guard her. She had not spoken since the abduction, and now refused the food and water he offered. She sat on the hard ground with her back against a tree stump, listening to the murmur of male voices and the chink of bridles as the horses were watered at the stream.

The Baron's shadow passed before her. In the full moon's light, he appeared hostile and threatening. This was not the gentle man she had been betrothed to for two years. He had kidnapped her without explanation! She would personally see that he was whipped within an inch of his life when her father rescued her. She would see the Baron brought to justice.

Lisette tugged her mantle close around her and laid her head on her knees. What had happened to the glimmer in her heart? Was it just a dream sparked by an ideal that didn't exist? Had her love for Jean been real?

When she stood to rub her numb legs, her guard mistook her action and in a flash Lisette's shoulders were grasped between his huge hands. The Baron must have warned him she would try to escape.

"Don't touch me," she ordered. She was trembling, but managed to slap him hard enough for a man of his size to feel. Pleased with herself for not succumbing to terror, Lisette persisted when he refused to let her go. She kicked his shin as hard as she could, making him groan in agony. But his fingers didn't move.

"You can release her."

The Baron's deep voice came from behind her. When the guard removed the restraining hold, Lisette spun around. She would show him how a member of the royal family dealt with insubordinates. She lashed out to strike him but Jean was quicker, catching her wrist just before her fingers grazed his cheek. In the moonlight, she saw the white of his smile.

"You are more spirited than I remember, *chérie*. You have matured since I last saw you. 'Tis fortunate we didn't miss your homecoming."

"You are no gentleman, monsieur." Lisette stood before him with a rigid back and clenched fists.

"Oh, but I assure you, I am," he said suavely.

"No gentleman would assault and kidnap me. Where are you taking me?"

"To our honeymoon cottage. My château at Avranches isn't far. But I warn you, behave yourself, or you will find my anger can be violent—it's even known to have been fatal."

"My father will not let this incident pass, my lord. Release me now and save yourself from his wrath." She said the words with as much confidence as she could muster from her weary body.

His arms wrapped around her waist, crushing her to his body. "I don't fear your father or any member of the royal family."

"What are you going to do, hold me for ransom? My uncle will strip you of your title and have you executed." As soon as she said the words, Lisette regretted her outburst. Jean's grip around her waist became a painful vise, and she knew she had enraged him.

"I have no intention of demanding a ransom for you." There was an edge of bitterness and disappointment deep in his voice. "Destiny has sent you right into my hands, and your fate is now at my disposal." To emphasize the point, Jean drew his face close to hers, his lips only a sliver away.

She cried out in hurt and anger as his strength squeezed the breath out of her. But Lisette wouldn't beg him to free her. Yet his stranglehold was so tight her head began to tingle and her world faded in a haze. She barely heard the voice of her guard breaking the hold on her.

"Stop it, Jean. You'll kill her!"

Lisette's body slumped forward, her head resting on his warm shoulder until her knees buckled and she collapsed into his arms. The Baron surrendered her to Paul's care once again.

The burly man lifted her onto the Baron's stallion, holding the reins until Jean mounted behind her. Escape would be nearly impossible, she realized. She had apparently pushed him too far. To further provoke him would mean risking possible physical harm. He was capable of murder, Lisette was sure of it.

The Baron paused as his scout reined in beside him. The man was breathless and his horse was lathered to a creamy white. "My lord, the Duc has evaded our trap."

Baron Jolbert looked up at Lisette. The light breeze tossed her long hair about her shadowed form, making her look wild and wanton. The strength of her gaze met his. In the glow of the campfire he read her conviction clearly. If she didn't try to kill him, she would try to steal away.

"Find the Duc and kill him." Although his command was meant for his scout, it held a special caution to Lisette. Jean resented her smugness.

My father will rescue me, she assured herself, trying to calm her despair. She had so many questions, and no answers. Why did the Baron kidnap me? What has my father done to make him so angry? Will I be imprisoned never to see the light of day again? Or die a slow cruel death? It was too gruesome to consider. At this point she believed Jolbert capable of anything. His monstrous behavior said this was only the beginning.

Chapter Three

Dazzling afternoon sunlight washed through the open doors to the balcony in blinding shades of yellow. Lisette traced the rose pattern in the drapes with the tip of her finger, then swept the heavy chintz fabric aside. She wrapped the yards of silk sheeting around her and tucked the tail end between her breasts; her clothes had been taken away the night before, leaving her naked but not unresourceful. Padding barefoot across the stone floor, she inspected the veranda. If there was a way out of Jolbert's fortress, she would find it.

The stone walls dropped a breathtaking fifty feet to a rocky shoreline. Waves curled and broke into a foamy white, disappearing in the strong undertow. The roofline brought no help for escape. Tiny clay tiles adorned the sloping peaks. This was no proper castle with strutting battlements where a person could tie a rope.

Lisette gave up on the terrace. Unless she had wings to fly, this was a secure prison. It made her think of the drifting of a hot-air balloon—the closest thing she'd seen to flying. The young Duchess had had a privileged seat next to her uncle when the first Montgolfier, so named after the brothers Jacques and Joseph who invented the flying apparatus, was launched over five years ago. The arabesque design on the billowing envelope was detailed with fleurs-de-lis, and the gondola was made from wicker. The possibility of flight had excited her, but her father wouldn't hear of risking her life in that "damnable contraption."

Walking back into her chamber, Lisette forced herself to concentrate on her situation. She would have to wait until dark and then pick the lock on her door with a hairpin. Her father's hobby as a locksmith was the only circumstance in her childhood that was shared with the Duc. Trying to please him, she became adept in the art and excelled to a point where she had teased her mother that she would make an excellent jewel thief. After that, her mother had forbidden her to use her talents, but the many times Lisette had escaped from her quarters at the school had prepared her for this day.

With no means of escape over the château walls, she studied the suite. The luxurious Persian rug was so thick her feet left prints. Yards of watercolor silk draped the gold lacquered Chippendale bed, and the light satin coverlet was the same soft blue color as her eyes. The cosmetic table was covered with a dyed royal-blue cloth overlaid in delicate chenille lace. Crystal decanters containing the finest perfumes lay beside gold-handled brushes on the chiffonnier.

"So, you were expecting me, after all," she whispered to herself. The plush room had obviously been designed for her; it was a strikingly beautiful decor done in her best-loved colors.

Her bottom lip drooped in a pout. Jean had probably had the room decorated months ago, before the feud between their families had begun again. But she wasn't meant to be captive here. This wasn't the way they were supposed to be reunited.

The dull echo of voices outside her door intruded

on her attention. With her ear to the keyhole, Lisette recognized the Baron's voice; the other she couldn't recollect hearing before. Lisette crouched beside the door to eavesdrop, but their grumblings were muffled.

"Blast that man!" She couldn't understand what was said.

"The Duc has eluded us once again," was all she detected. The Baron's curse was loud and clear. Couldn't any disagreement between their families be settled with a few gentle words?

The last thing she expected was the door to swing open without warning. Lisette fell to the floor with a thud. Staring at the Baron's scuffed boots, she had the urge to sink her teeth into his ankle. With all her courage, she stood up and smiled.

The Baron's eyes were hooded under black lashes. *Lord, he is handsome,* she thought. There was a hint of deviltry in his dove-gray eyes as he studied her. If Lisette hadn't felt the heat rise to her own cheeks, she would have loved looking at him for hours. He could pose for a sculptor with his aristocratically straight nose and hollowed cheeks, his ruffled shirt open to a smooth, tanned chest and his dark trousers making him appear lean and stately.

Her common sense returned. Defiantly, she lifted her chin. He had no right to keep her locked in a cell.

"Did you sleep well, *ma petite?*" He strolled into her room and made himself comfortable on the edge of her bed.

Lisette was appalled at his arrogance. "You should not be in here." She pulled the sheet tighter around her, not realizing that all it accomplished was to set off her figure before his admiring gaze.

"Mademoiselle, who do you think tucked you in last night? You fell asleep on my lap, if you remem-

ber." Her innocence amused him and he grinned
with self-satisfaction.

"You beast! You take liberties that would shame
any other gentleman. I have no doubt who tucked
me in last night." She would never tell him she
couldn't remember a thing after they had left the
camp. "I demand you leave this chamber at once.
It isn't proper for you to be in here." Her courage
momentarily faltered when Jean rose to his feet
and approached her.

"It certainly is proper for me to be in your boudoir. You are my prisoner. I will remind you to behave yourself. I may do with you now whatever I
please."

Her defiant nature took over. "You had better
explain yourself, monsieur. No fiancé would behave so . . . so insufferably. Why have you brought
me here? It was a cowardly thing to do, to wait and
ambush me while I was unprotected. You have the
gall of a ruffian and the manners of—"

"I wouldn't say it if I were you."

She saw his expression change to ire. He held her
slender shoulders in his grasp, firmly drawing her
closer to him.

"Why am I here?" she asked in a frightened
whisper.

"You will find out when it suits me to tell you.
Until then, I don't care what you think of me." He
let go of her and noted the red welts on her arms.
He hadn't meant to hurt her, but every time he
went near her, his frustration made him lose control.

Wanting to appease the fear he saw in Lisette's
eyes, Jean put his arms around her waist, and
when she didn't resist, he cuddled her close to him.
Her gaze focused on his mouth as he lowered his
head and brushed her forehead with a kiss.

"Don't fight me, Lisette." His breath was warm

against her cheek. Maybe she hadn't changed. His
beautiful young fiancée had become a woman and
at this moment seemed ready to be his paramour.

Lisette thought she was in a dream. She wished
he would stop talking and kiss her again. Her eyes
closed as his lips touched hers and the wisp of his
dark lashes brushed her cheek. The warm contact
made her hungry for more. Jean lifted her completely off her feet, and the room spun around her.
Her lips parted to his gentle probing, and her hands
snaked through his hair.

"You do remember me, don't you, Lisette?" She
yielded to his passionate embrace. The sense of
triumph made him withdraw and he set her gently
back on her feet.

The cold stone under her feet brought Lisette
swiftly back to reality. Disconcerted by her own
heady response, she walked back to the bedside.
Lisette needed distance between herself and the
desire he could arouse. She plucked a rose from the
flower vase on the bedside table and tore the petals
from the blossom.

The Baron withdrew a key from his breeches
pocket and unlocked the doors to the armoire. "I do
prefer you as you are right now, but the sight of a
young lady in a sheet would drive my hussars to
madness." He tossed a sapphire-colored dress on
the bed and paused beside the door. "If that doesn't
suit you, choose another you would like to wear for
dinner. Your maid, Anna, will help make the necessary adjustments. Though I could stay to help
you?" His eyebrows lifted playfully.

Lisette was furious. She reached down and her
hand closed over the fluted edge of the beautiful
vase. Without thinking about what she was doing,
she threw it at him. The Baron ducked and the pot-
tery crashed into the wall behind him; glass and

metal clattered to the floor. "I would rather starve in a convent than marry you!"

Jean slowly smiled. All that beauty possessed spirit, too. He would enjoy this battle. "I will stay and dress you myself if need be. Dinner will be served at six this evening, and if you're not ready, I will return to assist you."

Her head jerked up and she swept the heavy curtain of hair from her face. She knew he would keep his word. "There won't be any need for you to return. *Ever!*"

He locked the door behind him and his chuckle faded as he made his way through the halls.

"The man's impossible," she said in a huff, shaken by the close contact. She spent the rest of the day pacing in frustrated circles. By two o'clock she had resolved to be on a hunger strike. Shortly thereafter, a tray of fruit and Camembert cheese arrived, and her empty stomach won her over. Vanishing in the middle of the night was better than starvation. Somehow, she would manage it. By now, her father would be preparing a major attack, and she would need her strength when the scrimmage started.

The key in her door turned and a young, blond maid entered the room. "My name is Anna. I am to attend you, my lady." She curtsied and waited for orders.

"You may attend your mistress by helping her escape this fortress," Lisette said wryly. "I do not wish to be held captive while my lord Baron devises my certain demise. I demand that you help me, lest I have you arrested with the others when the King hears of this."

"I couldn't!" The young girl wrung her hands. "My lord would have my hide tacked to the château walls and he'd feed my corpse to the wolves." Anna quailed in terror just thinking of it.

Lisette caught a glimpse of a guard posted outside her door. He looked at her with round eyes and an open mouth as if she were a goddess while water was brought in for her bath. The door was promptly locked when the servants finished their duty. "It's a wonder they can do anything while they're drooling and stumbling over their own two feet," she snapped sarcastically.

Lisette bathed, and Anna brushed her hair until it shone in a red-brown halo down her back. It was fruitless to fight the wave of her natural curls, and the damp sea air would no doubt reverse the careful ministrations. It would take hours to heat a curling iron and arrange a coiffure that would be appropriate. Her natural style was unfashionable but necessary.

After the ribbons of her chemise were tied and the corset laced, the gummed linen pannier holding the skirt on either side of her hips was fastened into place. The gown of sapphire-toned chiffon draped over a satin skirt and Valenciennes lace gathered in rows from her knees to her satin-slippered feet. The square neckline was bare and revealed the rounded mounds of her breasts in a sinfully low décolletage. At the end of the three-quarter-length sleeves was a lace ruffle, and most scrumptious of all were the garters that had real gems sewn onto them. A carved ivory fan completed her attire.

Had she not been a prisoner, Lisette might have relaxed to enjoy the unexpected time with the Baron. She had to remind herself that she was above the kind of outburst she had displayed earlier. The uncertainty of her future had kept her nerves tightly strung, but tonight she would behave differently.

She was ready at six o'clock. Lisette decided to be contrite, and not let the Baron goad her into another tantrum. He could make her captivity quite unpleasant. But he couldn't force her to marry him, under just any circumstances; the Church wouldn't recognize the marriage, and the Duc would soon see that it was annulled. Yet Lisette also knew that he wanted her as much as she longed for him. It would take all her self-control to keep him from breaking her resistance.

Paul waited outside the door to escort her to the dining room. He regarded her cautiously. Though he spoke up on her behalf at the camp, she had kicked him hard enough to cause a limp. He kept his distance, lest she decide to attack again.

He led the way through the corridors of the château. She tried to pry information she needed from the stout guard. "You must be related to the Baron."

"I'm Jean's first cousin and captain of the hussars," he answered. "Also surgeon when need be, and a cook when I'm hungry."

Hussars were paid cutthroats and pirates, she mused. "Will Jean's father, the Earl of Normandy, be joining us for dinner, Paul?"

"He has been delayed in Paris," he said with a hint of a grin under his dark beard. He was impressed that she had remembered his name.

She mustn't let the Baron effect her sense of duty. Their relationship had changed drastically since the meeting long ago, and she couldn't think of him the way she once had, and she mustn't provoke his temper again. But when they entered the dining room, the arrogant smirk on the Baron's face made her have second thoughts about holding her tongue.

The hall was large enough to seat over a hundred people, and held a banquet table of polished mahogany that went almost the entire length of the room.

"Good evening, Monsieur Jolbert. I trust I am not late?" Her dress rustled as she crouched into a formal curtsy. Given the circumstances, she was composed, and the dress added to her feminine allure.

As she entered, Jean let his gaze slowly drop down to her décolletage, then swept it back to her blue eyes. His wide smile flickered in delight.

"You look beautiful, Lady Lisette." The defiant glint in her eyes was sublime. This mere slip of a child had all the grace and charm of women twice her age.

Now that he was rested, he could deploy all of his military training to find a weakness in her defenses. It wouldn't do any good to carry out his scheme unless he knew he could hurt her. Jean had become obsessed with carrying out the counterplay. If his *père* were incarcerated, the enmity between their families would never cease. As yet, Lisette hadn't questioned his father's absence. Jean thought that if she knew about the arrest, she could prevent his harassment by a few simple words like "Touch me again and your father loses a hand." She would hold that power over him, and *he* would be in a checkmated position. Her innocence was his salvation. Since she apparently didn't know about the Duc's attempt to destroy the Jolberts, he felt free to claim what was rightfully his. But there was still a twinge of doubt about her participation.

He had to know where her loyalties were before he would open up that secret part of his heart and tell her how much he loved her. If Lisette were in league with the Duc, Jean would have to deliver justice and destroy her as well as the Duc. Yet part of him already belonged to Lisette, and if his suspicions about her were true, all of his love and hope for their future would die with her. If he were wrong, he played a deadly game with an innocent woman's devotion, and he would forfeit something more precious than his newfound wealth could ever replace.

As he approached her he made a silent wish that she *was* the woman he remembered. In his dream, Lisette was a perfect wife and the mother of his children, not a ruthless wench who was out to crush him.

"I believe you're right on time." He offered to escort her across the room to the table. Jean wanted to touch her again. The years he had waited for her had been miserable, and now that he had her, he wasn't about to let go.

Jean held the chair out for her and pushed it in when she was seated. When he remained standing behind her, Lisette had to force herself not to turn around. It took all her concentration to remain unflinching as his hands caressed the nape of her neck.

He leaned over and whispered into her ear. "Such a pretty throat, mademoiselle."

Lisette sat perfectly still as his hands moved forward and ever so lightly stroked the small dip at the base of her throat.

"A woman is an unfinished masterpiece without her jewelry." He left momentarily, and then draped a string of pearls over her head.

Lisette bent her head to see the necklace and touched the creamy, smooth texture with the tips of her fingers. The string of pearls almost touched the bodice of her dress and clung daintily to the swell of her breasts. She let out a sigh of relief when he sat down at the head of the table. He was still within an arm's length of her, and seemed fascinated with the pearls reflecting the candlelight.

"Dazzling," he said softly.

Lisette broke the trance with an abashed laugh.

"They're lovely." It was true, and yet the weight of the necklace felt like a ball and chain.

He poured the wine and raised his goblet for a toast. "I drink to your superb loveliness, mademoiselle." He was amused at her formality as she rose and curtsied. "Are the accommodations to your liking, my dear?"

It would be so different, she thought, *if I truly were a guest in this marvelous house.* She smiled slyly and set her glass down. "It certainly isn't the dungeon I imagined you would throw me into, but then, who knows what you are capable of?"

Jean leaned back in his chair, leisurely sipping his wine. He looked deadly serious for a moment, then smiled a slow and easy grin. "There are many forms of misery, my lovely lady. I must confess, though, my dungeon was taken apart and now serves as a wine cellar for vintage port. It almost broke my cousin's heart to dismantle the room. Paul just isn't happy unless he's maiming someone. He still religiously dusts the rack, just in case it might be used again. Frankly"—he leaned over the table close to her—"I never did like mutilating someone before supper."

She didn't know him well enough to be able to tell if he were lying to her or not. The Baron was trying to badger her into losing control; she couldn't let him know he was succeeding.

His cousin Paul sat at the end of the table and looked up at the mention of his name. He had the biggest brown eyes she had ever seen. Would this man apply the hot irons to her tender skin? Or would the Baron claim the privilege? The rumors of his many victories while under the service of the King had never been mixed with terrorism. He was a respected gentleman at court. But, she reminded herself, no gentleman would kidnap a woman. Lisette had to keep her wits about her or lose this verbal battle.

"I, sir, drink to chivalry."

Lisette began to enjoy the dinner. The wine was excellent and she couldn't hide her ravenous appetite.

Jean leaned closer to her. "Do you like the *poisson?*"

"It's a little heavy," she ventured to comment.

"Shark always is." Jean grinned.

"How appropriate."

"Pardon me?" he asked politely.

"Oh, nothing." Lisette's mouth went dry. She finally swallowed the mouthful of the sea demon, washing it down with a full chalice of wine.

He filled her glass every time she emptied it, leaving her relaxed and light-headed by the time liqueur was served. The sweet aroma of apple orchards tickled her nose as she sipped the Calvados.

"This is delicious." She could hardly set the cordial down. The Baron's black mood had eased, and she was reminded again of the magic he could cast over her when he looked at her. He definitely had panache. His boyishly handsome face was further complemented by a square chin, and the small dimple in his right cheek made her want to see him smile at her again. Lisette figured she must be drunk; she wanted to flirt with him.

The Baron had learned more about her than she knew. She wasn't afraid of pain. But he still didn't know where her weakness lay. Somewhere under that marble surface was a vulnerable young woman who could be hurt. He would have to bait her again, and watch her reaction.

"This is my cousin's special recipe," he said casually. "He has discovered a unique fermenting process, perfecting the use of paralyzing drugs to a science. You see, it can't be detected through the full bouquet of the apple flavoring."

"Oh, I really don't believe you are capable of poisoning me, my lord." Lisette smiled in return to his dazzling grin. "It wouldn't be much sport to torture someone who was drugged." Her gaze met his in a deadly test of wills as she called his bluff.

Thankfully, Paul interrupted the Baron's retort, and Lisette enjoyed the chance to watch him while they talked. Set against the glow of a crackling fire, his profile was cast into deep relief. Her favorite fantasy had been touching his face and holding him in her arms. They had danced together in her fairyland romance, two people set apart from the world.

"I have something for you," the Baron said, interrupting her reverie. Dropping the serviettes on their plates, they rose from the table and he took her hand firmly in his. Hesitantly, she followed him to the fireplace hearth. There was a velvet box on the mantel, and he placed it in her hand.

Inside was the brooch he had given her long ago, except that it had been altered. The seal of the Jolberts had been scraped off. The scratches in the golden surface were felt deep within her. How dare he?

"What have you done!" she exclaimed in disbelief. The brooch had been given to her at their betrothal and was her dearest possession. He must have taken it off her mantle while she slept. "What have I ever done to you to deserve such a slight?"

"I could ask the same of you, Lady Lisette."

She mustered her courage to ask, "But you've kidnapped me. Why are you so angry with me?"

The glitter of fear and hope in her eyes almost softened his resolve to destroy the de Merets. But he had only to remember that his father was imprisoned to remain firm.

His silence was frustrating. Lisette couldn't get a straight answer out of him. He would crush her spirit if she let him, but her pride wouldn't allow defeat. In an act of defiance she closed the box and tossed it into the fire as if it meant nothing to her.

"It has been an interesting evening, Monsieur Jolbert." And with that, she turned and ran, not looking back. Lisette had to get out of that room, and out from under the deadly scrutiny of the Baron.

Paul caught up to her. He was frowning when he escorted her back to her room. The lady had won his respect by not backing down to the Baron's threats. He paused beside her open door.

"My lady, if you need anything, please ask for me."

"If I need anything?" Lisette was confused. Did he think she would call for him to break her legs, for God's sake? He was first cousin to the Baron. How could she trust him to help her?

The door lock clicked securely behind her. Lisette put two clenched fists to her temples. Why had Jean destroyed the brooch he had given her as an engagement gift? Lisette had almost made a total fool of herself thinking that batting her eyelashes at him would change his hatred for her family. The liqueur had gone to her head. She couldn't concentrate.

She slipped into a sheer white nightshift and tossed the pearls to her cosmetic table. Lisette walked out on the balcony to clear her head. The cool breeze tossed her hair around her face and she absently pushed it aside. Why would her father break the treaty and anger the Baron when they had worked so long for peace? Where was the Earl of Normandy? She knew that the Baron's father wouldn't sanction this kidnapping. Her emotions were as turbulent as the billowing clouds rimming the horizon.

From the rocky coastline below, the steady rhythms of waves breaking on the shoreline eased her nervous twinges of fear. The view of the sunset from the high balcony was magnificent; the huge orange sun appeared to sink directly into the ocean, sending shimmers of golden-red rays lazily dancing on the surface of the Channel. The heavens melted into a final display of peach and blue.

Momentarily held by nature's serenity and grandeur, Lisette didn't hear the Baron walk in and stop at the threshold to watch her. His breath caught when he saw her image against the sunset. The nightshift she wore had become translucent in the light. An angelic glow surrounded her shapely young curves. She was more beautiful than he thought possible. He had to know if she was still as pure in body as she had been the first time they met. Or had the de Merets' treachery robbed him of that, too? He would use her and cast her aside if she were no longer a virgin. And if she, too, were involved in the Duc's schemes, he would have to find a way to repay the de Merets and give up all hope of having his beloved Lisette until the end of time.

With a deep sigh, Lisette lazily stretched and turned to go inside. When she discovered she wasn't alone, a shiver of impending doom crept up her spine. Jean was wearing a long robe, open to reveal his naked chest. "What are you doing here?" She forced her voice to sound calm.

He smiled. "I should think that it would be obvious, Lisette. Fate played you into my hands, and my design for your future is scandalous. You will not leave my château without being . . . compromised."

The Baron was demanding the ancient rites of a

feudal warlord. It was archaic, in such a modern time, to claim her under the old laws. If that's the way he was going to behave, so be it. Lisette answered to the King, and it was to him that she swore her fealty. Within the bounds of the Baron's fief she was still one of the King's vassals.

"You have no authority over me, Baron Jolbert. The King is my liege lord."

"Your uncle can't help you if he doesn't know where you are."

He watched a flicker of horror weaken her stance. He had found what he wanted.

Chapter Four

"I am your betrothed! You can't do this to me! It would . . ." Lisette was aghast. A scandal of this kind would ruin her chances for marriage to anyone else. A virgin bride was prized above all. It was obvious now that he didn't intend to wait for the wedding ceremony to make love to her. Yet a gruesome fate awaited her when he tired of her. She couldn't risk being publicly branded as a prostitute and having her children rejected from society as bastards.

Suddenly she felt silly and foolish for loving him because he was handsome when all he wanted her for was her proximity to the throne. The Baron wanted to use her as a political pawn, not to love her for herself.

"Get out of my chamber," she insisted.

Jean crossed the distance between them in three long strides. He scooped her up into his arms, brought her inside the chamber, and dropped her on the bed. She attempted to roll away from him but was caught between his arms. He pinned her to the feather bed with his body stretched out over her. Before she could move, his mouth crushed her tender lips in a brutal kiss.

She should have been his. Now he would take

what was rightfully due him. His fierce temper flared when she bit his lip.

"Vixen, stop fighting. Accept your future with me."

"No!" Her breath came in shaky sobs. "I won't give in to your perfidy."

"You have lived your life by the honor of the feud, as I have, Lisette. Your disreputable father broke the contract." He shook with fury. "It is you who should fear the wrath of the Jolbert family."

There was a sinking feeling in her stomach. *"You* must have provoked him."

"Why? Because I supported a country free of tyranny? How could I not see the filth and poverty encouraged by my fellow noblemen?" The Baron's voice exploded in anger. "When is the royal family going to stop raping this country? Have you seen the families dying together on the scaffold?" He hovered over her, and she cringed against the pillows. "Try to imagine, just for a moment, a child you had brought into the world waiting for her turn."

"They were traitors, and stood trial." She clamped her hands over her ears. The nightmares of the execution she had witnessed still haunted her.

"They were all fools who dared to speak out against your uncle? Do you still dare to justify your family's actions?"

"My father had nothing to do with it."

"He supported terrorism by remaining silent."

Anger sparked Lisette into retaliation. "You can't hold me responsible for deeds of state." Her eyes burned every time she blinked. Emotionally spent, she covered her face with trembling hands. She couldn't bear the loathing in his gaze.

It was a moot point for Jean. Of course he didn't blame her directly. In all honesty, Jean realized he was taking his frustrations out on Lisette because she was a link to the throne.

"I apologize for treating you badly, Lisette. I just can't stand back and watch what is happening to France."

Lisette raised her head and looked directly into his gray eyes, her mouth dropping open in surprise. His tenderness always took her off guard, as on the day he had sent the flowers to her.

"What happened when you met with my father?"

The Baron stood up to pace the floor and thrust his hands into his pockets. The black fury that blazed within him couldn't be fully suppressed by the beautiful young woman he had waited so long to claim. The thought of the Duc arranging the fall of the house of Jolbert incensed him.

Lisette sank deeper into the bed. His silence was terrifying. She pulled her quivering bottom lip between her teeth to still it. If she wasn't careful, these could be the last few hours of her life.

Finally, he answered her. "You know all too well, my lovely lady." His voice was deep with sarcasm. "I found the note in your reticule, so there is no need to keep up this pretense of innocence."

Her chin tilted as she prepared to defend her honor. "I never had the chance to find out what the note was about." She wished he could hear the concern in her voice. His harsh stare softened. Again she asked, "What happened?"

"You have been betrothed to an English count."

"That's not possible!" She knew now why the feud would begin again.

"I didn't think your father was stupid enough to cross me," Jean spat. Evidently Lisette didn't know about the new arrangement, or else she was a very good actress. She seemed genuinely confounded.

"So that's why you're angry." Lisette didn't place any credence in her father's wisdom. And she felt betrayed by her Baron; he obviously thought she was a willing partner in this marriage scheme. "What makes you think I would agree to marry him?"

"You don't have any choice in the matter."

She knew he was right. If her father so desired, he could have betrothed her to an ogre. "Why did you have to meet with my father?"

"You don't know?" Jean wasn't sure if he could confide in her completely. "The Duc informed me that my father was arrested yesterday, on a trumped-up charge of treason."

"Oh, no!" Lisette had no idea what was going on. For the first time she felt compassion for the anguish the Baron was suffering, and an immoderate amount of self-pity because she was caught in the middle. "So you intend to use me to get him released?"

"I will have justice."

"I won't allow you to disgrace me."

Lisette shook her head and let her gaze drop to the coverlet. Her dreams of a happy wedding day seemed yet further out of reach.

Jean stopped short of telling her that only over his dead body would another man touch what belonged to him. He still had to know for sure if she was experienced in a man's bed.

"Have you ever been with a man, Lisette? If you lie to me"—his voice dropped to a deadly whisper—"I will not be responsible for what happens next."

The truth was her only defense. "No man has ever touched me, except you when you kissed me long ago. But you can't hurt me by raping me." It was a reckless statement that she instantly regretted.

Jean closed his eyes for a moment, a sad frown

on his mouth. She felt guilty for hurting him, and wasn't sure why.

"I won't rape you, Lisette," he said softly and opened his eyes to gaze at her. Rejoining her on the bed, he reached up and touched a lock of her silky hair, then traced the outline of her oval chin with the tip of his finger. "I'm not really a monster. It seems to me that we were both uninformed about your father's designs. Do you still want me, Lisette?"

"I have wanted you from the first moment I saw you. But I won't be used by you." She carefully noted that he didn't mention love or marriage. Was he just taunting her with his threat to compromise her? She still feared he would cast her aside if she gave in to desire now.

Lisette willed her body to remain rigid as he caressed her face. His lips touched the base of her throat and slowly moved to her ear, sending a shiver up her spine. Her fists clenched against the pounding in her chest. Jean's strong hands cradled her face, and the moist contact of his kisses on her eyelids was warm and tender. As much as she tried to fight it, the feeling of belonging in his embrace tugged at her heart. With her fingers spread apart on his broad chest, Lisette felt his brisk heartbeat. The gentle massaging at the small of her back nudged her intimately closer to him.

Jean wouldn't waste another moment fighting with her. Her resistance was wavering; he could see that in the imploring look of her blue eyes. Awed by the soft perfection under his hands, he stroked her body until she trembled against him.

Something was awakening within her. This was frightening, and yet she wanted more. She was helpless to stop him as he pressed her to the bed. "Oh, Jean," she moaned unknowingly. The Baron of her dreams was tenderly making love to her.

He eased the nightshirt from her body, kissing each new expanse of skin that was unveiled until she lay naked before him in the firelight. Her back arched as he touched his lips to her rounded breast and gently sucked the blushed tips to hardened peaks.

Knowing that only she could quench the fire that was burning within him, he wanted to please her. Taunted by the near touch of her lips on his, he sought the kisses that could inflame his desire to madness. With his fingers laced in her hair, he briefly touched the tip of his tongue to her parted lips. His restraint in taking her made him tremble as he held his own passions aside to woo her. He tossed his robe aside and lowered his naked body to hers. When there was no rebuke, he explored her tremulous mouth in thrusting strokes of adoration. He eased her beneath him and, with a hand at the small of her back, guided her to him.

He felt her terror as she clutched at his shoulders. His voice was pitched low and soothing. "I will be gentle, *petite.*"

His words were the cold slap of reality that reminded Lisette that Jean still wanted revenge on her family. It was heartbreaking to think he would utilize her for his justice. Lisette couldn't give in to the passion he ignited and let him make love to her. She pushed him aside and sat up abruptly, taking him by surprise.

"You're no better than my father," she said hastily.

Jean rolled over onto his back and stared at the canopy. Her rejection wounded his soul and angered him all over again. He was unable to move or speak until the shaking within him subsided. She shied away when he draped an arm around her back. He was still very uncertain if she had had anything to do with his father's arrest.

"You prod my temper needlessly, risking your tender hide. Perhaps there is a fate worse than death, and better suited for the Duchess de Meret."

"You are a despicable man, Baron Jolbert." She squeezed her eyes shut to blot out the tears of shame that were forming.

"Hush, my darling. I have no intention of hearing another insult on my behavior. There will come a day when you crave to be my mistress, of your own free will." He gathered her up into his arms and firmly guided her down next to him.

"I will never come to you," she swore, trembling. Yet there was truth in his words. Lisette was aware of the desire that caused pandemonium with her senses. Relaxing in the glow of his misty eyes, she let exhaustion untangle the tension in her strained muscles. "Never," she repeated softly.

"Thus we shall unite our families in blood. You will carry my child, or we will go to war," he said quietly, tenderly stroking the dark cloud of hair that spilled over the pillows. The thought of her carrying his child seemed a fancy that would never come true.

Jean held his thought of revenge. The beauty of her shapely body had kept him from abusing her and taking her violently. He still didn't know if the charge the Duc had made was verified. Was the Earl arrested? His men hadn't returned from Paris when he retired, so there was still a reasonable margin for skepticism. For now, the Duc was in an immobile position. He couldn't kill the Earl as long as Lisette was Jean's hostage.

Soon the deep, even breathing reassured him that she was sleeping. The light violet shadows under her eyes were an indication that she was fatigued. He hadn't wanted to claim his bride like this. A code of honor prevented him from raping an unwilling female. But with this woman, Jean felt he had a right to consummate their relationship, if not their marriage. It was an undeniable claim that even she couldn't fight.

You will come to me, Lisette. Until then, I will make certain there is no way you can escape.

The troop quarters in the château were silent with sleeping men, except for one who decided it was a good night to get drunk. Paul was slightly inebriated himself when his quiet evening was disturbed by the entrance of an old friend.

"Where have you been?" he grumbled at the Marquis. "You were missed after the meeting this afternoon. Jean threatened to have you flayed alive if you hadn't returned by morning."

"I was in Paris for a few hours." The Marquis squirmed out of his coat. The pain in his shoulder and back hadn't been helped by a swift ride in the dead of night. "Jean is going to kill me anyway. I arrived in Paris too late. Lady Lisette was already gone. My brilliant plan to kidnap her has been foiled."

"I know," Paul chided. "She is here. We found her quite by accident, just after the meeting broke up."

While the Marquis breathed a sigh of relief, Paul did not. "Well, was she blond, brunette, or a saucy redhead this time? You'd better get your story straight before you see Jean, and hope his captive has put him in a better mood." Paul took a long drink of brandy and wiped his mouth with the back of his sleeve. "If I were you, I would start praying to the Holy Mother for mercy."

"I have never prayed so hard in all my life," the Marquis snapped angrily. "And she had white hair, if you want to know."

"Mon Dieu! You have decided to romance older women. I will have to hide my sainted mother."

"Don't be absurd, Paul. There was a riot at the school and the old schoolmistress fainted on me. I have strained myself somewhere, I'm sure." He checked for damage and found a large purple bruise on his ribs. "See, I have proof. My back feels like there's a dagger stuck in it." He groaned.

"Tsk, tsk." Paul shook his head. " 'Tis a feeble story."

"But true, I assure you. It would have taken no less than six Arabian stallions to move that enormous woman. The gardener finally rolled her off of me. *Merde,* what a relief! For a moment, I even swore off women." Tomorrow he would have to face Jean, and the Baron wouldn't be in good humor if Jean's earlier mood was any gauge.

Paul shrugged and poured a full goblet for himself and one for Michel. The Marquis downed the brandy in one gulp. "Shouldn't we go up there to defend the lady?"

"Not on your worthless life, Michel. I value my hide, and Jean is already touchy on the subject of the Duchess. Have some more brandy." Paul was tired and grouchy.

"He wouldn't actually hurt her, would he, Paul?" The Marquis realized Jean would probably kill them if they disturbed him now. All they could do was worry.

"I don't think so." Paul sighed heavily. "He is angry, though. I wouldn't want to be in her place at this moment. She was terrified when we rode back to Avranches, and I am sure she had no idea why she was brought here, until now. Jean is trying to scare her." Paul thoughtfully twisted a stray curl of his beard. "I believe he has found a formidable opponent this time."

Michel opened another bottle of the aged liquor,

spitting the cork at a man who snored loudly. "Is there nothing we can do?"

"Perhaps there is." Paul smiled. "If we can keep him busy enough to leave her alone for a while . . ."

"Maybe she can learn to like him." Michel's eyebrows rose mischievously. "She might get used to him. It is possible, isn't it, Paul?" He wasn't sure at all that the young Duchess could actually like Jean, let alone love him.

"The only thing we need to worry about is Jean catching us at it," Paul growled. "He can get wicked when he wants to."

Michel smiled widely. "Still, discreet insubordination is so much healthier than an open challenge of war. If we buy them some time to get to know each other, who knows, it might work out for the benefit of everyone concerned." The Marquis paced, thinking over the matter.

"Sit down, you whoreson, you're making me dizzy."

Michel was used to Paul's threats and didn't flinch as the insults were hurled at him. "What has put you in such a foul mood?"

"She put up quite a struggle when we kidnapped her. That feisty little woman almost broke my leg, and she tried to hit Jean. I just pray for her own sake that she has calmed down a bit."

"She tried to *hit* him?" Michel's sandy-brown brows raised in disbelief. "And I had to miss that," he hissed. "One small woman against the mighty Black Baron. What a sight that must have been." He picked up his lute and strummed ever so lightly. "I will have to write a ballad about this." He finished the brandy and leaned back in his chair. "After I get drunk."

"A song must have an end, Michel, and we shall have to wait and see the outcome. I believe this is

just the beginning of our problems. Prepare yourself, the worst is yet to come."

Michel brushed cobwebs from Paul's dark hair.
"Where have you been?"

"Dusting the rack, religiously," Paul answered
crankily.

"The only trestle you have ever dusted is in the
wine cellar." Michel grinned. "He threatened her
with torture?"

"She called his bluff." Paul yawned, exhausted
from the events that had passed. "Did you find the
Earl? We had no way of knowing you were already
en route to Paris, and sent an envoy to escort the
Earl back to Normandy. If the Duc was misinform-
ing us about the arrest, Jean wanted his father to
come home."

"The Earl was definitely taken into custody."

Paul vented his fury by throwing the bottle of
brandy against the wall; it shattered into a thousand pieces and left a sodden stain on the stone. He
stumbled to his bunk, passing out as his head
touched the pillow.

"What a waste of good alcohol." Michel was sure
Jean wouldn't like the news he brought back from
Paris. But the Marquis would have to give a full
report in the morning.

Michel was pleased to hear that Lady Lisette had
obviously made an impression on the Baron and his
cousin Paul. Otherwise, Jean wouldn't have remained at the château and sent his men to Paris,
and Paul wouldn't have given her anything more
than a passing comment. Somehow, they had
passed each other on the road, and Michel had
missed finding out that Lisette was safely in the
Baron's care. If he had known, he would have returned posthaste, and not stopped to pay a call on
a certain brunette who gave a marvelous massage.
He could have saved himself some agony; Michel

had had to vault off a second-story balcony when the lady's husband returned home at an unusually early hour.

The Marquis stretched out on his bunk and covered his head with the pillow. "This is going to be a long night." Secretly, he was very taken with the young Duchess de Meret. He had always known the moment would come when she would lie with his friend, and if he was honest with himself, the thought made him a little bit jealous. He had watched her in the two years that Jean was away, keeping his distance so that she didn't know she was being observed. Lisette was loyal to her country and the Baron, he was sure.

Chapter Five

Slow steady breathing in her ear woke Lisette from a deep sleep. The candle had burned itself out and pale moonlight outlined the man next to her. She didn't move, for fear of waking him. His arm still lay across her stomach, possessively holding her close to him. While he was asleep his face had softened and no longer appeared sinister. A lock of dark hair fell across his forehead, and Lisette felt a sentimental urge to push it aside. But she resisted. She was nothing more than a passion's pawn to Jean, to be used as an instrument of war.

A heavy tear splashed down her cheek. Lisette knew what must be done. With a parting look at her love, she eased from the bed. He rolled to his back and the deep breathing continued. She found Jean's robe at the end of the bed and wrapped it around her to ward off the night's chill.

There was a guard outside her door, and no other way out of the château except for the balcony.

The doors to the veranda were still open; Jean hadn't bothered to shut them after carrying her to bed. The stone wall was only waist high. She brushed aside the deep green ivy clinging to the walls and leaned over the balcony railing, viewing the nasty rocks below.

The waves seemed to lure her seductively to

their fatal embrace, draining the strength from her body. The warm summer night brought back disturbing memories of her beloved Baron, the one who had danced beside her on Midsummer Eve and given her all the passion a woman could want. A brief smile toyed with the corners of her mouth. If she jumped off the balcony . . . Lisette could envision the Baron standing over her broken body with nothing left but his own consuming hatred.

Never before had a de Meret yielded to the Jolberts. To think of herself subjugated under the rule of that—that barbarian. Unthinkable! Defeat was unknown to a de Meret. The fog of self-pity vanished. In her previous inspection, Lisette must have missed the trellis supporting the heavy vines on the side of the building. She hoped it was sturdy enough to hold her weight.

" 'Tis a very long drop and not a pleasant landing, my darling."

His deep voice startled her and she twirled around to face him.

His arm slipped around her waist. "Do you think I would allow you to kill yourself?" He shook her angrily.

"I have no intention of jumping because I want to be there the day you are executed for kidnapping me."

He carried her back to the bed, her inert form slumped over his shoulder, and dumped her amidst the rumpled blankets.

Lisette attacked. With every blow of her small fists against his wide chest she repaid him for her shattered dreams. "I hate you! I hate you! Oh, how could you do this to me when I . . ." Unable to move, she clenched her teeth together. Provoking him into another argument wasn't worth the energy it exacted from her. He wouldn't rape her or kill her; now she was sure. But he wanted her to be hum-bled and to beg for his affection. And that would never happen.

Jean pressed her against his body. Until now he hadn't realized how far he had pushed her. It took a desperate mind to seek escape in suicide, and he wanted her . . . alive.

Lisette shivered against him. The powerful body next to hers was sleek and rippled with muscles. The desire to touch him made her ache inside. What would happen if she did? It was madness to want him, knowing he was her enemy, yet within her was the need to know more. Why did her stomach tremble every time she thought of making him her lover? Were the rumors of pain or ecstasy the girls at school giggled about true?

Cradled by his powerful arm, she began to relax and she cuddled up against his side. A feeling of security banished her fears. The palm of his free hand kneaded the muscles in her back, then moved down her side to cup her derrière. Unable to stop herself, she tipped her chin up so their lips could meet. The first touch of his mouth brought a tingle of desire. His fingers moved across her belly to her thighs, where he caressed the tender skin in long strokes of torment.

For a long time they lay in silent embrace. He shifted his weight to his elbows, gently kissing her captivating face until the twilight of sleep closed her eyes. He eased the robe from her shoulders and tossed it to the end of the bed. Relishing the opportunity to see her mouth soft and peaceful instead grim with determination, he wanted to touch those rosy lips with his. If only she hadn't been so blasted innocent. Soon she would know the depth of his passion.

"Chérie." His soothing tone left intact the veil of half sleep.

She answered slowly, as if it took a great deal of

effort. *"Oui?"* She was dreaming an old, wonderful dream of her wedding day, when she would marry the man she loved.

"You said, 'How could you do this to me when I . . .' What is the rest, my little sea nymph?"

Her voice was barely a whisper. "When I have loved you for so very long." Not realizing what she had admitted, Lisette never knew how thoroughly her words disturbed the man beside her.

Jean couldn't get back to sleep; her confession stirred his emotions. Could he believe a sleepy admission?

With his hands clasped behind his back, he paced the room. Every time he turned back he glanced at her sleeping form. If he had stayed in France, he wouldn't have been able to keep his hands off her. Yet the sacrifice of his leaving for Spain had played directly into the hands of the Duc de Meret. The Duc had found another man willing to pay for the privilege of marrying her. But Lisette belonged to him, and for the Duc's treachery, he would destroy the house of de Meret.

In a few weeks she would turn eighteen, and then her fate would lie in his hands. A child no longer, she *would* become his mistress.

Jean answered the soft knock on the door. Paul was standing in the hall, fully dressed.

"Simon has sent word for you to meet him in Rouen," Paul whispered. "He said it was urgent, a matter of life and death." He peeked at the form on the bed. She appeared to be fast asleep.

She became fully awake as it grew strangely quiet. Lisette had heard the knock, and the slight squeak of the door as it was opened. They left the room, and she stretched out on her back, staring at the shadows on the canopy. Muted voices drifted from the hall.

"What am I going to do with her? How I'd love

to get the Duc on the tip of my rapier." The Baron's voice was filled with the need for revenge.

The grumbling voice of his cousin retorted, "We have plenty of natural resources around for water torture. Or we could hitch up the stallion and have her drawn and quartered. Well, what are you going to do?"

"If you're not going to be helpful, please hold your tongue." The Baron wasn't in the mood for humor. "What is the news from Paris?"

Lisette felt a giggle shake her flat stomach and rock the bed. She could envision Paul thoughtfully stroking his beard while the Baron ranted and raved. What would they do to her, indeed? The men moved down the hall, and it wasn't long before Paul returned to secure the door. His gaze met hers and his eyes twinkled in mischief. He silently saluted her and closed the door, locking it behind him.

Somehow, she missed the Baron's warm body next to hers. In this strange place beside the sea, she could dream of happier days and sun-filled afternoons. They could have been divine together.

Her life was changing too fast to understand. What did she care for politics or feuds? She would give everything she owned for one genuine smile and a moment of his attention without fear of retribution. Her heart ached, suspecting it would never happen.

Lisette drifted in and out of a restless sleep until Anna brought in her breakfast. She had been certain she could never eat again until she got a whiff of fresh yeast pastries and creamy churned butter.

"You look tired," Anna offered sympathetically. " I brought you something to cheer you up. Do you like strawberries?"

Of course she did. The young Duchess thought

she would kill for a taste of oatcakes smothered with strawberry jam, but she'd never admit it.

"How about a cup of hot tea?" Anna prodded.

That sounded good, too. "I might try a little."

"Good. It will put the color back into your cheeks. The Marquis has promised to take us riding on the seashore today, and I'd feel terrible if you didn't eat something first."

Lisette had control, even though the aroma of buttered cakes and fresh, juicy berries drifted from the plate to assail her senses. "A lady only nibbles" had been a prime directive at the school, and one of the hardest lessons Lisette was forced to learn. It wasn't easy to hide her healthy appetite. The butter oozing off the pastry to form puddles on the plate was a severe temptation to her training. But, crumb by miserable crumb, she maintained her dignity.

"Who is the Marquis that will take us riding this morning, Anna?" Perhaps Lisette would know the name and could seek help from him. Her family was well known as royalist, and anyone in the King's grace wouldn't refuse her plea for help.

"The Marquis Michel le Maire is the Baron's friend. He has joined us for a time. What will you wear today, my lady?" Anna giggled and opened the doors to the armoire.

Beautiful gowns of all colors caught Lisette's attention. Velvets and satins, silks and brocades, all exquisitely styled and dripping with yards of lace and expensive ribbons.

"Whom do they belong to?" Lisette asked as she tossed the sheets aside and slid her arms into the wrapper the maid held out to her. Lisette pulled a yellow taffeta gown from the closet and held it up to her body. In the mirror, she saw how her auburn hair was set off by the golden sheen of the gown. It was a striking sight. She laughed with delight.

Anna clapped her appreciation. "They all belong to you, my lady. The Baron has seen to your every need. This room, in fact, was decorated just for you. My lord thought you might like it."

" 'Tis very elegant." Lisette saw a fondness for the Baron in the young girl's eyes. Anna looked plain in the dull maid's uniform, her yellow hair tucked under her cap. She seemed no more than fifteen. Yet, as Lisette watched Anna, she got the uncanny feeling her maid was far wiser than the young woman at first appeared.

Lisette had to face reality. The Baron was not planning on a wedding as long as he could torment her. She was not a visitor, and soon he would no longer simply threaten violence to achieve his revenge on her family.

She had to leave the château before her will failed her completely. Somehow, she must find a way out of the fortress.

Anna answered a tap on the door and stepped aside to let the guest enter. Didn't anyone have any manners? Lisette didn't know the brash young man, and she wasn't dressed.

"You may come in," she said pointedly.

"Bonjour, mademoiselle. My name is Michel. Jean asked me to look after you while he is away."

He took her hand into his and lightly touched her fingers to his lips. His warm brown eyes smiled at her, and without meaning to, she smiled in return. His hair was a mass of curls that sent ringlets in every direction. It was softly brown, almost blond, she thought.

"Shall we ride this morning, ladies?"

Lisette dressed before the Marquis could change his mind and decide it was too risky to take her off the grounds. While they toured the château she took note of everything she saw. There were six turns to get to the main entrance. She persuaded them to stop in the kitchen for a picnic lunch, and she noticed a door leading to the courtyard.

Lisette swung the gate shut after Anna passed through. It was perfect—the gate was well oiled and didn't squeak as it closed. But a pair of giant wolfhounds were caged next to the kitchen, and the slightest noise could set them off.

Lisette was stunned when they reached the gardens. She inhaled deeply as they walked the stone paths smelling the fragrant red and white roses which edged the far end of the garden. Cloistered flower beds of rainbow hues adorned the grounds, and the walls were covered in dense ivy. Brass crosses peaked the clay roof of the château, and a bell tower stood over the gateway. The design was reminiscent of the time of the Norman invasion, complete with a moat.

"It's lovely," she breathed easily.

Michel clipped a white rose and pruned it for her. "The blossom is plain next to you, my lady."

He smiled warmly and escorted her to the stables. A small voice in her head warned that this man could rival the Baron's attentions. He was gallant and soft-spoken, a trait she had come to appreciate after the fury she witnessed within the Baron.

A pudgy-faced boy stood back and gaped as they passed. Lisette was surprised when Michel spoke to him by name and tousled his dark hair. Servants in Louis's palace weren't treated this well. They performed menial chores, and were never spoken to except to be given their master's commands.

The boy's reaction to Anna further surprised and intrigued Lisette. He bowed slightly as they passed, and her young maid nodded. Was there

more to this maid than they were telling her? He
spoke in a language she didn't understand.

"What did the boy say?" She tugged on Michel's
arm, slowing him down to get a moment of privacy.

"He has waited for the grand lady of the house
to arrive, as we all have. I told him you were the
lady." He patted her hand, dismissing any further
questions.

Lisette noticed the stall marked Midnight Blue
was empty, and she guessed it belonged to the Baron's Arabian. She missed her speckled-gray gelding. He had been a good-natured horse. When
Michel led a chestnut mare out of the stable she
immediately ran over and stroked the strong neck.

"Oh, she's gorgeous."

"Her name is Morning Glory," Michel said
softly. "She is the same color as your hair. I guess
that's why Jean couldn't resist her." It gave her a
tingling feeling in her stomach to consider the Baron would think kindly of her. The Marquis helped
her mount and Lisette felt the thrill of riding a
racehorse for the first time in her life.

Lisette found she had a deep reverence for the
men who had conquered the savage elements and
founded Normandy as their home. The beach along
the north shore was edged in sheer cliffs and the
coastline rugged with small inlets and grottoes.
The sea stretched as far as the eye could see, and
glimmered in a deep, rich blue.

Morning Glory jumped a rickety picket fence and
cantered beside Michel's gold racer. Lisette wanted
to ask where the Baron had gone, but thought that
if she asked, she might not like the answer.

Michel chose a direction leading south, instead
of east toward her home province, Meret. Preoc-
cupied with thoughts of home and a path of escape,
Lisette barely noticed as the afternoon passed into

long evening shadows. Soon they had to turn their horses back.

While the livery boys unsaddled their mounts Lisette gave Morning Glory an apple, straining to see what was beyond the stone bridge. She didn't know any more about the lay of the land than she had this morning. It would be dangerous, but she would have to try.

Michel directed her into the library and poured them both a glass of wine. Dark, richly grained wood covered stone walls, and everywhere she went thick Persian rugs covered the floors. The estate dripped of inestimable wealth.

Lisette strolled through the library. She sipped the Burgundy wine and viewed the paintings of Jolbert ancestors. When she found the portrait of Jean, she stood rooted to the floor. The likeness was perfect. There wasn't a flaw in that noble nose or any waver in the hard, square line of his chin. The dark-haired Baron was a rogue amongst his flaxen-haired ancestors. His eyes were a paler version of the deep blue eyes of the lords of Normandy.

The room was filled with armory of the barbaric warlords who had once fought for the northern province. There was a helmet with red and gold plumes and a gorget mounted on top of a pillar. Beside it was an antique hauberk of chain mail on a valet with a stout cudgel leaning against it. The tunic and club were from another time, reminding her again of the Baron's belief in the old laws.

Beside the painting of Baron Jean-Charles Jolbert, ninth Baron of Avranches and heir to the title of Earl of Normandy, hung a painting of her. Lisette had posed for that portrait, believing it was for her father. An unsettling fear crept through her nerves as she turned and faced Michel.

"Where did the Baron get this painting?" Had he already ransacked her home? There were no lim-

its to what the man would do to get what he
wanted.

"Actually, I ordered the portrait for the Baron—
with your father's permission," Michel added for
clarification. "The artist was commissioned over
two years ago. The image doesn't do you justice, my
lady."

Lisette ignored the flattery. "I don't remember
seeing you at the palace." She felt her cheeks warm
in a blush when he took her hand in his and kissed
her fingers.

Michel grinned. "Let me start with the first time
you fainted. It was during an execution and your
uncle was correcting you on your manners at social
functions."

Lisette held up a hand to stop him. "I remember
that day all too well. Why didn't I ever see you?"

"I believe you had eyes only for my friend. If I
didn't believe that, you wouldn't be alive today."

"You would have killed me if I had been unfaithful to the Baron?"

Michel turned away disgusted. "No, my lady, I
couldn't hurt you in any way. Jean would have
claimed that right himself."

Her beloved Baron would have killed her. The
threats were real. She had to know the rest. "Is he
planning an attack on my father?" She didn't
really expect Michel to answer.

"I don't believe so. Jean already has what he
wants."

She knew he meant to reassure her that no further action was planned against her family, but instead the reminder was frightening. The Baron
already had a de Meret captive.

"Will you help me?" she pleaded.

"For reasons that I cannot tell you, I won't help
you leave this château." His tone was firm.

"But you have been at the palace and know the

King will be angry at your friend for kidnapping me. The Baron will be arrested. Do you want to see your friend in prison?"

He shook his head. "I have kept you too long." He evaded her question and called for Anna to escort her to her room. Special care was taken to lock her in again.

Michel collapsed against the wall outside her door. He had almost forgotten his loyalty to Jean. The Baron didn't know it yet, but his heart was already pledged to Lisette. Michel had no doubt that his friend dearly loved the Duchess. "If this madness doesn't stop soon," Michel swore under his breath, "I'll take her away and marry her myself." Perhaps he had fallen in love with her? He pushed the thought aside. Jean would have him shot at dawn if he knew what Michel was thinking.

Chapter Six

Lisette had committed to memory every door and courtyard of the château since her ride with Michel. She chose what she thought was the safest route. It was too risky to get a horse from the stables; her escape would have to be on foot. She wore her own riding habit, which had been cleaned and returned to her.

The Baron can't accuse me of taking what isn't mine, she thought bitterly. Lisette plumped up her pillows and arranged them to resemble her still form under the covers.

After the house fell quiet, she lay awake. A hairpin would serve as a key. With silk slippers on her feet, she could elude pursuers without a sound. She squinted, peeking through the keyhole. Her guard had retired and the hall was empty. Exasperating moments slipped by before the tumblers gave way and the pin slowly turned in the old lock. She silently cursed the creak that sang out from the hinges as the door opened.

Laughter floated up the stairs from the men's quarters. Oil lamplight glowed from the wing of the château that housed the Baron's troops. Lisette had to pass by their door to get to the kitchen.

Feeling with her fingertips along the rough stone wall, Lisette made her way to the staircase.

The steps were hidden in shadows, and the dim light worked to her advantage. She passed the men's quarters unnoticed. Each step took her closer to the kitchen door leading to the garden. Her excitement mounted, and soon she was almost running through the halls of the château.

Lisette reached the kitchen and found she was not alone. Her heart lunged into her throat. The old cook slept on a cot in the corner with a cat nestled beside her. Lisette had disturbed the feline. Afraid his friendly greeting would wake the cook, Lisette found a scrap of meat and tossed it to the oversized beast.

The bolt on the door squeaked when she moved it. She stopped to listen, hearing only her own heartbeat and the loud voices of drinking men echoing through the château. Before she could stop him the cat sneaked through the open door and set the dogs barking. Following quickly behind, Lisette passed through the door, closing it after her. She crouched in the shadows, pressing against the château walls, as the cook came outside to investigate the ruckus. To Lisette's horror, so did Michel.

The cook scratched her head and yelled back to the inquisitive men. " 'Twas only one of the cats." Michel dismissed the clamor and went back into the château. The dogs were more interested in the cat than they were in Lisette. And soon the curious cook gave up, went back inside, and crawled into her warm bed.

Lisette was out the gate with no more than a whisper of her skirts as she raced headlong into the night. Running until she thought her chest would explode, she took a moment to rest until her breathing came easier. As Lisette looked back the château loomed up ominously against a cloudy sky. The eerie sight caused goose bumps on her arms.

She could easily get lost; her sense of direction was already confused in the darkness. The terrain seemed to have changed since her excursion with the Marquis. Yet she felt she must put at least five miles between her and the château before morning.

Silver moonlight highlighted the tall stone statue of a man. Even in the dark she knew it was a Jolbert. The profile was unmistakably Norman. Somehow, she had stumbled into the family graveyard. The west wind rocked the bell in the tower, as if an unseen hand announced her arrival. Lisette gulped hard, her throat tight and dry. The churchyard, now crumbling with decay, was a foreboding scene, and she slowly backed away.

An owl screeched overhead and Lisette clamped her hands over her mouth to stifle a scream. Something brushed past her skirt. She reached a shaky hand down and swept cobwebs aside. Everywhere she turned, a statue seemed to watch her. Feeling along the clerestory wall of the old church, Lisette finally found an opening and was through the iron gate in an instant. She bolted for the shelter of the forest.

Stopping again to check her direction, she found the orange shadow of the moon over her shoulder. The thought of pursuit terrified her. What if the dogs were set loose? Paul would find out by morning she was gone, and his horse could travel much faster than she could run. Could she be a safe distance from the Baron's clutches by morning?

Lisette ran for her life.

Branches struck out at her with long, spiked fingers, scratching her face and arms as she tried to brush them aside. She trudged along until the earth beneath her feet seemed to suddenly disappear and she tumbled forward down a steep embankment. She lost her cape, and her skirt tore as she crashed through the underbrush, snapping twigs and loosening gravel. Finally, she rolled to a stop.

Lisette lay at the bottom of the hill unable to move for a few agonizing seconds. The sleeve of her dress was held on by a thread and she pulled it free and buried it deep under the leaves so as not to leave a trace for any pursuers.

With dirty hands she brushed the leaves and twigs from her hair, smudging her face with mud. Only superficially scratched and bruised, Lisette picked up her torn skirts and set off in a direction that felt right. A brilliant streak of lightning highlighted the forested hills of Normandy. The approaching storm would pass right over her.

Desperation crept into her mind. It was so dark she could barely see her hand in front of her face. The terrain seemed familiar, and she had an uneasy feeling that she had come this way before.

Lisette stopped. Her skirt billowed as she spun around. The moon was hidden behind thick clouds. She held her breath in those few moments as she waited for nature to illuminate the countryside. Was it possible she'd turned back on the same path? Her answer came swiftly. The statue in the graveyard stood before her; a monolith of death. She had gone in a circle!

Tears stung her eyes. Lisette backed away from the statue, turned and ran. But her foot caught on a tree root, twisting her leg, and she stumbled to the ground. Tears streamed down her scratched cheeks. Lisette gave in to them finally. Lying in a disheveled heap, Lisette sobbed and beat the ground with her fists. "I will never forgive you, Jolbert. Never!" All her pretty dreams were gone. The beautiful wedding and the summer balls in Paris beside her handsome fiancé disappeared. It was an apparition of her childhood fantasies. Escape meant her only chance for revenge.

Lisette found she felt better, at least emotionally. But pain shot up her leg when she put weight on it. She was furious with herself for letting the Baron provoke her to such a desperate act.

"First, I will have him whipped. Then slowly tortured over a roaring fire. That arrogant, overbearing, pompous dictator can find his pleasure elsewhere. I would no more have him for a husband now than I would care to have the pox!" Feeling victorious now that she had properly thrashed him, Lisette hoisted up her skirt and slowly moved onward.

Her ankle swelled to twice its normal size, making it difficult to walk. She had to stop to rest. As she regained her strength the aroma of food brought her attention to her empty stomach. She let her nose lead the way through the darkness. Dawn would soon come, and with it the Baron riding furiously behind her. She needed sustenance before she could go much farther. The sight of a fire brought a sigh of relief.

A lone figure stooped next to the blaze. Lisette's mouth watered at the thought of something hot to eat. The man beside the fire appeared startled when Lisette hobbled boldly into his camp. He had been eating. The few wooden utensils he had in his lap dropped to the ground as he stood.

"Monsieur, I am lost and hungry. My father will pay you well for my safe return," she implored, stopping short of telling him the Baron Jolbert was after her.

He motioned to her. "Come, sit beside the fire and warm yourself. Why, you're nothing but a child." He kicked the remains of his supper aside, providing her a comfortable place beside the fire.

Lisette warmed her hands over the small fire.

The food bubbling inside his iron pot could have been gruel for all she cared. She took the wooden bowl he offered and graciously accepted the watery porridge. It was sticky, almost unpalatable, and stuck to the roof of her mouth. But she was ravenous. As she sat there, using her fingers to eat, Lisette couldn't help wishing for the basic comforts of a hot bath and a maid to wash her tangled hair.

Her host moved behind her and she strained to look around the camp in the darkness. An animal that had once resembled a horse but now had thin legs and a swayed back was tied to a tree beside his camp.

"Your father would pay for your return?" the man cautiously inquired.

"Oui, if you can grant me safe escort and the use of your horse." It bothered her that he stayed behind her. Although he seemed to be busy rolling a blanket, she got the weird feeling that his eyes never left her back. Nervous, she turned around. The smoke from the fire made him appear demonically evil as he approached. He had a wolfish smile, and his cheeks were greasy.

"You must be in a hurry to see your father, to brave the night all alone."

"These are desperate times."

"For a peasant, maybe." He scratched the stubble on his chin as he watched her.

Lisette couldn't move as he loomed before her.

"If your father would pay me well to get you back, think of the frolic we can have before you return," he snickered, staggering toward her.

The Baron quietly entered Lisette's chamber. He had finished his business with Simon and ridden hard, eager to return to his lovely captive and resume the seduction. He lit the candle beside the bed. His back ached from the long hours of riding without rest. The thought of returning to Lisette had driven him to ride through the night. She slept so soundly that she didn't move when his boot dropped to the floor. He pulled the shirt from his arms. When she still didn't move, he slapped what should have been the curve of her hip.

He ripped the coverlet from the bed and threw it across the room. Pillows were tucked together to resemble a sleeping form, and a powdered catogan wig lay on the headrest. She was gone. He checked the armoire and found nothing. Nor was she hiding under the bed, or behind the tapestry. Jean had thought there was something wrong with the lock when he opened her door.

"Paul!" His bellow echoed through he halls. "Search the house. She has fled."

Jean wouldn't leave anything to chance. They searched everywhere. What if she had taken her own life? The balcony was empty, and in the dark, the rocks below offered no sign of her.

"Search the beach, too," he angrily ordered Michel.

"I can't find her," Michel reported. He had dressed within minutes and searched everywhere. From attic to cellar, the house had been torn apart.

The Baron drew his black brows together. If she had managed to get out of the house, she would be headed east, toward Castle Meret. He would have her back soon, he vowed, or someone would pay for her escape with his hide.

Paul's voice boomed through the château. "We found the trail. She's headed through the gardens."

The Marquis slumped against the doorframe and let out a sigh of relief. He guessed by the vehement look from the Baron that he would be blamed for her escape. Michel might live to see another day if they found her unharmed. If not, Jean would kill him, and Paul would say a few words over his miserable corpse at sunset.

Twenty lanterns blazed along her trail. It headed due east.

Lisette rose and stepped back a pace, edging closer to the fire.

"Lost, eh?" he taunted. With a jump, he grabbed her. "I always wanted me a highborn wench with soft skin."

Lisette screamed and pounded on his back when he tried to kiss her. The taste of his slimy mouth made her gag. She sank her teeth into his bottom lip and pushed his disgusting body away from her.

Enraged, the man raised his hand. "You little witch! I will make you pay for biting me." He cursed again and caught her around the waist when she tried to run.

With her back to his chest he hauled her away from the fire. Remembering what she had done to Paul, Lisette raised her knee and pointed her toes, bringing the heel of her boot backward sharply against the man's knee. Free at last, she stumbled toward the horse. In her exhaustion, she clung to the horse's mane. Her head felt as though it were being lifted off her shoulders. She was going to faint.

He crushed her against his filthy clothes and dragged her back toward the fire. She cried out in agony as he threw her to the ground, knocking the wind out of her. He climbed on top of her, tearing the bodice of her dress.

Lisette was sickened by the foul smell of him. She couldn't fight him; his strength was three times hers. While his lead-heavy legs pinned her to the ground, she looked for anything she could use to clobber him. Her terrified mind worked in slow motion. Lisette fumbled through the dirt and found a rock that was small enough to fit into her hand and jagged enough to be a weapon. She had only to wait for her chance.

One of his grimy hands held her down by her hair while the other pushed her skirts up over her thighs. His face went down to her chest, and with all of her strength she brought the rock down on the back of his head.

His body sagged against her. Blood gushed from the wound, glittering in a crimson arch. She hit him again, just to be sure he couldn't get up.

Lisette crawled out from under his inert form. Her stomach wrenched as she wiped the blood from her face. Her wide, terrified eyes never left the pauper. With shaking hands she pulled the shredded remnants of her bodice together.

The sound of approaching horsemen heralded her final defeat. The Baron had found her, she was sure. Dazed, she stood beside the horse, unsure of which way to run. She knew she wouldn't make it twenty feet before the Baron would have her surrounded. A thought crept into the back of her mind. What if the Baron didn't know she had escaped yet? It could be the Rouen guard that patrolled the area.

She nervously looked back at the prone figure of the peasant. He hadn't moved. She had knocked the man senseless to protect herself. But what if he were dead? Her head hurt, thinking of what could happen to her next.

A man dismounted and walked up in front of her.

Scraping up the last morsel of her pride, she held her head high. The dark figure of Baron Jolbert stood before her. As she feared, she was completely surrounded.

"Come to me, Lisette," he said gently.

Indecision wavered in her mind. Could she trust him? Her thoughts were wrapped in confusion. Not knowing where to turn her eyes, she stared at the brass buttons on his black coat.

He had heard her scream and would never forget the shrill sound of terror in her voice. The torn dress fell open to reveal reddened skin and the first signs of bruises.

"I want that bastard," the Baron proclaimed with a low growl. He would personally pull the man's limbs apart with his bare hands. "Keep him alive."

Michel brought a blanket from the pack on his horse and stood next to his friend. The young Duchess trembled where she stood. The troop passed beside her. Out of respect for their lord, they didn't stop to gape. A look of helplessness quivered at the corners of her bruised and bleeding mouth as the Marquis watched her.

The Baron ran his hands over her head, looking for any serious cuts. "This isn't her blood, Michel. She must have wounded the man who attacked her." He poured water from his canteen into a *mouchoir* and dabbed at the stains on her face until he was certain she wasn't hurt.

Michel silently thanked the Holy Mother that he would live to see another day. "The door was locked, Jean. Anna wouldn't forget and leave it open. I checked it myself, before I retired."

"That hardly matters now."

Jean sensed Lisette couldn't speak, even if she wanted to. She stared at him, and yet her beautiful blue eyes were focused on nothing at all. The sight of her battered body infuriated him. No man would ever have the right to touch her perfection, none but him. He possessed her. His respect for her had been earned almost at the cost of her life, he thought grimly.

"Where is that bastard?" the Baron growled.

Paul heard the fury in the Baron's voice and

grinned with pleasure. "He's dead. She crushed his skull with a rock. We had to bury him."

"Indeed." Jean would never underestimate her again. Reaching out to Lisette, he stroked her cheek with his thumb, then cradled her head between his hands and gazed into her azure eyes.

"Come to me, Lisette," he repeated slowly.

He wanted her homage. It was a public declaration acknowledging the Baron as her liege lord and allowing him to put her under his protection as his vassal.

"I didn't do anything to you," she cried out. "I trusted you."

Jean was guilty as charged. He accepted the blame for her anguish, and silently chided himself for not seeing her faultless virtue. His doubts and indecisions were inconsequential now. At this moment, all he cared about was the woman he loved. "We'll find a way to work this out, Lisette. I will protect you from those who would bring you harm."

Her dream surfaced from misty memories as the huskiness of his voice seductively lured her to him. She couldn't go through another night of terror. His arms were an invitation to disaster, but she didn't care. She let herself step forward into that tender embrace and collapsed.

Triumphant, Jean smiled.

Chapter Seven

Michel hooked an arm over the oak banister railing. His chin rested on the back of his hand as he observed the Baron. Jean gently cradled Lisette in his arms and carried her up the stairs to her chamber. "She'll be eighteen in a few weeks," the Marquis commented idly to the captain of the troop who stood beside him.

Paul and Michel overheard Anna's scolding tongue as she met the Baron in the hall. "What did you do to her?"

"*I* certainly didn't beat her, Anna." Jean swept past the maid, entering Lisette's room.

The waxed tips of Paul's mustache curled upward. "We could always give him lessons on the finer art of love."

The Marquis squirmed at the thought of teaching the Baron *anything*. Long ago they had come to terms with who would win the battles between them. The Baron always triumphed.

"For a man who doesn't believe in kidnapping, Jean sure learns fast. He should be sweeping her off her feet, not taking her prisoner."

Paul gave him a sidelong glance of disbelief. "Women need a straightforward approach. Jean should haul her off to the chapel. Marriage is what

they both need to settle them down, after she realizes who's the lord of the house."

Michel's eyes rolled heavenward, then settled
upon his muscular friend. "She'd never marry him
now. Look at the way he treats her. It's almost
criminal. Lady Lisette would melt in his arms if he
gave her a little kindness."

"And then break his knee. You know how feisty
she can get." Paul remembered all too well. His leg
was still bruised and sore from her kick.

As Jean reached the head of the stairs their
voices became a murmur. "Your brother Simon has
agreed to help us keep Jean busy," Michel announced.

Paul thoughtfully stroked his beard. "I wonder
what information Simon has on the Duc de Meret."

"Simon had some interesting news," Jean said
as he descended the stairs. "The Duc doesn't know
that I have his daughter. Darias was informed of
the kidnapping, and couldn't care less. It seems
that Lisette's cousin has plots of his own that the
Duc doesn't know about."

"But for what purpose would it serve Darias to
forsake Lady Lisette?" Paul didn't like the latest
developments.

"He wants something from me," Jean said bitterly. "Darias forged the note to Lisette, insisting
that she return immediately, and signed it with
her father's seal. It was damned convenient we
found her that afternoon. Almost as if it had been
preordained by a third party."

"The Duc is submerged in his own political aspirations and doesn't know what his nephew is
doing," Michel snorted.

Jean explained further. "I didn't do what Darias
expected of me. By feudal rights, Lady Lisette belongs to me. I was enraged when the Duc broke the

contract. Darias must have speculated that, under the circumstances, I would marry her immediately and claim what I had paid. He didn't think I would take out my revenge on Lisette. Darias wants to destroy me, but not before he can secure an heir to Normandy. Let me put it this way. What if Lisette did bear a Jolbert child, then she accidentally died?"

"Murder?" Michel spoke up. "It's too incredible to believe Darias would kill his own cousin."

"Is it really so hard to believe?" Jean questioned. "Darias could benefit from an alliance between our families. If Lisette's uncle and father become victims of the revolution, they would leave Lisette to the mercy of her malicious cousin. If the Duc and King are killed, Darias becomes her guardian and able to control the future of France. And if she should have a fatal accident . . . well, then Darias would achieve total power.

"He couldn't kill her off, though, before she bears a Jolbert child to inherit the Normandy wealth and the proper bloodline to the throne." Jean's smile was sad. "Lisette doesn't know of her cousin's true plans to sit on the throne. As yet, Darias doesn't have the funds to manage the costly campaign. But he's using the Duc as his puppet and his patron, and when the time is right, the Duc will disappear and Darias will step in to take his place."

"An illegitimate heir wouldn't possess a solid claim to the Jolbert wealth," Paul pointed out. "What if you didn't marry the Duchess?"

Seated on the stairs, Jean braced his elbows on his knees and rested his chin on his knuckles. "Darias had my father arrested to ensure the heir is legitimate. He figured I would be impulsive and marry her immediately. The Duc probably believed my father was guilty of treason and secured the *lettre* with loyal intentions.

"If I marry Lisette and have a child, my *père* is dead. Darias has got to get rid of both of us before he can have access to the Jolbert fortune. There isn't much time to find my father before Darias becomes impatient."

Paul interrupted. "Since Darias has an inkling of what your estate consists of, and any fool can assume the inestimable wealth of the King, it would be well worth his time to wait a year for an heir."

Michel loved the intricacy of Darias's thinking. "Soon after the nuptials, he'll probably slip a bodkin between your ribs some night when you least expect it."

Here was Jean's chance to point out his worst fears. "Maybe Darias would take the honor of murdering me. But what about Lisette doing the deed? She would be in a perfect position to kill me. She would have plenty of motive with Darias offering her wealth and power. It has to be considered, either way. It's an honor to be a queen mother."

"I don't believe it," Michel scoffed.

Jean stretched his long legs out in front of him and braced his elbows on the stairs behind him. God, how he hated politics. There was a *lettre de cachet* issued with his father's name on it that was scribbled in the King's hand. The King wouldn't argue with his brother, and had probably issued the order without knowing what Darias was planning to do with it. Darias had a perfect escape; he had covered every angle, except one. Jean would take Lisette to Spain.

Was she still the sweet, innocent young woman he had met years ago? Or was she baiting him into believing she was still a virgin? He would find out if she still had her maidenhead first, then decide whether or not to marry her. As for trusting her? He simply couldn't now that he knew of Darias's schemes.

The Baron and his father had discussed the possibilities of marrying a number of young women. Over two and a half years ago, Jean paid a call on the King to resign his commission in the military when he observed Lisette as she strolled by dressed in her finest for an appearance at court. He was instantly attracted to her, and wouldn't accept another for his bride. Jean's father tried to point out how the de Meret's royal lineage might be a threat to Jean's life. But Jean was headstrong. He had found his dream come true and wanted her beyond all reason.

Jean had to find his father and leave France before the revolution swept over the countryside. The Duc wasn't counting on the peasants turning their wrath upon the nobility. This was the one flaw in Darias's device that Jean could count on. A civil war was brewing, one that could change the future of France. Anyone standing in its way would be crushed.

Outside, a steady rain tapping on the balcony door seemed to hum along with Lisette, while inside ripples of bathwater swirled around her. Lisette washed and combed her hair, hanging it over the edge of the tub to dry in the heat of the fire. She held a sponge over her face and let the water trickle down her neck. She was alone in the room, and enjoying the sound of rain tinkling against the windows and the fire crackling, until a key turned in the door.

Knowing her privacy was soon to be invaded, Lisette grasped for the only weapon she could find. A sponge—hardly a defense that would be a threat to his life, but a deterrent nonetheless.

The door swung open and the Baron entered. He carried a large, oval platter laden with food and drink. An ankle-length robe dusted the tops of his slippered feet, and his hair was damp and mussed.

She aimed carefully. The sponge hurtled through the air. Jean ducked to put the tray down just in time. The sponge smacked against the stone wall, then fell to the floor.

"Don't you ever knock?" Lisette sank deeper so that her shoulders were under the milky water. "Your manners are deplorable!"

"My, but you are testy this morning, Lisette," he teased. "Do you need another outing like the one you had last night to convince you of the need for my protection?"

"This is imprisonment, and you know it." She forced her voice to sound stern. It was hard to be angry with him when his devilish grin focused on her. "Please call Anna back. I want to get out now."

His smile brightened and he bowed before the tub. "Your valet, my darling. I am at your service." He held the sheet of toweling out for her, noting the crimson blush in her cheeks. When she hesitated he sighed tediously. "You can't stay in the tub forever."

Lisette quickly rose, snatched the sheet from him, and wrapped it around her body. His nimble fingers caught a strand of hair clinging to her wet body and slowly pulled it back, over her shoulder. She couldn't meet his steady gaze. Standing before him with nothing more on than a sheet left her feeling unsure of herself.

Jean chuckled and scooped her up into his arms. In two easy strides he was beside the fire and gently set her on her feet. The thought of ripping the sheet off and making love to her caused his heart to pound in his veins.

He could kiss her earlobe and work his way down to her inner thigh. In a dream he had imagined her long legs encompassing him in the throes of passionate lovemaking. She would stand over him and ease herself down. Her fluffy hair would toss in the wind as he kissed and tormented the dark patch at the crest of her thighs. Wickedly, she would brush his chest with the peaks of her breasts until his manhood thrust upward into the velvet recess of her body. He licked his dry lips and let out a shaky sigh. Maybe she wasn't ready for that part of his dream.

His broad hands lingered on her bare shoulders, smoothing the beads of water away. While he massaged the aching muscles in her neck, her head fell back. His lips followed the trail to the delicate hollow at the base of her throat. The fresh scent of her newly bathed body filled his head. With lazy determination, his kisses wandered over her throat, to soft, moist lips. Greedily, he pressed her slight form to his. They were bonded by a fierce need to have each other. But he would wait until she was ready for him.

Lisette stood still as he vigorously rubbed her dry. She tried to fight the attraction she felt, the desire to touch him. Jean handed her a goblet of warm wine. She hadn't realized how hungry and thirsty she was.

He tossed aside the linen serviette covering their breakfast and offered her a chair. "Perhaps some food would brighten your mood a little. I seem to recall you have quite an appetite once you get started. My cook is very talented. I promise the hot scones will make your mouth water. Would you join me, my lady?"

Jean couldn't take his eyes off her beautiful body. Her dark auburn hair fell in a silky waterfall around her nightshift, and the firelight sent flickers of light dancing over her soft curves. The tightly clinging fabric showed off her shapely figure as unmistakably exquisite.

Lisette began slowly eating, and soon found that her vision was blurred. His soft gray eyes stared at her. But she held her head high, proud and defiant. She noticed a bitter taste in her final swallow of wine and was angered that he would stoop to using drugs to keep her there. Her strength of will seemed to be disappearing, and she feared his charm would overpower her efforts to resist him.

When he rose and came to her side, the apprehensive twitch in her stomach started again. The warmth of his arms sliding around her was exciting. The euphoria of the drug made her body tingle. When he picked her up, the room started to spin. She clung to him, helpless to stop the whirling void of passion.

She had known that they were meant to be lovers from the first moment she met him. She longed for his touch and tempting mouth on hers again, and, casting aside all fear of revenge, she wouldn't let go when he laid her on the bed. Instead, her arms slid around his neck and pulled him down until their lips met in joyous harmony. Her rounded curves pressed to his, yearning for his hands to caress her. She found it so easy to forget everything and succumb to his charm. Tiny shivers pulsed through her lips as he teased her with little kisses. He was taunting her by nuzzling her earlobe and tracing the line of her jaw with the tip of his tongue. A trembling sigh of desire eased from her lips. His head bent to the full swell of her breast and nibbled the dark shadow of her nipples through the filmy material of her nightshift. Her leg slid between his thighs and her knee rubbed against the swell there.

Jean looked up to see the wicked gleam in her eye.

"Love me," she pleaded breathlessly.

It's the laudanum doing this to her, Jean

thought, although he didn't question his good fortune and stretched out above Lisette, pressing her deep into the soft feather mattress. He flinched when she lightly bit his shoulder and her fingers gripped the taut muscles of his back. Their lips touched in intense passion, and her legs parted at the pressure of his knee, allowing him passage to the soft folds of her womanhood.

The yearnings of her body had become a reckless desire. Her cheek rested against the silky pillows and her eyes closed, suspending her dreams in her mind.

"L-love me again," she slurred.

His hands clenched into fists when he realized she was groggy from the laudanum. She would probably never even remember his torment. He sighed in frustration. If he could find something to smash at this moment . . .

Jean rolled on his side and propped his head on the palm of his hand. Her lips parted to protest, but his finger silenced her. His light chuckle shook the bed.

"So, *ma petite,* the kitten in you is really a wildcat."

Her pride wounded, she retaliated hastily. "Why won't you just leave me alone?" Why did he always have to laugh at her? She rolled away from him, trembling until the longing subsided and the peace of sleep calmed her.

Her covered her with the quilt and got up to place another log on the hearth. He stared at the fire a moment, his mind drifting back to the gentle rise of her breasts as she opened her arms to him. He hoped that the laudanum in her wine had brought to the surface signs of her true feelings for him.

Her disappearance had scared him. What if she did manage to escape him again? He couldn't bear to think of what fate Darias had in store for her.

She seemed so innocent. Even if she did conspire with Darias to destroy him, he was certain she didn't realize what she was doing. Was it his destiny to hold paradise in his arms, then have it disappear?

Oh, my darling, if you knew how much I wanted you.

Jean wanted her to be happy with him. He *had* treated her badly, but wanted to make it up to her by showing her how much he cared for her. Perhaps that would help her to be less frightened of him. Her birthday was a few weeks away, and he would find something special to give her. It would be a gift from that part of him that dearly loved her. For now, he wouldn't consider his doubts about her loyalty.

Daylight cast the clear sky in a light shade of blue. The rain clouds moved inland to water the crops in the fields.

Jean sat on the edge of the bed and smoothed Lisette's cheek with the back of his hand. She looked so peaceful while asleep. "We were supposed to be married in a few weeks, Lisette. If you knew me better, you'd see my concern goes further than our love and happiness. Our country needs us, and yet we must get away from this chaos before it overtakes us all and destroys everything we have worked for.

"I was angry when your father told me I couldn't have you. We are very much alike, my spirited lady. We both obey the rules of propriety, but are not afraid to defy authority if we know we are right."

Chapter Eight

Lisette rarely saw the Baron in the following weeks. He refused to allow her out of her room, and the solitude annoyed her even more. She wanted a confrontation with him, not silence. Anna was with her continuously. All Lisette could learn from her was that there was "trouble" and the men were seeing to it. The maid smiled, though, as if she knew more than she was willing to tell. But no matter how hard she pleaded with Anna, the maid would not help Lisette escape. According to Anna, the Baron was a saint.

A sturdy bolt was nailed to the outside of Lisette's door and a guard posted day and night. The Baron was not taking any more chances with her. He wanted her kept alive to continue his revenge on the de Merets.

Lisette became cross and irritable from sleepless nights. She heard the Baron enter his chamber late at night, but he was always gone when she rose the next morning. If Jean had continued to seduce her, it wouldn't have been long before she gave in to the desire to fully explore the realm of sensual delight.

Early that day, she yelled and banged on the door until the guard had to get Michel to settle her down. Lisette insisted on seeing the Baron, and

Michel bowed and informed her that Jean would be sent for.

Lisette was unable to eat, her stomach twisted in an anxious knot while she awaited the Baron's return.

Anna worked all morning altering a gown for the Duchess and held it up as she finished. "Do you want to try this on now, my lady?"

"Leave me, Anna," Lisette curtly dismissed her. "I don't want the dress or anything else the Baron offers. If you can't help me gain my freedom, then get out of here!"

"But, my lady, I cannot leave you," she implored.

"Get out!" Lisette screamed. Anna tearfully obeyed. Lisette felt like a wretch for scolding the maid, but every moment reminded her she was a captive, held against her will, with a promise of a scandalous future. She wouldn't make it easy for Jean to taint her by quietly waiting. She wanted her protest known, and he would have to discuss the terms of her captivity.

Lisette paced the length of the balcony several times before her temper cooled. Her birthday was tomorrow, and it was supposed to have been her wedding day as well. The lost hopes added to her sullen mood.

The door to her chamber burst open and she shrank back against the stone rail. She guessed by the glowering expression on the Baron's face that he wasn't happy about her request. Jean stood in the threshold, looking like an angry cavalier who was about to whip his horse. He tapped his riding crop in his open hand, and her mouth dropped open in terror. He looked so angry she thought he would kill her. He crossed the balcony and his hands clamped over her shoulders in an admonishing grasp.

"Not a word," he warned. "You will hold your tongue when talking to Anna, or *lose it.* Do you hear me? She volunteered to be your handmaid, and I will not tolerate your threatening her. *Mon Dieu,* have you no heart at all? She's only sixteen years old, and her life has been shattered!"

"And you haven't disrupted mine?" Lisette had held her own temper at bay as the furious nobleman shouted at her, but she could contain it no longer. "How dare you speak to me like this?" she shouted back at him. With his powerful grip, the Baron lifted her off the floor. His teeth were tightly clenched and his voice low.

"Don't try to use Anna to escape me, Lisette." He dropped his hands and turned away.

Jean needed to calm down. He watched the sea gulls on the Channel until the anger in him subsided. There were enough petty problems in the province to keep him busy, and he now realized he had neglected Lisette. The bread queues had been growing longer. It was a desperate time for the peasants who were hungry.

A miller was suspected of hoarding grain. The Baron's judgment had been stern; the miller had to sell the hoarded grain at half the inflated price of twelve *sous* for a four-pound loaf of bread. It was a tiring duty to rule the province and keep the serfs from killing each other. Even this far removed from Paris, the grumblings of an angry nation were felt.

When he finally spoke, his voice held a melancholy tone. "Anna's very young. I pray she can forget the horror she's seen in her youth. Someday I'll tell you more, but for now, I beg you to treat her with kindness."

Lisette felt a wave of shame. It wasn't the maid but the Baron that had upset her. She stood behind him and lightly touched his shirt sleeve with her hand. "Tell me what happened to her."

"It's better that you don't know. When the time comes, we'll talk about it. For now . . . ?"

"I will grant her every kindness."

Lisette wrung her hands in despair. It was a daily agony, wondering if her father was still alive, wondering what was delaying his rescuing her from the Baron. Her father *must* be fretting over her disappearance. Perhaps he had fallen into one of the Baron's traps and no one knew of his demise. Lisette could easily envision a hundred different ways for the Baron to have secreted the Duc out of the country, never to be seen again.

What was preventing her kin from storming the château? The answer was simple. No one knew where she was. And by now the Duc might think she was dead.

She silently scolded herself for not waiting for an escort the day she left the school. Once again she had reacted emotionally, not thinking of the consequences.

But how could she ever leave Jean?

"I don't understand what is happening to me," she whispered. "When can I go home?"

His rage spent, he sighed deeply. A smile touched his mouth. Jean finally understood her problem. How could she know what was happening to her when he wanted to make love to her one moment, then wanted to strangle her the next?

He wasn't certain that Lisette was involved in the de Meret treachery which broke his heart. Yet it disgusted him to think a man of honor could lay hands on a woman and want to hurt her. How could he make her understand the risk involved if she escaped again and her father took control of her? Or why the Jolberts had wagered so much to make her his bride knowing her bloodline could destroy them? The marriage offered the Jolberts and de Merets peace between their provinces, a chance for happiness. The Baron had loved Lisette when she was a child of fifteen, and now at her coming of age he was even more deeply in love with her. She was worth the risk of his own life to make her his wife.

"You will stay with me always, Lisette."

"Until the day your revenge on the de Merets is satisfied and you cast me aside?" she asked quietly.

"You arrived at an unfortunate time, my lady. When I found you that afternoon, it was after your father informed me that you were promised to another. I have too much invested in you to allow that to happen."

"If money is all you want, it can be repaid."

"It isn't that easy, Lisette. Your father wants to destroy me. The only reason I am still alive is that I have you here with me."

Lisette suddenly felt torn between going home and staying with the Baron. How could she choose between the two things that she loved the most? It was a cruel twist of fate that she would have to make the decision.

"There is something else you should know, Lisette. The reason you and your father are alive is only because of *my* intervention. There are mercenaries freely roaming France. Some of them are under the King's influence, but not all of them care what happens to the throne; there are many revolutionists who find your blue blood reason enough to kill.

"We will talk about this later." Jean moved to answer a knock on the door. He accepted the message from his man, stepped out into the hall, and yelled for Michel. The Marquis appeared moments later and Jean handed him the missive.

"Prepare to leave for Paris at once," the Baron ordered.

Michel looked questioningly to the Duchess. "Will the ladies be sent ahead to the ship?"

"She goes with me." The Baron's tone indicated that he wouldn't argue with them. "Anna will be sent to le Havre." Michel paused a moment, then left the room.

When the Baron faced Lisette again, his dark brows drew together in a frown. "Listen to me carefully. We are leaving for Paris today. I have business there that won't wait. If we become separated, you are to go directly to the ship at le Havre harbor. It is called *Homeward*, and it sets sail as soon as we board. The *capitaine* will know who you are and keep you safe until I join you."

"Why should we be separated? Where are we going on a ship?" She had no intentions of leaving France.

"We're going to Spain," he answered calmly. "It is against my better judgment to take you with me to Paris, but you have proven to be a wily character and I dare not leave you behind. We will be able to find refuge in Spain until the rebellion ends."

"Why Spain? Couldn't we go to Austria or Germany? Are you not loyal as a feudal baron to stay in France and help the King?"

"My loyalties no longer are to France but to our destiny, my darling." His disposition softened. "Your safety is not all that's at stake. Anarchy has swept over France, and I want to be safely out of the country before the bloodshed begins."

Lisette began to understand how serious the unrest was. She considered going to Paris. In a city of thousands of hungry peasants, she would have another chance to flee the Baron.

As if he understood what she was thinking, he wrapped his arms around her and held her tightly to him. "I don't intend to let you out of my sight for a moment. It is too dangerous for you to contact anyone before we leave. There are spies for both sides of this political struggle, and you could lose your pretty little head if you fell into the wrong hands." He smacked a kiss on her forehead, barely able to resist the temptation of making love to her. They had both tasted the depth of their passion, and if she didn't give in soon, he was sure he could lose his mind from wanting her so much. "Spain won't be so bad. Just think of the long nights we will spend together en route."

She pulled free of his embrace, still feeling the beat of his heart against her cheek. Lisette swept her auburn hair back and met his gaze evenly. "When we reach Spain, what then? Will I spend the rest of my life seeking forgiveness for something I have no control over? I beseech you to forget your revenge on my family. I had nothing to do with the break in our contract."

Jean's smile was that of a man who was about to say something from deep within him.

"I want you to come, Lisette."

How could she argue when he was smiling at her?

Was her sleepy admission of love for him another de Meret ploy? Jean wondered. Could he trust her? She was still a de Meret. He couldn't erase the years of loyalty to her father and the throne overnight. It would take time to show her the error of royalist ways.

Anna stood in the doorway, trying not to interfere in what she thought was a lovers' quarrel.

Jean saw the maid enter and took the bundle she carried. "Your new wardrobe has arrived, Lisette." He held shirt and breeches up to the young Duchess. "You are to put these on and braid your hair. Hmmm, maybe a chapeau would do if you could get all of your hair under it. I will see what I can find in my wardrobe."

Knowing it was useless to argue, she inspected the garments. "Am I supposed to wear these?" She held up the worn leather breeches, a frown wrinkling her nose. "I am a woman, not a boy!"

Jean's glance skimmed over her body. "I am well aware of that fact, my lady. It is for your safety. The clothes are a disguise to hide that beautiful figure, but you will also need to conceal your long hair." He left to see to it.

Lisette tossed her gown and chemise on the bed and changed into the light linen shirt. The vest was tight and she couldn't get the wooden buttons fastened across her chest. The breeches didn't fit too badly with a leather belt to hold them on. Her own riding boots were taken out of the armoire and she gratefully put them on. Lisette braided her hair tightly and pinned it to the top of her head.

When she finished dressing, Lisette took Anna's hand and guided her over to the bed, and sat down next to the young maid.

"There is so much happening to me that I don't understand, and all this talk of an uprising is frightening me." Lisette smiled at her. They seemed to understand each other without words. The Duc didn't allow her to associate with people her own age except for the girls at the school or her cousin Darias. Lisette's relatives were of the royal family, which lived by the creed "Friendship is one of the pleasures in life not suited to royalty." Anna could be useful, Lisette speculated. Sooner or later, the maid would help her.

Admiring the costume before the mirror, she wondered what the Queen would say about her wardrobe now. She could just hear Marie's speech on the proper *étiquette* for the young ladies of the court.

Jean returned carrying a cloak and beret. He asked her to turn around as he inspected the fit of the breeches. She felt like a horse being bought at market. At any moment she expected him to open her mouth and examine her teeth. What held her attention was his reaction when he touched her shoulders. He seemed to take care not to hurt her. Should she try crying and pleading to seek escape from him? Or remain obstinate and demand her release? She decided to try both and see what his response would be. Her last resort would be a challenge of war. It was her first thread of hope since Jean had announced they were leaving France.

The back of his knuckles pressed to her chest as he finished buttoning her shirt. The full curve of her tender bosom brushed the back of his hand, tempting him to rip the shirt from her and cup the gentle mound in his hand. Could he hold back the fierce passion welling within him to ease her over that threshold of innocence?

Lisette felt the warm contact against her skin. It made her breath catch, thinking that he could touch her and ignite the unbidden flame surging within her. She couldn't look at him as the heat spread to her breasts and left an aching feeling within her. Her nipples were taut against the linen shirt, their tips outlined in the sunlight. Lisette's eye lifted slowly to meet his gray gaze. He had laughed at her for wanting him, but now his eyes held the softened lines of longing. He knew the secret of unlocking her desires, and Lisette would forsake everything she held dear to be with him.

He said something she didn't quite hear. It broke the magic holding her spellbound. "What did you say, monsieur?"

"We will just have to hope no one notices your well-endowed chest, mademoiselle," he repeated.

Covering her hair with the beret, he noticed the rose-colored flush on her cheeks. It brought him a small amount of satisfaction to see that she was as easily flustered as he was. Finished at last, he handed her the cloak. "This isn't the latest fashion, but it's passable."

Lisette followed the tall nobleman out of the chamber. "Where is everyone?" The once-crowded rooms were now empty, and their footsteps echoed in the long halls. Outside the château was the same deathly quiet.

"The men are out on a mission," he answered sharply. He gave last-minute instructions to the few men who remained.

Lisette waited beside the gate until Jean finished his business. She gave Morning Glory a pat on the neck in greeting. With the freedom of breeches she didn't need any help mounting. Riding was easier and the horse seemed more controllable. Cantering beside the Baron's black Arabian, Morning Glory had to be reined tightly. Once off the Baron's property they could easily fall prey to a highwayman, and she wasn't looking forward to another meeting with a villain.

They were headed east, toward her home, and her spirits brightened. The sunshine brought out a glow on her cheeks. She had missed the fresh air and open fields while cooped up in her chamber at the château.

Jean watched her mood change and had to wonder if he should have taken her out riding more often. In the past two weeks he had had to attend to a thousand small crises in the province and he had missed being with her.

Lisette caught a glimpse of the Baron watching her out of the corner of his eye. He smiled indulgently as Morning Glory gracefully jumped a fence.

He turned the horses to the north to avoid the

Duc's property, and Lisette's mouth dropped in a frown, betraying her emotions. This was not a pleasurable journey, Jean reminded himself. He had important business in Paris, though her big, blue eyes and slim thighs in breeches certainly didn't make it easier to remember his duty.

Morning Glory seemed particularly spirited this morning and needed to run. Lisette gave in to her horse, and with a slap of the reins to the thoroughbred's flanks, they sailed over the ground, the gold and brown countryside becoming a blur as the horse picked up speed.

There was a river a mile away; if only she could reach it before Jolbert! The race was on! Her hat dropped to the ground and her hair fell, still tightly braided. She was sure she would win and teach him to contain his arrogance.

It took Jean a moment before he figured out her plan. He gave her a brief head start, and then with a smile he urged Midnight Blue into a gallop. Using a trick he had been taught in Spain, Jean hooked a foot in the stirrup and leaned over the horse's side to snatch the beret where it had fallen on the ground. There was a quarter of a mile left when he pulled up beside Lisette, and slowed her horse to a walk.

"You dropped your chapeau, my dear." He handed the cap back to her and released her reins.

"I would have offered to race you fairly, my lord, but I haven't anything to wager," she answered, breathless. Lisette sat back disgusted. His stallion could have run a race around her and still won without getting winded.

"It wouldn't be fair to match my horse against yours. But since I *did* win, a kiss from my lady will be my reward."

Lisette couldn't help but smile. "You weren't

worried that I was escaping, were you? Someday I will race you and win."

"Ah, but you lost, and I shall have my reward from the fair maiden. The kiss can't be just any, but one from the heart," he stipulated. "How did a young lady learn to ride the way you do?" Jean didn't know her as well as he thought he did.

The words of praise sent a quiver to Lisette's stomach. "Before I went to Paris my cousin Darias and I would race the fields surrounding Castle Meret."

"I've met your cousin. Is he an heir to Meret?"

"He's a third or fourth cousin and not *that* closely related. I'm the only heir to Meret." Lisette clucked, disgusted at the thought of Darias being a blood relative. Her cousin had the peculiar habit of sniffing opium; it made him clever one moment, and snide, vindictive the next. And he always tapped a golden spoon on an ornate silver box, urging her to try the sticky brown substance with him.

Darias had always resented Lisette's position. If it hadn't been for her, he would have inherited the de Meret province and been lord over all the adjoining land; Lisette was the last of the line and Darias the next-closest male relative. The thought was unnerving to Lisette. Castle Meret with its green fields filled with grapevines was all that she could ever call her own. Yet if anything happened to Lisette, her cousin would rule her demesne.

Thinking about Castle Meret made Lisette homesick and sad. It meant remembering the heartbreak of losing her mother at a young age, just when she needed another woman to talk to the most. What would happen to her when she gave in to the Baron's demand to make her his consort? What would it be like to bear her first child?

When they stopped to water the horses, Lisette decided it would be a good time to pay off the wager.

She was standing at the crest of a small incline, her face almost level with Jean's face. He wanted a kiss, straight from her heart. Well, then, if she never had any other memory of him to savor, it would be of this moment.

Lisette cradled his face between her hands and kissed him. At first it was a shy touch, but as she drew closer her embrace became more tender and passionate. Her hands snaked through his dark curls and her tongue reached for the warm recesses of his mouth.

Jean stood perfectly still as Lisette withdrew. This lady showed profound emotion; she trusted him and loved him. Her kiss was a candid statement of her soul, and left him so deeply moved he was speechless.

"Will you allow me to contact my uncle before we go?" His pause gave her hope. "The King will be worried about me and he should know I'm still alive." She broke off as Jean shook his dark head at her.

All thoughts of kissing him again vanished. Instead, she pondered the possibilities of getting a message to the King.

Michel focused the telescope on the figures beside the river. He lowered the scope beside him. His mouth hung open in surprise. "I don't believe it, Paul. She's kissing him!"

The surly captain tossed his empty waterskin aside. "Knowing that woman, I'd say she's trying to bite him."

"Don't be such a pessimist."

Paul took the telescope from Michel. The figures beside the river seemed peaceful enough, but he still doubted what the Duchess might be planning.

"Stop leering at them," Michel scolded. "I told

you it was only a matter of time before love conquered all of our problems."

"I wouldn't turn my back on her," Paul warned.

Michel brushed the summer dust from his ivory satin coat. The Baron had handled the situation as he would have. Michel dismissed the notion that Lisette would actually try to kill his friend. "You'll see," he assured Paul.

"Double the guard surrounding them," Paul ordered the troop of men he commanded in Jean's absence. "If my cousin lives through the night, perhaps you may be right."

"Of course I am," Michel said, without a thread of conviction.

Chapter Nine

Lisette turned away from the Baron. She hid her anger by tending to the horse. Why does he continue to confuse me? she thought. Every time she believed he was remotely human, he squelched her romantic idea of him and the proud, arrogant side of him emerged.

While they continued the journey she let her mind drift over the past few weeks. At the moment, they were treading a ticklish middle ground between the heat of anger and passion. She would accept either being thrown into the dungeon or a proper marriage proposal, but not the uncertainty of not knowing where she stood with him.

The extremes of their emotions drove her crazy; he wanted her physical attention, yet claimed her merely as a political pawn. She needed for them to be legally bound in order to consummate her desire for Jean. Lisette wanted to wave the evidence of alliance under Prissy's nose. It was a small reprisal for the two years of suffered criticisms.

The last rays of sunlight faded to dusk when they reached a large alcove hidden in the rocky banks of the river. Tangled roots from a huge oak tree clung to the rocks, creating a niche completely hidden from view. Lisette hoped they would go directly to Paris without stopping.

"We will take cover for the night here, Lisette."
His hands braced under her arms as he helped her
down. While Jean bedded down the horses outside
the shelter, Lisette surveyed the mossy floor of the
alcove. It seemed clean, but she didn't like sleeping outdoors. Why couldn't they stop at an inn for
the night?

He seemed to be testing her endurance. But she
didn't complain about the lack of facilities and
tried to make herself useful tidying up the mess
from their supper. Neither of them dared to be the
first to break the silent truce. Lisette bathed her
face and neck in the river, and was allowed a few
moments of solitude to take care of nature's little
nuisances.

"Don't get lost," he warned.

She returned to their campsite still maintaining
an apathetic façade. Jean's grin was infectious
though, and the look in his eye disarming. He laid
out a blanket, sat down, and pulled his boots off.
He motioned for her to lie down beside him.

"I would prefer to sleep alone."

"The night air can get chilly. I was hoping that
you would keep my feet warm." Jean held his hand
out and guided her down beside him on the blanket.

"Must you be so close to me?" she protested.

"Shhh, *chérie,*" he murmured in her ear. "You
must be quiet. The echoes from the alcove can be
heard to the river." She was being stubborn; a distraction was in order.

His mouth touched hers as he eased her down
next to him. The curve of his lips nudged the corner
of her mouth and she closed her eyes, afraid that if
she opened them she would fall under his spell
again and her body would betray the ache in her
womb.

The booming sound of gunshots was faint at first,

but grew louder. The Baron caressed her neck and didn't seem interested in the battle headed their way. Lisette pushed him over onto his back and sat up. "Don't you hear it?" She held her breath for a moment until a loud blast rang out, not half a mile from them.

"Aren't you going to do something?" He removed her vest and let her hair down, taking no notice of the struggle.

"Lisette, lie down." He pulled her backward and continued to undo the buttons of her tunic.

The garment was open to the waist before she was aware of what his nimble fingers had accomplished. "There is someone out there," she said, angry at his nonchalance. "We could be murdered in a moment, and all you can think about is undressing me. You must do something!"

"I assure you that I am doing everything humanly possible. This last button is stuck inside your breeches and 'tis frustrating when it won't give." He traced a line around the circumference of her plump, creamy breast, determined to gain her attention. The last button finally gave way, but she held on to it, resisting him.

From her position under him, she viewed his smile in the firelight. It exasperated her to think he wouldn't protect her. "Are you going to do something about the fight going on outside this cave?" she persisted.

"No." He kissed the tip of her small nose.

"Why not?" She was shocked at his attitude. "You will get us both killed!"

With his arms around her, Jean's chuckle rocked them both. "Surely you didn't think I would travel with such a treasure as you without a guard?"

"Then those are your men out there?"

He was annoyed at her persistence. "Yes, those are my men out there. They won't let anyone near

us. Paul and Michel are just having some fun." He
pressed his lips under her ear. The battle sounds
stopped and silence once again reigned. The tunic
slipped from her shoulders, and he brushed the
flimsy linen aside.

Lisette had no doubt Paul and Michel were hack-
ing and maiming some poor soul to death.

She tensed as Jean's lips met hers. Lisette tried
to concentrate on seeking revenge, but his mouth
brought forth a tumult of emotions.

"No," she groaned and tried to roll away from
him, but his strong arms didn't allow it.

"Yes, my sweet." He spoke her name so softly
that she turned to him.

The spiced fragrance of his hair reminded her of
coveted scents from the Far East. He turned her
hand palm up and kissed each fingertip in turn.
The new sensation left her skin tingling from the
warm, tender contact. The raspy stubble of his un-
shaven beard prickled her fingers as she explored
his face. He was much too thin, she thought, looking at the hollows beneath his high cheekbones; his
form was whittled to sleek sinew and muscles,
making him appear lank in the hips and broad in
the chest.

Jean held Lisette's hand up to his, palm to palm,
and his fingers were a full inch longer than hers.
"This is what is known as a saint's kiss."

It was delicious to nestle with him and not fear
him. Her hand wandered down his neck to his chest
and lingered on the rhythmic pulse beside his
heart. She explored his mouth, running her tongue
over his straight teeth. He was trembling, she realized. Lisette continued with tormenting flicks of
her tongue until he groaned, and she clutched the
rippled muscles of his back as intensity curled
them together. Her legs parted to the pressure of
Jean's thigh, and for the first time she noticed that

she was half naked. When had her tunic been taken away? The flames surging through her loins was consuming her and her head spun in confusion, as the past and future melted away.

"Will you relent and become my mistress, *ma chérie?*" Jean's voice was pleading.

"What did you say?" The chaos within her stilled. Reality flooded back, and with it the purpose of her presence with him. She jerked free from his arms. Lisette retrieved her shirt from the marshy floor of the alcove and yanked it over her head. She had come close to submitting. Disgusted by her lack of will, Lisette fought back the shiver of disappointment.

"What are you doing now, Lisette?" Jean's voice was unusually cold.

She tugged the shirt down to the tops of her thighs. "I'm getting a drink of water. What do you care?"

"If you go outside like that, my men may not bring you back unmolested. They are camped outside, and something as beautiful as you"—he sat up and slapped her backside—"won't make it ten feet."

"I fail to understand the humor—oh, I see." She let her voice rise so that it could be clearly heard. "You can defile me, but no one else may intrude on your property? How dare you flaunt me like a common whore before your family and men?" She sat down on the edge of the blanket and sobbed into her hands. It didn't take much effort to cry in a loud, racking wail. She reeled away when he tried to touch her again.

"Lisette." Jean raked his fingers through his tousled hair. "Why is it so important to you to remain chaste? Isn't it natural for me to want you?"

"Perhaps it's because that is all you have left me, Baron Jolbert."

Someday, she thought vengefully, *I will even the score between us. For what you have done to me, Jean Jolbert, the cruelest end would be a mercy.* The image of Jean on the rack brought out a crooked smile on her lips as she devised a thousand gruesome deaths for him. It didn't matter that she couldn't think of the crime he had committed; it was enough to believe he was a scoundrel. If he tried to touch her again, she would turn on him and try to kill him herself.

"I would not sleep soundly if I were you," she whispered, noticing a small rock lying in the sand. It would be useless to hit him only to be captured again by his men, but it gave her a sense of power just to say the words. Duchess Lisette de Meret curled up on her side, hugging herself against the cool breeze and shunning the warmth of Jean's arms.

Chapter Ten

Her eyes opened slowly, and instinctively she snuggled closer to the warm body that stirred next to her. The dim pink light of dawn filtered through the opening of the alcove, casting soft shadows against the roots of the ancient tree that sheltered them. Lisette silently chided herself as she rolled away from Jean's arms to her back; sometime during the night she had wriggled out of her clothes and moved from her cramped position into Jean's embrace. She stretched her aching muscles, rubbed her eyes, and sat up.

Jean's deep voice startled her.

"Let's start this romance over again, Lisette. You are very special to me, and there is nothing common about you." Jean took her hand between his and kissed her fingertips, hoping she wouldn't refuse his request.

It was all or nothing, starting right now. Loving him was easy, fighting him impossible, so why not become his mistress? Virtue was innate, not something that could be taken from her.

In her silence he had to wonder if she would refuse him. The doubt troubled him. They had come too far to hide behind the fury of revenge.

"I want you to know, my charming mink, that I

will never fail you. If you need me, I'll be there for you."

Tears welled in her blue eyes. Her chin dipped to her chest, and under the pressure of his finger, she raised her head.

"Trust me, Lisette."

"The only advice I can remember from my mother was never trust a handsome man who has coupling on his mind. She told me a man would say anything to get a lady into bed, and then have an acute attack of amnesia shortly thereafter."

"Do you believe her?" Jean stroked away the tears on her cheeks with his thumb.

"Non. I don't want any false promises. I want your word of honor to leave my father alone."

"You have my oath that I won't kill him." Maybe just break every bone in his body, Jean thought to himself.

Her gaze locked on his gray eyes, and her mouth trembled with unspoken endearments. Wanting him was her folly and her ecstasy. The concerned wrinkles around his brow had vanished; Jean didn't look at her with mistrust anymore. Gingerly, she put her arms around him.

Jean rocked her against him. He was happy, truly happy for the first time in his life; the woman he cared about had yielded to him. He smoothed the wisps of hair from Lisette's face as he grinned from ear to ear.

"I have a surprise for you."

Lisette didn't want to let go. "What is it?"

He released her long enough to produce a small box with a blue satin ribbon. "This is for your birthday."

Lisette took the box, and having no patience with opening gifts, tore the ribbon off. Inside was a diamond ring surrounded by emeralds. She surveyed the expensive gift with awe. It was an exact replica of a ring her mother had worn until her father had taken it into Paris and sold it for a few *livres*. It meant more to her than he would ever know. Jean took it from the box and slipped it upon the third finger of her left hand.

"Until the time comes when our relationship can be handled properly," he spoke tenderly, "you'll have to be patient with me."

Lisette cried with delight and clasped her arms around her Baron. The moment for him to claim her had finally come. All the grief of the past few weeks disappeared. Under the warmth of her azure gaze, Jean felt he could conquer the world.

A single ray of sunshine cast a halo around Lisette. For a few moments Jean lay motionless, committing to memory the tilt of her head and the light blush on her cheeks. He inhaled deeply and the scent of wet, musty earth laced with a touch of her jasmine soap filled his chest. Her long, dark lashes lowered under his adoration and brushed against her ivory skin. Unceremoniously, he slipped the tunic over her head and cast it aside.

Her fingers toyed nervously with the frayed edge of the blanket. She could deal with the angry side of him but never knew what to expect when his mood softened and his gray eyes filled with tenderness. She longed to brush aside the lock of dark hair that fell across his forehead, but the gesture seemed too bold. For the moment it was enough just knowing that the man she cared about would be lost without her. And in helping him find a resolution to his revenge she would also find herself.

Her lips were cool and soft as he kissed her; her hair like fine silk as he rubbed the wavy auburn strands between his callused fingers. The hourglass shape of her body was outlined in the dark blue blanket, and, laying beside her, Jean

smoothed over her voluptuous curves with the
palm of his hand.

Lisette felt safe and secure cuddling close to him.
Feeling daring, she ran her fingertips from his earlobe to his shoulder. She took his soft groan as encouragement and this time followed the same path
with the tip of her tongue. The effect was more dramatic, causing Jean to shiver. There was so much
about him yet to discover—so much still unknown.
Lisette was only just beginning to understand the
power of her own sexuality.

"Stealing the enemy's tactics is fair play, Jean."
Her voice was ragged, her breathing rapid and
shaky as his tongue delved into the shell of her ear.
Lisette licked her lips and released the pent-up
sigh that had been held within her too long. She
knew now without being told when he wanted to
taste her lips, or when she needed to tip her chin
up so he could tantalize the dip at the base of her
throat.

The blanket clutched to her chest fell, releasing
her lush bosom to Jean's capable hands. He was eager to promise with kisses what he couldn't say in
words. He kissed her temple and his lips brushed
her hairline. "Let me love you, Lisette."

His plea was husky and endearing in its intensity. There was nothing she could withhold. The
sweet anticipation started with a small flame in
her loins which soon consumed her with its
strength.

"Please," she begged. Was it something she actually said out loud, she wondered as he continued
with little kisses on her eyelids, or was it something she only thought?

She lay back on the blanketed floor of the alcove,
her legs wound around his and the coarse hair on
his legs tickling her toes.

Jean wanted to love her and comfort her through

their first time together. She was like green tinder and had to be coddled and protected before the passion fire could catch and eventually build to a blaze.

"I wish this didn't have to hurt you," he murmured, burying himself within the warm folds of her body.

Lisette called out his name in a tortured whisper. The cry of her lost innocence made him withdraw for just an instant as the tips of her nails clawed at his back, evoking a little agony of their own in retribution.

Jean took her hands into his and whispered encouragement. He caught the tear rolling down her cheek with his tongue, and kissed her eyelids with such gentleness that her heart swelled with unsaid vows of love. Easing her through the sting of penetration, he slowly brought back the raging desire with a slow and easy rhythm. "Trust me, Lisette."

An amorous moan replaced her terrified cry. He could feel excitement mount as her hips rose to meet his. And she smiled as she became lost in the delirium of his easy thrusts. It made him want to please her even more.

The muscles in his back flinched under her touch. His sleek body glistened in the morning's heat as he held his own needs aside to slowly undo the tender wraps of her maidenhood. Mercifully, he shuddered and collapsed in her arms, wearied from the need to withhold his passion for her sake. When it was over, he lay down beside her and took her back into his arms and held her tightly against him.

Lisette clung to him. Her cheek rested on his chest, and for a while she basked in the fulfillment. The warm glow of satisfaction spread over her and relaxed her against his side.

Jean wasn't so totally engrossed in his passion that he hadn't known the pain had been almost unbearable for her. His pity for her discomfort had made him spill his seed deep within her as quickly as possible. The rose-colored bloom on her cheeks had paled. He silently chided himself for not waiting until they were in Paris with the benefit of a real bed and bath for her comfort.

She opened her eyes and looked up at him. "Was it terribly disappointing? I'm not much of a seductress."

"You were wonderful, Lisette. It's always difficult the first time."

"Was it difficult the first time for you?"

Her blunt question was a little unnerving. *"Non.* It's not the same for men."

With special care not to further embarrass her, Jean poured water from his tin cup onto a handkerchief and removed the streaks of blood on her inner thighs.

Her mouth dropped open and her eyes grew round with wonder as he stood and dressed. She couldn't force herself to look away. It was mesmerizing to look at him. Hardened muscles in his back gave him grace of movement, and his long legs were tapered by years of riding horseback. His dark hair curled just below his ears and twisted in a dozen directions.

"Your breeches, my lady." He produced them at arm's length, teasing her to stand up and take them from him.

Lisette draped the blanket around her, struggled to her feet, and gingerly took the breeches from him. "Turn around."

He did as she asked, but it was the wicked side of him that made him turn back, just for one more glimpse of her luscious body. "I have seen you undressed before."

"Have you no honor?" she reproached. She pulled the vest over the tunic, and masses of tangles tumbled forth. "I should make you brush my hair."

Jean's eyebrows rose in delight.

Lisette pushed past him, sure he would be willing to assist her. Her mind had been made up to become his mistress in the wee hours of the morning. Unable to sleep, she had tried to come up with any possible way to stop the forthcoming bloodshed between their families.

The whole charade of dressing her in breeches seemed ridiculous to Jean; he should have put her in the family carriage with fine velvets to ease the journey, not put her on a horse and forced her to ride like a man. It had to be an excruciating new experience for her legs to straddle the horse, and then for him to make love to her without giving her a proper rest.

There was always a disquieting humility associated with making love to a virgin. He walked to the river and dived into the water, letting the thoughts drift with the current. He should have taken her into Paris like a queen, not his paramour.

The diamond sparkled when Lisette held it up to the light. Her dreams would be fulfilled and she would stand beside her *ami.* Patience wasn't one of her stronger virtues, and she didn't intend on making it easy on him while waiting.

She emerged from the secluded alcove. Her hair had fallen from the braid that had been pinned tightly to her head. While they made love his hands had wound into her hair, and it now consisted of nothing but tangles. Setting the folded blanket down on a rock, she took the ivory-handled comb he had packed for her and started working on the mass of unruly ringlets.

Jean stood beside her, naked to the waist and clad in his breeches. He gave her a wet, smacking kiss, glad at the opportunity to do so when she wasn't angry with him.

"You're very beautiful, *ma chérie.*"

"I feel beautiful when you look at me."

He took her hand in his and kissed her wrist. "We'll be able to sleep in a decent bed tonight. With any luck, we'll get to Paris at sunset."

" 'Tis still morning. There's plenty of time to get to Paris."

Jean's smile broadened. "I think you'll find the ride . . . uncomfortable."

His rich voice distracted her with songs of the seafaring life as he pulled his tunic over his head and raked his fingers through his hair. Lisette knew the effect she had on him when she brushed up against him and brought the passion to life again. His manhood nearly burst out of his breeches.

"Now who's distressed?" she scolded in a playful banter.

"Ye're a wicked wench," he reprimanded lovingly. He was searching for his other boot while he continued. "And not at all the blushing virgin I almost married."

"Almost?" she questioned, afraid of what he would say.

"A man doesn't marry his lover," Jean informed her as casually as if he had just said the water is blue. On the outside he managed to make his words sound cavalier, but on the inside Jean was uneasy about deceiving her.

The bottom of her stomach felt as if it had dropped to the ground.

"Of course not," she intoned spitefully. "He doesn't have to."

Chapter Eleven

Lisette was drawn to the spiral of smoke drifting over the treetops. To her surprise, just around the bend there were over a hundred men on the riverbank and a big fire going. Michel walked out of the crowd to meet them.

"Good morning, m'lord. Paul wants to speak to you." Michel shook his head at Jean's questioning glare. "I'm sorry, Jean. We haven't been able to locate your father."

Jean and Michel had sent word to every prison in France, trying to find the Earl. There was still no word from Simon, who watched the coast, that Jean's father had been taken abroad.

"Perhaps you could use a hot meal, Lady Lisette?" Michel took her arm and led her to the fire as Jean disappeared among the waiting men on the riverbank. Michel escorted her to a blanket laid out for her. "Best wishes on your birthday," he said to her privately.

Lisette remembered there was a party planned at the palace that she wouldn't be able to attend. She nodded, too numb to say anything. The Baron had made himself clear. There wouldn't be a wedding. She felt naïve and gullible for having thought the ring meant their engagement would be announced. Instead, he had used it to trick her into

becoming his mistress. She couldn't feel more humiliated. She would make him pay for his decep-
tion.

Jean's sultry mood was disturbing. She watched
the tall Baron in the troop of men, and even at a
distance she could feel his power over her senses as
he glanced at her.

Her stomach tightened into an anxious ball,
making it impossible to eat. Was it her own appre-
hension she was feeling? Did he already know of
her intentions to challenge him? Could he predict
her actions that well?

When Jean finished his business with the troop,
he went to join Lisette, who seemed to him to be unusually nervous this morning. She was learning to
trust him, but she was still skittish. It wouldn't be
much longer, though, before she would be his completely. He regarded her carefully and wished that
he could confide in her.

"May I join you, Lady Lisette?"

"Do I have a choice?" Her leg quivered where
they touched. She deliberately moved over to give
him room. "What was all that noise about last
night?"

"Just some rioters my men intercepted." He took
a drink from a tin cup and offered some to her.
What her words didn't say, her eyes did. She was
confused; the tiny wrinkles above her brow formed
an expression all their own.

Jean reached out to stroke her soft cheek, and
their gazes met. What he hadn't been able to de-
fine in her eyes, he could now see plainly. There
was defiance in her even stare. She was still retal-
iating against his power over her.

"You will like Spain, my darling. I certainly
wouldn't think of leaving you here. You are much
too beautiful to leave behind to fall prey to the revolution."

Goaded, Lisette stood up with her feet apart, determined that he would hear her out. "I have no intention of going with you, not on your terms. Of all the gall! Telling me I will like going to Spain with you, when you are giving me no choice in the matter. What kind of man are you?" Angered beyond control, she didn't back down as he towered over her. "Any man of honor would have properly challenged my house and met in battle instead of kidnapping a helpless woman. You should be strung up, you barbarian! I would never marry you when you haven't given me a chance to defend myself. You have forced me into your bed because you are stronger than I am. I call you out as a coward, Monsieur Jolbert, and now demand to meet you in battle."

The entire camp watched and waited in tense silence as a crimson fury flushed the Baron's face. "Does she know what she's doing?" Michel whispered.

"I don't think so," Paul answered. "It may take all of us to disengage his hands from her pretty neck this time."

Jean held her arms tight behind her back, bending her slightly away from him. He had to restrain himself from using his strength against hers. "I seem to recall you begged me to make love to you."

She couldn't deny it but wouldn't back down.

"For your information, your father broke the treaty with me, and by feudal rights I am allowed recompense for his treachery. I took every precaution not to draw de Meret blood before the treaty was properly broken. Don't tempt me now, Lisette. My time and effort were wasted in obeying the laws. My father hasn't been found. No doubt the Duc arranged for his mysterious disappearance. Where did they take him?"

"You know I don't know what you're talking about," she stated with absolute clarity.

"The Duc de Meret wants to destroy me, but not before he can get his hands on the Jolbert coffers. I won't give you up. I will find and rescue my father. And I will take what rightfully belongs to me."

Lisette knew he was referring to *her*.

Her voice choked with emotion while she made her last plea. "Will your honor be satisfied when you have humiliated me? Will both of our fathers have to be sacrificed before this senseless feud will come to an end? What about what rightfully belongs to me? If we married, there would be no cause to continue the battle."

Jean's hands clenched in confusion. It had to be another de Meret scheme. Until he could sort out the thoughts that made him doubt her, Jean swept the notion of her innocence aside.

"There won't be a wedding, Lisette."

It was futile to continue to argue. Her last resort—to be his mistress—would be the only way to avoid bloodshed. Her knees felt weak, as if they would buckle under the weight of her irrevocable decision.

She realized the entire camp had seen the exchange. The men murmured their approval at the way their lord had handled the young woman. They waited for further reaction from her, ready to flay her alive if she didn't accept defeat and give in. Though Paul had to be physically restrained.

Lisette stared at Jean. How could she have been foolish enough to love him? Jean had not been smiling at her, but laughing at the innocent girl who longed for him. He had made his position clear from the beginning, and she had clung to her romantic daydreams. She was nothing more to him than a piece of property.

Jean hadn't missed the defiant tip of her head or her proud stance before him. Even in breeches her figure was elegant. "It would do you well to learn obedience, Lady Lisette. You have the insolence of youth, which could someday threaten your life."

"And you have the arrogance of a savage!" She expected the earth to open up and swallow her before the next words could be voiced. In the history of the feud between the Jolberts and the de Merets, neither side had ever given in to the enemy's demands. Lisette would be the first traitor to her ancestors. But for now, she could endure anything for the sake of peace. Later, she would consider the humiliation she would suffer by her peers when it became known that she was no more than a concubine to the Baron.

"I w-will become your mistress."

"What a noble act to save your father's life."

"Not just my father's, but *your* family's blood, as well. Just remember, if a child results from our unholy alliance, and may *le bon Dieu* forgive me if that happens, he will also know of his father's disgrace. Don't delude yourself into thinking this is out of love for you, but rather out of a need for peace." She turned on her heel and returned to the riverbank alone.

"Touché," Michel whispered and released Paul. It wasn't easy, holding a mountain back while the winds of love raged between Jean and Lisette. When the Baron approached, Paul and Michel stood beside their horses, arms akimbo.

"I think it's useless to believe she will learn to like him," Paul grumbled. "Do you have any more clever ideas?"

"This may take longer than I figured," Michel whispered. "He's very obstinate."

"He does lack style," Paul agreed. "I have seen him with a lot of women in my life, but never has one upset him so much. He's confused by her motives. Is she a de Meret pawn, or his blameless fiancée?"

"I say she's above suspicion until proven guilty."

"You were saying?" the Baron growled from behind them. Paul and Michel slowly turned around. Jean toyed with the hilt of his rapier, his agitated stance suggesting he wouldn't mind working some of his anger off on them.

Michel had seen that look before and warily backed up. He mounted his horse, still watching his friend, then saw that Jean was smiling under that scowl.

Michel breathed a sigh of relief. "I volunteer to go on ahead to Paris. There are several ladies I know of that may have some information about your father."

"He'll probably come back with some new disease to pass on to us," Paul grumbled.

Jean turned to his cousin. "I suppose you also have an opinion concerning my rapport with Lady Lisette?"

Paul stroked his beard, grinning. "No m'lord. I thought he put it adequately."

"I'll shave your beard with my sword yet."

"That you may. Are you certain you have won the battle with the lady? It seems that you received more than you bargained for."

"Perhaps." Jean's mutter dropped to a whisper. "When we find the Earl, then we will know."

Paul took charge of the Baron's black Arabian and ventured on to Paris. So as not to be conspicuous, the hussars would wait for Jean outside the village of Rouen, where they would all rendezvous, then journey on to the coast.

Jean and Lisette were alone.

Lisette walked to the river and let her troubled mind relax. As she splashed cool relief on her face and neck, the sticky heat of mid-July dropped in beaded circles on the river surface. With the burden of decision past, her heart felt free. The thought of becoming his mistress didn't seem so bad when she remembered her dreams about him.

She couldn't deny that she had wanted him to make love to her—she wanted to consummate their relationship, but within the sanctity of marriage. But, for now, to finally have peace between them was worth any sacrifice she had to make.

A violet wildflower was tossed into her lap.

"I meant what I said earlier, Lisette. I'll always take care of you and be there when you need me."

It was a small morsel of his affection for her. For the moment, it was all she needed. Later, he would *have* to give her so much more.

She peered up at Jean's face and smiled, sharing a tender look with him. He took her hand and pulled her to her feet, drawing her against the length of his torso.

With his arms wrapped around her, Jean buried his face in her hair. Somehow, the victory didn't seem as sweet. The long years of loneliness had left him weary. How could he tell her he needed her soft form next to him? A man wasn't supposed to possess emotion. Did she know he lost all sense of order when she graced him with one of her dimple-cheeked smiles? Could he ever tell her of the dreams of unrelenting desire that woke him in the middle of the night in a cold sweat?

Jean was determined to find his father and free himself and Lisette from the Duc's hold. Only then would it be safe for him to call her his wife.

Chapter Twelve

With Jean's impeccable sense of direction guiding them, they avoided the open roads and followed the river. The sights and smells of the open markets surrounding Paris filled her senses with thoughts of food and comfort.

As the sun set, an eerie gloom was cast over the city. Shops were closed and there wasn't a soul in sight. In the two years she had spent in the city, Lisette had never known such unusual quiet. Normally, the streets were filled with merchants calling their wares and hawkers who promised instant youth and vitality to anyone who could swallow the snake oil in brown corked bottles. Romance of all kinds flourished in the parks, where affairs were often a public display. It wasn't unusual to see two men embracing in the park. Lisette was sure that while she was in disguise as a boy, it wouldn't be noticed when the tall Baron lifted her down from Morning Glory and pecked a kiss on her mouth.

Her muscles throbbed from fatigue and the long hours of riding. When her feet touched the ground, her legs buckled.

Jean held her lightly against him. She was exhausted, and desperately needed the repose of a soft bed. With little effort he swept her into his arms. Entering the familiar inn, the nobleman glared at a peasant who noticed Jean's affections toward the young rake he held in his arms. Michel emerged from the crowded room and held a tankard of ale aloft.

"We have been expecting you for hours." The Marquis had worried that evil had befallen them along the road. Paul had left them alone, and it was a miracle that the Baron and Duchess were both still alive, when Jean had threatened to strangle her and she to smash his head with a rock.

"Call the maid," Jean ordered. Lisette's eyes were already closed and she rested peacefully against his chest. The patrons parted in silence as he strode the length of the tavern. There were old friends there waiting to meet with him, but Jean wouldn't acknowledge their inquiries until his charge was safely tucked into bed.

Lisette didn't want to wake. All the agony of decision was behind her. Now that she had given her word to stand beside him, she wasn't about to change her mind. He laid her down and the cool sheets lifted the haze of sleep.

"Stay here and get some rest," he said softly. "The maid will be here to help you, *petite*. I'll be back shortly." His voice drifted over her sleepy form.

The door closed and Lisette sat bolt upright. He wouldn't leave her there, would he? She couldn't bear to think he could be parted from her.

The maid appeared with a bundle of clean clothes in her arms, and Lisette quickly bathed and changed. She let her hair fall free and tucked the white peasant blouse into the dark blue skirt. She opened the door, and to her surprise the hallway was unguarded.

The tavern had closed its doors for the evening. Her heeled boots clicked against the tiled floors.

When she reached the top of the stairs, muffled voices drifted to her ears.

Her sense of alarm heightened when a voice angrily rose, seemingly directed at her Baron.

"I have done all that I can," a man shouted from the dining room.

Lisette tiptoed down the stairs. The room was dimly lit, with two dark forms at a table in the far corner. They were Paul and Michel. Her vision centered on the broad form of Jean's back as he lounged against the *barreau.* Another unrecognizable man in a green-striped nankeen jacket and blue-and-white-striped waistcoat stood next to him. His was the voice threatening her love. They didn't notice she had joined them; she remained hidden in the shadows.

When he turned to face the Baron, his profile was outlined in the candlelight. His lips were full, and he had a generous mouth set above his white cravat striped with red. She guessed his eyes were green but wasn't sure in the distance across the room.

" 'Twill be up to you to get yourself out," the man continued. "Getting into the Bastille is easy; it's getting out that's more of a problem, especially because of the *lettre de cachet* that has your father's name on it."

Lisette thought she would faint. Jean had told her the truth. Her father had gone to the King, and Louis had issued an order for the Earl's arrest. There was no chance to defend oneself against such a warrant. Offenders were sent directly to prison with no trial.

"It won't be as difficult to get my father out of the Bastille as you believe," the Baron interrupted. "Are you sure that is where you last saw the Earl?"

"I'm sure. The guard picked him up after an

evening of wenching and drinking. We were come
upon suddenly, and I had no time to defend your
father. The Duc is disclaiming any involvement.
And there's something else you should know.
When questioned about his daughter, he said that
she's finishing her education in England. But the
rumors have it that *you* murdered her. In either
case, the Duc doesn't seem in the least bit annoyed that she has disappeared. There's a new
magistrate in the de Meret province. It's a young
man."

"Could it be Darias?" Jean questioned.

"That sounds right. I met him once, and he's a
strange one. The boy has an opium addiction. He
was given full privilege in governing the province
while the *parlement* is in session and the Duc is detained in Paris. The Rouen guard was put under his
direction and they have vowed to have you delivered to him within a fortnight for questioning. If
you ask me, the Duc doesn't want the girl back,
even if she's still alive. He has that boy set up like
a king."

Lisette gasped. The Duc had betrayed her. No
wonder there was no rescue party tracking her
down. She was expendable as far as her father was
concerned. The Duc wanted Jean Jolbert ruined,
and what better way than to demand a high bride-
price for the betrothal, and then accuse him of treason?

Jean was right; her life wasn't safe in her family's hands. Her father had always wanted a son,
and that slimy little rat Darias had wormed his
way into her father's good graces. Oh, how she
loathed him!

The utter treachery of the false charges against
the Earl smacked of Darias's strange ways. Darias
had probably written the note asking her to come
home. Yet she found it hard to believe that her

father could turn her fate over to her deranged cousin. But in her heart, Lisette knew it was true. Darias knew of the scheduled meeting with the Baron, and had guessed at the length of time it would take her to travel. He must have known she would forgo all reason and leave Paris immediately. The fastest route from Paris would take her directly into the path of the Baron's troops.

Lisette didn't know how long she remained in the shadows of the staircase. The last thing she remembered was Jean's warm arm wrapping around her back as he picked her up.

Jean laid her on the bed and backed out of the way. The Baron wasn't sure what was wrong with his lady. Paul had some knowledge of medicines and herbs.

"Do something," he ordered his cousin.

"She's in shock," Paul reported.

Jean swore under his breath. "She must have overheard us. I wonder how much she knows about her cousin."

"Brandy is all she needs now," Paul prescribed. "And a wedding ring. When are you going to marry her?"

"And give Darias what he wants? My son will not be controlled by the royal house of de Meret."

"Then leave France tomorrow," Paul warned.

"Not before I find my father."

"Are you going to tell her you can't marry her because her demented cousin wants your son conceived before he hangs you?"

"No. I don't trust her."

"She deserves to know," Paul pressed. If anyone else had tried to talk to Jean in this manner, he wouldn't have lived to see the sun rise.

Jean held Lisette's hand in his, contemplating the birth of his offspring. He was especially hopeful for a female child. A daughter could be coddled and spoiled, not like a son who had to bear the burden of the Jolbert name on his shoulders. A little girl, the image of her mother, would suit him just fine.

"You're probably sterile anyway," Paul grumbled and stalked out of the room.

Jean smiled at Paul's impatience.

He pressed the cup to her lips, and her eyes fluttered open.

"Is it true?" Lisette had to know.

"Is what true?" Jean eased down on the bed next to her.

"My father has abandoned me? I figured it out. Darias probably sent me the note hoping you would kidnap me and kill me so that he would then have cause to destroy you."

"Lisette," Jean said softly, "I assure you that you're safe with me and he won't get the opportunity to come near you. Paul and Michel guard our every move. It's me that he wants."

"But that man said my father wasn't even annoyed that I was missing! It doesn't make any sense."

"If the Duc announced that you were missing, he would have to inform the other noble houses of his breach of our marriage contract. The Duc wouldn't risk public disfavor. Not with a revolution brewing and the populace searching for a strong leader."

"Then why break the marriage contract? Why tell you that I am betrothed to another?" Lisette prodded.

"Your father is ill advised by your cousin. Darias wanted to enrage me into action. If no one else knew of the break in the betrothal except me and I drew the first blood, then the Duc could proclaim a crime had been committed. I didn't do as he wished, and that, I believe, is why my father is

missing. Darias still wants something from me."
Jean stopped before telling her the child she would
be carrying would be heir to an even greater fortune than her cousin suspected.

"What does he want?" Lisette was confused.

"When we reach Spain, I'll tell you everything
you want to know. Remember this, Lisette." Jean
held the ring to her view. "I gave you my word to
be there always. Will you now give me yours?"

The old bonds to her father fell away. Lisette no
longer felt an obligation to the royal house of de
Meret. Jean had given his word to protect her, and
her heart too, was pledged.

Lisette held her arms out to him. "I gave it long
before you asked for it."

Jean felt safe from the old, brooding memories of
the years spent apart from his lady trying to amass
a fortune. With Paul and Simon beside him, Jean
had become fabulously wealthy, but what a price
they had paid for it; their meanderings had left an
indelible mark on all of their lives. All Jean wanted
now was to hold the woman he cared about. She
could make him forget everything.

Lisette undressed slowly, partly because she still
felt uncertain about her relationship with him, and
partly because of the way he looked at her. The
hard lines of his mouth softened into the faintest
smile. And his eyes, those gray orbs that could send
her reeling in fear, now beheld her with a tenderness that hadn't been there before.

The bathwater had grown cool, but he didn't
seem to mind and finished his toilette in record
time. He washed the dust from the summer
drought away and took special care to shave the
whiskers that raked her skin raw.

Stripped to her chemise, she folded the blouse
and skirt and draped them over the back of a chair.
She was nervous. This was worse than being a new

bride and not knowing exactly what was expected. After the pain of losing her virginity, would he expect to continue so soon the physical abuse of her tender body? No wonder the gentlewomen of the nobility sent their husbands off to whores for the evening.

Refolding her clothes, Lisette caught him watching her from the mirror where he stood shaving. He was smiling, and not watching where the blade of his razor moved. Blood trickled down his square jaw.

"Do you see what you do to me?" he teased.

Lisette took the toweling from his fingers and dabbed at the cut. "It serves you right."

Her hands trembled as she touched him. Why did wanting him cause that ache inside?

Jean was oblivious to the gouge on his chin. As he held her safely within the cradle of his arms, the scent of her hair filled his head. He understood her hesitation.

"It will be better this time, *chérie*," he promised.

Lisette felt the blush warm her cheeks. She hadn't wanted to ask that question. She would probably soon know anyway.

"Are you sure?"

"Absolutely. I won't hurry you, and I won't break if you touch me."

He took the towel from her fingers and wiped the shaving lather from his face. It was baby soft, and a dark shadow still lingered on his upper lip. Her hands rested on his bare chest while he finished, and she realized she wanted him to hurry. The gnawing desire within her became more unbearable by the moment.

"What is happening to me?"

The throaty timbre of his voice was soft against her ear. "Let me show you, Lisette."

Slowly, so as not to frighten her, Jean brushed

the straps of her chemise over her shoulders, bent
his dark head to give her a love bite, and then
licked the lightly freckled skin. It gave her goose
bumps down her spine. Only her deep breathing
kept the chemise from falling to the floor. Anxiously, he tugged at the ribbon nestled between her
breasts, and the fabric dropped to the floor. Wrapping his arms around her bare form, Jean stepped
back to the bed and lowered her down to the feather
mattress.

It wasn't enough to be caressed. Lisette sought
the inside of his thigh with the palm of her hand.
His muscles tensed under her teasing gesture, and
she soon heard a purr of pleasure come from deep
within him. Instinctively, her fingers began to caress him in a most provocative way. This new sensation brought her as much excitement as it
seemed to do for him. Leaning over him, she bent
to kiss him.

Jean reached up and framed her face between his
hands. His control was almost gone; he could stand
to wait no longer.

Lisette fell under the spell of his lips trailing
fires to the peaks of her breasts. His mouth closed
over the cinnamon nipples and bit lightly, then
suckled the tormented mounds into hardened bliss.
Her hands wound into his dark brown hair as the
kisses feathered across her belly. The tip of his
tongue unmercifully sought out the hollows between her hips, then moved to the crest of her
thighs.

Lisette's body responded to every nudge of those
deft fingers moving over her heated skin. She
moved as he bade her, curling her legs over his
shoulders, and could have died for the pleasure he
gave her. Her eyes closed against the intensity of
his hot tongue delving into her. He eased kisses
over her lost maidenhead, soothing the torn flesh

with the tip of his tongue. "Please, Jean," she begged, trusting that he knew how to end the agony within her.

He entered her quickly. The wet velvet recess of her body welcomed his intrusion as each tiny shiver of orgasm pulled him deeper within her. The rhythm mounted and rocked the old feather bed as each thrust took them further into that realm of total, mindless ecstasy. Jean's kisses lingered on her warm, soft lips until his control broke and he ground against her hips. Finally able to free himself of the ache within his loins, he shuddered. Lisette's cry called out to him, and then she, too, went limp with exhaustion.

Feeling settled in the afterglow of satisfaction, she sought out with spry fingers the contours of his back, caressing the sweat-soaked skin with tenderness.

Her first sniffle was muffled. She had been loved so sweetly by Jean that it sent her affections into wild delirium; Lisette was unable to hold back the sobs of happiness.

The sound of her crying made his heart sink. Jean braced his elbows beside her head, kissing the tears that fell.

"Did I hurt you, Lisette?"

She shook her head.

Jean nuzzled her ear and brushed the hair from her face. "Then I don't understand. Why are you crying?"

She wiped the tears away with the back of her hand. "Because I can't ever go back." Fresh tears fell down her reddened cheeks. "I can't change what has happened. It was supposed to be beautiful."

Jean was confused. "It wasn't pleasing?"

Lisette knew what he was referring to and it made her blush. "It was wonderful."

"You enjoyed it?" he asked.

"Oui," she responded, clinging tighter as the sobs racked her body. "It was wonderful. I didn't know that making love could be so good. But you must hate me."

Jean rolled to his side, shaking his head at the illogic of young women. "Why would I hate you?"

"Because I should have come to you without hesitation, no matter what the circumstances. I was your fiancée, and you had every right to take whatever privilege you wanted with me. I called you every name I could think of, trying to forget the pledge I had given you when we were betrothed. Why didn't you force me?"

A smile wrinkled his brow. "I liked it better this way. And," he teased, "I have heard worse names. Do you have any regrets, Lisette?" Jean took her hand in his, kissing her palms.

"I do have one regret."

His hand closed on hers. She wouldn't still leave him, would she? He had to be sure. "What is it, *mignon?*"

Lisette turned to the shelter of his arms and rested her chin against his chest. "I should have told you how much I love you."

Jean's smile widened. "You should have?"

"Then we could have made love right away. We wasted so much time fighting each other when we should have been in bed."

He couldn't feel more like a wretched monster than he did at this moment. She had been honest with him; he was sure of it. Lisette had openly declared her heart to him, and only a tiny twinge of his doubt remained.

"I guarantee"—Jean leaned over her sleepy form, kissing her soft shoulders—"that I will make up for lost time."

"Promise me?" she said quietly.

"My oath as a gentleman. I will make love to you at every opportunity." He would keep his word, or die trying.

Chapter Thirteen

Lisette was drawn to the slim ray of light flowing between the heavy satin drapes. There was some excitement on the street which ignited her sense of adventure. The sounds of a milling throng could be heard engaged in high-pitched merriment. If there were a riot forming, the voices would be angry, but these sounds were different—happy sounds that pulled her out of the bed to gaze out the window to the square below.

There, in the middle of the plaza, was the most delightful sight she could imagine. A hot-air balloon lumbered in the morning breeze. It stretched four stories off the ground! The envelope was elaborately detailed with Greek scrollwork in brilliant reds and blues. Straw was being burned to give the balloon the lift it would need to get into the air, and the basket prepared to give some lucky onlookers a ride.

Lisette had been at the very first launching of a balloon and she never forgot the exhilaration it gave her to think she might drift into the clouds. Since her father refused to let her ride in it then, she wasn't going to let this opportunity pass her by.

Surely Jean wouldn't refuse her anything, not after the night they had spent together. It had been nearly dawn before she allowed him to sleep; she found she had an insatiable appetite that only her handsome Baron could fulfill.

"Jean!" Lisette bounced on the bed. He didn't move at her first prodding. Impatient, she shook him again. "Wake up. You have to see this."

"What is it?" He smiled. Through closed eyes his blind search found the soft form of Lisette and tenderly cuddled her close to him. "Don't wake me up for anything short of civil war being declared."

"Wake up, lazy," she pouted. "There is something outside that could threaten my life!" There, that did it. His eyes flew open in an instant. He lurched out of the bed and glared out the window.

"It looks like my head feels, bloated!" he stated gruffly. "This is what could threaten your life?" He turned back to Lisette, and she shrank back against the pillows from the sinister look he gave her. Jean rubbed his aching head. Why had he had so much to drink on an empty stomach? He was ravenously hungry and tired, he realized. Having a young woman to please took a great deal of strength.

"Don't be angry with me." Lisette eased off the bed. She watched the crowds on the street below scurry about. It was a spectacular day to be alive.

Jean reached out and took her into his arms. "God, Lisette. I thought half of your uncle's army was outside the inn." He touched his lips to her temple and breathed deeply of the scent of her hair. "I was ready to fight all of them to keep you."

"All?" Lisette's arms went around him; his words gave her a sense of belonging to the man she cared about more than life itself. She loved his gray eyes, his hollow cheeks, and, most of all, his delectable touch.

"They would have to fight me, too, to get me to go back." She tipped her chin up to place a kiss on his shoulder. A scar was soft under her lips, so she kissed it again, hating anything that would hurt her beloved.

"Isn't it marvelous?" She sighed.

Jean had lost interest in the balloon. His lady stirred something in him he thought impossible after a night of pleasing her. She surprised him in her eagerness to learn. It wasn't enough to lie still and be caressed. She wanted to make it good for him. And it had been very, very good.

Lisette knew what was on his mind the moment she saw the look on his face. He didn't seem to care what happened outside the window. He didn't see anything past her loving smile. Suddenly, the balloon could wait. It would take time to get the balloon ready to launch into the clouds, she thought.

Hours later, Lisette emerged from the cocoon of passion. She tossed the silk coverlet off her body and draped it over the brass footboard.

"I'm starved," she announced. A thin sheen of perspiration glistened on Jean's chest. She had just put him through his paces. She giggled. Could she help it if she were a willing student of his fine arts of desire?

"I'm too weak to move," came his voice from under the sheet. "Just leave me here to die."

Lisette rummaged around the room to find her boots. She pulled on the skirt and milkmaid blouse that she had nervously draped over a chair the night before. Her stockings came next, and there was still no sign of movement from her exhausted partner. "Don't move. I'll get you something to eat."

"I couldn't budge if I wanted to. You'll have to fight the armies today, Lisette."

Today Lisette felt she could conquer the world.

Jean dozed, peacefully unaware of the situation in the dining room.

* * *

"You heard me, Michel." Lisette was firm. She wouldn't take no for an answer.

"Does *he* know about this?" Michel's face was alight with mirth. She shook her head, and he hooted with laughter. "I can't wait until he finds out."

Lisette looked at Paul. "What about you? Will you give me your word to keep my secret?"

Paul stroked his beard. They knew something about the Baron that she didn't. Still, it was a hopeful sign. Jean had given her the engagement ring, and Paul doubted they had been sleeping until noon. "I promise not to tell him unless he asks."

"That's not fair," Lisette scolded the huge man. She wasn't afraid of Paul anymore. She picked up the tray of food. There were enough delicious morsels to feed a league of Jolberts. "I'm counting on you two," she called over her shoulder as she climbed the stairs.

Paul roared with laughter. "Wait until she finds out he won't get into the thing."

Michel was already grasping at his stomach as the peals of merriment continued. "We have a quest, at last." Michel's mind drifted for a moment, then he smiled. "It's a perfect wedding gift for the lady. Why didn't I think of it before? What else do you get someone who already has everything she could possibly want?"

"When Jean finds out," Paul warned, "he's going to slit your gullet."

"This time, it will be worth it. Did you want to tell the lady the mighty Black Baron is afraid of heights?"

"Like you're afraid of the water?" Paul reminded him. "We drew lots to see who gets to dunk you into a tub this time. I won the repugnant task."

Michel tossed the chair aside, and the room cleared of inquisitive patrons. He drew his rapier and stepped into fencing form. "It's all in the stance," he warned Paul. "Try to touch me, and you'll lose your beard."

"You've probably got scurvy by now. Why won't you just get into the tub?"

Michel's expertise with his rapier was unmatched by anyone except Jean. Paul had strength, but Michel employed a dexterity that remained unrivaled by anyone of the fine houses of France. "It's uncivilized."

"You're only making this harder on yourself," Paul cautioned. He hurled the table aside, taking care not to meet the point of Michel's rapier. "Stand still, you little buzzard."

Lisette put the tray down on the bed. Jean stirred under the covers. The scones were freshly baked, and she had a sneaking suspicion the maid would have preferred to deliver them. The Baron was well known to the innkeeper. The cook knew exactly what he wanted to eat, and accepted no intervention from Lisette. The young Duchess had finally won the battle on the strawberries. She loved them even if Jean didn't. The cook and maid didn't seem interested in Lisette's preference. Jean's selection was all that mattered. The little snip of a maid had issued some guttural oath before running out of the kitchen. Lisette had refused to let the girl enter the Baron's chamber and attend him. She saw now that she would have to change some of his habits.

"Jean." She was pensive. "How many women am I going to have to fight to keep you?"

"Dozens." The form under the sheet chortled.

He was laughing at her again. Lisette bit into a big, juicy berry. Her small hand slid under the sheet and tweaked him.

"I mean it. How many? The maid nearly slit my

throat for the chance to bring you breakfast. I think I should be forewarned."

Jean couldn't wait. The aromas drifting from the tray drew him from the cocoon of sleep. He plumped the pillows behind his head, deliberately evading the penetrating gaze of his lady. "My cousin thinks it would be a miracle that anyone would want me."

"Your cousin isn't a woman." Lisette sat on the edge of the bed, toying with the satin coverlet. There was a green-eyed streak of jealousy flaring that she hadn't known she possessed until now. If it weren't beneath her dignity and station to resort to a catfight, she would have torn the maid's hair out.

Jean curled her fingers around his hand. "I can't change the past. Would you have preferred me to take a vow of celibacy until you reached an agreeable age?"

"I would have considered it. Will you please hurry and get dressed? I have a surprise for you."

"Oh?" Jean questioned. "What surprise?" He had a feeling that keeping up with Lisette was going to be a debilitating experience. Jean ate greedily. He would need his strength.

Lisette tucked the fine threads of her hair under the beret. Jean wouldn't allow her to leave the inn without the disguise. In breeches again, it was her turn to tease and tempt. As they strolled the square arm in arm, the looks the Baron got were worth the loss of her feminine appearance. He could dissuade even the casual onlookers with one fierce glare. She clung to him in adoration, and that made the snickers worse.

Jean looked at this cousin. "I see you decided to shave." Lisette had no way of knowing the effort it took Jean not to laugh. Michel's hair was still dripping wet, and Paul looked years younger without the beard.

The balloon was finally ready to launch. The envelope was swaying high above their heads. The only thing that would stop the launch was heavy winds.

Lisette heard the nasal twang of Mistress Prissy long before the woman's hefty flanks came into view. It was a sound that would be forever etched into her memory, a bad seed that couldn't be forgotten. She didn't want to meet up with Prissy. Not now. In her heart Lisette knew she loved Jean, but the woman would never let her forget the depths that Lisette had fallen to. A kept woman! Lisette knew that Prissy would tell everyone of her disgrace, from Versailles to the bakery the woman frequented. Lisette dodged behind Jean's broad back. With Paul beside the Baron, it was a wall of humanity that kept Prissy from view.

Michel remembered the mistress. The nerves in his back screamed at the thought of another encounter with the woman. He also knew that Jean didn't want Lisette recognized, and the mistress would spot her immediately, disguise or no.

The Marquis Michel le Maire had to think fast. Jean picked up on his signal to depart immediately. Lisette was helping by remaining out of sight, but the woman was within a few yards of them and the Baron would have to back off quickly.

Jean turned his back to Prissy, and Lisette slid in between him and Paul.

"She ruined my surprise," Lisette seethed. "I had it all arranged."

"The wind is picking up. It wouldn't have been safe for a balloon ride." Jean was happy to miss this surprise. "I have an appointment, Lisette. Paul will take you back to the inn. Stay there and get some rest. I'll be back soon."

Lisette looked directly into his gray eyes. "You'll be back soon? Where are you going?"

"It's a business engagement that can't wait." He offered no other explanation.

It was going to be easy to get himself arrested; people were arrested every day now for "subversive" activities. But could he get the information he needed before he came out of the prison? The peasants were becoming angry. The Bastille would be taken within the week, and that should provide him with plenty of time to locate his father inside the fortress walls. The guards would talk if bribed, and Jean had made sure they were happy. The revolution would provide him with an escape. He only worried that Lisette might try something foolish and leave him.

"Wait for me, *ma chérie,*" Jean requested.

"No." Lisette was definite. "I won't let you go alone." Panic constricted her stomach. Her sense of *déjà vu* was heightened when she saw the balloon. It was somehow linked with their destiny. She was terrified she would never see him again. "Take me with you."

Jean guided her through the crowds. He couldn't take her with him into the prison. Paul would take care of her until he was able to meet her outside Paris. "I can't take you with me, Lisette."

"I'll leave," she challenged.

"You promised you wouldn't."

"That was before you decided to put me in the care of your cousin. I won't wait for you to return. Please, don't leave me." Lisette couldn't explain her fear; she only knew it was there.

Chapter Fourteen

Jean drew her away from the sidewalks, into the inn. He was furious with her for insisting he remain, and with himself for not being able to entrust her to Paul's care.

Lisette almost tripped up the stairs behind him as he pulled her along to their room. In his black mood, she wasn't about to tell him she had the unsettling feeling that once parted, their paths would take different directions.

Jean had made his decision. He had to make contact with his father before anything else happened. There wasn't time to argue with Lisette. He lifted the crystal decanter and poured himself a drink of brandy, and one for Lisette. It was a sneaky, underhanded thing to do, but he didn't have a choice. He opened an envelope and emptied sleeping powder into the snifter he would give to Lisette. Paul would take her to meet him outside Paris, where they would hastily depart for Spain.

Lisette felt she had won the argument when he didn't make any effort to depart. She would gladly endure anything but losing him.

They sat on the bed and he shifted his position to face her, handing the snifter to her.

She had to fight the warm, lethargic feeling he aroused every time he came near her. She decided conversation would be a good diversion from the sensuous direction her mind was taking.

"Why is Paris so quiet?"

"The tension is being felt everywhere."

"When did the militiamen start wearing cockades of red and blue in their helmets? That isn't the color of the old Bourbon families."

"It's the symbol of the revolution. The people have combined the colors of Paris with the white of the old families. The cockades are secured with a white band, joining the old France to the new."

"Paris looks like it's under martial law," Lisette pouted. "Did you see the barricades in the streets?"

"There are frequent riots here, and most people stay behind locked doors after the curfew."

"Things can change so quickly. It doesn't seem that the National Guard is effectively protecting the city if everyone is afraid to leave their homes. Aren't they arresting the agitators?"

"Lafayette is soon to be appointed head of the guard, and he will have his hands full, I assure you. Most of the insurrectionists are friends of mine, and although they are ruthless, they also have France's welfare in mind."

"But they are treasonous cowards! How could *you* have anything to do with them?"

Again, he wished that he could trust her and tell her about his family's involvement. "My dear Lisette, you have lived too long in the house of a royal family. I support my friends because they have lived in the poverty France has become. Your uncle is a fool, and any man with enough power could easily have the entire country at his feet. There are hungry people starving to death, and Louis ignores it. The day will come when a nobleman's privileged birth won't exist and all men will be equal."

"You are a nobleman," she protested. "You have

lived with all the privileges and rights bestowed on you by the King as a feudal baron."

"Only because I, and every generation before me, have fought for France." He was becoming irate at her defense of royalism and shook his head. "You don't understand."

"We have a *parlement* for the needs of the people, but without a monarch to lead them, what would they do? Who would rule them? They have no experience in matters of state. It has been this way since the beginning of time; our people know nothing else. What will you do with your child? If there ever comes a day when we conceive a son, he would have the potential to be a king, a monarch like the one that you are fighting against. Isn't that a privileged birth that could do some good for the people?"

"I am not breeding a monarch!" he shouted at her. "My revenge has nothing to do with your title, Duchess de Meret." Jean was angry, but more for his own lack of foresight. She had trapped him, and he knew it. If he married her, their child could sit on the throne, inheriting the kingdom from his mother, which angered Jean even more. "I'd rather breed a bastard than a king, Lisette. The child would never be able to control France, born as a bastard. It's the only means that I have to protect us from those who would use your lineage and my fortune to gain the throne."

He couldn't marry Lisette nor tell her that he'd managed to set up an underground made up of volunteers who snatched noble men, women, and children from the hangman's noose. If Jean told Lisette that he, and several others who were close to him, rallied for aid from the King of Spain, they'd all be doomed if Lisette escaped them and gave this information to the King.

Jean instantly regretted his outburst. He thrust

his hands into his pockets and paced the floor. How had Lisette managed to get him so angry? Whether to marry her or not to marry her—that was the question that was driving him mad. One moment he wanted to wring her pretty little royalist neck, and the next he wanted to take her into his arms and apologize for hurting her.

Her big blue eyes filled with tears, and his resolve broke. She had told him she loved him, and he was ranting like a rutting bull. He hated himself.

"You must think I am a monster. I give you my word of honor—our child will inherit everything I own. All of Normandy will obey him as their rightful lord: the castle and the province will all be his to command while we retire to my villa in Spain. Everything but a throne—I swear it."

"You can't change my heritage. I don't know why you wanted to marry me if you hate my family so much."

"Because I wasn't marrying your family, Lisette. I want you, not your lineage."

Just when she was sure she should hate him, he said something wonderful and she forgave him again. Lisette would wait until they reached Spain. After that, if he didn't answer her questions, she'd find a way to escape him.

She swallowed the brandy. It warmed to her body temperature and burned in a liquid fire to her stomach. She found the chair a comfortable distance from his brooding mood.

Paul knocked on his lord's chamber, hesitating when the voices within stopped to a chilling silence. The Baron's visitor wouldn't wait any longer. Paul knocked again, then admitted him to the Baron's chamber.

Lisette drifted into a world of her own. Her heart ached with the knowledge that Jean would never marry her. Wait until our relationship can be properly handled, he had said. Handled how? Could she be further humiliated? She doubted it was possible.

The conversation in the room buzzed on around her. Lisette had to concentrate hard to understand what was being said. Jean's guest pointed out that terrorism would safeguard the revolution, and Jean's brows snapped together in disapproval.

Jean stared at his comrade. "Maintaining terrorism will exchange one life in bondage for another. If you try to rule with cruelty, you will become the enemy of the people you represent."

"The people understand force because Louis has used it on them for so long. The *robe de noblesse* who started this revolution didn't count on the Third Estate gaining power. Now that the *parlement* has started the melee, it will be up to us who represent the majority to control and reorganize into a strong nation. By whatever means it must use, France will become a mighty European power again. I intend to see to it that Louis loses his head. We don't need the nobles or their constant bickering to get what we want."

"Then the rumors are correct. You have withdrawn from the *parlement?*" Jean pressed.

"The Third Estate has declared its independence from the Paris *parlement* and formed the National Constituent Assembly." He smiled with pleasure.

"It is an assembly built totally by anarchist peasants and Jacobin incendiaries," Jean hissed.

"Therein lies the strength of France." The Baron's guest was confident of his power and let himself relax while his opponent smoldered.

"You have nothing to gain. The Girondist liberals have called out the Royal Guard on you and stunted the movement you began."

The other's temper flared. "For that stupidity we will answer with a riot of incredible proportions. At dawn tomorrow, it will paralyze the city. Paris will not so soon forget our strength. The idiots who govern the people had only to listen to our pleas, but they chose not to, and now we will seize control."

Lisette was frightened by this odd visitor. His threats were real and aimed at the royal family. She shivered as she watched them argue. The fate of her country was at stake, and Jean seemed to argue for the royalty. If she weren't skeptical of the Baron's sentiments, she would be proud of him.

"And what will you do with the government once you take control?" Jean asked quietly. "You haven't the finances to control that which you take. In doing this you will estrange the real wealth and power of France, the *noblesse.*"

" 'Tis only a matter of time before we are joined by the wealth. You will see, Jolbert. France will become a strong nation again as a democracy, not a monarchy."

These men were talking blatant sedition. The door was guarded by Paul, and there was no threat of immediate arrest. But if their conversation were overheard, they could be reported.

"What are your plans? Total annihilation of the royal family to get what you want? It won't work."

"It will with the strength of the peasants behind us. Soon every member of the King's family will feel our power as we send them to the scaffolds. There won't be another generation of monarchs to rule France, only the people, the true citizens."

Lisette was relieved she hadn't been formally introduced to this rebel. She had the urge to run to the palace and disclose this information to the King before the threats materialized. Jean's restraining hand on her arm held her there. She was confident Jean would not allow this man to do an injustice to her family.

Jean's guest hesitated with his hand on the shoulder-high door handle. " 'Tis regrettable that we have come to a parting, *mon ami.* Someday we will meet again, and you may not have a choice but to join us. I would be careful if I were you. The Duc is still a powerful man. From what I can learn, 'tis a game of power, and anyone holding the pawn meets certain death. If you stay in France with a royalist wife, you'll die."

"We will meet again," Jean assured him. Paul escorted the man out of the chamber. Jean paced with fury. He had always known Lisette's lineage could be a greater liability than an asset. It was even more urgent that they depart for Spain.

Lisette felt extremely tired. She could hardly hold her head up. The threat to their lives was plainly stated. If only she weren't so sleepy. She needed to think about what the man had said.

"Jean, who was that?"

Jean briskly turned to face her. "He is a Jacobin terrorist who doesn't care who gets murdered to get what he wants."

"Why are you so angry? I thought you were both on the same side, against royalism."

"We are against royalism, Lisette. He just does things differently than I do," he snapped.

Lisette noted that he hadn't answered her question. She kept quiet while he paced the room. Her body sought to stretch out on the bed and fall into a deep sleep. She stared at his hands tightly clasped behind his back. The muscles in his arms flexed and strained against the fragile linen of his tunic. From the chair where she sat, his tall, dark image was frightening. She knew well enough his strength when he was roused and his intensity warned her to keep quiet. When he didn't react to the knock on the door, she stood, forcing her sluggish muscles to work, and opened it. Paul walked in and waited for the angry nobleman to speak.

"We leave immediately. By this time tomorrow, Paris may be burned to the ground if that imbecile has his way. We'll have to continue with inquiries about my father. Have the horses ready in ten minutes."

"Yes, m'lord." Paul turned and left.

Lisette floated over the floor to the door to answer yet another knock. Her feet didn't seem to touch the boards as she swung the portal open.

The Baron stood by the window, deep in thought. A sudden movement on the street momentarily held his attention, his hand nervously resting on the hilt of his rapier. There were too many men on the street for comfort.

He turned to Lisette too late. The door opened and the room filled with soldiers. Lisette was grabbed tightly across the shoulders, and a pistol was pressed into the soft flesh of her neck.

The Baron vaulted into action as the men entered the chamber. His rapier had flashed out and two men lay dead on the floor. A quivering outcry came from Lisette and Jean ceased his struggles.

The lieutenant holding Lisette tightened his arm across her shoulders as the Baron stepped toward them. Jean moved to the center of the room directly in front of her. He kept his icy gaze on the guard.

The lieutenant stepped back a pace out of the Baron's reach. "You are under arrest." The Baron raised his rapier to duel. "Curse you, Jolbert. There is no way to win. My men will kill you. Where is your guest?"

"Gone," Jean reported. "If you hurry, you can still catch up with him."

"Jean!" Lisette screamed as the troop moved in

on him. She feared for his life and her arms went out to him. Flashing lights sparkled before her in a million colors. She slumped forward, falling to the floor. The lieutenant had neatly brought the hilt of his sword down on the top of her head.

"She's a pretty one," the lieutenant mused. "The executioner will thank us kindly for this one. Bring her along to keep His Lordship company."

Chapter Fifteen

Paul and Michel watched the arrest from the stables. Unable to help, they remained out of sight and waited until the guards passed by.

"Well, he got into the Bastille," Paul growled.

"What do we do now?" Michel asked.

"Didn't Jean say there was going to be a raid on the Bastille in the morning?" Paul grumbled.

"Yes, he did," Michel agreed. "There doesn't seem to be anything we can do tonight. For the Baron, I mean."

"Nasty turn of events." Paul nodded. "We'll just have to wait until tomorrow to help Jean out of this one."

"I didn't know Lady Lisette was supposed to go into the Bastille with him."

Paul scratched his naked face and cursed Michel again for shaving his lustrous beard. "She wasn't. I was supposed to take her to meet him outside Paris, and he would escape from the prison."

"You don't say." Michel grinned. "I don't think it worked."

Paul drew two bushy eyebrows together. It was obvious the plan to get Jean into the Bastille alone had failed. Michel was living dangerously to even mention it.

"Say, Paul, do you think we should be involved

in the raid tomorrow? It would be great sport, and just think of the exercise we can get."

"Politics! Bah!" Paul hated to become involved in anything that wasn't for the betterment of the Jolbert family. He lived and breathed to protect the heir of Normandy. His personal life would wait until Jean was safely on his way to Spain. Still, this was a golden opportunity to tip the scales of justice. Peasants weren't adequately prepared for open warfare. He was. So was Michel.

Their discussion was dropped as three maids from the inn passed by. One of them was instantly enamored of Paul. She was a small, dark-haired woman and sumptuously well rounded. She caught his attention by running her hands down his arms, cooing at the size of him.

"Mon cher." The maid gave an excited laugh, and Paul took her into his arms. "Such a bonny man."

Paul had a duty to the Baron, but he wasn't crazy.

Michel had a woman on each arm and knew the night wouldn't be spent in planning the attack on the Bastille. The Marquis didn't ask their names. One of the young women happened to have a bottle of wine. The little temptress offered warm red lips to his, and suddenly all thoughts of the impending revolution vanished.

Paul didn't need further provocation. He took the pretty little woman over his shoulder and climbed the ladder to the hayloft.

"Have you no pride, Paul?" Michel reprimanded. The Marquis shook his head. The man didn't have any caliber. Paul always took the direct approach. Michel knew differently. Women liked to be wooed and caressed, promised the stars and given the moon. He was a gentle lover with his easygoing nature; he was easy to please and well skilled at pleasing. The fact that he had two women to contend with didn't sway him. They didn't seem to mind sharing his talents, so why should he object to his fortune in sweet-smelling women?

"Easy, ladies." Michel laughed. They were already undressing him. "There is an empty chamber that I know of. Care to join me?"

Need he ask? Michel took the drink of wine one of the women offered. It was going to be a long night, from what he could tell.

Jean looked around the torchlit cell inside the Bastille. There hadn't been further resistance to the arrest. Jean had had too few men there to fight. Why hadn't he sent Lisette safely on her way before the soldiers had time to find him? If they had been taken to any other prison, their escape would have been difficult. At least here they had only to wait until the riot started in the morning. Lisette was dropped on the floor beside him, still unconscious. He said a silent prayer of thanks that she had not been recognized.

"Enjoy the accommodations while you can, m'lord Baron," the lieutenant said greedily. "You won't be here for long. There will be a special inquiry for the great Black Baron this evening." The guard smiled as the Baron was shackled to the wall. The lieutenant leaned over Lisette and touched his fingers to her neck to feel for a pulse. "She's still alive. Such a pretty head to lose. Charles Sanson will undoubtedly regret cutting it off. Perhaps I'll come back later and enjoy her while she's still alive." His wicked laugh echoed down the hall as he left. "Or I'll wait until they bring her back for burial. It doesn't matter to me." Jean was sick to his stomach thinking of what the man implied. The door clanged shut and they were left in total darkness. This wasn't the worst prison he'd seen. At least there was a skinny little window to brighten the room when the sun came up. The danger Lisette was in prevented him from rebutting the lieutenant openly.

"Bastard!" Jean seethed. He had made special arrangements to be arrested by a man whom he knew worked at the prison. He had been betrayed.

The stone floor and fourteen-foot-thick walls made the prison a cool relief from the summer heat. The straw bed though probably flea-infested was a small convenience.

Knowing the raid on the Bastille was planned because his father's friends had learned of the Earl's arrest didn't help the Baron to dispel a certain amount of guilt. The simple peasants who would be putting their lives in danger didn't know the riot was planned by men who held positions in the *parlement,* men who dearly wanted the Earl released.

Lisette's hand groped to her aching head. She winced at the throbbing pain. Her eyes opened to inky darkness, and she blinked hard to focus. There were rats squeaking nearby, and she cringed instinctively at the sound. An overwhelming stench burned her nose and throat. She tried to brace herself and sit up.

"Jean!" She covered her face a moment with her shirt, choking for a clean breath of air. Something furry touched her arm and she recoiled, sick to her stomach. "Oh, Lord, where am I?"

"We're in the Bastille, Lisette." It was Jean's soft voice next to her.

She waved her arms in a wide circle, fumbling through the darkness to find him. "Where are you?" She crawled on her hands and knees toward the sound of his voice. "I can't see," she whispered. Her hand found something warm, and she jumped backward. She touched it again at his encouraging words and followed the shape of his leg. "Jean? Are you all right?" Her head reeled and spun as she moved. She thought she would sink into unconsciousness again as twin talons of pain clamped onto her head.

His soft chuckle shook his body. "So, *chérie,* all I have to do to get you to stop calling me monsieur is to get arrested and shackled to a prison wall? It's something I didn't think of, I'll admit."

"Stop teasing me. Are you hurt anywhere?" Her fingers went through his hair, checking for lumps, and down his chest, gently probing for damage. "I haven't found any holes in you. Were you hurt?"

"My darling Lisette. All this concern for my well-being almost makes getting arrested worth it." He flinched when she pinched him in the ribs. "I am quite well. How does your head feel? I thought he broke your skull, he hit you so hard."

"I . . . feel like I've been drugged."

Jean felt like a rogue. "You were drugged, Lisette."

She wanted to hit him. Nothing short of a punch in his straight, aristocratic nose would suffice this time. "Was it necessary?" she seethed.

"You have every right to be angry. I just didn't want you to come into this prison with me. It would have been safer for you to await my return outside Paris. Tomorrow, when we get out of here, you will understand what I mean." When she failed to respond, he nearly panicked. "Lisette? No, don't pass out again. Stay with me, love. This place is terrible, and I miss you."

Lisette fought back her rage. He had called her love.

"You drugged me," she choked. "Damn you. When can I ever trust you?"

Jean had expected the anger, but not her open disgust. "I thought only of you."

"Why were we arrested?" Lisette followed his arms to the shackles holding his wrists. "I thought you had friends in all the right places."

"We weren't exactly arrested, my dear. The King wants to talk to me about my loyalties, that's all. I didn't obey the order he sent me to come to the palace during the investigation of my family. The National Guard is none too choosy about who is brought to this place. The soldiers are scouring Paris for anyone who even speaks to revolutionists. My best-laid plans have gone askew. I had a friend who was supposed to escort me into this prison, and then get me back out again before sunrise. I'll remember his name for a long time. He betrayed me, and for that he'll die."

"You really aren't in a position to threaten anyone," Lisette pointed out to him. She clutched her aching head, sorting out what had happened through the pounding thunderstorm going on in her brain. "I am going to call the guards and get us out of here. My uncle won't stand for this kind of treatment to a member of his family."

"Have you forgotten that you were at the same meeting I was? Your uncle will have no authority in this matter. You will stand trial, just as I will, as a renegade."

"Treason!" she gasped. "How did this happen to me?"

"More innocent people have died here than in wartime just because they had to steal to feed their families, or were murdered because they were considered dispensable by the nobility. The peasants are being cheated out of everything they own. Their only hope of justice is the revolution."

"I see what you mean," she said softly and swallowed the bittersweet tears that welled in her throat. She had been a spoiled brat long enough.

Jean felt torn between protecting Lisette and

rescuing his father. The Earl of Normandy was in
the prison—probably within a few feet of them—
and Jean was powerless to help. If he did manage
to get free, he couldn't leave Lisette alone in the
cell while he searched the Bastille. She couldn't be
left to defend herself against the onslaught of rioting peasants.

"We must be prepared if our guard returns. He
has promised that your remaining hours will be as
unpleasant as possible." As a herald of the dawn,
a tiny beam of light from the window above their
heads pierced the darkness. "I wouldn't want you
to be raped while I stand by, forced to watch."

"I don't intend to let that happen." She removed
the long, sturdy hairpin holding her braid.

"What are you doing? Lisette?" She started
working on the shackles. With a look of determination that bespoke her frustration, Lisette turned
the old lock and his left arm dropped free. She
crossed his body and freed his right arm.

"I see how you escaped your room at Avranches." He was reminded again of his respect for
the lady's cunning. Jean inspected the lump on her
head, and she groaned with pain.

"Are we really going to be executed?" Her heart
was heavy and sad. "Just because we met with a
Jacobin?"

"It's not uncommon, *petite*. Whole families are
being sent to the scaffold for that reason, and less.
Little children and innocent wives have died
bravely and knew only that *le Roi le veut,* the King
wills it." Deep emotion faltered in his voice as he
spoke to her. It was a different, caring side of him
she had not seen before. Her small hand slid into
his. It didn't seem to matter anymore that she had
relented and become his mistress. Their quarrel
seemed a minor tiff. The country was going insane

around them, and leaving for the sunny shores of Spain sounded better all the time.

The hours crept by, and there still was no sign of their guard. Jean was beginning to think they would never get out of the prison. Lisette slept, nestled against him, until the first of many gunshots was heard throughout the prison.

Seemingly without reason, laughter welled up in Lisette. She laughed until tears were streaming down her face and she lay limp in Jean's arms. She could feel him smiling at her as the giggles subsided.

"What do you find so funny? You are locked in a dungeon cell and talking of such serious matters as murder and treason." He had to wait until she stopped tittering to pull her back into his arms. "Perhaps that bump on your head did some damage, after all."

"I just find it ironic. I told you I would be there the day you were executed, but I didn't expect to be the next person to mount the scaffold."

"We won't be executed, Lisette. Didn't you listen to him say there was an attack planned on the Bastille today? Woman, where does your mind go? At times you seem a thousand miles away and the prettiest smile curls on your lips. I have often wondered what you are thinking about." Jean kissed the small hand clutching his. He couldn't tell her that before he left France her father would be his prisoner and would be killed for the injustice he had done to the Jolberts. Lisette would never forgive him. It was better that she didn't know.

"Do you ever wonder what it would have been like if we had married?" she queried slowly. "I have."

"Marriage to you is the only thing I thought about for two years, Lisette. While you were at the school—"

"Why did you pay for my tuition?" she interrupted.

Jean guffawed. "The mistress had to be bribed to keep you there. It seems you gave her a rather hard time of it. I wanted you kept apart from any . . . influences." He paused.

"What influences? I didn't get to go anywhere except to dine with my uncle. Have you ever had to sit through one of those dinners?"

"But it worked." He chuckled. "While you were learning the finer graces, you didn't have time to find a young man to fall in love with."

"I see." She marveled at his thinking.

"I didn't know you had already fallen in love with me," he said hesitantly.

Her back went rigid and she sat up to face him.

"I think, sir, that you are as much a spoiled brat as I am. You always get your way, never thinking of what might be given willingly without your demanding it."

"You freely became my mistress."

"You insisted on it."

"Do you mind being my mistress?"

"No," she pouted.

"I'm glad that's settled." He drew her close to him. "You're right. I am spoiled."

"And arrogant," she added, settling against his warm body and winding her fingers through his.

"Maybe just a little arrogant."

"Don't forget handsome," she added.

"Handsome?"

"Sinfully."

"You're very beautiful, Lisette. Until my father disappeared, I thought of nothing else but the day I could finally claim you."

Lisette hadn't denied her loyalty to her family but continued to defend them. Jean was a patient man, but if she didn't see the need for a revolution soon, he would have to continue hurting her to protect himself. Jean knew it was only a matter of time before the accusations made by the Duc became formal charges. To remain on French soil would mean giving fate a hand, and Jean intended to cheat the executioner and leave for Spain before his luck ran out.

Lisette never questioned the absence of his hussars. Fortunately for him, no one else had been able to link the disappearance of doomed noblemen and their families to the Baron. Jean was always careful to be where Darias's spies could see him when a nobleman was snatched out from under the executioner's sword. It was through the help of the King of Spain, and a particularly beautiful Spanish countess, that he routed the rescued families out of France with a new identity.

"Rest for a while, my darling captive. And if you can get that door open, we can escape this doomed fortress."

Chapter Sixteen

"May I remind you, my lord Baron, that we are both captives at the moment." She laid her head down on his chest. *I am destined to love a man who will destroy me,* she wearily thought. *I can always escape him later if we escape, and if I become enceinte, I could always abort the child.* She had heard of it being done by courtesans and knew it was an ordeal a woman didn't want to face. *But, oh, how I would hate to take the life of our child, bien-aimé.*

Time had stopped when Jean had abducted her. It seemed as if months had passed, but in fact it was only a few weeks. "What day is it?"

"The fourteenth of July. Are you ready to open the door?"

They both froze as boots thumped down the hall. Their cell door banged open and the lieutenant entered. "I see the lady has recovered."

Jean had had enough warning to make it appear that his hands were still restrained in the chains. "How is the riot progressing?"

The lieutenant focused two powder-blackened eyes on the Baron. "So, you knew of the riot?"

You might say I was instrumental."

The guard laughed wickedly. "It was all for nothing. We moved your father last night, after you arrived." He turned to Lisette. "I have been given permission from the commandant to do with you as I please."

"I've heard that before," Lisette said in an indifferent tone.

The guard made a move to take her. With his back to Jean, he didn't notice his rapier sliding form its sheath until it was too late.

Lisette screamed. The man fell to the floor with his throat slit. She turned her back. "I hate the sight of blood! Why did you have to kill him?"

"Would you have me politely excuse us?" Jean drew the man's pistol and checked the chamber before handing it to Lisette. "There's only one shot, Lisette. Use it well."

He handed the pistol over to her and kept the guard's rapier for himself. Jean counted the prisoners as they ran down the hall. Through the dim torchlight they glimpsed seven men being held, and not one of them was the Earl. "Freedom is near," Jean called over his shoulder to the prisoners.

There was an unnatural silence as they slipped down the hall to another door and a long staircase. The steep descent seemed to go on forever as Jean took the steps two at a time, pulling Lisette with him. When they reached the door to the courtyard, she was out of breath.

"The guards are probably all busy on the parapets," Jean said with anxiety in his deep voice. He let her rest a moment to collect her strength. Wrapping her in his arms, he lightly kissed her mouth. "If I don't make it out of here, find Paul. He will help you get out of France to safety. You are wanted for treason," he lied. Jean couldn't allow her to escape him now. If she did, there would be no way to get her back from her father. "Remember to stay behind me."

"I'm scared," she whispered.

"Trust me, darling. I would never allow anything to happen to you. I pray my luck holds through this day, lest we both fall prey to the revolution. If anyone asks you to identify yourself, dear little *citizen*, you are a peasant."

She nodded.

The courtyard was a sight she would never forget. Instantly they were rushed by guards. The Baron cut a path through the men, and they were almost to the portcullis when a deafening roar came from the crowd outside. The gate fell under a cannon blast.

Lisette was caught in the massive stream of people. Jean's grip on her slipped and she was pushed to the front of the angry crowd as hundreds of peasants entered the courtyard. Anyone who stood in the way of this human wall would be either slaughtered or trampled.

Lisette screamed uncontrollably for Jean. She was near fainting as a hideous nightmare became a reality. Jean's arm slid around her waist and he lifted her off the ground. He pressed his way out of the crowd and into the street before setting her back on her feet.

"We'll never get out of this alive." Jean's hopes were dashed as he watched the streets filled with rioting people.

Lisette splashed her face with cold water from a fountain, hoping to bring herself out of shock. When she looked up, she recognized the square. She had escaped it before. "Follow me!" She took the lead, directing their path down alleys and over fences until they were a safe distance from the worst of the tumult.

"Stop, Lisette," Jean panted. "How on earth. . . ?" he questioned.

"Training," she answered, panting herself.

Their refuge in an alley seemed safe enough. She slid to her derrière, gasping for air, her elbows braced on her knees as she rested.

Jean sat next to her, turning her dirty hands over in his. "Gads, ye're a mess."

"Dungeons don't seem to agree with me. Silks and velvets are more to my liking."

"Someday I'll drape you in the finest silk. Spain is much too hot for velvets."

"How soon before we get there?"

"Within a month, winds permitting. I have a cousin who occasionally pirates the coast, and he will escort us."

"You do have an odd family. If your cousin is anything like Paul, he is probably preying on some poor, misbegotten soul for his income."

"You will be surprised just how much he is like Paul. I fear getting you there may be only half my problem. Keeping you to myself will be twice the battle once Simon gets a look at you."

"Simon?" She tried the name on the tip of her tongue. "That doesn't sound like a buccaneer's name. I had always thought you were well suited to the high seas and a pirate's life."

Jean chuckled lightly and rested his elbows on his knees. "I prefer solid ground under my feet. But Michel was with us when Simon was washed overboard by a large squall. The Marquis went in to save him."

" 'Twas a brave thing to do."

"That it was, considering a shark had his eye on Simon. To this day Michel refuses to bathe in anything larger than a basin and he refuses to eat anything caught in the sea. The men have a terrible time getting the Marquis to bathe in a tub, so they draw lots to see who gets to dunk him. Paul lost the last round. But, being adept with a rapier, Michel retaliated this time and my cousin lost his beard."

"So that's what happened to Paul." Lisette giggled. "I didn't want to ask."

Jean was trying to think of anything but Lisette's slim body next to his. There was a bright flush to her cheeks, and her hair was loose and fluffy about her shoulders. Despite some griminess she couldn't have looked more vibrant and alive than she did now. Wanting her caused his pulse to beat erratically. How could he find desire in the back streets of Paris so enticing? He shook his head, dispelling the thoughts of ripping her clothes off and making mad, passionate love to her right there.

There was something thrilling about escaping from danger. The excitement awakened Lisette's senses to the Baron's sheer masculinity. She turned to face him and, taking his face between her hands, she pressed her lips hard against his. Temptingly, she flicked her tongue against his until he drew her roughly against his chest. The excitement of his unleashed affections sent her pulse racing through her body. Her head fell back as he kissed the base of her throat.

It took all of Jean's self-control to set her upright. His breathing was uneven for a few moments while his heartbeat calmed to a normal pace.

Lisette's lip dropped to a pout and she sagged back against the wall.

"You have a dirty face, sweetheart, though it hardly mars your beauty." Sitting on his haunches before her, he wiped at the smudge on her forehead.

She opened her mouth to speak and a strangled "Ahhh!" stopped her heart. A guardsman had come from nowhere with a shovel raised behind Jean's head, to hit him. She watched paralyzed in horror as the shovel crashed down on Jean's head. Her hand tugged out the pistol and her world spun in slow motion as the guard raised the shovel again.

Jean rolled out of the way. His mouth dropped open in astonishment as he watched Lisette draw the pistol out.

"No!" she screamed. With both hands to steady the weapon, she held out her arm straight, aiming at the man's chest. The gun slowly hissed, and the crack that followed hurtled a ball through the smoke, penetrating the center of his chest at point-blank range.

The guardsman stumbled backward, clutching the crimson stain. His eyes rolled back and he fell to the cobblestone street, dead before he hit the ground.

Lisette couldn't believe what she had just done. It was a matter of survival, a brutal necessity that she kill him before he killed Jean. She fought the queasy jerk in her stomach and tore a strip from the bottom of her skirt, winding it over the gash on Jean's head.

"You're a brave woman, Lisette." Jean was filled again with awe at her courage. "I'll get a horse . . ."

"I feel sick." Lisette broke his hold on her arm and ran farther into the alley. Her stomach wrenched. Lisette hadn't known she was capable of murder.

For a fleeting moment she had had a glimpse of a peasant's life, of their fight for survival. Staying alive was all that counted, no matter what it took. It was a hard lesson to learn, especially after her secluded life. She thought of Louis sitting in a plush palace while she waited out the riot in a filthy alley. She had come from that elegant world and Jean had given her a rare glimpse of what was really being done to France. Lisette was grateful to him for opening her eyes, and furious because she was helpless to do anything about the desperate plight of the peasants.

Lisette brushed the hair from her face. She felt better, or perhaps tougher was a good description. To her surprise, Jean led a horse down the alley. "You could be hanged at dawn for stealing that horse," she admonished.

"I didn't steal this wretched creature," Jean defended. "I merely offered it a chance to follow me."

"And you no doubt tempted the nag?"

"Woman, you insult me. The carrot in my pocket had nothing to do with its decision. The poor, homeless creature needed a friend."

"Do you have another carrot? I'm starved."

"We'll dine in leisure tonight. For now, let's get out of Paris."

"What have we here?" a deep voice rumbled, and they stopped, slowly turning to face three men. They weren't guards, but peasants out to slay any noblemen they came across. The pistol now tucked into Jean's breeches was useless with the shot already fired.

Lisette would have to use her wits to get out of this one. "Stand aside, citizens. I must get my wounded friend to safety."

Jean was about to say something, but closed his mouth instead. She never ceased to amaze him.

"State your name or die," a husky man bellowed. "If ye be a nobleman, 'tis your last hour in this world."

"It matters not what my name is. We have just escaped the Bastille, and, as you can see, it wasn't without injury." Their presence started to draw a crowd. The streets were patrolled by armed citizens, wearing the cockades of red and blue.

They grumbled between themselves and challenged them again. "For what crime were you arrested."

"Our charge was treason," Lisette proclaimed proudly.

Jean was speechless.

"Can you identify yourselves?" the leader questioned.

"My empty belly is my identification," Lisette bristled. "Isn't it enough that we've nearly died for the revolution?"

"Faith, citizen," the man seemingly designated as spokesman answered, "you may pass."

The streets were strewn with toppled carts. The riot had spread over the entire city as the frenzy struck both nobleman and peasant. It was a slow contest to pick their way through the back alleys, but the riot was not to be avoided. Everywhere they turned there was blood and death.

A horseman approached and people scurried out of his way. "The Bastille has fallen!" he called and disappeared into the streets, spreading the news. In his hand was a pikestaff adorned with . . . someone's head.

"May *le bon Dieu* forgive what we have done this day," Jean said softly; he, too, prayed that this terrible hot day in July would come to an end.

Mercifully, it started to rain.

Chapter Seventeen

Lisette tore a strip of fabric from her tunic to make a bandage for Jean. The blow on the back of his head had stopped bleeding and a nasty lump had appeared. Not having slept for more than a few hours in the past three days, Jean wearily agreed to take some much-needed rest while she kept watch.

She took her boots off and wiggled her toes in the damp grass. The rain had ceased, leaving the sky a brilliant canopy of sparkling stars and the air humid with the rich scent of moist earth. The grassy glade where they chose to wait for Paul was a short distance from the road that would take them to Rouen. She hoped Paul would be coming along shortly. Their clothes were wet and she wanted to feel dry and warm again.

When she finished dressing Jean's wound, she laid his head in her lap and affectionately stroked the mass of dark, wavy hair. It was the first time she felt she had control over him. He was sleeping and she could have easily escaped, but she couldn't bring herself to leave him. Lisette was in love with him. *He will use you* echoed through her turbulent emotions, but Lisette didn't heed the warning.

She accepted now that her family had betrayed the peace treaty between them when her father re-

fused her hand to the Baron. Her attitude had
drastically changed since their first meeting. She
would behave like an adult and not threaten him
like a child.

Lisette sighed deeply and sifted through Jean's
dark hair with her fingers. She felt more mature
and confident than she had in months. Yet there
was no future for her; only the present counted and
what Jean meant to her. She could never delude
herself into believing he was in love with her. She
bent and kissed the corner of his mouth. Someday
she would have to leave him because her heart
couldn't take the strain of loving him and knowing
he didn't return her feelings.

No matter how hard she tried to forget her
dreams of a home and marriage, they always
seemed to rise to the surface of her consciousness
to haunt her. It was evident he wanted her physically, but he wouldn't make a commitment to her.
Perhaps he did care for her in a special way, but it
didn't change the situation between them. She was
still a royalist and Jean was not. The one thing
they shared as a common goal was to find his father
and leave for Spain.

Jean's eyes fluttered open. Dark lashes rimmed
the crystal gray of those gorgeous orbs. He touched
the bandage over the wound and with a loud moan
he sat up.

"How do you feel?" She had a sneaky feeling he
had pretended to be asleep just to see what she
would do.

"I feel as if I got hit with a cannonball."

"How long have you been awake?" She stood and
brushed the grass from her legs.

"Long enough to feel that kiss. You make a better surgeon than Paul, and you're prettier, too."

"When are you going to stop teasing me?" With
her hands on her hips, she gave him a stern scowl.

In one swift jerk of her arm, he had her neatly in his lap. "When you stop blushing, my darling."

Lisette wound her arms around his neck. "What a character you are, Jean. First you scare me half to death kidnapping me, then you drag me out of prison and drop at my feet, and I have to kill a man to save your life. The saints have their hands full keeping you out of mischief."

He smiled, tipping the corners of his mouth in a playful grin. "That was a good shot. I fear I didn't know what I was doing when I kidnapped you, but I doubted you would willingly accompany me today."

"So you were awake and just baiting me to try to escape you?" she cried in anguish. "I will get even with you someday, Jean."

"You will, will you? We shall see, little woman. As for the royalty, I wonder if they are still in power. Do you still believe in a monarch, Lisette?"

"To say that I didn't would be saying that I don't believe in myself. You can never change my background. I am not a frightened little girl anymore."

"I think I will still sleep with one eye open, just in case you do change your mind and split my head open with a rock." Jean chuckled.

"I wouldn't do that." Lisette lowered her lashes coquettishly. Her lips were parted invitingly.

Jean ached from wanting her. He rolled her over on the grass, pinning her outstretched legs to the ground by sitting on her knees with his legs tucked under him to support his weight. With her hands in his, his lips were free to explore the skin under her tunic with his kisses. She writhed as he brushed his lips over the peaks of her breasts. The flimsy material did nothing to hide her arousal.

"I'll get even with you," she moaned softly. "This is torture."

"Tell me you want me, Lisette."

"No," she answered impishly.

His hands continued to taunt and caress the contours of her body. "Tell me, Lisette, how much you want me to make love to you."

Lisette gritted her teeth together. He wanted her total submission. Her body had already given in to him. Her tunic fell open, leaving her breasts gleaming in the moonlight. When his hands moved down to her breeches, her agony was unbearable. "I want you," she breathed. It was a ragged sound in her chest.

"What do you want me to do?" His head lowered to kiss the hollow of her hip.

"Make love to me," the answer came quickly. The stars above were blocked out by the shadow of his head as he finally bent to take her lips to his. She ached with a need that only he could fulfill. Their clothes were cast aside and sweetly he entered her, rocking against her fragile form until they clasped each other tightly in a shattering climax.

Lisette lay under the stars completely naked. It seemed too soon when Jean handed her breeches back to her and urged her to put them on.

"Paul should be arriving soon. And I wouldn't want to share my little wood nymph with him."

They heard Paul's approach long before he came into sight. The burly man shouted at someone, and from what Lisette could guess, he was about to murder the unseen person.

Jean took a good look at her. The bloodstained shirt was tied in a knot and revealed her slender waist. A deep frown hid the jealous surge. He would not share more of his beautiful woman than he would have to. Jean checked the pistol. He had reloaded it before leaving Paris, and the shot remained in place.

"Why didn't you shoot me, Lisette?"

"I didn't feel it was in my best interests, and Paul would be angry with me," she replied.

"Or mine," Jean agreed. He signaled to the approaching men.

The familiar voice of Paul rumbled over the pounding hooves. He yelled at a man who bent over his horse while the captain held the reins, leading him. The tirade of curses was aimed at Michel, she realized as he briefly raised his head to retaliate.

"Hold your tongue!" Jean yelled back at Paul and stepped to the side. They got a surprised look from the captain, followed by a wide smile.

"What is wrong with Michel?" she asked beside Jean.

"I'm dying," Michel groaned.

"Then it has to be from syphilis. He had too much wine and one feisty woman too many." Paul shook his head. "Disgusting scrap of humanity."

"I'm sure I'm going to die," Michel groaned.

"The greatest battle in a decade is being fought, and I have to save your decaying hide!" Paul chided him.

"If you had left me alone, I would have gladly lain down and joined my ancestors."

"If you ask me, you already have. I should have left you in Paris to suffer your *adieux* to the ladies."

"That would have been unmerciful."

Lisette was genuinely concerned. "Are you in pain?" She couldn't help but notice the swollen eyes as he slouched in his saddle. "Gads, you look horrible."

"A woman with a kind heart. Nay, my lady. 'Twas the arms of a young woman that nearly broke my back. My head is throbbing from the sweet nectar of too much wine."

"This"—Paul slapped Michel hard on the back and almost knocked him from the saddle—"is

France's Casanova. This blackguard has slept with at least fifty percent of the female population of our good country. It's a wonder he hasn't been killed in a duel—he's been called out by a good many irate fathers. Last week, it must have been four duels in a single morning. They were standing in line to do him in, and I had to save his life! May the Holy Mother forgive me."

Michel perked up a little. "What a comparison! Casanova is in his sixties, while I am still in the prime of my youth. I see no reason to insult me by comparing me to an old man."

"Gentlemen," Jean sternly interrupted, "you can discuss Michel's fidelity later."

"He looks awful," she whispered as Jean helped her mount Midnight Blue. "Can't something be done for him?"

"Paul could shoot him, I guess." Jean chuckled and mounted the horse to sit behind her. "It won't last long. I assure you he will recover."

"Or I'll gladly bury him," Paul snickered.

Jean glared at his cousin. "What is your report?"

"There is a large patrol of the King's soldiers riding fast and headed this way."

"Were you followed?" Jean asked quietly. They had lost the advantage of remaining ahead of the patrol, and he silently chided his cousin for delaying them. He motioned for them to take cover in the thick underbrush while the troop passed.

"No, my lord. They don't appear to be pursuing us or to know of our presence. We would have been here sooner if it wasn't for—"

Jean silenced him with a look that bordered on hostility. "I will expect a full report of your activities later."

Michel collected his strength and answered slowly. "We spent the night interrogating the maids, trying to find out who turned you in to the king's soldiers. Shortly after you left, your friend from the Bastille arrived."

Jean waved him into silence as the royal patrol came into view. Lisette shivered against his chest. The royal soldiers brought back the horror she had witnessed at the Bastille. She buried her face in the Baron's shoulder to block out the memory.

Jean lifted her head with a finger under her chin and stroked her cheek tenderly. "I will keep you safe," he whispered. "Trust me." He lightly kissed her pale cheek and hugged her closer to his warmth. The sky had clouded over again and the rain refused to be held back. Thank goodness Paul had thought to bring their traveling possessions, including a warm cloak for Lisette.

The last of the troop disappeared, and Paul leaned back in his saddle. "Whatever they want, it must be important to use a patrol of that size."

"With no scouts," Jean said thoughtfully.

"What does that mean?" She turned to Paul, curious at the significance of this.

Paul grinned at her. "A large escort troop without scouts means that someone already has what they want. They wouldn't call a patrol of that size out unless the person is an important one and they fear an ambush."

Jean chuckled at the exchange between Paul and Lisette. "Didn't that school teach you anything, Lisette?"

"A course in military tactics is not a necessary prerequisite for entry into the *haut monde,* my lord Baron. However, had I known it would be put to use as I fled for my life, I wouldn't have wasted my time learning to needlepoint."

Paul chortled with laughter. "I have never heard anyone put you in your place so nicely."

"That she did." Jean still had a lot to learn about

his beautiful captive, and his sense of foreboding
told him it would take a lifetime of study to figure
her out. What had changed her? The nervous
young girl had disappeared and a determined
woman now sat on his lap. It would take a wizard
to understand women, he thought wistfully.

The next three days were spent in a cat-and-
mouse game of pursuit. The Baron caught up with
the royal soldiers without their knowledge. Jean
and his men moved in a direct line for the port, with
the soldiers heading for the Rouen fortress, riding
parallel to them. He ordered his men to halt in a
position high above the fires of the royal troop
camped in the valley.

Jean recalled eight of his men to guard her. Lisette got the feeling the entire troop was always
within hailing distance, though she never saw
them. The Baron directed the eight men to guard
her life with their own, and Lisette was pleasantly
surprised when they accepted the duty eagerly.
She had thought they hated her family and would
shoot her at dawn before protecting her life.

She marveled at the Baron and Michel. They
were both titled lords. Yet both of them lived in
their saddles without a care for the discomfort of
having the hard ground to sleep on. They could
perform the simplest of duties, including preparing a hearty stew for the men to eat. Cooking had
never been Lisette's forte, and Michel teased her
that she might have to try it someday. It was a good
feeling to know that the men who rode beside her
cared for her as well as the Baron.

The most disturbing fact that she learned during her time spent with the Baron was that his private army consisted of men trained to kill at his
command. She winced when they gave her a dem-

onstration of how to best a guard and slit his throat without giving him a chance to cry out for help.

The Baron's hussars were patient with her when she balked at their teachings, and were jubilant with praise when their coaching sharpened her shooting skills. If she did something right, they clasped one another and boasted which one was actually responsible for the remarkable feat. And if she did something wrong, they sighed and started over, discussing which one of them had given her the incorrect instructions.

The Baron stood by as marshal over all. Even Michel would back down when Jean was ruffled. It took a powerful hand to stay his troops, when their purpose in life was to hunt the enemy, and kill without a second thought to the man's life. It was disturbing to Lisette because Jean had enough wealth, and a powerful army of mercenaries, to gain control of whatever he wanted. The thought that maybe he wanted the throne for himself had crossed her mind, though she dared not speak of it to anyone. Since Jean had declared his freedom from French rule, she was wary of mentioning her family.

Jean was watching the patrol's movements in the valley below. Lisette broke his concentration as she strolled over to him, having finished her supper. All it took was to have her beside him, as she was now, kneeling in front of him, her hands on his thighs, to pull his thoughts away from everything else. His fingers lazily traced her glowing face. Lisette's presence made Jean think of whether or not to marry her before leaving France, or, indeed, whether to marry her at all. If he married her and her heart still belonged to France, she would betray him, and Jean's father was sure to be killed. Yet if he didn't marry Lisette, her love would turn to hatred. He wished with all his might that he could trust her.

Jean had made certain they were well guarded, but he sensed that Darias would find a way to kill him if his defenses were lowered for a moment. Jean's trip to Paris had proven unfruitful; the Duc was at Versailles and had the other noble houses to guard him. If Jean made any public attempt to call the Duc out, the Duc de Meret would rely on the *parlement*'s intervention. Jean would not be able to defend himself in view of the *lettre de cachet* issued against his father. It was a vicious circle, with Lisette caught in the spinning center. If only he could decide on what course of action to take. His indecision was becoming a daily torment.

Jean's fingertips rested on Lisette's jawline. She was too young to understand the politics of old, desperate men when there was a throne at stake. "Is there something wrong, *chérie?*"

"Oh, no. Not at all, except . . ." She wasn't sure how to approach the subject with him while he still didn't trust her to go off on her own.

A smile tugged at the corner of his mouth. Most of his troop was out keeping a constant surveillance on the soldiers camped in the valley. "Except what? What is your desire, my delicious darling?"

"I would like to take a bath in the river." She spurted the words out, waiting for him to say no. "I promise I won't be any trouble to you or your men. It's just that I've gone three days, now, without washing properly."

"You aren't any trouble, Lisette." Jean chuckled at the gleam in her eyes. "Of course you can bathe in the river, but not alone. It wouldn't be safe to let your beautiful body out of my sight. I will have to accompany you."

As soon as he had given her permission, she dashed over the ridge to the river. The Baron stopped to give orders to his men guarding the horses. "Do not disturb," he commanded and knew they would die before invading his privacy. He reached into his saddlebag and brought out the finely scented soaps he had obtained while in the Orient, one for Lisette that smelled of jasmine, and one for him that had a spicy scent to it.

Lisette dropped the leather breeches and vest on a rock and rinsed her shirt in the swirling water. She eagerly plunged into the deep, cool water and dropped her head back to clean her hair. Floating on her back, she leisurely counted the stars in the sky. Relaxed and enjoying herself, Lisette didn't know she wasn't alone. The river had a demon, which latched itself onto her leg and pulled her under.

Jean's lips were pressed to hers as he stood in the chest-high water, drawing her with him. Lisette wrapped her arms around him and held tightly to his warm body. "I thought you were the river demon. Where did you come from?" She turned back to the bank and still couldn't figure out how he had joined her without her seeing him.

"I just dived in and look what I found. You forgot the soap." Jean's arms held her while she bathed. The river had a good current, and without his weight to hold her down, she would lose her footing. Jean found himself wishing he were the bar of soap sliding over her arms and chest.

When she finished, Lisette started soaping his arms and shoulders. "Hold still." She gulped as he dunked her. Lisette found out something new about her lover. Jean was ticklish. Her fingers were swift, lightly roaming the contour of his ribs until he shook with laughter. It pleased her greatly that she could make him smile outside of the obvious quenching of lust that they shared. He was in a playful mood and dunked her again. This time she came up spouting water at him. She rinsed his chest and arms, hesitating a moment as a thought came to her lips.

"When do you and your men have time to shave?"

His hearty laughter shook her. "Before you wake every morning there is a scene that you wouldn't believe. The men fight over the razor, fearing you will wake up before they have all finished. You have caused quite a change in those young rogues. They have been on their best behavior, for your sake, hoping to find themselves in your good graces. The eight men I chose to guard you were there the day we kidnapped you, and from what I understand, if I had chosen to toss you aside, they were ready to keep you. You see, they simply idolize you."

Lisette felt overwhelmed at their generosity toward her. "Would you have tossed me aside, my lord Baron?"

Jean pressed his lips to the pulse at the base of her neck. "How could I stay away from you?" he groaned, needing her more than he could ever put into words. "I want you with me, Lisette. Forever."

"As your concubine?"

"Would you love me any less if you remained beside me in everything but my name?"

Lisette swallowed back the disappointment that tugged at her heart. "I don't know."

"Let me convince you that you don't ever want to leave me." Jean didn't want to hurt her. God, how he hated himself for causing her a moment of pain. The feeling of love for her came easily, but marrying her could mean giving Lisette a power over him that could prove disastrous until they were safely out of France. But if he waited too long, Jean would lose her.

Chapter Eighteen

"Do you think your men adore me enough to help me escape you, Jean?" She smiled and tugged at a dark lock of his hair. He carried her out of the river and laid her down on the bed of soft moss and a blanket that he had thoughtfully remembered.

"I would flay them alive if they helped you escape, and they know it." He kissed her gently at first, but as his hunger for her grew, Jean roughly pulled her close. She was no longer afraid of his aggressive caresses that brought her sexual awareness to a pinnacle, and she relaxed in his strong arms.

Lisette was in a playful mood and giggled when he kissed her neck. "What if I screamed for help, monsieur? You are taking liberties on my person and perhaps . . ."

"Perhaps what?" Jean's grin widened.

"Perhaps I do not want you to take such liberties, and maybe someone would rescue me if I screamed."

"If you screamed you would have a valleyful of royal soldiers down on us before you know it. And besides, you're totally naked, Lady Lisette. Are you so brazen?"

"Who are you to speak of shamelessness?" She

rolled him over on his back, straddling his hips, and lightly bit his chin.

"Scamp! I am trying to avoid that patrol, but if you desire, go ahead and scream. I am sure they will appreciate rescuing you from my passions. But then . . ." Jean was enjoying this time with her more than she knew.

"But then, what?" She was kissing his ear when she abruptly sat up and looked down at his serious face.

He lazily stroked her back. "But then, if you persist in calling me monsieur, I might have to call them for you. I feel like an old man every time you call me monsieur, as if we should be sitting on a divan and balancing china teacups on our knees and exchanging polite conversation while a chaperon sits yawning from boredom. It's much too formal for an occasion such as this." To prove his point his lips covered her nipple and gently suckled. His pearly smile glimmered in the moonlight as he lay back and softly laughed. From his position under her, his hands were free to roam the silky skin of her stomach and cup the gentle mounds of her breasts.

"You are a scoundrel, Jean. And not a gentleman." She clucked her tongue at his arrogance.

"You offend me, mademoiselle. And yet you stoop to be seen with a man of my reputation."

She had resumed nibbling his ear and sat up, curious. "My lord, what kind of reputation do you have? A lady has to be careful with whom she is seen. Perhaps I shall have to call the royal patrol, after all."

"If you do, history will repeat itself, my dear. I will have to kidnap you all over again. My reputation is at stake if I don't."

Laughing, Jean tickled the soles of her feet. The rush of warm blood surging through her body tingled her senses. His touch could inflame her to madness; it was a wonderful frenzy that captured her in the fire of desire. The splendid length of his rigid body brushed against her, and his lips tormented her mouth with a slow, sensual kiss. He delicately explored her lips with the tip of his tongue and probed farther into her delectable mouth. His hands wound into her hair as he taunted the silken luxury within. She realized with acute astonishment that he was shaking against her, controlling passion that could sear them together.

Lisette could break that control. The thought that she had a power of her own to dispel that blasted control of his crept into her mind. But she wanted him to make love to her. This time she wouldn't allow him to walk away from her without the memory of what they could have been burned into his body for eternity.

A glitter of excitement lit the depth of Jean's eyes as Lisette slid her hands over his wet, slick chest, then pressed him down on his back to revel in his supple form. She straddled his hips and tucked her legs to support her weight, lowering herself onto his lap. She ignored the throaty groans coming from her beloved and took a deep, shivering breath, not wanting the loving to start too soon. Her fingers pressed against his lips, stilling his protest as she continued the agonizingly slow process of seducing him. A gentle breeze picked up the ends of her hair and dried the long strands, causing them to toss around her head. The moon was still low on the horizon and cast a silvery light over her crowning glory as her head fell back and revealed her milky slender throat.

The river sighed and gurgled beside them as waves slapped to the shore. It was the the only witness to her revenge. Lisette brushed the peaks of her breasts over his stomach and thighs, kissing and licking the dips and curves of his tautly drawn muscles, inching her way to his hip.

Her lips brushed his manhood. Jean cursed and grasped her shoulders, stopping her. "I will not waste what could conceive our child."

Why did he have to remind her of what the future held for her? It stung to the quick to think of them having a child out of wedlock. But Lisette obeyed him.

She took him fiercely into the velvet recess of her body and rode him as if to suffocate the pain that he had caused her. Jean saw the anger in her, lashing out at him in a frustrated cry of lost dreams and forgotten hopes. She wanted a physical pain to blot out the torment inside her heart. Later, she would be able to speak of her fury. Now, because she trusted him, he couldn't allow her to abuse herself. He clasped her hips, slowing the pace. "Easy, sweetheart," he cooed affectionately.

"Isn't this what you want?" There was a bitter edge to her voice that couldn't be mistaken. She roughly took his hands away and held on to them. "You have everything you want and gave me nothing in return. *This* I take from you as ruthlessly as you took my innocence from me."

"At what cost did I obtain it, Lisette?" He brought her clenched hand to his lips and brushed her knuckles with a gentle kiss. "Have I lost you so soon, my precious darling? What more devotion could a man give to you than to cherish you above life, home, and duty? You are the reason for my being. Without you, I am lost."

His proclamation diffused the anger boiling inside her. Lisette realized her emotions were tipping from depression to a wild yearning for the Baron. She didn't understand the bouncing of her feelings from one extreme to the other.

"I need you, Jean." She blinked back the heavy tears that filled her eyes. "I'm afraid that some day I'll wake up and you'll be gone."

His grip on her hands tightened. Jean's voice was shaken with anguish. *"I will never leave you. I swear it."*

Lisette shivered as the heartache drained away. Each thrust of his hips made her gasp against his passion. Her nails dug into his skin, leaving tiny trails of blood where her hands, clasped to his, braced against the unrelenting need for release.

"Stop!" Lisette screamed. She couldn't bear the sensation coiling her frame into a spring, constricting her muscles into spasms of ecstasy. "Stop it, please," she begged.

Tears stung Jean's eyes, and his nostrils flared as his chest heaved for a breath. He spilled his seed deep within her womb. Why had he found his piece of heaven on earth, just to bring harm to the person he loved the most? He gulped for another breath to control his emotions. Lisette collapsed against his chest, her head resting on his shoulder. He could feel her tears drop to his warm skin and wanted to kiss her agony away. Tenderly, he straightened her legs so that she was lying on top of him.

After several minutes had passed, Jean sighed deeply and kissed her soft mouth. "Oh, my sweet, what you do to me!"

Lisette stretched out on her back next to him. "I thought it was what you were doing to me." Lisette wiped the tears away with the back of her hand. She would never be able to forget him, her first and only love.

"Do you want my child, Lisette?" His tone was melancholy.

"That is a funny thing to ask when it has probably already been done. I have only seen childbirth once, and it scared me terribly." She shuddered at the memory. "I am not sure I will be as brave as she was and not scream as if I were being cut into little pieces."

"Who was she, *belle?*"

"She was a servant in my father's house." Lisette's tone drifted with the memory. "The maid worked all day scrubbing floors and then, with a small cry, announced her time had come. Right there in the hallway, she gave birth. My mother was ill at the time and there were few women in the house to help her except me. I was no help to her. It was quite a sight, since I had no concept of birth or the pain of it."

"Was it her screams that frightened you?" Jean quietly asked.

"No, she didn't scream, or cry out even once. But in her eyes was a dull look of agony. I held her hand, helpless to stop the woman's pain as the child was born. It was the helplessness that scared me." Lisette remembered the birth in vivid detail, and it left her wary of ever wanting to be in that situation.

"Fear doesn't help." He kissed her fingertips and held her tiny hand in his, marveling at the small size. "Don't be afraid, *petite*. The pain is soon forgotten and in its place is a new life."

"I am not sure of that. I never forgot her pain, and I expect that when my time comes, if ever, I will scream so loud the English will hear it across the Channel."

"You haven't answered me Lisette."

Lisette had no skill in lying. Her body stiffened. "What would you have me say, my lord? That I would gladly have your child although it would ruin me? I thought a man of your capabilities would have several children by now."

He chuckled at her diversion, noting she had not

given him an answer. "I shall take that as a compliment."

"I doubt very much that you lived the life of a celibate priest while you were roaming around the world. While I went to church and remained your faithful fiancée, I will wager you were out wenching and gambling with your friend and cousin."

"Lady Lisette!" Jean was shocked. "Where did you learn to talk like that? It's almost indecent to hear a proper woman even mention gambling, let alone wenching. What could you know about such things, anyway? The school you attended didn't teach you that."

"That it didn't," she agreed. "Your men did. I'm hardly what you would call a proper woman. While we're on the subject we might as well discuss my position as your whore, as well. That is the proper term *n'est-ce pas?*"

"No," he said definitely, angrily. "It is *not* so."

"Then what would you call it? What is the proper word for the conduct unbecoming to a young lady who is no longer able to give her husband sole right to her purity? I gave it to you because of foolish dreams, full knowing what would happen to me if I did. Women are branded with hot irons for being whores. I saw it happen once. The woman passed out from the iron touching her skin, and I vomited from the smell of burning flesh. You asked me if I wanted your child. I will ask the same question of you. Would you want something that would destroy you?"

"I would never allow anything to happen to you." She had every right to be angry with him. He had asked her to be his concubine and he would give her everything within his power to give but his name. It was the only way to keep them alive until they reached Spain. He couldn't forsake his father by telling her that he loved her more than his own life. "I hope that someday you will understand my reasons."

"Then I too hope you understand mine. I can't bear a child while unwed. It would destroy me."

Jean got an inkling of what she was talking about. "What are you saying, Lisette? Would you take the life of the child? Could you allow a butcher to rip the child from your womb before it was born?" He couldn't believe his lover could do it. It was too incredible to be true. Anyway, he would never give her the chance to do it. But Jean wanted her word, to know she was as bound by her sense of honor as he was not to harm the child.

Jean knew it was expecting a lot to even think that his son or daughter had already been conceived. It had taken years of disappointment before his mother was able to bear a son to the Earl. Maybe it would take as long to produce the next generation of Jolberts.

There was a way to handle stubborn women.

"Who is to say that a child already exists?" he said suavely. Lisette instantly responded to that. She heaved a sigh of relief and stretched out next to him, with an arm bent under her head as a pillow. Her innocence didn't include training on what to expect in a pregnancy. He knew of a few signs, outside of the obvious one of morning sickness. Her breasts would become fuller. He carefully inspected them now. Two ivory globes winked back at him. They didn't appear to have changed. They might be slightly swollen because of his earlier attention to them, but they were basically the same. He ran his hand down her belly. It was still flat, and pressing on her abdomen didn't produce any sure sign of a child.

Lisette giggled as he inspected the distance between her hips. It tickled to have his hands moving over her skin. "If you want to know," she inter-

rupted his probing, "I feel fine in the mornings."
Lisette felt better, knowing she had told him what
she would do if she found herself facing a pregnancy. It helped to ease the anger away. His fingers slid into the secret recess of her body and
instantly brought the need to have him alive again.
Her legs wrapped around his slim hips in a fer-
vored response.

"You provocative little scamp," he lightly murmured and nuzzled her earlobe. "You drive me
crazy, Lisette." She was sore, and he was gentle as
they moved further into the sensual abyss.

He brought her almost to the climax, then slowed
the pace. "Not yet, *chérie,*" he whispered, delaying
the moment she begged for, knowing she would
shred his back to ribbons when he withheld it.
"Answer me now, Lisette. Will you have my
child?" He withdrew from the warm, wet haven of
her body when she hesitated.

"Yes!" she cried. "Don't stop now."

"Your word, Lisette. I want your word you will
not harm our child. You *will* bring it life." He tan-
talized her further by sliding deeper within her,
then slowly pulling back. It was all the convincing
she needed.

"You have my word, I will not harm our child."
She wanted to kill him for making her wait another moment. She clung to him as the shuddering
sensation enveloped her body. Her back arched in
a final, joyous physical triumph.

They both relaxed, spent and exhausted from the
effort. Once she could think straight again, her
fury rose. She dressed quickly, presenting a cold
shoulder.

Jean reluctantly got to his feet and, not wanting
to face her, stood behind her and wrapped his arms
around her.

"Let go of me," she hissed. "You arrogant rogue! That was a dirty trick."

"But it worked, didn't it?" He grinned at her. "You did give me your word, and you are now bound by honor."

"That I wouldn't hurt our child, yes. But I didn't say anything about you!" She pushed him backward as hard as she could, and with a splash he was back in the river. While he floundered she sat down and pulled her boots on. How had he won so easily? It was unnerving to know he could get any promise he desired out of her while engaged in the throes of love. Now she was bound by honor to bear his bastard child.

She slipped the damp shirt over her head and pulled the vest over her shoulders. Jean struggled to the riverbank; he was soaking wet and looking like a drowned rat. "You know something, Jean?" she said, smiling sweetly at him. "You don't look scary at all, soaking wet and naked."

"I deserved that, my sweet. Remind me the next time I get you angry with me to watch where I am standing." He pulled his breeches on and walked barefoot. Jean picked a wild daisy and dropped it into the deep cleavage between her breasts. "We have to find you some new clothes, my lady. You are driving my men into the local brothels at an alarming rate."

"That's all I need," Lisette fumed. "One hundred and three sex-crazed men."

Chapter Nineteen

Lisette followed the Baron back to his makeshift campsite. The troop had returned, and moonlight clearly outlined their cloaked, shadowed forms on the hillside. There was a great deal of jesting exchanged between the men as they huddled into a circle. As Jean and Lisette approached, the troop parted.

The resounding gasp of every man there should have warned Lisette to turn away. She noticed that the mouths of the men were agape at their discovery.

Michel was at the center of the ruckus, with a prisoner lying at his feet. He lit a torch and held the illuminating light beside the prisoner's head.

At Michel's feet was a young woman! The Marquis had put a gag in her mouth to keep her quiet, and bound her hands behind her back. Her bare feet were tethered together by a leather strap. She let out a vicious growl as Michel attempted to remove the gag, and kicked at the Marquis. He backed up a pace and gingerly reapproached the prisoner.

"I won't hurt you." Michel attempted to assure the angry woman that he meant no harm to her.

Straight black hair hung to the prisoner's waist. Her skirt was made of brilliant red silk with a

shimmering hemline of gold doubloons that were
pierced and sewn onto the fabric. Long silver beads
hung from her earlobes, grazing her shoulders. The
plunging neckline of a white peasant blouse lay
open in a deep V, with the strings used for tying at
the neckline undone and brushing the nipples of
her breasts. With the short gathered sleeves pulled
off the shoulders, the bodice of her dress would fall
to her waist if the prisoner took a deep breath, Lisette thought. The young woman struggled to sit
up, and bare feet and thighs glowed in the torchlight. There were three long strands of pearls
draped around her neck and clasped at the side of
her throat by a diamond brooch. Her blue-gray
eyes, outlined in kohl, glittered back at them as
they viewed her. Every time the Marquis got close
enough to touch her, the woman hissed her displeasure and Michel withdrew his hands.

Jean smiled at the woman. The prisoner finally
noticed the Baron's presence, and her struggles
came to an abrupt halt.

"Alexia!" Jean instantly recognized the prisoner. He knelt beside the young woman and released the gag. He cut the bonds at her hands and
feet.

A breath of time later, Alexia stood before the
Marquis and turned her tongue on him with a
vengeance. "How dare you touch the royal concubine to the King of Spain! You'll be roasted over a
slow fire for having the audacity to lay hands on
me. I should slit your throat for this indignity." She
rubbed her wrists where he had tethered her. Her
wrath on the Marquis spent, she dismissed the
stunned man with a wave of her hand.

Alexia launched herself into the Baron's arms.
"You look wonderful, you antiquated hunk of
manhood."

"I'm not that old, Alexia." Jean hugged her so

exuberantly it took Alexia a moment to regain her
footing.

Lisette sensed this woman was more to her Baron than a casual acquaintance. Jealousy coursed
through her as she watched her rival plant perfect
carmine lips on his mouth. It was disgusting to
watch him reciprocate. The men circling Jean and
Alexia drooled in a blatant display of lust.

"Older but better, *mignon,*" Alexia purred.
"What luck to be captured by the most handsome
man in France."

"I didn't think you would get my message so
soon, Countess." Jean warmly smiled at her.

"What message? I got lonely after you left me at
the *hacienda.* You did promise to return shortly."

"I was delayed," he explained. Jean glanced at
Lisette, and if looks could kill, he would have been
dead in his tracks. "May I speak to you privately,
Countess?"

Alexia put a hand on her hip and saucily walked
away, the Baron close behind her.

Lisette was furious at being ignored by the Baron. He hadn't even introduced them, just whisked
the wench away for a private audience with her.
Lisette felt an overwhelming hostility toward the
wanton Countess who flaunted herself before the
Baron's men. Was he now contemplating keeping
two mistresses? Lisette's vehemence was riddled
by doubts about his motives. Would he take her to
Spain and keep two women at his beck and call?

"Where did you find her?" Lisette directed the
question to Michel. He hadn't stopped grinning
since he had returned.

"She was following the royal patrol," Michel
said faintly, his mind evidently on his prisoner.

"The Countess would make a nice addition to
your vast collection of women," one of the younger
men spoke up in jest.

"Alexia makes a collection all by herself." There was a wistful tone to Michel's voice. The men drifted away to water their horses. While they walked, Lisette heard them discuss the possibility of the Countess becoming enamored of Michel.

When Jean and Alexia returned, Alexia was given food and water, then directed to rest beside Lisette.

The Countess eyed Lisette with disdain. "You have forgotten your manners, Jean. Who is your beautiful page?"

"Lady Lisette de Meret." Jean made the introduction so casually it was as if he regretted the meeting between the two women. He left them alone while he issued new commands to his men.

The Countess made herself comfortable on the blanket, sitting a safe distance from Lisette. Jean's voice rose over the grumbling of his troop.

"You're getting grouchy in your old age," Alexia called out to the Baron. She cocked her head to get a good look at Lisette. "So, you are the Duchess? Since Jean won't introduce me, I will. I'm—"

"Alexia," Lisette broke in. She was trying to handle the situation with dignity. "Why were you following the royal patrol, Countess?"

"Ah, a woman who dispenses with silly formalities and gets down to business." The Countess crunched into an apple, and as she slowly chewed, her ruby mouth curled into a smile. "In answer to your question, I was looking for someone."

"It appears you found who you were looking for," Lisette countered easily.

Alexia tossed her head back and laughed, in a deep, rich sound that came from her throat. "Who? Jean-Charles? That was just a stroke of luck. The man I am looking for is Viscount Moursives."

"I don't know who he is," Lisette stated.

"He was last seen going into the Rouen for-

tress," Alexia said sadly. "I have to get him out of
France before they take him to the Conciergerie
prison for execution."

Lisette was surprised. "What crime did he commit?"

"He didn't commit any crime other than believing in freedom. You really don't know much about
politics, do you? Jean warned me. Why didn't I listen?" The exquisite gray-eyed Countess shook her
head. "In the last six months many good families
have been unjustly accused of treason and sen-
tenced to death. I have smuggled twenty-six people
out of France. I take them to Spain, where King
Charles grants them amnesty. You must have been
in a convent not to know what is going on around
you."

"It was nearly that," Lisette agreed. "I was in a
finishing school and only allowed minimal contact
with the outside world." Lisette set her thoughts
of jealousy aside for the moment. "Why would King
Charles of Spain grant them amnesty when he has
a peace treaty with King Louis?"

"King Charles doesn't know they're in Spain.
Every person is given a new identity. That way, the
King can honestly say he honors the treaty with
France."

"And Louis can't charge the King of Spain with
unlawfully harboring political prisoners." Lisette
frowned. This Countess was not only beautiful but
courageous. "Why are you helping the French nobles, Countess?"

"Some of my favorite people are French." Alexia
laughed again and tossed her black hair over her
shoulder to cascade down her back. "Someone has
to, and I'm definitely kept occupied. Charles is
thrilled that I finally have something to do, and I'm
not driving him mad anymore. I think he is hoping
France will keep me detained for a while."

Lisette had to wonder at the personal reference to the King of Spain as Charles. Jean returned and offered his hand to help her up, but she ignored him.

"Are you ladies ready?" The Baron felt Lisette's cold glare focus on him. He would have some explaining to do after they set sail. It wasn't easy being surrounded by beautiful women, although he was sure his men didn't see the problems of keeping two spirited women at bay. From what he could tell, it wouldn't be long before they would be in the throes of a fight. Jean would have to send Alexia on her way to Paris before Lisette got a chance to question the Countess.

"Where are we going?" Seated in front of the Baron on Midnight Blue, she was comfortably settled between his strong arms.

"To the Rouen fortress," Jean whispered in her ear. Her cold-shoulder attitude annoyed him. He wanted to wring her neck for it. Hadn't they just shared a special evening together? He often wondered what she thought after the loving was over. Did she still hate him? Or was it true that she loved him?

The torment she caused him was beginning to rage out of control. When they were alone, she gave herself freely. Surrounded by his family and friends, she became distant. Jean needed to know her affections were honest. It bothered him that she considered herself his concubine.

Jean had wanted to meet with Alexia, but not in front of Lisette. The Countess had been warned to remain in Spain. Now he had two feisty women to protect, and it wouldn't be easy, knowing they were both willful.

Lisette ignored him as punishment for his rude behavior. She hadn't given him more than a few clipped words since they had departed. Now that she understood her rôle in his life, she would escape him. This time, she couldn't let him know what she was thinking. Lisette could remain aloof until the opportunity presented itself. He trusted her now and gave her the freedom of being unguarded.

Jean bent his head to nibble at her neck. She turned slowly, looking at him askance in the moonlight.

"What are you doing, Lisette?" She had a strange look on her face, as if she were trying to decide something important.

"I was just looking for wrinkles."

"Did you find any?" Jean cuddled her closer to him.

"Yes, I did. But they give you character."

He pinched her derrière in retaliation. "Scamp."

The Marquis didn't seem to mind that Alexia had been given into his care. The petite woman sat on his lap and he couldn't stop grinning.

"How old are you?" Alexia asked of her benefactor.

Alexia taunted Michel with every bite she took of that wretched apple until the core was finally tossed aside. Her small frame felt delicate against him as they rode the path etched into the rocky hillside. If he had known this was the woman Jean had invited him to Spain to meet, he would have accepted the invitation without delay.

"I'm twenty-eight," he finally answered.

Lisette looked up at Jean. "Just how old are you?"

"I'm antiquated."

"I would have guessed at least thirty-five." Lisette soon paid for her repartee as he pinched her backside much harder this time. She knew he was thirty-two, and enjoyed the jest.

The horses had to pick their way around the

rocky slopes to the fortress. A wash of moonlight highlighted the path they chose until heavy clouds gathered and blocked their only source of light. The mood of the men changed as they scouted the area between the royal patrol and the fortress; they were serious soldiers again. Jean picked an area that would give them the best advantage, and the men set to work on the ambush. Ropes were strung across the road to unseat approaching soldiers. Their pistols were put back into their saddlebags. The crack of the ignited powder would draw the attention of the royal patrol camped a couple of miles from the site of the ambush.

Jean took Alexia aside. "Don't tell Lisette anything about our underground involvements," he warned.

"Why can't she know?" Alexia had an uneasy feeling she had already said too much.

"Lisette is a royalist and still supports the cause of the monarchy. If she knew we were involved in helping condemned nobles to flee France, she might try to inform her uncle."

Alexia didn't say a word. She had already told Lisette enough to have them all convicted of treason. Alexia made her decision based on loyalty to the Baron. She would have to get rid of Lisette to ensure their safety.

A brilliant streak of lightning flashed in the blackened clouds, followed by a grumble of thunder. The air was heavy with moisture and an underlying excitement as the final preparations were made. Lisette was positioned high on the hill overlooking the road, with an excellent view of the impending battle. She caught a glimpse of the Baron's arrogant swagger from her perch on the hill. Her stomach felt as if butterflies were dancing. The anticipation seeped through her bravado, and she clenched her bottom lip anxiously between her teeth. Lisette rubbed at her temples, trying to avoid a headache as her nerves melted into jelly. She worried that something would go wrong and Jean would get hurt.

Jean took a last-minute look around to check the men's positions, then climbed the dirt hill to Lisette. He placed a pistol in her hand and issued his final instructions to her.

"Stay here, out of sight, Lisette. Try not to use your pistol, but don't hesitate if you find yourself in a life-threatening situation. Be ready for a hasty retreat. We only want to free the Viscount and gain access to the fortress, not get into a major battle."

Lisette put the weapon down on a tree stump. It was her only defense against the Rouen guard if they had to withdraw. "Are you leaving me unguarded?"

Jean cleared his throat with a nervous cough. "It would be safer to send you to Simon, but I can't spare the men to guard you. Alexia will stay with you."

"I don't need *her* to watch over me." Lisette resented his apparent trust in the Countess. "After what we went through in Paris you can be assured I am capable of defending myself."

"I know you are." Jean chuckled softly. He reached out and closed his arms around her. Her heartbeat raced against his lips as he kissed the gentle curve of her neck. The jasmine essence drifted to his nostrils and he inhaled deeply, cherishing the scent of her. "You smell good," he whispered.

"You're awfully calm," she chided.

Michel ran up the hill to where they were standing. Jean reluctantly released Lisette. "What is your report, Michel?"

"There are thirty men escorting the prisoners out of the fortress. Paul is ready to hold the patrol back should they be warned of the ambush. The Viscount is among the Rouen guard; so is the Earl of Normandy."

Jean's body became rigid as steel. A flicker of disbelief wrinkled his dark brows. They had found his father, and all his heartache would soon be forgotten.

His grin held her in its magic. Lisette saw his look of joy and felt his happiness with him.

Jean swept her into his arms and twirled her around. "My sweet Lisette. We will board the ship at sunset, and be in Spain before the winter sets in."

Lisette's feet touched the ground again as he quickly pulled away. They heard the approaching horses before the shadows of the Rouen guard appeared on the distant hillside.

"Take your position, Michel," Jean ordered, and the Marquis disappeared into the underbrush.

"Can I trust you to stay here and out of trouble, Lisette?"

"I promise to stay out of trouble." She kissed him fiercely, sealing the bond between them. Lisette didn't want to admit that she had had a premonition that he would be captured and she'd never see him again.

Her lips tingled from the warm contact when she pulled away. She didn't want to admit that she was worried about him. He was concerned about the ambush and his father. He didn't sense that she wouldn't be there when he returned.

"We'll be leaving for Spain by dawn, my darling. I believe once you see the home we'll be sharing you won't ever want to escape me."

Lisette touched her fingers to her lips and blew him a kiss as he worked his way down the hill. As she watched him leave, her heart felt as if it were sinking to her toes and an utter sense of depression

set her feelings in a spin. They would board his ship
by dawn, and then there would be no way of getting out of his clutches.

"This is your opportunity," a soft voice prodded.

Lisette turned to find Alexia standing behind
her. The Countess fingered an ornate dagger and
sauntered behind the ridge of underbrush that
lined the hillside. "What are you talking about,
Countess?" Foolishly, Lisette followed Alexia behind the cover of wild raspberry bushes.

"I heard about your attempt to escape. This is a
perfect opportunity. Jean is detained, and I
wouldn't stop you. As a matter of fact, I'll be happy
to help you."

"Why?" Lisette didn't trust the Spanish consort.

"Let's say that I think a highborn consort is un-
suitable for him. He needs someone who knows
what his life has been like and will offer him something other than treachery for a bed partner."

"You would gladly provide that for him,
wouldn't you, Alexia?" The Countess scoffed and
turned her nose into the air. They were alone at the
top of the hill. Jean's men were all in the vale,
ready to ambush the troop. The fortress guard appeared. While still a mile away, they were clearly
visible with torches flaming their way.

With a loud clash of thunder, the rain started
and the distant torches were doused. Alexia slowly
circled Lisette, like a panther making ready for the
kill. "You're not good enough for him, Lady Lisette. Why don't you leave?"

"Because I don't like being told what to do, especially by a gutter-born Spanish ..." Lisette
couldn't say it.

"Ah, *caramba*, but you do have some fight left in
you. Jean said he had tamed his French consort."

Lisette was dangerously close to losing her temper and becoming physically violent. She knew

what she meant to Jean and didn't have to tolerate
Alexia's sarcasm. Her fury was just below the sur-
face; it wouldn't take much more prodding to get
Lisette to do something rash.

The rain had turned the wooded hillside into a
mudslide. Lisette was soaked to the skin by the cold
night rain, and miserable. Alexia padded barefoot
in the slippery earth next to her. There was little
Lisette could do to persuade the Countess to leave
her alone.

"Alexia," she said at last. "Why don't you turn
around and I'll leave. You can have him all to yourself, and then *you* can take care of his needs."

"So!" Alexia seethed. "It is true that you would
escape even after bedding the Baron! I didn't believe Paul when he told me your relationship with
Jean was intimate. Now I do." What Alexia left out
was that Paul had warned her not to interfere in
an "intimately dangerous situation!"

That did it. Lisette couldn't contain her anger
any longer. Was her relationship with Jean casually discussed between the men of the troop? It
was an insult that sent her temper into a boiling
state of rage. Lisette slapped the Countess across
the face, sending the woman reeling backward.

When she recovered, Alexia pounced. She hit Lisette's jaw with an open hand, knocking her down
on her backside. Together they rolled downhill in
the slippery mud, with feet kicking and teeth biting. Alexia got a wicked blow in, smacking Lisette
on the cheek with her closed fist.

Lisette rubbed her cheek and struggled harder
to stop the Countess from inflicting any more pain.
There wasn't an area of Lisette's body that wasn't
dripping with water, wet earth, and matted leaves.
They rolled again, this time stopping on a ledge
that would take them directly into the vale below.
Lisette had the upper hand, since she was six

inches taller than Alexia, but she had made the mistake of letting the Countess pin her to the ledge. Alexia was spitting mad, and what she lacked in height she made up for in experience. A handful of Lisette's hair was lost to the Countess's grip. Lisette screamed in anger and pushed Alexia off her, over the summit of the ledge into the vale.

Jean's troop had ambushed the guard, and they were sure of a victory, until he heard Lisette's scream. The distraction was all his opponent needed to turn the tide against the Baron. The Rouen guard pinned Jean to a tree with the tip of his rapier pointed at Jean's heart. The Baron was disarmed and forced at gunpoint onto a horse. The Rouen guard was lucky enough to have the Baron separated from his troop.

From her vantage point Lisette watched Alexia slide down the muddy hill, then saw the guard leap on her. She pitied the poor man. Alexia was in no mood to be taken prisoner a second time that day. The Countess was a hellfire of sputtering anger. She maimed the guard, his knife sticking in his arm before he finally subdued her.

Lisette was terrified. Stumbling through the underbrush, she was uncertain of which way to run. Her hair dripped beads of water from the heavy rain. She brushed the curtain of auburn locks aside and blinked against the onslaught of water rushing into her eyes. She clawed her way up the hill, her boots sinking in the mud at each step of the way. She reached the top and crouched down.

The Baron was surrounded by Rouen guards. She swore under her breath. This wasn't the way she was supposed to have escaped. Now she couldn't possibly leave. A hand reached out from the underbrush and clamped over her wrist. Lisette was pulled into the dense thicket. The hand belonged to Michel, she soon realized. He pressed a finger to her lips, urging her to be quiet. She did as he bade her, and lay beneath the biting thorns of the bush.

The Rouen guard's order rang through the night air. "Tell your men to cease and desist, Baron Jolbert, or I shall kill you."

Jean ground his teeth together. His troop had been alert to the danger of capture and had scattered at the first sign of defeat. He had ordered his men to leave the area if any harm came to Lisette or the Earl. The hussars would make sure she was out of harm's way before abandoning the area. Where had they taken his father? Somewhere before reaching the ambush, the Rouen guards had split up and had taken their prisoners on a different route. Why hadn't they known it was a trap? What had happened to Lisette? His hands were bound and he was put on a horse.

The Baron's worst fears were realized when Alexia was pushed into the midst of the Rouen guard. Her captors helped her mount a horse and held the steed's reins while the men were reassembled. From the torn clothes, he understood she had put up quite a fight. Where was Lisette? Had she been safely escorted from the area by one of his men?

There were no other prisoners taken. The Baron's men had scattered as soon as their leader fell captive.

The *capitaine* of the Rouen guard looked up at Alexia. "Your cousin is waiting for you at the fortress, Duchess de Meret. We are here to rescue you, not to hurt you."

Jean breathed a sigh of relief. While they thought Alexia was the Duchess de Meret, she was safe. They would discover her real identity when they reached the fortress. It wouldn't give them much time to devise a means of escape. Hopefully, they would be too busy torturing him to bother with Alexia.

Alexia quickly picked up on Jean's nod of agreement. She would pretend to be the Duchess until they reached the fortress. Alexia focused her attention on the captain of the guard. Her long black eyelashes fluttered coquettishly. "I had no way of knowing you were here to rescue me, Captain."

The Countess was smart enough to know it was too dangerous to try for escape now before Paul and Michel could help.

Lisette was uncomfortable, cramped under a prickly bush. Michel wouldn't let her move a muscle as the guards searched the area. She watched the guard form a human barrier around her Baron and Alexia. While Jean had his hands bound and a guard had taken his reins, Alexia was free to control her horse. That puzzled Lisette. She could clearly see them as the torches were relit. Torches relit? If the torches had been doused by the rain, they would be too wet to relight? But not if they had been purposely doused. Why wasn't the Earl of Normandy in the midst of the prisoners? It had been a trap, she realized too late. The guard had effectively lured Jean out into the open. While they probably thought they had the Duchess with them, they would soon find out their mistake. By then, they could both be dead.

Lisette couldn't let them kill Jean. She had to get into that fortress and get him out before the guard sent him to prison in Paris.

"Sacré Dieu," she whispered, thinking about what it would take to get into the fortress. Lisette needed a miracle.

Michel was uncomfortable in a different way. Lisette was snuggled against him, creating a swelling in his breeches. He was sure his amorous feelings for the Duchess would shorten his life by decades if Jean found out. To resist the lovely body next to his took a paragon of virtue.

Michel had never claimed to have any scruples. Grasping the moment, he brushed a kiss on Lisette's lips.

Lisette smiled into the night. The kiss had been nice.

Chapter Twenty

Michel forced Lisette to wait until the Baron's troop returned before allowing her to leave the sanctuary of the underbrush. Paul's voice could be clearly heard over the falling rain. Why did it have to pour? Lisette pulled the clinging hair from her face and wrung the tangled and muddied strands of excess moisture. Alexia had torn her shirt, she realized. There were two buttons missing, showing an indecent amount of cleavage. Mud was caked on her arms and legs. Lisette felt filthy.

She slid down the hill, coming to a stop beside Paul. "We have to rescue him before . . ." Lisette couldn't think of what would happen to him if the Rouen guard managed to keep him captive for an extended period of time.

Paul was astounded. He looked down at the Duchess's pleading gaze and and shook his head in wonder at it. She had wanted to kill Jean, hadn't she? He didn't have time to think about the fickle emotions of young women. "Do you have any idea how difficult it is to get into the Rouen fortress, mademoiselle?" Jean and Paul had discussed every possible avenue of attack. With the exception of walking through the drawbridge, it was impregnable.

"Well, *oui,* I do have an idea on how to get into

the fortress. We could take a wagonload of supplies through the gate," Lisette rambled on. She didn't want to waste a moment. They had to get him out of there before the Baron got a chance to taste the cat-o'-nine-tails. She didn't want him tortured.

"It might work." Paul stroked the beginnings of a new beard. The scratchy stubble on his chin was still in a pathetic state. Marie, his *amie* in Rouen, had complained about it two days prior to this sorry attempt at an ambush.

Marie had finally given him the garments he requested. Although they were for Lady Lisette, Marie had put up a screaming fight over clothing another woman, thinking it was Paul's paramour. It took hours of reconciliation, and a promise the clothes were for the Baron's woman, not his. Marie had fangs of jealousy that surprised him. Paul had always been a roamer. But he was getting older, and the little wench made him pay in a way that he would remember for all the days of his life. It was dawn before he was finally able to ride away, totally exhausted from the intimate demands she had placed on him. The thoughts of Marie had been ever present in his mind, and threatened to distract him again.

Paul had warned Jean that there would be an ambush. Damn, he thought, if only he had known the ambush would come from the opposite direction. The Rouen patrol hadn't stopped to claim their dead. The bodies of more than a dozen militiamen lay in the mud.

Michel noticed a fatally wounded guard who clawed at the grumbling earth, soaked with rain. If they weren't in the presence of a lady, he would have slit the man's throat, merely for the anger he suppressed. Jean had been captured, and they were forced to ride against the fortress. Michel unsheathed his rapier, placing the tip of the deadly

weapon on the back of the guard's neck, directly in
line with his spine. It would be a painless death,
and a mercy compared to what his fellow citizens
were going to be inflicting on the Baron.

"Hold your sword, Michel," Paul ordered. The
young man held an uncanny resemblance to the
Marquis. If one did not look directly into his face,
he could pass for Michel. Paul considered Lisette's
proposal that they walk through the gate. It might
slip the gatekeeper's notice, to pose Michel as
wounded and now returning to the fortress. The
problem would be getting as many of the men out
of the fortress as they could. A diversion was
needed. Several minutes had already ticked by,
and time was a dangerous element when one faced
torture.

Lisette had given him a moment to think over
her plan. There wasn't any time left. "Well?" she
pressed the captain. "Will it work?"

Paul nodded in agreement. "I can't think of another way to do it, Lady Lisette. When Alexia was
captured, they thought they had you. It won't take
them long to figure out their mistake when your
cousin Darias realizes he doesn't have you back in
his hands. I think it would work. If we sent you
with our troop to the hills . . . ?" he continued
thinking out loud. "The Rouen guard would follow
you, thinking they could yet get you back."

Lisette quickly chastised the burly captain. "I'm
going into that fortress with you."

"No, you won't," Michel broke in.

"Oh, yes, I will," Lisette corrected the Marquis.
"Do you know the layout of the inner chambers?
No, I didn't think so," she automatically answered
as the Marquis shook his head. "I have been inside
the fortress before. I know where they will be taking him."

Paul had been inside that fortress so many times

he couldn't count them. Now that it was under de Meret control, the Jolberts had pulled out completely, save for a few agents inside the old castle just for emergencies. It had been their men inside the fortress who confirmed to Jean that his father had arrived at the castle and would soon be transferred to the Conciergerie prison in Paris.

Yet he liked seeing Lisette's fierce loyalty to Jean in the lady's determination to accompany them. If he let the troop go on by itself, Darias might believe she was still among the Baron's private army. It was a snap decision, one he was sure Jean would soon be threatening to have him shackled to a wall for, but a necessary one. The Baron's troop would lure the Rouen patrol into the hills of Normandy, then turn and do battle, thus detaining the bulk of the soldiers. That would give them time to escape, and Paul would be able to protect Lady Lisette.

Michel turned the guard over with the toe of his boot; he lay spread-eagled on the ground, with a severe wound in his chest. Jean must have inflicted the mortal injury. It was perfectly executed with one quick thrust. Michel so admired Jean's ability with a rapier.

"Don't kill me." A plea, gurgled with blood, rose in his mouth.

"What of his uniform?" Paul asked.

"It is still serviceable," Michel answered. The Marquis looked up to Paul and nodded. They understood the necessity to end the guard's suffering, even if the lady didn't.

The captain ordered a horse brought forward. Midnight Blue, the Baron's black Arabian stallion, would allow no other rider than a Jolbert.

Lisette was given a suitable mount, and then, under Paul's direction, turned away from the site of the battle. Ten men were selected to remain as a personal escort if the rescue was successful, while the rest of the troop was directed to ride to the hills of Normandy.

As the troop passed before Lisette she noticed the intense looks on their faces. They seemed to know without being told what was expected of them. The men of the troop tipped their tricorn hats to her as they passed, and she nodded her thanks until the last of them disappeared into the wooded vale. Mounted beside Paul, she waited for the Marquis to join them.

Minutes later, Michel was buttoning his new coat, strolling up to them as if it were a casual change of clothing. The helmet was too big and kept sliding down on his forehead.

"What took you so long?" Paul grumbled.

"I had to give him his last rites!" Michel was a fanatic for giving a man his last opportunity to cleanse his soul before meeting his maker. The guard had a lengthy confession, and died before his many sins were listed. Michel's only hope was that when his time came, someone gave him the same respect.

"Now all we need is a supply wagon." Lisette directed her gaze to Paul. "Do you have any friends in Rouen?"

"That I do." Paul heartily laughed. "Although once she gets a look at you, she may pull a pistol out on me."

Jean awakened from the fog of unconsciousness with a start. Cold water splashed over his face, dripping into his mouth, giving him the fluids his body needed. He couldn't open his eyes; they had been pasted shut with his own blood. The guards had been accurate with their blows. The fracture of his skull left him with one hell of a headache and several loose teeth. He was tethered between two whipping posts, his feet dangling inches off the ground. His arms were numb. He had been dreaming while he was unconscious. The luscious form of Lady Lisette was in his thoughts. Was she all right? Alexia had been instantly recognized for a fraud. They had taken her away and locked her in the tower, where Darias could further interrogate her. That would be later, Jean thought, after they were finished with him.

The guard before him tapped a coiled whip in his outstretched hand. He was running out of patience with the stubborn Baron. "You are a guest at Rouen fortress, monsieur. Abducting a member of the royal family is a serious charge. Where have you sent her?"

Jean's jaw hurt when he tried to move it. That had been the first blow inflicted. Darias had used the butt of a thirty-pound broadsword to do the damage. He spat out blood from his bleeding tongue, cursing the guard. The Baron had been stripped to the waist and then tied to the posts. Before succumbing to their torture, he had killed three more guards, buying a few more precious moments of time.

Darias pulled Jean's head up by his dark hair. "I don't like to ask a question twice, my lord. Where is the Lady Lisette?"

Jean prayed for either rescue or a speedy death. He didn't like the man who stood before him. Gathering his failing strength, Jean spat in Darias's face. It was a last attempt to cling to his stubborn pride. What was left of his self-esteem was soon lost under the biting sting of the whip. Welts swelled and bled from the savage leather. The pain was unbearable. His knuckles were white holding to the cords that held him aloft, stretching the skin of his back like a taut canvas, and the guard was the artist who left streaks of a red sunset against his bronzed flesh.

Jean was still conscious when the whip ceased. He fought the buzzing sound in his ears to hear what was delaying the wicked cat-o'-nine-tails. The guards were arguing with Darias. The Baron's troops had been seen fleeing for the hills of Normandy. They could catch up to the troops and bring the Duchess back.

Darias strolled up to Jean. Although he hadn't done the despicable act of whipping the Baron himself, Darias assured himself he would return to finish the duty. "You can rest for now, my lord Jolbert. When I return, we'll see how long your obstinate nature will withstand the hot irons."

Jean couldn't see Darias walk away. He needed rest, and let his body sag.

Lisette clenched her teeth and endured every jarring bump of the wagon. She was dressed like a peasant in an old, torn black shirt and a shawl over her brilliant puce-colored hair. Marie had suggested that Lisette should leave the dirt and twigs in her hair, to keep up the façade that she was a peasant. A peasant wouldn't have time to take a bath, and wouldn't consider it before the week ended. Paul was terribly gallant to the young woman who had sacrificed the rags to Lisette. He had charmed the clothes right off Marie's back in exchange for the promise to return and properly thank her someday. After all, Lisette thought, he was a Jolbert, and Jean certainly hadn't had much difficulty in getting her to abandon all sense of morality.

The Rouen guard had sent word to the royal patrol and joined forces. Together, they followed the path made by Jean's troop directly into the forested hills of Normandy. The hussars led them on

a merry chase while Lisette was still safely in the
care of Paul Jolbert. It left the fortress with a skel-
eton force, just enough men to maintain the huge
estate, and they would be too busy to notice another cart approaching the gates.

Paul didn't like the turn of events. Michel had
his disguise of a Rouen guard, and Lisette looked
like a plump and pregnant baker's wife. But he had
to remain hidden under the tarp covering the supplies. He didn't like it one bit. Paul should be protecting Lisette at all costs; her life was worth twice
his or Michel's. From his position behind the cart
seat, he could see Lisette's ankles but very little of
what lay ahead. No, he didn't like it one bit, he reminded himself again. It was too risky, come to
think of it. What if Lisette was recognized? There
were too many possibilities to consider, and it made
him grumpy. Things weren't going as well as they
should have.

Lisette reined in the old nag that pulled the cart
and hailed the gatekeeper to lower the drawbridge. Without further identification required,
the bridge was lowered. The man inside the gate
performing the menial task hadn't even asked her
name. Lisette had asked the name of the local
baker, just in case she needed it. Getting inside the
fortress seemed easy enough. The rain had become
a steady drizzle, and the cart jogged against the
muddy trail. She knew where the kitchens were located. Michel jumped from the seat and disappeared into the side entrance to one of the halls of
the square structure. Set above the rise of the valley, the Rouen fortress was an ominous reminder
of the oppression of the local peasants. The cart
bounced once as Paul made his exit, and he, too,
vanished from sight into the fortress walls. If all
went well, they would return in the time it would
take her to unload the supplies.

Her back had never felt worse, and her hands were blistered and tender when she finished her task. Lisette had given Paul and Michel all the time she dared. It had taken her an hour to deliver the supplies into the storehouse. The fortress cook had called on the help of a stableboy when Lisette appeared to be taking her sweet time at it.

By the end of the hour, Lisette was getting worried. There was no sign of Paul or Michel. To wait any longer would be dangerous. She had to try to find Jean or Alexia. Paul and Michel would get to Jean first, believing he would be in the worst danger. That left Alexia to Lisette. Where had they taken her? Did they already know of her identity? Lisette rubbed her sore back. The cook came out and paid her ten *deniers* for the delivery, and she noted that he cheated her out of her rightful pay.

"Hold on there." She held a brash tone to her voice. Her belly was plumped up with pillows, making it appear that she was soon to burst with child. "How could you cheat a missus in my condition?"

"I paid you what the other baker gets." The cook smiled. There was a definite loss of teeth showing in his grizzled grin.

Lisette didn't agree. "My uncle told me what to collect." She held out the coins and a tear glistened in her blue eyes. "This isn't enough."

The man hobbled back into the kitchen to fetch the rest. It never hurt to cry, Lisette had learned long ago. Even the hardest of hearts couldn't take her tears. It had worked on the Duc often enough. Jean was the only man who never appeared shaken by crying.

There was still no sign of Paul or Michel. Lisette decided to try to find out what she could. The cook returned and paid her the full bounty for her bread.

"Thank you, kind sir. Is there a private place

where a lady could rest up before the journey
back?"

The cook looked at her and scoffed. "You ain't no
lady. A lady gets married before she tumbles with
her *beaux*. How many men you had? Never mind,"
he grumbled, "I don't want to know. You can water
your horse before you leave, but you better be gone
before His Lordship returns. Now we got two
women prancing through the battlements," he
said, disgusted. "The one locked in the tower didn't
like my cooking, and now I got one ready to foal."
His grumbling was heard long after he had entered the kitchen doors.

Lisette skipped over the threshold, following the
path Paul and Michel had taken. The hallways
were deserted, and it wasn't long before she found
her answers. Paul was bracing a man's form
against the wall. A stab of fear sank in her stomach. Lisette gasped at the sight of her Baron. He
had been beaten and was unconscious, his handsome face swollen and bleeding. Paul carried him
out of the building over his shoulder, and Jean was
draped in the uniform Michel had worn.

Michel had come from behind her. She hadn't
seen him until he was holding her arm and leading her out of the building. He had found himself
a new change of clothing, and now posed as a lieutenant.

Lisette didn't balk. "Where is Alexia?" She
wouldn't leave the fortress without the Countess. She would hate herself for it in the morning,
but she couldn't leave the woman to her cousin
Darias.

"We couldn't find her." Michel swore softly.

"The cook said she was locked in the tower," Lisette offered.

Paul and Michel exchanged a look of surprise.
Michel was the first to regain his calm. "I think I

can get her out. Paul will take Jean, pretending to be burying him."

"I think you'll need my help." Lisette was firm. "I can pick a lock faster than you could."

Michel stared hard at the young woman. "So that's how you got out of your room at Avranches? I should have known. All right, you can come with me."

Paul heaved the Baron over his shoulder. He whistled a cheery tune while he walked through the gates. He even saluted the gatekeeper when he called that he would be detained in the graveyard that lay outside the old castle.

Jean was cooperating. He hadn't moved or uttered a sound, even though Paul was sure Jean was being jostled into hell itself while slumped over his shoulder. There were several cracked ribs and a busted head, from what Paul had been able to tell. The Baron would need time to heal. They wouldn't be able to move him to the port for a few days.

The Rouen guards had returned to the site of the ambush and claimed their dead. The gravediggers were busily hefting shovels of dirt. They watched another man approach the area, and one of the two beggars hired to do the job wiped at his brow with the back of his shirt sleeve.

"Merde, not another one!" The man rested against the handle of the shovel, eyeing Paul with disgust.

Paul didn't say a word. He silently passed the two of them, with no more acknowledgment than a dip of his hat.

"I guess they ain't done with that one yet," Paul heard one of the men say.

Jean wheezed when Paul set him down. Paul was worried that a lung had been punctured while Jean was being carried out of the fortress. The ten men selected to stay behind brought a blanket and some cognac. Assessing the damage done to Jean, Paul clenched his hands into mighty fists. If the Baron died, he'd tear the fortress down stone by stone.

Chapter Twenty-one

"You're not walking right."

Lisette had an easy gait. Her hips didn't sway in a provocative way, as Alexia's did. Her stride was that of poise and dignity. "What do you mean?" she questioned Michel.

"You are walking like a lady born to wealth. A gutter strumpet doesn't hold her head up, and a pregnant one doesn't have grace of movement. Try walking with your belly outstretched, and waddle a little, would you?"

Lisette had forgotten how much she liked Michel. She corrected her posture, stooping to the occasion, and tried to walk as if the pillows stuffed into the skirt had taken over her body. It produced a laugh from Michel just when she needed it most. She was nervous while strolling the halls of the Rouen fortress. Michel was the calm one. He draped an arm around her and whispered, "Relax. We could always tell them we *intend* to get married."

"Just when I was beginning to wonder if you'd ever get around to asking." Lisette picked up on his humor, though inside she was shaking with fear. What if they were discovered? As yet, anyone who walked by didn't give them more than a passing look. Michel was born to command, she guessed.

When a guard noticed more of her figure than he liked, Michel ordered the man back to his business. The incredible part of it was, the men never argued or challenged his authority. His earth-brown eyes twinkled in mischief as he winked at her.

She loved him in those frightening moments. Lisette had come to trust him completely. He would never hurt her. It was always Michel who could make her laugh when she wanted to kill Jean, or cry because she hurt. No wonder half the women in France wanted Michel for their paramour.

Finding the room Alexia was located in was easier than they had first believed. All Lisette and Michel had to do was follow the noise. It sounded as if furniture were being torn apart and battered against the door, and the streaming gutter curses were all in Spanish.

Lisette waited around the corner to the door to Alexia's room while Michel accosted the guard outside her door. She didn't have to ask where the guard had gone. She heard a thud, and a groan that spoke of pain.

"You didn't kill him, did you?" Lisette whispered as Michel dragged the unconscious man down the hall. She pulled the sturdy pins from her braid and slid the thin iron metal into the old lock.

Michel shrugged. "I didn't have to. He needed a nap."

Lisette gave up after four pins lay broken on the stone floor. "I can't do it, Michel. This lock is more intricate than the one at the château."

"There's a difference?"

"This lock has several ... tumblers." Lisette heard the commotion die. Alexia was quieting down inside the room.

Michel heard approaching steps before they saw anyone. He pulled Lisette to her feet and wrapped his arms around her. "Don't say a word." he warned.

The old cook came up the back stairs. "What are you doing here?"

"She has kindly offered to help us calm down the prisoner." Michel said suavely. "Do you have the key?" Michel tucked Lisette behind him.

"Well, I do have to deliver her breakfast, and she has been none too kind about my cooking."

"I will see what I can do," Michel offered. He accepted the key from the cook and opened the door, admitting Lisette into the chamber. Michel remained outside while the breakfast was delivered, studying the cook for the advantage he would need to distract the man in conversation.

Lisette stepped into the room and put a finger to her lips. "Alexia, be quiet," she whispered.

"I don't believe it." Alexia groaned. "Why did it have to be you of all people to get me out of here?"

"Michel is with me." Lisette set the tray down on the chair. The table had been demolished. "Just stay in here after I'm gone. The cook will think that Michel relocked the door."

"I'd rather be boiled in oil than be *obligée* to you, Lady Lisette. Where is Jean?"

"Paul already took him out of the fortress." She could feel her face pale. Her cheeks were chilled and her hands started shaking again. Lisette realized she was playing her part rather well, for an amateur actress. Her stomach hadn't felt well for the past few days, and this escape wasn't helping matters any. "I already regret getting you out of here, Alexia. If you prefer to stay . . . ?"

"No." It was all Alexia said. She turned her back to Lisette and continued staring out the barred window.

Lisette compared the room with the one she had been locked up in at the château. It was bare except for a cot and a table that was now in splinters and a small cane chair. Not at all like her beautiful suite at Avranches. Jean had taken care of her in style. If she could repay him for his kindness, it would be by helping Alexia escape.

In the hall, Michel chatted amiably with the cook. The Marquis put the key in the lock and appeared to be securing the door. He also made a mock check, pretending to attempt to open it, just so that the cook would believe the solid door didn't move.

Michel handed the key back to the cook. "There you are, then. The prisoner has been taken care of. Sometimes it takes one woman to understand the needs of another."

"I guess it must be so," the cook muttered. He tottered down the back stairs when Michel and Lisette moved down the hall.

"I want you to go back out to the wagon," Michel whispered into her ear. "And wait beside the well. I'll bring Alexia out to you."

Lisette didn't pause. She was terrified of being held a prisoner inside the fortress. When she escaped the Baron, she would go directly to Castle Meret, posthaste.

The only nag that pulled the empty cart slowly lunged into action. "Move those old bones," Lisette commanded. She was rewarded with little or no reaction at all. They needed a racehorse, not a mule. She went directly to the well and drew a bucket of water for the horse. The cart was beside the stables. While the horse drank its fill she waited. She held to her own courage in those desperate moments. Jean had been hurt, but he was still alive.

Her belly appeared so large, and it made her think of bearing Jean's children. Lisette would look the way she did now. Although it was only a disguise, she found she liked the thought. How exciting it must be to share your body with someone who would grow to become a man or a woman. She had once believed that together they could sire a dozen children. Now even one child had become a bitter battle between them.

The cart creaked with the newly added weight of Michel and Alexia crawling under the tarp. Lisette hadn't seen them approach.

Her first reaction once they cleared the portcullis was to whip the nag into a canter. Lisette quickly decided against it. That would bring attention to the wagon. Her palms were sweating against the leather reins. The Rouen fortress battlements were ever present as she looked back. She couldn't press the poor beast too hard. With her sunbonnet pulled over her eyes, she kept her head down and her shoulders slumped. The rain had left the air fresh as springtime and the road a horror of puddles filled with murky water. The gray dawn became a misty morning as the sun rose in the east.

Their fresh mounts were waiting just around the bend in the road. Lisette released the wagon back to its owner and took the bundle of her clothing into the bushes. She threw the dress aside and changed into her breeches again. She was urging the horse into a gallop before Michel and Alexia were ready. Lisette couldn't wait any longer; she had to know what had happened to Jean. Paul had told her where they would meet. It was an old barn that would house them until Jean recovered. *If he recovered!* The worry crept into the lining of her stomach, causing the nausea to begin again. Lisette was exhausted. She hadn't stopped to eat or sleep while Jean was captive. It had been the day before when they last stopped to rest and fill their bellies.

Tears started of their own volition. If she had

been able to control herself and not let Alexia rile
her, Jean wouldn't have been distracted. It was
surprising to find out he was human and could be
defeated. He told her he lived a charmed life, but
why did his luck have to go bad now? It was all her
fault, and now she would have to help free him from
the threat of the *lettre de cachet.*

She was also angry because he had a Spanish
consort and hurt that he thought the two women
could become friends and share his affections like
good sports. The Duchess de Meret had pride, if
nothing else left to her. Riding ahead of Michel and
Alexia, she gave in to the need to cry. The ring Jean
had given her was tucked into Paul's pocket. Well,
she thought, he could just keep it. She wouldn't live
her life in the shadow of another woman.

Why did she have to care about Jean? Why was
waking in the arms of the man she loved worth the
heartache he invoked? Why couldn't she bring herself to stay in the fortress and wait for her cousin
to take her to Castle Meret?

The miles became a blur of tears and frustrations. Could she go on in a romantic triangle, with
the Countess nipping at her toes every time they
were alone? Yes, she could go on forever. Jean's affections, those he could give her, were all that mattered. It was worth the loss of her pride. She loved
him. It seemed simple enough, to open her heart
and let her emotions decide what direction her
head would follow.

The barn appeared on a distant hill. It was de-
crepit, its stone and mortar base in ruins. Rough
wooden planks held the weathered roof together. It
looked to her as if a good wind could blow the building into the next province. Lisette dug her heels
into the horse's side. Her mount was already a
creamy white and frothing at the mouth from her
relentless flight from the fortress.

Lisette was only vaguely aware of the men riding alongside her. She recognized Jolbert's men. They helped slow her horse when she reached the barn, and took charge of the mount when she leaped down and ran to the open doors.

The air inside the barn was speckled with hay dust. Sunshine peeped through a hole in the roof, and rays of light danced around the dirt floor. Paul was at the far end of the structure, bending over a small fire. Lisette had paused in the threshold. "Where is he?"

Paul took in her pale cheeks and distraught frown in an instant. Lady Lisette looked as if she had ridden hard and fast. Mud clung to her legs and boots, and her hair was streaming madly about her head.

"Jean is sleeping." Paul offered her a cup of water.

Lisette turned it away. "I want to see him." Paul motioned toward the steps to the loft.

"You won't be able to wake him for a few hours," the captain warned. The lady didn't seem to care. She wearily climbed the steps.

Paul hadn't thought about it before, but he did consider her reaction now. There was a definite fear in her eyes. Maybe that was all it took for her to become the Baron's lady. Paul and Michel hadn't thought of that. While they were trying to get Jean to romance her, they had no idea that she was truly concerned for his welfare. If they had known his battered appearance would have brought out this kind of reaction, they would have accommodated her sympathies sooner. Paul could easily have given Jean a few bumps and bruises. After all, Jean had been hurt worse in a bar brawl than he was now. Paul's fears had been laid to rest once he got a chance to examine his cousin closer. Before sinking into healing sleep, Jean had instructed him to give them privacy when Lisette arrived, and prepare warm water for a bath for the lady. Who was he to argue with Jean?

Lisette descended the stairs. She was satisfied that Jean was sleeping comfortably on the bed of straw and was on his way to recovery.

Paul brought out some clean clothes for the lady. Holding the garments up, he tried to recall from his previous experience with women in what order they came off. He poured the warmed, jasmine-scented water into a tub. It wasn't the best of accommodations with only a round metal tub to bathe in, but it was suitable while they remained hidden and Jean healed.

Lisette passed up the food, preferring a flagon of wine and a chunk of bread to nibble on. The barn had been cleared out by its previous inhabitants and swept clean. There was a crate for a table. The stalls were filled with Jolbert horses. An area in the rear of the barn was blanketed off for her bath. She set the flagon down on the dirt floor and pulled her boots off. The tunic and breeches dropped into a heap on the floor. She eased her tired body into the warm, scented water, relishing the luxury of a bath.

Alexia's voice interrupted her toilette. The Spanish countess demanded to know what precautions had been made for Jean's recovery to go undisturbed. Lisette scrubbed her body until it tingled. Why couldn't Alexia just do as she was told and go to Paris as Jean had wanted her to do? Lisette didn't want to have another run-in with Alexia. Her emotions were at their rawest point. Patience was a virtue given only to priests and kings, not Lisette. She wanted the Countess out of her life, and to keep Jean for herself.

Lisette soaped the muddy strands of her hair and scooped water with her hands to get as many of the bubbles out of her hair as she could. She reached out for the extra bucket of water to rinse her hair.

"Is this what you're looking for?" Alexia asked, a bucket of water in her hands. The Countess had invited herself into Lisette's secluded corner of the barn.

Lisette blinked back the soap stinging her eyes. "What do you want, Alexia?"

"I want you to leave Jean alone."

"He doesn't seem to feel the same as you do."

Alexia poured the bucket of cold water over Lisette's head.

Lisette wasn't expecting the water to be cold. It made her gasp, then shoot out of the tub, grasping for the toweling Paul had left her. "Get out," she demanded of Alexia.

"I will." The Countess sauntered out of arm's length. "I just wanted to make sure you understood where I think you belong. Go back to your father, Lady Lisette, and leave Jean alone. He's not right for you."

"That's up to him to decide," Lisette countered. "Didn't Jean tell you to go to Paris? Isn't it obvious he doesn't want you around?" She watched Alexia's eyes light with anger. She had finally hit a nerve, and the Countess couldn't deny it.

"I have no doubt we will meet again," Alexia said in parting.

The curtain fell back and Lisette was left alone. She didn't put the blouse and skirt on. Instead, she donned her chemise and wrapped the blanket around her. She was tired and needed some rest. Jean wouldn't be awake for hours, and she wanted to be refreshed when he awoke. The barn had emptied of Jean's men. They were outside, and from what Lisette could tell by eavesdropping, Michel was escorting Alexia to Paris.

Au revoir, she thought. Lisette climbed the ladder to the loft. Jean had kicked his blanket off. His naked, bronzed body was a direct contrast to the golden straw that made his bed. His eyes were still swollen. Paul had placed a cold compress on his head. Lisette put the cloth in the basin of water left beside Jean. She squeezed out the excess water and placed it back on Jean's head. He probably had a terrible headache. There was a huge purple bruise above his right eyebrow. Someone had deliberately hit him with a solid instrument.

Her senses came alive when she touched the contours of his body. His ribs were bound with strips of sheeting, and there were so many cuts on him she couldn't count them all. Paul had left behind a jar of laudanum salve that she gently applied to every mar on his beautiful physique.

"Lisette?" Jean groaned.

"Shhh." She pressed her fingers to his lips. "I'll take care of you, but please get some rest."

"Sleep," he cooed from his drowsy state. "Not without you beside me, *chérie.*"

"I'm right here." She placed his hand in hers. "I'll stay with you."

"I'm very angry with you."

"What have I done to upset you, *mon ami?*"

"You risked your life," he spoke softly. "Why did you do that for me?"

"Because your cousin probably would have stormed the castle. I couldn't wait that long to get you out." She dabbed the laudanum salve on his cut lip. "Why did you let them capture you?"

"I didn't see any choice in the matter. I am not so foolish that I don't know when I'm outnumbered, and to resist would have meant my death."

"Are you in pain, Jean?"

"My eyelashes don't hurt." He moaned, and it was a heart-wrenching sound to her ears. "I can't see anything yet."

She noticed his eyes didn't open when he talked, and started to worry that she had kept him awake too long. Lisette fought the tears that wanted to spill. Why couldn't she stop from crying? Lately, it was all she could do to keep her emotions in check. She feathered kisses on his jawline and held his face between her hands.

"I didn't want them to hurt you," she finally admitted with a sob. "Oh, Jean. What have we done to each other?"

"You didn't do this to me." He reached out to draw her soft form to him. His lady stretched out next to him on their bed of straw. It made him think of Spain and a house that had been built for them. They would be safe there, away from the devious plans of her father and cousin. Lisette cried in muffled sobs against him. Would she still leave him if he gave her the opportunity? The question had never been answered. In his heart he knew that if she left him, he would slowly die inside. The laudanum Paul had given him eased the pain his body suffered, and holding Lisette beside him gave his heart joy. He sleepily stroked her back and arms. "Stay with me, *ma, belle amie,*" he breathed against her hair.

Lisette felt him sag against her form as he fell into a deep sleep beside her. He had called her "my love," but did he mean it? The dreams of her beloved fiancé had surfaced again. She could endure anything if he loved her and only her. She finally did fall asleep, drifting into memories of her tall Baron dancing with her. The haunting melody of a waltz swirled around them, and he was gone. He had disappeared in a puff of smoke. She frantically searched for him, to no avail. Alexia appeared and grabbed her arm, trying to drag her to the balcony. It was only a dream, Lisette reminded herself. It wasn't real. Jean was beside her.

The nightmare ended, and a noise pulled her from slumber. She reached out and touched Jean's bare chest. His skin felt hot to her fingertips. Paul knelt beside them, with a hand to Jean's head.

"Is he all right?" she questioned. Lisette had been covered, she realized. Paul had probably noticed their covers kicked aside and provided her with a wrap. She was clad in a chemise, and thankfully allowed some modesty.

"Will you help me turn him over?" Paul sat back on his haunches and studied the Baron. Jean was still sleeping and wasn't aware of them. "He shouldn't be this feverish."

Together, they carefully turned the Baron over onto his stomach. Lisette saw the puffed streaks on Jean's back for the first time. "He's been whipped!"

Paul put a hand on her arm to steady her. "He'll be fine after he gets some rest."

Lisette didn't believe him. Her stomach turned. Lisette rolled away from them and doubled over as the heaves held her in their merciless grasp.

It took several deep breaths and the wet cloth that Paul offered to control her stomach. Lisette rested until the queasy jerk in her tummy subsided.

"I-I didn't know," she stammered.

Paul considered her carefully. Lisette was pale, and violet shadows had appeared under her eyes. "I think I will have two patients on my hands if you don't get some sleep, my lady."

"You don't understand," Lisette tried to explain. "I told him I'd see him whipped for what he did to me."

"You couldn't have meant it," Paul offered for her. His tone was as gentle as a kitten's.

"Oh, but I did. I wanted him to feel vulnerable, as I did. I thought nothing could hurt him. He was always so self-assured that I wanted to find a way to have my revenge. Everything that I wanted to happen to him has come true."

Paul was beginning to understand. "Now you regret your oath of vengeance?"

"I do regret it. Why did this have to happen to us? It should have been a summer filled with beautiful memories, not a war to separate us. He should have been mine, Paul." Lisette wasn't afraid to admit her claim on the Baron. She had made a commitment to Jean long ago. "He belongs to me," she repeated, in a softer tone.

"I believe that is what Jean said when your father told him you would marry another." Paul smiled. It was a good feeling to know the lady cared about his cousin. He had misjudged her. Lady Lisette had no care what happened to the throne or what fortunes could be gained or won. She loved Jean; he was sure of it. Her remorse was evidence of her true feelings.

Lisette resented her father's intervention in her happiness with the man she loved. Yet to believe her own father could have used them both in a scheme to gain the throne for himself was unthinkable. She was the Duc's blood, his only child. Now that Lisette had inherited her mother's title and come of age, her world had suddenly changed. Gone were the carefree afternoons spent riding the grape-filled fields of Meret. She sorely missed the innocence of youth.

"Will we be safe here, Paul?" Lisette felt better. Her stomach had calmed down. Paul offered her a flagon of wine and a chunk of fresh bread smeared with cheese. Lisette was ravenously hungry. She forgot the *étiquette* she had learned at the school and gobbled down the tasty morsels.

"The troop will keep the Rouen guard detained for a few days. That should be long enough to get

Jean back on his feet. When he recovers, we're sending the two of you to the port at Le Havre."

"We're?" Lisette questioned.

"Michel and I must locate the Earl of Normandy."

Paul had the Jolberts' arrogance, she mused. Evidently, Alexia wouldn't be joining them. Lisette would be able to have Jean all to herself.

"I see that arguing with you is a lost cause," she teased.

The captain reached into his pocket and produced the diamond ring Jean had given her. "I think you might want this back."

Lisette couldn't bear to wear the ring again. It represented her belief that Jean would marry her, when she knew he wouldn't. "Would you keep it for me?"

Paul was puzzled. He did as she asked and pocketed the ring again. Why wouldn't she wear the engagement ring? Didn't she know of the wedding planned on the island of Las Palmas where she would marry the Baron? He didn't like this one bit. Was Jean still toying with the lady's affections and clinging to his vow of vengeance on her family? Paul reasoned that when his cousin recovered, Jean would have a few questions to answer, and Paul wouldn't be asking them in a pleasant manner.

Chapter Twenty-two

Three days later, Lisette woke to the timbre of Paul's voice. The burly captain was involved in an argument, she guessed by the angry tone of his voice. Some poor soul had crossed the captain, and he brought loudly the lack of discipline to the man's attention.

She stretched in her bed of straw and immediately noticed Jean was not beside her. The sun was already high in the afternoon sky and washed through the hole in the roof to light her loft. Jean had recovered his strength with her tender care. His fever had diminished the day after they arrived at the barn, and he soon found his appetite again. But although his stamina returned, he had changed in his attitude toward her. Her once-loving Baron had become cold and distant.

While she had been able to hide the nausea from Paul's watchful eye, she took care to nibble a chunk of bread every few hours to keep the squeamishness at bay. It seemed to help the most. The queasiness ceased by late morning, and she always felt wonderful through the evening. Her turbulent emotions were the hardest to contain. At first, Lisette was logically able to pass off her tears as relief at Jean's recovery from the fever, but as her condition continued she knew she was pregnant.

The girls at the school had warned one another of the symptoms. Lisette had mentally listed them and found they all applied. Her breasts were tender, but not engorged yet. When Jean touched her chest the night before, she reeled from the gentle massaging. He had taken care with her after that. Her excuse was that her flux was soon due. Lisette already knew that time of the month was past, and she had no sign of the red warrior that cramped her stomach into a painful ball. It brought out a disappointed grunt from him, but she gave a sigh of relief that she still was the only one who knew. She wanted to wait until he was fully re-covered before telling him about the child.

Also, there was the matter of the marriage cer-emony needed to prevent the child from being brought into the world as a bastard. She didn't really believe Jean would want his son or daughter born without a title.

Lisette dressed in the skirt and blouse Marie had donated to her. She climbed down the ladder and boldly walked to the group of Jolbert's men. Her bare feet and slim figure mader her appear small and frail next to the brawny gents of the troop. She sought out Paul, the largest of the men in the barn.

Seeing him made her gape. "What happened to your eye, Paul?" Black and purple rimmed his eye, and the stubble of a new beard was clean-shaven again.

Paul shrugged it off. "It's nothing."

Lisette felt the turn of his back to her as a per-sonal affront. Their new rapport seemed gone. Paul's attitude closely resembled Jean's. He was indifferent to her.

Jean finished laying the powder charges beside the open road leading to the old barn. He would be ready for the Rouen guard. This time, there would be no mistakes made. His troop would soon return, and Lisette had to be safely out of the way by then. Jean wouldn't take any more chances with his lady's life. So far, his luck had held out and Lisette hadn't been recognized or captured. She had to be sent on to Spain without him. It was the only way he could keep her safe.

He entered the barn and came to a stop inside the portal. His men were sitting on the floor with her, exchanging stories of battles while she ate. There were several blankets folded to·make a pillow under her firm posterior. The scene before Jean made him proud of the men who saw to her comfort. The young Duchess had become endeared to their hearts with her gentle words and gay laughter. The hussars adored her, and maintaining control had been difficult of late. They wanted her to remain; he wanted her sent ahead to safety. It was an argument Jean won only because he commanded them.

"I see your appetite has returned, Duchess." When Jean entered the barn, the men rose in respect for his command. After the disagreement with Paul, there wasn't a man there who would ever challenge him again. His cousin scowled at him, and Jean gave him a truculent look.

Lisette set the wooden bowl of stew aside. There was an ominous tone in Jean's voice that warned her to be careful what she said to him. "I see you're back on your feet again, my lord."

"Your concern for my welfare is touching, Lady Lisette. You can leave for Spain with the peace of mind that I am fit. You will be ready to travel in a quarter of an hour."

Her regal pose didn't sway as the men moved to let them stand face to face. If she didn't know how angry he was, they did.

Lisette felt the bottom drop out of her stomach.

He was ordering her to leave France without him. Paul had lost the argument, she realized. Jean wasn't about to let anyone else command his troop. He would never leave without his father.

From what Paul had told her, the Earl had disappeared from the face of the earth after the ambush of the Rouen guard, and Jean was determined to destroy the Duc de Meret for this insult.

Lisette was afraid she would lose Jean forever if she left him now. Her last hope was that he would listen to her plea. Swallowing her pride, she kept her distance from the man who could turn her emotions against her. He would try to make her angry, she knew. Jean would attempt to see to it that she did as she was told. He wasn't counting on her strength of will.

"I will stay with you," she said softly.

"You will go with your escort to the port and board the ship." This was harder on him than he thought possible. She looked so damned trusting with her big blue eyes filling with tears. Jean steeled himself against her supplication. His mind was made up.

"You made a promise to me, Jean. You said I would always stay with you. Will you break your word to me in front of your family and men?"

Paul nodded in agreement. He liked the young Duchess. She had taken a sound tactic, reasoning with Jean, although he personally believed Jean was beyond reasoning. The Baron would have a mutiny on his hands if he weren't careful. The hussars had voted to accept Lady Lisette as Jean's wife, whether Jean wanted her or not.

"What is a man's word when given to his consort?" Jean balked at the sound of what he said. He didn't like hurting her, but didn't see any other way to get her to go on to Spain without him.

Jean's words cut through her. The barn had become deathly silent. Not a man in his troop would come to her defense. "You don't mean that," she whispered, her voice cracking with tormented emotions.

"I have grown weary of you, Lady Lisette. Simon will escort you to Spain, where you will wait."

"Wait for what?" Her courage was faltering. "To do your bidding? Nothing has changed, has it? You still intend to find and kill my father, don't you?" He didn't answer her. His gaze was steady with hers, a battle of wills Lisette would lose.

"I killed a man to save your life, Jean. Isn't that worth something to you?"

Jean remembered the alley in Paris where she had shot a man. "I know what you did to save my life."

He didn't want her to suffer the same treatment from Darias that he had. If her cousin managed to get her back under his control, Lisette would be tortured. Jean had tasted the salt of his blood through the sting of the whip, and couldn't allow Lisette to be kept in constant danger. He knew she wouldn't make it easy for him.

"Keeping you out of trouble is a full-time occupation. Twice now I've had to abandon my plans to rescue my father because you were in danger. Sending you to Spain uncomplicates my life. Paul will take you to the port."

Lisette was dismissed without further explanation. Jean turned on his heel, ordering several of the young men to accompany him. When he walked out the door, so went her hopes. There was no chance to tell him about the child she carried within her womb. Jean had used her and cast her away as he had promised to do the first night she was held captive at the château. Lisette felt empty inside, as if Jean had taken all of her love with him. He had betrayed her. She stood perfectly still, star-

ing at the dirt floor. Her silent curses weren't for
Jean, but for herself. Why had she believed in him?

She was humiliated beyond reasoning.

Paul led Lisette's mare out of the barn and tethered the horse to the hitching post. Michel had finally returned from Paris, and Paul snorted in
response to his questions.

"What is going on?" Michel was stupefied. "I
just passed Jean, and he's in a foul mood. Now that
I see you, I can guess why."

"You needn't dismount, Michel. I want you to
take Lisette to the port. My cousin needs me."

"Where is Lady Lisette?" Michel was beginning
to understand what had taken place.

"She's still in the barn. But . . ." Paul didn't try
to stop him. Michel dismounted and entered the
barn.

Michel's glance found Lisette standing in the
shadows. He approached her slowly, taking full
note of her shaken figure. Michel held his hat in
his hand, afraid to speak. His anger was held in
check as he studied her face.

She wouldn't tell him what had happened. He
could see it, though, without words to tell of what
had transpired. He knew the Baron wanted her
sent to the port, but didn't believe Jean would hurt
her to accomplish the task. That is, until he saw the
dark lines under her eyes. There was a blank look
on her face telling him what he wanted to know.

Jean asked too much to expect Michel to ignore
this breach of gentlemanly conduct. Lady Lisette
had given the Baron her love, and Jean had cast it
back in vengeance. Jean wouldn't get away with
this.

"Lady Lisette," he said finally, "I would like to
be your escort." He gallantly offered her his arm.

Confused, she looked up to his brown eyes.

Michel smiled. "I understand Paris is beautiful at this time of the year."

Lisette's pulse pounded against her ribs.

Michel swept his hat before him. "I have great news from the *parlement*. Feudal rights have been abolished. Thus, Jean has no claim over you, Lady Lisette."

"Do you mean it, Michel?"

"I certainly do. And, as a gentleman, I will not condone Jean's continually harassing you. If it is your wish, I will take you to Paris."

Lisette fell into his arms. "Oh, Michel. Thank you for your help." When she had a moment to recover from the shock, she found her anger rising. "How long have the feudal rights been abolished? Did Jean know of this?"

"He couldn't possibly have known, Lady Lisette. It has only recently been decreed, and if I hadn't been in Paris, I wouldn't know myself."

The Marquis was very fond of Lisette and loved Jean like a brother. But this complex romance had gone on long enough. Jean had been given plenty of chances to claim his lady out of love. It was Jean's choice to send her away. Michel would see her happy yet. The Marquis would remain close to Lisette when he returned her to the palace, just until Jean came to his senses and asked for her hand like a proper fiancé.

"Your uncle didn't know there was one feudal war still being fought, my lady. When I explained your dilemma, he supplied an escort. There is an angry general waiting to accompany you to Versailles, where your father is waiting to greet you."

"Michel, where is the Earl of Normandy?" Her hopes had returned. She had a friend, after all.

"I was hoping you would help me locate him."

"Once Jean has the Earl back, he will have to

leave my family alone." There was a spring in her
step as she neared the door.

"Lady," Michel called her back. He shook his
head and impatiently tapped his foot on the dirt
floor. "You can't let Jean see you looking so ra-
diant. Couldn't you look angry or something? How
about a pout?"

Lisette calmed herself. Michel was right. If she
left the barn with a smile, Jean would suspect
something was going wrong with his plan to send
her to the port. Michel wasn't as tall as Jean, but
he had a quality about him that tugged at her
heart. She had once thought he could rival Jean for
her affections. He was a dear friend, and Lisette
would forever be in Michel's debt, but she could
love only one man.

Jean stood off in the distance as Michel and Lisette mounted their horses. There was a guard of
five who would take them to the port. Lisette took
a long look back at the dark frame of her Baron riding his black Arabian. A part of her life would always be with him in the secret child she kept in her
belly. Jean would get his father back. In the final
moments she looked at him, Lisette vowed to see
to it that he had his family returned. When the
Earl was found and returned to Normandy, she
would go into seclusion until the child was born.

Michel knew the general was impatient.
Through one of the court courtesans, he had
learned of the muster the King had ordered to re-
claim Lady Lisette. The Baron would soon lose her
anyway, he reasoned. He was betraying an old
friendship in taking her to her uncle, but he hoped
it was one that would spare Jean another battle.
They spurred the horses into a gallop in a direction
that would take them to the port. Once out of Jean's
view, they would double back and Michel would
present her to the general.

She didn't look back. Lisette followed Michel's direction to the wooded hillside, feeling free for the first time in two months. When they came to the top of the hill overlooking the barn, they reined in their horses. She flinched from the noise as explosions ripped across the valley. Smoke columns rose in the summer sky, at first red with fire, then turning white and hanging on the valley floor. The blue and red coats of the royal soldiers stuck out against the white background. Jean was caught in a trap and completely surrounded. The barn was set apart from the battle until it, too, exploded into flames. The cover of smoke completely veiled the valley below.

"Where is Jean?" Lisette was getting nervous. The battle raged in the valley below, and somewhere in that tangle of death was her lover.

When the men who guarded them voiced concern about the victor of the battle, Michel gave them leave to return to the Baron.

"The battle goes well for Jean, Lady Lisette."

"How can you tell?" She couldn't see anything but a blur of bodies and horses.

"Jean has the advantage. He's prepared for the Rouen guard. Those explosions were calculated to give them cover."

Michel knew more than he would tell Jean or Lisette. Simon had been under siege by the King's guard, and had to put out to sea. He wasn't waiting in the port. The King was anxious to have his niece back at the palace, and had provided Darias with the men he needed to free Lisette from the renegade Baron. The Duc de Meret was busy with his political aspirations, and completely unaware that his daughter hadn't been sent on to England as Darias had informed him.

Michel's conference with the Duc had been short. The Duc de Meret swore he didn't know what had happened to the Earl of Normandy. As Jean suspected, Darias had managed to gain control of Meret province with the Duc's blessings and the King's permission. In taking Lisette back to her uncle, Michel hoped to accomplish two things. The first, to have the *lettre de cachet* with the Earl's name revoked. The second was to give Jean time to think of what he was doing to Lady Lisette. Michel could see the love they held for each other, even if Jean was too stubborn to admit it.

Michel would trap Darias in his own schemes to control Normandy and Meret. He needed Lisette for bait to draw her cousin out into the open with his treacherous plans.

The Marquis would send word back to the Baron that he had been met on the road by the King's guard, and rather than send her to the palace alone, he had proclaimed himself her rescuer. He hoped his friend would understand when he told Jean the truth. Michel would wait until Jean was over the brunt of his anger, then send his reports of what was happening at the palace to the Baron.

Lisette turned from the scene in the valley. Part of her felt she had betrayed Jean. Once again the de Merets would hurt him. Hopefully, the Earl would be returned to Normandy and peace would once again reign in the northern provinces. Her uncle had a soft heart when it came to her requests. She would ask Louis to free the charges against the Earl of Normandy. As for the bounty the Baron had paid for her hand, Lisette would find a way to repay him. She didn't know how yet, but she knew she would try.

His final words still stung her pride. He had grown weary of her, and somehow this hurt worse than being cast aside. She had opened her heart to him and thought they shared something special when they made love beneath the stars. It was her own dreams that had betrayed her love for him. Lisette wouldn't make that mistake again. She was a quixotic fool for loving him, and for her vengeance, he would never know of their child.

Lisette vowed to take the secret of the life they had created with her to the grave, rather than let him know. He had asked that she tell no one, and Lisette would comply, not even telling Jean. She had almost made a terrible mistake in loving him so much; Lisette thought he loved her in return. There were no more feudal rights for him to claim over her. The was no more war between their families. She would make restitution for the financial damages to the Jolberts somehow, she thought. Never again would she believe in the tall man with gray eyes.

Michel and Lisette rode through the hills at an easy pace. The Marquis sensed her depression and had the solution to brighten her mood. If he delivered her sulking and looking forlorn to her cousin, Dairas would know something was wrong. Lisette had to be thinking her future looked pretty bleak. Michel didn't want anyone associated with the de Merets to know the intimacy Jean and Lisette had shared. There was too much at stake if she carried a Norman heir.

Michel could remedy her unhappy mood. He slowed the horses to a walk. "I have a present for you, Lady Lisette."

Lisette had been drowning in self-pity and hardly heard the Marquis. "A present for me?"

"I think it's something you desire beyond anything else." He had meant to pique her interest, but noticed the pallor his announcement caused. "Will you talk to me, Lisette?"

She bristled at the thought. Lisette trusted Michel, and hadn't discussed her feelings about Jean with anyone else. Riding sidesaddle, she could easily face Michel, but she couldn't raise her head.

"I loved Jean as a memory, and the dream of him that I had created, Michel. In reality, Jean is bitter and angry with me, and will never return my deep affection for him."

"I think," he answered softly, "that my friend is a fool, but that he cares for you more than he will ever admit. Jean is driven by duty."

"Duty to whom?" Lisette had never really known the Baron. He was still as mysterious to her as he had been the first day she met him.

"His loyalties were to France, and for many years he served the King faithfully. When he was ordered to perform acts of terrorism for the good of the kingdom, Jean followed his orders. He questioned the King's judgment when he was ordered to massacre a family. The King insisted every living member be murdered to protect the good of France. At that time, Jean resigned his commission in the Black Musketeers, and I soon followed. That gave Jean freedom to seach the world for a place where he could rest and forget the things he had done." Michel loved a good tale, and this one got better. "He wanted a wife to share his life of peace with, and you were chosen. Jean offered his suit to your father, and the Duc turned him down. It would be an advancement of rank for Jean, and the Duc didn't like his old enemies the Jolberts having the control that marrying you would bring. So Jean tried again. Even after being turned down three times, he pressed to marry you. The day he met you, his face glowed with happiness. I saw in my friend the peace he had always wanted. But there was the matter of the bounty the Duc demanded for the betrothal, so once again Jean had to take up arms to gain his fortune. He put out to sea and became a pirate—"

"Mon Dieu!" Lisette gasped. "I don't believe it."
She quickly explained to Michel's inquisitive gaze.
"While we were in Paris I told him the buccaneer's
life suited him. I thought he'd make a devilishly
handsome pirate."

Michel noticed the warm regard for the Baron in
Lisette's voice. "Jean and Simon," he continued,
"built a fortress on the island of Las Palmas. That
was where Jean was sending you."

"To a pirates' hideaway? How very exciting!"

"Most of the Jolbert family is there already.
Only the Earl remained in France because he felt
he could do the most good in working to reorganize
the government."

They rode in silence for a little way, and Lisette
thought about what she had learned about Jean.
He wasn't the hard man she had imagined him to
be.

"About your present." Michel got her attention
back.

"What is it?" Lisette was squirming with curi-
osity.

"It's a Montgolfier, a hot-air balloon. The em-
blem on the envelope shall be of the combined
houses of Jolbert and de Meret."

Lisette forgot her own troubles as she envisioned her very own hot-air balloon. She didn't care
what design was on it. "When can I see it? Can I
take a ride in it right away? It will be my first flight
into the heavens. Do you know that Louis thinks
it's marvelous how they can soar, but my father
thinks it's a doomsday weapon? I can't wait to see
it. When will it be ready?"

Michel held up a hand to stop the barrage of
questions. He was thrilled she looked forward to
returning to Paris. "You shall see it as soon as it's
finished. That should be in about a month. You'll

have to see your father, Lisette. I know it won't be easy for you."

Lisette wasn't thinking of the Duc de Meret. All that danced before her eyes was the drifting flight of a hot-air balloon.

Chapter Twenty-three

Lisette was at Versailles within the week. The King was on a hunting expedition and was absent from the court. During the King's truancy, his secretary held the court of *petit lever*. At precisely eight o'clock the ministers and officials were admitted to present their requests. Lisette was late. She had overslept, and spent a miserable hour controlling her unsettled stomach. It was nearly noon, and time for mass to be said.

Lisette was granted an audience in the King's secretary's private apartments. The court household was dismissed, leaving her alone with him. She felt confident that once her business was accomplished, she could retire to Meret in peace.

Clad in a borrowed dress, Lisette dropped into a formal curtsy. The King's secretary was detained with the man she knew to be Charles Sanson, the executioner. Seeing the man so famed for his merciful decapitations gave her goose bumps down her spine.

Lisette was annoyed they hadn't noticed her. Cramped in the unnatural position, her back and legs ached. The King's secretary was a slim man, with dark eyebrows and a mustache that was trimmed into a thin line above his upper lip. His graying hair was covered by a catogan wig, and his capot coat and satin breeches reminded her the ill-fitted dress she wore was seasons out of style. The black dress was vaguely reminiscent of a matron's habit with a lace fichu to cover the low neckline. Long sleeves turned a sweltering August afternoon into a steam bath as perspiration trickled between her breasts.

The secretary scanned the papers spread over his desk. "How long will this take to complete?" He directed the question to the executioner.

With his beret nervously clenched in his hand, Monsieur Sanson continued to stare at the floor. "A few months, if I can find the financing to complete the project. This instrument has been used in other countries, and my reports state that it is more efficient than the sword."

"Complete it as scheduled," the secretary ordered.

"If you might remind His Majesty, I have not been paid in months. I don't have the funds to purchase the materials. My creditors are unwilling to wait much longer for payment. They are threatening me with debtors' prison."

The secretary took a quill from the marble holder on his desk and wrote a note on a piece of parchment. He sprinkled sand on the wet ink, then tapped the grains free and stamped the document with the royal seal. The missive was handed to Monsieur Sanson.

"This should hold them off for now. When the treasury has more money, you will be paid. You have the King's letter of credit until then." He tossed him a small bag of coins. "Complete the guillotine."

Monsieur Sanson collected his papers, bowed, and left the office.

The secretary finally noticed her. "You may rise,

Lady Lisette. I have been informed that you escaped an ambush."

"Oui," she answered, keeping her eyes down. "If I may confide in you, that you may inform my uncle?"

The secretary crossed the sparsely furnished room to the window. He was testy today because he would rather be out hunting than seeing to the affairs of the state. The Duchess de Meret followed him to the sanctuary of the window seats. It was partly due to the palace spies that he chose this informal setting to greet his lord's niece. There were pages in the room who would remember their words verbatim, and repeat them to anyone who would listen. The palace inhabitants and servants thrived on intrigue, and what better form of gossip than to hear the details of the ambush that abducted a royal lady of the court? The young woman was still as innocent as a rose, yet contained all the beauty she would possess in the full bloom of years to come. Seated beside her, he gave her hand a pat. "You may speak freely."

Lisette took a deep breath for courage before launching into her story. "What I bring to you is a problem that I cannot find a way to make restitution for without my uncle's help. A terrible injustice has befallen the Jolbert family. The Earl of Normandy has been accused of treason, and a *lettre de cachet* has been issued against him. My father broke the engagement to his son, the Baron Jolbert, because of the charges against the Earl. Jean-Charles Jolbert has paid the bounty demanded of him, and now he has been robbed of his rights under our marriage contract. I beseech the King to withdraw the *lettre* against the Earl and restore his favor to the Jolbert family. They are loyal subjects and have served France faithfully."

"Lady Lisette," he began, "it is not for you to distress yourself when it comes to matters of state. The charges against the Earl were well founded, and witnesses to his treason testified against him."

Lisette wouldn't accept defeat. "Witnesses can be bought. Think back on your own friendship with the Earl. Hasn't he supported the King's rally for gradual reform of the government? He has been a friend and adviser to my uncle in the past, and his views were not so radical as those of some men who walk freely in our city streets."

He explored another angle. "Is it your wish to wed the Baron Jolbert?"

"No, my lord. The Baron Jolbert is too angry with my family to desire me for his wife. His only wish is to retire to his estates and live out his life in peace, as it is mine to return to Meret."

"You are too young to be a heartbroken recluse."

"It is my wish," she spoke softly. Her chin dipped to her chest. Facing the rest of her life alone seemed simpler than telling anyone of the secret affair between herself and the Baron. "My uncle must help me locate the Earl of Normandy and return him to his family, or there will never be tranquillity in Meret."

"We shall have the matter investigated." The secretary's voice was a whisper. He reached to her back and touched the braid that held her hair. "And what will become of you?"

Lisette cringed when he touched her. "I have considered a convent." The comment took hold. Any man who fancied himself a gentleman wouldn't try debauching her if he knew she considered becoming a nun.

He withdrew his hand. "I shall be notifying you as soon as possible."

Lisette completed the perfunctory curtsy and swiftly exited the secretary's apartments. She

hadn't liked seeing him alone. Where was her
father when she needed him? When she had arrived at the palace, she hadn't wasted a moment
before writing to her father to explain that she had
returned and to request an audience with him. He
hadn't answered her letter. The Duc was evidently
too busy with the *parlement* to come to her.

Michel, sweet Michel, hadn't left her side except
for the evenings when the ladies sent requests for
his company. She had yet to figure out how he
managed to have a willing female every few miles
en route to Paris just waiting for him to make an
appearance. The Marquis had pledged his loyalty
to her and kept his word. His character was beyond
reproach, if she overlooked his gambling, wenching, and wife stealing. Other than a few minor
flaws, he was a perfect gentleman, and she trusted
him implicitly.

The halls of Versailles were bustling with servants. Everyone and anyone who had a title was out
hunting with the King. That suited Lisette. She
was the only member of the royal household who
remained at the palace. Her riding boots clicked
against the tiled floors. Michel was where she had
left him, except that he was no longer alone. He had
a pretty blond maid tucked into his arms.

Lisette paused beside the arched doorway with a
hand on her hip to display her impatience. Michel
disentangled the woman's arms, kissed her hand,
and promised to see her again very soon.

"Don't you ever worry about social diseases?"
she reprimanded sternly.

The Marquis matched her rapid pace as she
made her way down the halls. "I think about it occasionally," he teased. "Well." He abruptly
stopped her with a hand on her arm. "What did the
man say?"

Lisette knew Michel was as anxious as she was

to find the Earl. "He said the matter will be investigated. I want to find Jean's father and clear his
name."

"You asked him to revoke the charge also?" He
thought it was monumental that she cared enough
about Jean to try to find the Earl, but to try to withdraw the *lettre* was outrageous.

Lisette nodded. "I hope to restore to Jean all that
was taken from him."

Michel was pleased. He wrapped her hand
around his arm and set a slower pace. "Speaking
of my friend, he sent this for you." The Marquis
placed a letter into her hand. "I hope you don't
mind that I sent word to him that you had arrived
safely at the palace. Jean was really quite angry
when he couldn't find you at Le Havre."

Lisette's palms were cold as she tucked the linen
envelope into her pocket. She hadn't thought Jean
would allow her to leave him. She had expected
him to be lurking in the shadows to execute her
second abduction.

They turned down a dark corridor, and Michel
took her hand and kissed it gently. "If you had torn
the letter into pieces, I would have taken you back
to your suite." Lost for words, the Marquis backed
away.

Lisette didn't need to be told Jean was within a
few feet of her. She could feel his gaze, and knew
so well the quicksilver flutter of her senses coming
to life, turning her will against her. As she stood in
the center of the corridor, her first reaction was to
run. Her tongue licked dry lips. Lisette had to face
him. In the past week, he had been ever present in
her thoughts and actions. Praying there would
come a time when she could forget what they had
shared, she slowly turned to the man standing in
the shadows.

"I hardly recognized you." Jean's voice was a whisper, drawing her closer. "Lisette?"

"Do I look so different?" She spoke softly, so as not to draw attention from the servants passing through the great halls. He drew her into the shadows beside him with a gentle tug on her hand. Lisette wouldn't allow him to wrap his arms around her. Jean could no longer claim that she must rectify an injustice against his family. With feudal laws abolished, there was nothing he could do to force her to rejoin him. Seeing him reminded her of the passion that had occurred between them. He looked the same. His dark hair was tousled, and for the first time in their many days together he hadn't shaved.

"Non," he breathed slowly. "You don't look any different. You're still the most beautiful woman I have ever met."

Her breath stopped as the muscles in her chest tightened. He reached up and stroked her cheek in a gentle caress. Reality was a sour wine that left a bitter taste in her mouth.

"Even more beautiful than Alexia?" She couldn't recall how many times she had thought of Jean finding consolation in his Spanish consort's arms. The image of the two of them together haunted her nights until sleep was forgotten and all she could do to stop the reflections was to anxiously pace through the night.

"Alexia?" he questioned. "I can't stop thinking about you, Lisette. You must hate me for what I said and did to you."

"I could never hate you," she said honestly.

A smile twitched at the corners of his mouth. "Come back to me."

Lisette stepped back. "I can't leave the palace. There is unfinished business here that still needs my attention."

"Do you realize you said 'I can't' instead of 'I won't'? You still care for me, don't you, Lisette?"

"I loved a dream, Jean. Not what you have become."

"I will never regret what I've done to claim you."

Lisette knew he was speaking of the bounty he had raised for her hand. "Must you remind me that I was purchased? Why can't we just forget what happened between us? There is nothing but heartache for both of us in our memories."

"There is no future for me without you. I cannot forget the nights we shared beneath the stars. You were my goddess and my love."

"Non!" Her voice rose. "It's too late to make me believe you love me. You're only saying it now to get me to go with you to Spain."

"How could you not know it, Lisette?"

"You said you had grown weary of me. You would send me to Spain, knowing I would die a thousand deaths worrying about you. It was you who said you would not marry me. I offered myself to you out of love and a hope to avoid a war between our families, but you rejected me and clung to your damned honor. It is my sincere hope that your honor is keeping you warm at night, among other things." Her last comment was thrown in for spite. Alexia was probably rejoicing that Lisette had left the Baron's company.

"I'm a bastard for hurting you," he admitted. "It was my wish to keep you safe. If I had asked you to go on without me, would you have?"

"I would have stayed beside you, as I promised to do."

"Do you think I could live with myself if you had been the one to be taken inside the fortress and whipped like a common criminal?" He let her think about what he said for a few moments. "You're right. Honor makes a cold bed partner. Come back to me and let me make it up to you."

"I told you that I have business here."

"Then I'll wait."

"You can't stay at the palace. Someone will see you and tell my uncle."

"We're old friends."

Lisette angrily stomped her foot. "You'll ruin everything."

"If you need me, I'll always be within hailing distance. Remember me, my love." Jean slipped through the door and was gone.

She threw up her hands in frustration. Jean would be back; of that she was sure. Why did he have to show up now? Lisette was finally getting a grip on her stormy emotions, and seeing Jean just brought up all the visions she was trying to forget. At least he couldn't approach her in public. If she guessed correctly, he was still wary of being brought in again by the Paris guard for questioning.

Blast him, she silently raged. She had forgotten about mass, and the court would notice she was missing.

Lisette pushed the thoughts aside. It was the dinner hour, and today she would dine at the King's table. Her uncle was a fanatic about dinner being served at precisely twelve-thirty. Michel was found; he was leaning against a wall engaged in conversation with . . . Alexia! Lisette steered her direction to avoid them, but fate wouldn't allow it. The Countess dogged her footsteps.

Alexia put a firm hand on Lisette's arm, pulling her along. "You are going to be late for dinner, and the court would frown at your breach in *étiquette.*"

"Let go of me, Alexia," Lisette fumed.

"As I was saying," the Countess continued, "your already scandalous reputation would take quite a beating from the gossips if you miss dinner as well as mass. Of course, I started the gossip, so I should know. Don't worry, my dear, it is only rumor that Louis shackles his dinner guests to the table and applies hot irons to their feet. Hurry up, Lady Lisette; you walk like a turtle."

The Countess halted their pace to pin a white lily on Lisette's dress. "This is the latest thing in the court. Only the bravest women wear them, because it's provocative and represents faith in the monarchy. Your uncle would insist, although I think it's a death sentence if anyone outside of this palace finds you wearing one."

"What are you doing here?" Lisette followed the Countess through the Hall of Mirrors. Her reflection bounced back to her in a dozen different angles. "You should be arrested for treason for the things you have done."

"Your King can't arrest me. I have special permission from Charles of Spain to be here. Jean asked me to look after you. He isn't happy with you for letting him think you went to the port. Actually, he put it a little differently, but I don't think you've heard some of the more expressive words he used."

Lisette inhaled to retaliate, and got an elbow in her ribs. They entered the dining room, and she had forgotten to curtsy. The mistake was noted by a frown from the head of the table where Louis's secretary sat. "I'm going to tell them you are a traitor," Lisette whispered as they sat down on stools. The table formed a semicircle to admit the servants who would bring the meal.

Alexia considered the threat and brightly smiled. "If you do, then I will announce to the world what you were doing with Jean that night on the river. Your reputation wouldn't live past the disclosure that you pushed a naked man into the river."

"That is blackmail," Lisette hissed. It was embarrassing to think the Baron's troops knew what they were doing that night. What was worse was that she had been so willing.

"*Sí*, it is. Smile; all the eyes of the court are on you."

Their whispering was noticed by the lords and ladies seated at the table. Lisette was sure her cheeks had turned crimson. Her black cotton dress was plain and dowdy, mortifying her in the room full of elegantly dressed people. Tomorrow she would see her solicitor and arrange for a new wardrobe. She wanted to crawl under the damask tablecloth and hide until then.

Alexia crunched Lisette's toes painfully under her slippered foot to get her attention. The Countess was speaking to a man who sat across the table from them.

The Spanish Countess sipped from the goblet of wine. "Normally, her uncle would introduce her, but under the circumstances, I shall. Lady Lisette, this is Sir Robert Wolling, of England." Alexia beamed her sarcasm. She didn't necessarily want Lisette to meet the man, but to get her to look across the table and stop staring at the silver plates. It had taken a lot of manipulation to get them all at the same end of the table. Luckily, the King wasn't there.

Lisette shyly nodded through the introductions. Her gaze followed Alexia's direction to the figure sitting several seats away at the end of the great table. The man Alexia wanted her to see was easily recognized. Dressed in a gold-embroidered coat with a lace cravat at his throat sat the Baron Jolbert. Lisette choked and covered her mouth with her serviette. He had changed his clothes, and a powdered wig now covered his dark hair. With his face still as tanned as ever, she thought he looked magnificent. It was good to see him dressed in something other than black. But his arrogance amazed her. If he were recognized, the guards would be called and he would be taken away. How did he think he could get away with it?

Lisette had to force herself to look away from the Baron's charming smile. The dinner was over, and she had hardly eaten a thing. Her stomach growled in dismay.

"Will you join me for a walk in the gardens, Lady Lisette?" Jean held his hand out to help her up.

Lisette was pulled to her feet, leaving all hopes of staving off the starvation in her belly. "What are you doing in here?" she asked testily. If she had been able to eat, she might have been more sociable.

Jean couldn't help but smile. He knew her appetite hadn't been quenched. "I have a picnic planned in the gazebo, Lisette. Would you care to join me?"

She didn't hesitate. Her stomach ruled her head. "You didn't answer me, Jean. What makes you think you won't be arrested?"

"The King is out hunting, and no one wold notice another gentleman at court. As to what I am doing here, I am romancing you, Lisette."

"You can't do that."

"I certainly can. I intend to leave France with you beside me. My friend has insisted this be done properly."

"I'll get even with him." Lisette pursed her lips in anger. Michel had turned her over to the enemy.

"Did I ever tell you that you look adorable when you get angry, Lisette?"

Lisette was escorted to the courtyard where a phaeton hitched to a pair of matched Barbs stood ready for them. Jean helped her into the carriage and settled beside her. The driver took the reins and cooed to the horses, prompting them into action.

True to his word, there was a picnic lunch set up in the park. Under the graceful bows of the ornate structure, she found hot scones and strawberry jam waiting for her. A succulent roast turkey and sweet cakes filled her empty stomach. They didn't have a care in the world when Jean opened a bottle of champagne and poured the drink into crystal glasses.

"To your health." She held the glass aloft in a toast. The ambrosia tasted of summer-sweet grapes, and the bubbles rose to tickle her nose. A short distance from them a minstrel played a lute in soft, romantic songs of lost lovers. Jean made polite conversation and inquired about her father. He shook his head, disgusted that the Duc de Meret hadn't answered her letter.

He became the man in her dreams again. But this time, it was real. The Baron who sat beside her was congenial, not the angry man she had met just two short months ago. He spoke of his family who had been taken to Spain. There were so many cousins to keep track of that Jean had to take a head tally when they boarded Simon's ship. There were only two first cousins, Paul and Simon. Forty-seven second cousins rivaled for good spouses and needed constant supervision. Jean couldn't count how far the family expanded after that. They numbered so many that Jean had had to build his own small city on the property he had purchased on the island of Las Palmas.

Lisette relaxed. The champagne worked its magic on her tangled nerves. She listened, surprised at how little she really knew the man she thought she loved.

"You'll never be bored, my sweet. You will be

mistress of seven houses in four different countries. Also, there are the visits to the Spanish court and the numerous other dignitaries who are requesting our attendance."

"So many." She sighed.

"I like variety, *petite.*"

In your women as well, she silently noted. Alexia was younger than she, but they were both spirited. The afternoon sun sparkled on her hair in hues of copper and gold, and her face held a special glow he hadn't noticed before.

"You have never looked lovelier, Lisette." Jean lay beside her. He propped his head on the crooked palm, enjoying the chance to look at her when she was happy. His legs stretched out as he relaxed. The park was nearly empty at this time of the day when the mothers took their children home for an afternoon nap. The late hours of the day were meant for lovers, and an unwritten law existed preventing those who strolled the lush paths from disturbing couples who reclined on the grassy knolls.

She was dwelling on the compliment. There was a mystical rapport building between them that she couldn't deny. They had shared paradise, and the longing for their lovemaking was prominent in her thoughts. The ache within her loins cried out for him.

"How can you think I look lovely when I am dressed as I am?" she said in afterthought.

A mischievous smile lit his mouth into a smile. "Because I know what lies beneath that dress, my dear."

"Oh." She could feel her cheeks grow warm again.

Jean leaned closer so that their lips were a breath apart. "I want to kiss you, Lisette. I fear my whiskers would tear your skin to ribbons."

She pulled her bottom lip between her teeth. "Is this the start of a new beard?" She wasn't sure she would like the harsh whiskers brushing against her tender skin.

"Don't you think I'll look distinguished?" he teased.

Lisette loved his face. He had the sort of features that never seemed to age. That boyish glint of a rogue would always be there. Her fingertips brushed the raw surface of his face. "I think I like you better without a beard."

He gently touched his lips to hers. Jean pulled himself upright so that he was sitting beside her. "No beard?"

She shook her head. "No beard."

The Baron stood and offered her his hand to help her up. "I have to take you back before someone starts asking questions about where you've gone."

Lisette didn't want to leave.

"Don't pout, my darling. I promise we'll see each other again." Jean tugged her to her feet and started walking her back to the carriage. "I am honoring your need to stay in Paris. I am a patient man, but don't make me wait too long."

"You're not staying at the palace, are you?" She had spent a pleasant afternoon and regretted returning to her dreary apartments at Versailles.

"No, I'm not that crazy. If you need me, ask Michel to send for me. I have already met with your uncle, and I won't be arrested again." Jean had paid the King's ransom for his freedom.

"I meant it when I said there was unfinished business here that needed my attention."

"By unfinished business do you mean getting Darias out of Meret?" Jean hadn't wanted to ask what she knew of her cousin's intervention in her province.

"What are you talking about?" She was perplexed. "Has Darias already taken over my inheritance?"

"Ask your father," Jean suggested, hoping to stay out of a family squabble.

"That I will." Lisette was alone in the carriage as it left the park. Jean didn't follow her back to the palace. She had so much to think about. What happened in her absence? The Duc had a lot of explaining to do, and Lisette wanted some immediate answers.

Lisette stopped in the hall outside her room at the palace and reached into her pocket. The note Jean had written her was short and to the point. It said *I love you.*

Chapter Twenty-four

Lisette stood in the doorway of her room. She shook her head, disbelieving the scene that was taking place inside the room. She slammed the door shut behind her, and Anna dropped the brushes she was unpacking. Everywhere Lisette looked was the Baron's influence. Her bed had the same soft blue silk quilt that she had used while she was at Avranches, and the thick Persian rugs covered her bare floors.

"Who let you in here?" she demanded of Anna.

"I did," Alexia purred. The Countess was sprawled on the divan with a glass of wine in one hand.

"How dare you invade my privacy? I'll have you both arrested for this."

"You beast!" Alexia rose from the couch and held Anna's oval face between her hands. "They would send her to prison or behead this young lady for a criminal offense. How could you be so vile? Just because you're irritable this evening is no reason to pick on Anna. She has tried her best to make you comfortable. After all, the room could use a little improvement."

Anna had tears sparkling on her pale lashes. Lisette couldn't have her arrested. "Then I will dismiss her." She felt a surge of pride. She had managed to slide out of Jean's manipulations.

"You can't do that either. Jean-Charles would beat her for leaving you even if she were dismissed. You must accept her and your liveryman."

"My liveryman?" Lisette felt trapped. "How can I have a liveryman, Alexia? I don't even own a horse. Paul shot mine. Of course, you wouldn't know that, because you weren't there."

"He felt terrible," Alexia assured the Duchess. "Jean sent Morning Glory to you, and Paul will manage the beast."

"Where does this end?" Lisette wearily conceded. The King wouldn't be back for several days, and in that time the Jolbert family could infiltrate his court.

Jean and Michel patiently waited outside Sainte-Chapelle while Lisette confessed her sins to the priest. The day had turned blistering hot, and they had had to delay the first launching of Lisette's balloon until the weather cooled.

Jean paced the sidewalks, waiting for her to come out. "If I said all the penance the priest gave me, I'd be on my knees until I was seventy years old."

Michel agreed with the priest's wisdom, but tactfully changed the subject. "I see you decided not to grow your beard."

Jean glared at Michel. "She didn't like it."

The Marquis raised a silver flask to his lips and heartily drank of the fiery brew within. Lazily he reclined on the driver's seat of a rented carriage. "I thought about growing a mustache."

"Don't bother. It wouldn't help. Where have you been for the last week?"

"Ah, she was a sweet young thing."

Jean scoffed. "I'll make a wager that you can't even remember her name, can you, Michel?"

Michel emptied the flask. "No, I can't say that I recall what she said her name was." He raked the sandy curls on the top of his head as a hundred different names went through his memory. He honestly couldn't revive an image of the lass.

Jean turned and paced the length of the stone walkway again. "I always wondered if you didn't have something crawling around in that hair of yours. Don't you ever use a brush?"

"Brushes are for horses. My, but you're grouchy today. Did Lisette turn down your proposal again last night?"

Jean refused to answer. All week long he had been on his best behavior, and still she turned him down. Patience was his strong point, although that was becoming sorely tried of late. He wanted Lisette back in his arms again.

Michel laughed to himself. The Baron was in love and finally admitted it. "I'm taking her to meet her father today, Jean. Why don't you wait at your hôtel, and I'll bring her there when she's finished?"

"That serpent," Jean seethed. "The Duc has made her wait for a week to see him, proclaiming to have pressing *parlement* duties to attend. He's been padding the royal throne for himself, and Louis doesn't see it."

Lisette emerged from the chapel to find Jean waiting for her. When she confessed the intimacy of their relationship, the priest had urged her to marry the Baron or not to see Jean again. She was reminded of her duty to her country and obedience to her father. Absolution was given, and she envisioned herself on her knees for the next two years to say all the penance she received from the priest.

Somehow, she couldn't bring herself to tell the good
father about the illegitimate child she carried.

That secret was shared with only one other liv-
ing soul. Lisette had confided her condition to
Anna. The maid had promised not to tell anyone or
Lisette swore to have her arrested and executed.

Her day had a bleak outlook. What the priest
asked of her troubled her. Marry him or stay away
from him, that was what she was told to do. How
could she marry him when she was still so unsure
of him? Jean asked her every day, sometimes even
twice a day, to become his wife. It was the nagging
doubts about his relationship with Alexia that
stopped her. Jean wasn't open to questions about
the Spanish Countess, claiming that Lisette already knew too much for her own good. Yet living
her life without him seemed impossible.

Lisette liked the Baron who took long walks with
her and went to the opera with her. He fell asleep
during a symphony and woke with her elbow in his
ribs. Knowing she was angry with him, he kissed
her hand and said he would cherish the bruise forever. How could she go on being angry with him
when he was so charming?

He was her friend during these days at the palace when the other nobles whispered about her
scandalous abduction and treated her as if she had
the plague. Lisette and Anna would sit for hours
giggling about the latest rumor the maid had heard
about Lady Lisette and her dramatic life. Mistress
Prissy, the schoolmistress, was privately tutoring
the young Princess, and was the worst source of information. Prissy never got it right or knew the full
story. By the time the hottest gossip got back to Lisette, the truth had been distorted into a vicious lie.

At the moment, she didn't want to talk to Jean.
The pain she relived in telling the priest of her love

for the tall Baron was still too fresh in her thoughts.

As if reading her deliberation, Jean helped her into the carriage but didn't follow. "Was it that bad, Lisette?"

She gave an exasperated sigh. "I will talk to you later, after I've seen my father."

"If it's any consolation, the priest wasn't any easier on me."

A sarcastic laugh resounded from her throat. "I'm sure between the two of us he's heard quite a tale in the past few days."

Jean was glad to see her sense of humor was still there. "If I might offer a bit of advice?" He hesitated briefly, then charged ahead. "Be careful of Darias, Lisette. He has more power than your father realizes. Not only does he control Meret, but he is ill-advising the Duc."

Lisette always suspected her cousin would worm his way into the Duc's good graces.

Jean didn't want to tell her, but he thought she should be prepared for the worst. "Ask your father, Lisette. If I'm wrong, he'll deny the boy any rights to Meret. But if I'm right, you no longer have your heritage."

Lisette held her quivering chin high. Jean mounted his borrowed horse and rode off, disappearing into the city streets. She knew what Jean was trying to say. If Darias did control Meret, there would be no province for her to inherit; she would receive a small dowry and nothing more. Her better judgment told her that Jean was right. And he stood nothing to gain by lying to her. Yet Lisette vowed that she wouldn't be cheated out of her birthright.

The driver had promptly left to spend an hour in a local tavern, leaving Michel to defend the team of Barbs. When the driver returned, the Marquis surrendered the reins to him and climbed into the carriage, sitting across from Lisette. With his charge released, Michel couldn't suppress his gleeful mood.

"What are you grinning at?" she angrily snapped.

"I have to wonder why you need to see a priest for forgiveness, my lady. You were kidnapped and ravished against your will."

"Jean didn't rape me! It's because I was a willing partner in his scheme of revenge that I came here."

Michel sat upright with a start. "Thank heavens! You really do love him, don't you?"

"I could have you whipped, Michel."

"I was right," he said in wonder, and fell back against the cushions.

"If you repeat that to anyone, I will have your heart plucked out. Understand?"

Michel persisted. "If the Baron is right and you have lost Meret, why not denounce your heritage and rejoin your love?"

"He is a renegade," she said softly. "I have a duty to France. My uncle wants me to be a saint incarnate so the other young women in the court have someone to look up to. I love this country," she said solemnly.

"Will your duty and honor keep you warm at night, or relieve your loneliness in your old age? My friend is mad to have you back with him. He will do anything for you if you come with him of your own free will."

"I just wish I could trust Jean. When he told me that he loved me, I would have followed him around the world. That was before I found out the happy couple consisted of three, not the cozy twosome that I had imagined. Jean won't tell me anything about

Alexia because I already know too much. I love him, to be sure, but not enough to share him."

She glared at Michel in response to his deep rumble of laughter.

"Forgive me, my lady. My friendship with the Baron is the reason for my humor, not your anger. The troop will never forget the night Jean discovered you weren't at the port. They searched the area for three days, and didn't rest until Alexia sent word that you were expected at Versailles. Once again, Jean is a victim of a misunderstanding. Alexia pampers him in many ways, although not in the Baron's bedchamber."

"Then why has Alexia warned me to stay away from Jean?" Lisette was relieved and confused at the relationship between Jean and Alexia.

"Probably because you represent a threat in a different way. She has had him all to herself for two years, and now she must share him with you. I know my friend doesn't intend for the two women in his life to live together. Jean had a *hacienda* built for Alexia, should she decide to remain in Spain." Michel felt it was not his place to reveal any more to Lisette about Alexia's relationship with Jean.

"It still doesn't make sense," Lisette pouted.

"Trust me, Lady Lisette. Jean loves you."

"He loves her, also."

"Not the same way." Michel hoped he had put her fears to rest. It was ironic that Jean had lost her because of his relationship with Alexia. The Countess was very possessive of Jean; that much he had seen with his own eyes. It vexed him that Lisette wouldn't fight for her love. She accepted defeat by Alexia before the war had begun.

Lisette sighed. "I just don't know what to believe."

"You know in your soul that he loves you."

"Jean is still a stranger to me," she argued.

"I was there the day you were betrothed to my friend, and I saw the joy in him."

Lisette tipped her head curiously. "I don't remember seeing you."

"No doubt my presence was missed. Neither of you would have noticed if the earth had opened up that day and swallowed us all. The love you shared was evident to all of us who watched the event. Believe in the man who loves you, Lisette. It was not my purpose to distress you, only to counsel you on the love of my friend. His foolish pride has nearly destroyed us all. More foolish than he, I stood by and silently watched the discord between you grow until I loved you, and ached for a swift resolution between you and Jean."

"Michel?" she questioned. He tenderly took her hand in his. "Are you in love with me?" She brushed a stray curl from his forehead, understanding why he was so irresistible to women. Gentle Michel of profound emotion could easily claim her heart if it didn't already belong to Jean.

A smile brought out the warm lights in his brown eyes. "I do love you, in my own way." He brought her palm to his lips and kissed it sweetly. The warm contact was broken. Michel abruptly withdrew. "I apologize for my actions. I had no right."

It was her turn to laugh, and she relished the moment. "Your sin is forgiven and my honor is saved. In truth, I enjoyed it."

"If that small act of my deep affection for you had been witnessed by the Baron, I have no doubt this would be my last day on earth. Jean has warned me that if I forgot myself and made love to you, he'd have me horsewhipped. The one time I mentioned your beauty, he sat me down and drew diagrams of the torture he would put me through. His eloquent descriptions were enough to bring me to my senses."

"Jean has no claim on me. I may kiss whomever I choose without fear of rebuke from him."

"You may not fear him, but I do." Michel took out his silk *mouchoir* and dabbed at the beads of sweat on his forehead.

"Would you?" Lisette was astonished at his confessional. "I mean, would you want to make love to me? After bedding half the women in Europe, how could you find me desirable? Why, every time I turn around there is another woman in your arms."

"Jean would kill me if he knew I thought . . . never mind. Your beauty is enough to turn a man's senses into butter. I would marry you myself if Jean would let me live through the ceremony."

The carriage reached the Hôtel de Ville where the Duc had taken up his residence while in Paris. The towering walls stood three stories high. A clock and bell tower strutted from the peaked, red-tiled roof, and an arched gateway admitted them to one of the finest hôtels of the *haut monde*. The rooms within housed the Mayor of Paris, celebrated officials from around the world, and wealthy nobles from the far corners of France who gathered to discuss world politics.

Lisette was a bundle of nerves. Michel held her cold hand in his and prompted her forward to her father's suite. The pieces of her life were falling into a neat little puzzle. No wonder her father didn't see her in the years she was at the school. The Duc was busy molding a surrogate son to take his place and didn't have time for a daughter who would marry after leaving the finishing school.

For a moment she thought of her father as an evil man. The Duc had robbed her Baron of his marriage contract, defending such a ruthless action by obtaining witnesses against the Earl and having the King issue a *lettre* to have him imprisoned. The Duc was found guilty of embezzlement by Lisette's standards.

The King had replied to her request, and the Earl was being cleared of all the charges against him. The document was being drawn up by the King's secretary, and she would present it to Jean within the week. Lisette had won a small victory against the men who controlled her life. Now she would strive to regain control of Meret. It was her home and promised to her by the Duc.

Michel knocked on the door for her.

The Duc's valet admitted them into the salon. Michel made himself comfortable on the peach-tinted, brocade-covered settee while Lisette nervously paced the length of the room. Heavy sea-green-colored drapes blocked the warmth of the afternoon sun, giving the room a dismal appearance. She fingered an ivory statue of the Greek goddess of wisdom, Athena, that stood four feet high. Lisette wrinkled her nose and frowned at the Italian wrought-iron scrollwork around the pink stone fireplace. There was a painting, or at least what she would call a torrid example of a bad copy, of Michelangelo's *Leda* hanging on the wall.

Michel chuckled at her observation. "This room housed one of your grandfather's courtesans. Ostentatious, isn't it?"

Lisette scowled at him. Moments later, the Duc de Meret opened the door.

Philippe de Meret was awed at the little girl who had grown up to become a breathtaking beauty. He opened his arms.

"Missie. We have been apart too long."

Lisette didn't run into his embrace but kept her distance. She had forgotten how much she despised him.

Michel perused the man who entered with the
Duc. It was Darias, and they instantly recognized
each other. Michel had been with Jean the day the
betrothal was broken, as Darias had been with the
Duc. The Marquis surveyed the young man who
was the embodiment of the Duc de Meret. Darias
had the Duc's hair coloring and their eyes were the
same blue as Lisette's. Her cousin stood behind the
Duc, idly watching her. Darias had a volatile temper, and rumors had it that he was treacherous
when the mood struck him.

Michel had found out that Darias had promised
the King he would handle the situation and bring
about a settlement between the feuding families.
The King didn't know Darias's ambitions far ex-
ceeded controlling Meret. The Duc's province was
too poor to support Darias, and he knew he needed
money to control the throne. The Jolbert heir
would provide him with the funds he needed, and
the Duc's popularity would guarantee that he
would have a following when he took over. Darias
had planned the Duc's future out in detail, and had
managed to set his plotting into motion when he
forged the Duc's signature and Lisette was mysteriously called home.

Michel mused that Darias thought his deeds had
gone unnoticed at the palace. The Marquis had intervened, and the King had received an earful
about the gaining popularity of the Duc de Meret
and the peculiar habits of Darias. Michel had some
power of his own to deploy. Through the women he
bedded, he had secretly sent a warning to the King
to take notice of his brother, the Duc de Meret. He
knew how well gossip traveled when a young maid
thought she had found out a new piece of intrigue
to whisper to the King's servants. Discreet insubordination was so much healthier than an open
challenge of war, Michel had said before. It was a

code which he lived by. The Marquis hoped to undermine all of Darias's plots before the worst had come to pass and Lisette was totally within his grasp.

Darias was dangerous, but so were Jean and Michel.

Chapter Twenty-five

Lisette stood back and looked at her father. Without the peruke, his dark red hair had silver wings feathering from his forehead and temples. The years had aged him, but the spark of the man she once knew was still there. His body was leaner than she remembered, his cheekbones even more prominent than they were two years ago when she had bid him *adieu* and, like an obedient daughter, journeyed to Paris to attend finishing school. Dark lines were chiseled around his blue eyes, presenting a portrait of a man who lived well and laughed with vigor. If Lisette admitted the truth, it would be that she had idolized her august father in her youth. It was the Duc who could keep the hounds of hell at bay through childhood nightmares. While her mother had been stern, the Duc was a loving father. That is, she thought, until the day he sent her away.

There was an awkward pause as they surveyed each other. Lisette realized she had grown up and no longer needed the monsters chased away in the middle of the night. She wanted her fiancé back, and the life she had dreamed about for so long.

"You look tired, Your Grace," she said at last.

"The *parlement* keeps me busy."

"May I speak to you privately?" Darias lurked in the shadows.

The Duc noticed the Marquis Michel le Maire for the first time. Cool contempt passed between them as recognition dawned in the Duc's eyes. "What is this man to you?"

Lisette didn't like the tone of her father's voice. "The Marquis helped bring me back to Paris. He is my dearest friend and counsel. I owe him my life."

The Duc ignored her. He waved a jeweled hand at Darias. "Stay close, I shall want to see you soon."

Darias approached her with a blasé nasal ring to his speech. He kissed her cheeks, recoiling from the touch of a woman. "How nice to see you, Lady Lisette."

Her stomach threatened to turn.

Michel took his leave with Darias. They were kindred spirits in a strange sort of way; both men tried to direct Lisette's life, although of the two, Michel considered he had the upper hand. The Marquis certainly had more practice at playing the game. In his years in attendance at court, Michel had finely tuned his skills of verbal battle, deploying all of his tactics to keep one step ahead of the other nobles.

The Marquis eyed Darias with disdain. "Do you dress like that on purpose? The couture's seem to have left you in the lurch." Darias grunted in rage. Michel believed that Darias considered himself very stylish, when in fact he looked like a dejected rake who wore clothes several years out of style.

"For instance"—Michel sauntered down the hall with Darias salivating in anger—"your cravat is wilted. A gentleman of any honor wouldn't be caught dead in lace, unless of course it's Venetian, and it must be starched. Your hose lacks color, and your jacket is putrid. In fact, your whole wardrobe is tasteless."

Lisette heard Michel's speech. He was a dear, keeping Darias occupied while she pried some information out of the Duc. She turned to her father now that they were alone. With her mind set on the humiliation she had suffered the night she was abducted, she set aside all thoughts of making demure little comments. She was about to have a bold and perilous confrontation with the Duc, and didn't think she'd live to discuss it with Jean over tea in the afternoon. Of all things, the Duc most hated insubordinates challenging him. Lisette had no doubt she was considered dispensable. If she had really meant something to her father, he would have sent for her directly after her return to the palace, not made her wait like a servant.

"Why didn't you try to rescue me when the Baron abducted me?" Lisette demanded.

The Duc feigned innocence. "I didn't know the Baron had intercepted you and kept you prisoner. Darias informed me that you had been sent on to England as we had planned. He told me later that it was to protect my health."

"Why were you sending me to England, Your Grace? Did you find a new husband for me?" The icy edge of her voice was a warning that she knew far more than he imagined.

"A new marriage contract has been drawn up and you will wed a count in England." The Duc de Meret didn't like his daughter's scrutiny.

Lisette could see through all of his deceptions. She clenched her kidskin gloves in her hand, suppressing the desire to slap him.

"I want to know why you broke the marriage contract with the Baron. Don't try to tell me it was because of the Earl. There is no real act of treason in the Jolbert family. You took his money, set up a shipping port with the rights to the north shore the Baron granted you, and when it came time for us to wed, you changed your mind. What possessed you to do something that stupid? The Baron could have been a strong ally to you, but you insisted on turning the wrath of one of the most powerful families in Europe on us."

All her daughterly love was gone. A determined woman stood before the Duc, angry that she had lost her love because of the greed of an old man. She deeply resented him for his meddling. He was an opportunist, and Lisette saw him for what he really was. The Duc de Meret had no more decency than Darias.

"You impertinent little bitch!" The Duc regained his tongue. "Darias tried to warn me that you had become a willful wench. The Jolberts have become too powerful and represent a threat to me. They had to be eliminated. Under Darias's guidance, I have made a few changes."

"Speaking of my cousin, isn't there something you would like to tell me, Father? Are you going to make the announcement that he will inherit the province? You must think me a fool!"

The back of his hand stung her cheek. "I will beat you for your insulting attitude, Lisette."

Lisette stared out of tear-filled eyes. "It's true, isn't it? You intend to cheat me as well as the Jolberts." The Duc raised his hand again, and this time the blows were meant to hurt, not just punish her for the insinuations. Her arms covered her head in defense and her form crumpled to the floor.

He was furious and turned his anger against her. His foot shot out and kicked at her ribs. The agony was fierce. She almost blacked out from the pain that burned in her side. Lisette had to know the rest of her father's crimes.

"You sold me to the highest bidder, then renounced your promise to the Jolberts so that you could finance your path to the throne, didn't you,

Father?" From her position on the floor, her eyes shone upward to the Duc's.

"I have done nothing that wasn't for the good of France," he stormed. "You have no right to question my motives or actions. Your cousin will inherit Meret because it is his *droit* to do so, not yours."

"I detest the both of you. How dare you justify your acts of treason by professing to have the good of France at heart? Hasn't everything you've done in the past two years been with the throne in mind? I hear you are quite popular." Scorn rang clearly in her voice. "The Duc de Meret grants what his brother can't. You give the people your promise to reform our government and do away with the nobility, but they don't know it's to line your pockets with their gold and to sit yourself on your brother's throne. What will you do when the people call your bluff and find out what a dupe you really are? The great Duc de Meret lives on the handouts of the King and uses a sham marriage with his daughter to hire the cutthroats to do his bidding."

The fury boiled within the Duc, intensifying to a level of abomination.

Lisette saw the blow coming before his hand struck her head. She didn't move fast enough. A scream tore from her throat as his fist made contact and she was knocked off her knees and fell to her back, unconscious.

Michel moved as if struck by lightning. He had been toying with Darias, and now used the bodkin previously needed for cleaning his nails while berating Darias to attach his foe to the wall by a quick thrust of the blade between Darias's arm and side through his tawdry jacket. It nailed Darias to the wall behind him, immobilizing him. The Marquis left him there, dangling a foot off the blue-carpeted floor.

Michel threw the door open. He found Lisette inanimate on the floor with blood dripping from her mouth. The argument had been clearly overheard by the Marquis, but Michel couldn't imagine how he could have missed the sounds of Lisette being beaten. Several servants came down the hall to offer assistance. The Marquis had to get her to safety first, then deal with the Duc. In his own trembling fury, he didn't say a word. Michel stepped into the room, scooped the lifeless woman into his arms, and departed the scene before the anguished Duc could stop him. The gaping eyes of over a dozen eminent statesmen followed the broken form of Lisette as Michel passed through the elegant hôtel. There were gasps from the women and grumblings from the men not to interfere where the Duc de Meret was concerned. Michel's face was frozen in savage violence.

While astounded footmen held the doors open for him, Michel walked out of the hôtel. He effortlessly carried Lisette to the carriage, and once inside issued a command to whip the horses into a gallop. Michel had never felt so useless in his life. He held Lisette in his arms, and tears stung his eyes at what he saw before him. Why hadn't his plans for her happiness worked out? What did it take to get through to two stubborn people? While Jean and Lisette lived in a world of kisses reserved for lovers, reality was corrupt and greedy. A vicious game of truth or dare was turning them all into animals.

A drop of her blood fell to the white leather seat cushion. Michel swore under his breath and cradled Lisette to his chest. His cravat was soaked with her blood. She stirred, lifting a hand to her head.

Michel eased the prying fingers from the red-ness of her cheek. "Be still, Lady Lisette." His command was choked with thoughts of revenge.

Lisette forced herself to sit up in the carriage. "Take me back to the palace, Michel. I don't want Jean to see me like this."

"He is waiting for you." Michel was fed up with allowing the people he cared about to make their own choices when they were clearly all out of their minds.

"Let him wait. Take me to Versailles. I have had my fill of temperamental men for today."

Michel used a fist to bang on the carriage walls. "To Versailles," he ordered. With a murderous glint in his brown eyes, he turned on the seat to face Lisette. "Why did you prompt him to do this, Lisette?"

"I don't remember asking him to beat me!" She swayed against the seat. "How was I to find out the truth, Michel? Should I have asked him politely?" she offered. "Or just accept the lies?" She withdrew into her own mind. Michel was in a foul mood, and she ached all over. Her immediate fear was for her child. There was no pain in her belly, and she thought herself safe from losing her precious baby. Her mouth was swollen, and her lips still bled from being bumped against her teeth. Tomorrow she would have a blackened eye to show for her talk with her father.

When they reached the servants' entrance at the palace, Michel carried her up the stairs despite her protests. The Marquis strolled past the wide-eyed servants without a care for what they thought. It wasn't until she was safely tucked into bed that he released his charge. Michel tipped his hat and left her to Anna's care.

Jean and Michel would deal with the Duc de Meret within a fortnight. Michel walked the short distance to the inn where Jean was staying. The

Baron sat in the hôtel's sidewalk café with a glass of port for company. To those who strolled by, it was a serene picture of the café's tables filled with gracious ladies and gentlemen from the aristocracy. To those who looked closely, the Black Baron and a handful of trusted men relaxed at the tables. Michel easily approached his old friend.

"She saw her father?" Jean asked casually. His friend betrayed his contempt with tightly clenched fists.

"He beat her, Jean." He stated it in a matter-of-fact tone. "Lady Lisette will recover from the wounds her father inflicted. They are simple bruises and contusions, nothing like the scars on her heart."

Jean hadn't heard anything past Michel's admission that his lady had been bloodied by her father. Why had he let this come to pass? Jean lit a cheroot and inhaled deeply of rich tobacco leaves. He exhaled slowly, and a puff of smoke drifted from the outdoor café.

"I want the Duc destroyed." There was a cold, calculating glint to his gray eyes. "For Lisette's sake, I have left the Duc alone. That promise no longer applies. He must be politically and personally ruined." Jean set the glass of port to his lips, savoring the moment of revenge. "I want him run out of Paris like a common criminal, then brought to me."

Michel's hands rested on the golden head of his cane as he listened to Jean. Now that the Marquis had the order, he would utterly destroy the Duc de Meret. He nodded in agreement, and a smile curled on his mouth for the first time in several hours.

"As you command, my lord."

The Marquis rose from the wrought-iron chair and spotted Paul lounging sleepily in a chair tipped to rest against the whitewashed walls. He saluted his old comrade and left the café to return to the palace. There was a lift to his soul that he badly needed after finding Lisette trounced by her father. That would all change. Very soon now, Paris would be the host of the Baron's revenge. It would be the center of small talk at the best of soirées for years to come.

For once in his life, Michel passed the coquettish flirting of a palace maid. The Marquis was a man with a purpose, and hell-bent to carry out his orders.

Lisette impatiently plucked a rose from the garden path and tore the petals from the blossom, dropping them to the stone walkway. She had waited several weeks for the King to finish his investigation of the charges against the Earl, and to issue the orders for him to be free from the *lettre.* If only they could find the Earl. Her uncle had sent agents to every prison in France in desperate search for him, and as yet the Earl's whereabouts were still unknown.

Louis understood her reasons when she respectfully declined all social invitations until the bruises healed. Lisette was grateful to avoid the suspicious stares of the ladies in court.

Anna was her companion during Lisette's seclusion and her only true friend. The maid knew about the child and had won Lisette's trust for not telling the Baron.

Following the priest's advice, Lisette refused to see Jean again, and that made the loneliness worse.

Lisette wore the sapphire-colored silk dress that Jean liked so much. Anna had had to let the bodice out to accommodate Lisette's flourishing chest. Without the pannier hoops to support the yards of

silk gathered at her waist, the skirt trailed behind
her.

Lisette was pouting. The King was giving a costume ball in honor of a visiting dignitary, and she
had had to refuse without an escort. Michel was
Alexia's companion for the evening, leaving Lisette to sulk while the gardens filled with the drifting melody. Inside the brightly lit palace, the lords
and ladies sipped champagne and danced.

How she wished she could be there with them.
Her consolation was that her father's popularity
with the people had taken a turn for the worse.
After the episode when he had beaten her, the
parlement began to question some of his policies,
and it wasn't long thereafter when he was asked to
step down from his seat. His conspiracies were all
discovered, and he had to leave Paris a broken
man. In her silent world, Lisette had plenty of time
to think about her father.

It was with a startling realization that she found
she still loved him, even though he would give her
inheritance to Darias. Perhaps he had been mis-
guided and Darias was to blame for his treachery.
Her questions would be answered when she returned to Meret for a brief visit, then traveled on
to a convent until her child was born. Lisette
couldn't bear to stay in the same house with Darias. She would never give her cousin the satisfaction of throwing her out of her own house.

Lisette sat down on a stone bench in the garden
to reflect on the weeks she spent at the palace. She
had undermined her father's desire to wed her to
an English count. When the summons arrived to
take her to England, she wrote a letter to the Count
stating that she was entering a convent and
couldn't marry because her heart belonged to another. The other man in her life wasn't explained,
and she hoped the Count believed she had commit-

ted her life to the Church. It had stopped all further questions in the court regarding her morality. The King was pleased with her announcement, and she could finally have peace of mind knowing her father couldn't use her in another ploy to best some poor dolt who accepted her hand in a marriage contract. The Count's agent had called on the Duc de Meret before His Grace had left the *parlement* one sunny afternoon, and all of Paris had heard the conversation that left the Duc humiliated. He was called out as a coward and a cheat before the other nobles, and would never regain their trust.

Lisette was restless. She couldn't seem to focus her thoughts on any one thing before she was daydreaming about Jean again. Remembering his lovemaking started a tremble in the secret part of her that only he could reach. The dreams would wake her at night, leaving her drenched in a cold sweat. Lisette wanted him to come back and re-create that night of passion they had shared beside the Seine, and then, crazily enough, to go away and leave her in peace. How could she ever trust him again after he said he had tired of her?

Her head fell back and moonlight glistened on her throat as she groaned. Why couldn't love be easy? The stars above seemed tranquil. Why couldn't she borrow some of their repose and make wanting Jean cease to overcome her meditation?

"Be careful what you wish for, my lady." A dark figure spoke from behind one of the orchard tree trunks.

The sound was a healing balm against her ragged nerves. Lisette didn't need to see him to know that it was her Baron. How often she had heard that sensuous, deep tone touch her fantasy she couldn't remember. Jean was hidden in the shadows, waiting for her to call for him. "Where are you?"

"I'm on that star in the sky that just gave you your wish. I'm that whisper in the breeze that calls your name. Come back to me, my love."

Lisette smiled to her phantom lover. "I never knew you were such a romantic. Isn't it a gorgeous evening? I want to go dancing. That's what I wished for." She hugged her bare arms. "Wrap me in your enchantment and make me forget the hurting."

Jean came from his hiding place and took her into the sanctuary of his arms. She felt warm and vibrant leaning against him. "I never meant to hurt you, Lisette."

She pressed her fingers to his lips. "No, don't say it. Tonight I don't want to think about what has happened between us. Kiss me."

He touched her moist cherry lips to his and her arms went around his neck, pulling his mouth closer. To withdraw from the kiss seemed an unbearable effort. Her lush chest pressed against him, and he forgot the purpose of his visit. Starlight sparkled in her eyes, and her dark lashes fell slowly over the beautiful orbs and they closed. The blush on her cheeks was the color of a peach ripened in the sunlight to give a faint glow to the delicious fruit within. He had tasted the nectar of her innocence and wanted more.

"Dance with me," she breathed against his lips.

Jean couldn't stop as he, too, became entangled in the allure of the magic night spinning them in a cocoon of passion. The music started again, and this time it was a waltz composed by Mozart. He released her long enough to bow. "May I have this dance, Lady Lisette?"

She gracefully curtsied. "I shall have no other, my lord." One of her small hands was tucked into his, and the other lightly touched his shoulder.

His arm circled her waist, and the length of her

auburn hair tickled the back of his hand. The scent of jasmine rose from her perfumed breasts, filling his nostrils, and her silk-covered hips occasionally brushed against his thighs as they performed the steps. Jean's actions were automatic; he couldn't remember turning through the graceful stride of the waltz. His thoughts centered on Lisette. Her upturned face radiated a beauty that held him transfixed to the lovely woman.

Jean sensed that Lisette was in her dreamworld again, and even though she could remember the anger that had passed between them, she didn't want to. If he were completely honest with himself, he wouldn't want to think about what hurt they had suffered either. It was a night of paradise and promises, and at this moment, he was on that star in the heavens.

Chapter Twenty-six

Jean couldn't risk being seen in the gardens. The guests visiting the great hall of Versailles would soon start filling the garden paths with lovers stealing away for a private tête-à-tête. He maneuvered Lisette near the servants' entrance of the palace, never breaking the pace to alarm her. A smile of accomplishment twitched the corners of his mouth. She wasn't aware of anything else but his arms around her, and the contact of the warm kiss he expertly placed on the sensitive hollow beneath her ear. He let caution fly to the wind and explored the tantalizing full curve of her bottom lip with the tip of his tongue, and traced the perfect heart shape of her upper lip with deliberate ease. There was no resistance to his tongue as he parted her lips and probed within. Her eyes were a smoldering midnight blue, and her lashes lowered as the feelings engulfed her.

His chest heaved in a groan. She clung to him, igniting the fire of yearnings too long withheld. Guarded in the crooks of his arms, her body trembled against him, and he involuntarily answered her sexual hunger with his own. His eyes closed to still the desire to take her on the garden path. All he could think about was sinking into her and having her rose-petal softness sheathe his manhood.

With one arm at her back, the other swept under her legs and she was cradled in his arms. Jean bent his head to kiss her tender lips as he carried her up the stairs. He knew the location of her room as well as he knew his own name. There were so many nights in the past month and a half when he had paced outside her door, afraid that if he knocked she would refuse to see him. The guests and servants were all detained at the reception, and his dark figure went unnoticed at the palace.

A single tallow candle cast a glow around the room. Jean closed the door to her chamber with a kick of his foot. He stood her before him, and his breath caught at seeing her eyes, crystallized in smoldering passion to a smoky sapphire. His deft fingers found the line of buttons at the back of her neck, and one by one they were conquered. The gown fell open when his hands smoothed the fabric aside in a feather-light motion, falling on the floor in a rich blue cloud. The cinnamon peaks of her breasts strained through the silk chemise as he tested the weight in his hands, brushing the nipples with his thumbs in a gentle caress until they were hardened points tearing at the thin material. It was all so familiar to him, and yet different in a way that he couldn't explain. The contours of her body which he knew so well had taken on a womanly lushness that he devoured with his lazy gaze. Candlelight silhouetted the provocative sway of her hips in the gauzy chemise. She walked to the bed and threw back the drapes, then held him mesmerized while her arms crossed in front of her and she inched the chemise over her head, leaving her naked.

Jean divested himself of his garments. His gaze followed Lisette, fearing that if he looked away for a second, she would disappear and he would wake up from the dream and the agony of wanting her would remain. She poured them a goblet of wine. Their fingers touched off a spark as she handed the goblet to him and his hands folded over hers. He drank deeply of the fine Burgundy, then surrendered the goblet back to her. The temptress before him took a sip from the goblet, then tipped her head back and trickled a stream of scarlet wine down her lily-white skin. She put the silver chalice down on the nightstand beside her bed. His anticipation quickened as he saw the direction of the fiery liquid. It dripped from her nipple and coursed a path to the dark patch above her thighs.

His tongue licked at the drop that fell from her breast, and this time she groaned. Catching her up into his arms, he carried her to the bed and laid her back against the feather mattress. With her legs dangling over the side of the bed, he urged her slim calves around him as he followed the path of the wine. He found his delight in tasting her hardened nipples, then sought the haven of dark fur between her legs.

She mewed in response, winding her hands through his hair as his tongue flicked in and out of her, building a tension that crumbled into mind-shattering ecstasy. Lisette shivered against it, wanting it to stop before it consumed her completely, but she was already too late. Spasms shook her body and she was suspended in the vortex of sensual delight.

Her mind was crazed with needing him. Lisette writhed beneath his touch as fiery kisses branded her skin; this hip belonged to Jean, that breast was unequivocally his. He demanded ownership, and she gave herself to him for eternity.

"Let me have all of you," she pleaded. Leaning forward, she guided him and ever so slowly allowed his hardness to enter her, withdrawing when he eagerly acknowledged her ministration, sinking deeper into the wet velvet world within her that now readily accepted the intrusion of the full width and breadth of him. His feet were spread apart on the floor to give him balance, and his hands braced his body against the canopy. She wrapped her legs around him and started an indolent rhythm that teased and incited them both.

His body trembled from holding back. Jean withdrew from the warm, slippery haven and eased her body to the center of the bed. He gently bit her shoulder to punish her for the torment she caused. He had a little agony of his own to inflict, and grasping her hips pulled her down hard on him. She gave a muffled cry as the full length of him thrust into her body, clutching the sheets as his hands grasped her by the hips and pulled her up to meet the delicious extent of him. His love words took her with him into the realm of whirling orgasm.

Tears streamed down her cheeks when release finally unraveled her aching muscles. His seed was warm on her legs when he rolled over onto his back beside her. They were tears of relief that rushed from her eyes, and drops of regret. Together they were something special, but apart they were both miserable. Lisette pushed the qualms to the back of her mind. She reached across him and took the goblet of wine that was left on her nightstand to her lips, savoring the moment of fulfillment.

Jean had relaxed, but as she stretched across him her nipples brushed his chest, and the blood rushed to his groin all over again. He couldn't get enough of her. Every time he thought he would die from the blissful oblivion that always followed when he made love to her, she would make the tiniest of movements, and his senses went crazy. He brushed the curls from her face and framed her head between his hands.

This time, he was infinitely tender. He tucked
her body under his and her thighs opened to accept
him. She sighed in wistful surrender and wrapped
her arms around him and caressed the hard muscles in his back. The tissue inside her was dis-
tended and swollen. He had loved her too hard. He
reminded himself that she was a lady, and not like
the riverfront whores who were used to a man's
needs on an hourly basis. He slowly took her to the
summit. Pure joy glowed on her face as this time
they opened their innermost selves to relish the
moment of union.

"I love you, Jean," she whispered against his
lips. He lay beside her, smoothing the hair from her
face. They collapsed and fell asleep together, a harmony of two souls who had found happiness. Their
bodies and minds were joined in love and passion.

There was a phrase that crept into her drowsy
mind. *What God has joined, let no man part.* She
could almost smell the flowers in her wedding bouquet. Orchids were her choice; white against white
would be her wedding gown. It was the virgin white
of the old Bourbon families and her lineage. The
red and gold colors of the Jolbert banner curled in
the wind above them. It was a dream, she reminded herself. It lifted the fog of sleep, pulling her
to a conscious state of mind. They hadn't married
on that afternoon. That was part of the old pact between them. Now he wanted her to be his mistress,
or his wife in name, and yet not in his heart. Her
eyes opened to see him beside her.

"I love you, Lisette. Will you come away with
me?"

"To Spain?" she whispered.

"Anywhere you want to go, my love. I will take
you to America if you want to travel that far."

His breathy voice was warm against her ear. "I
wish I could trust you, Jean," she said honestly.

"Once, I would have gone to Spain or anywhere else you went because I couldn't bear to be without you. You make me feel things that I didn't think I could, but it doesn't matter if I love you, or you love me. I won't share you with Alexia, Jean. Will you promise me that wherever we went, it would be alone, without her?" Lisette clearly stipulated.

Jean was torn between the two women he cared about. He raked his fingers through his dark hair, silently cursing himself for allowing this situation to get out of control again.

"I couldn't ostracize Alexia; it would hurt her terribly if I told her I would never see her again. Please, trust me, Lisette. I love you, and it is you that I will wed. You don't understand the relationship that Alexia and I have."

"Then explain it," she demanded. Her throat constricted, and her eyes filled with the dew of new tears.

"I can't." He gritted his teeth in frustration.

"Then get out of my life!" She clenched her fists and beat on his chest. "I hate you for doing this to me. Why can't you stop making me miserable?" The sobs came easily. Jean snapped into action, holding both her hands in one of his. The months of holding her peril inside of her young heart spilled out in spiteful words. "Haven't you hurt me enough? You're nothing but a bloody bastard. May you rot in hell!"

Jean quickly released her hands. He charged out of the bed, yanked on his clothes, and stomped into his boots. He was trapped, and he knew it. To tell Lisette of his relationship with Alexia could hurt the Countess if Lisette wanted revenge. There were too many other lives at stake to risk the wrath of one heartbroken female. Even if it meant enduring Lisette's hatred, he couldn't tell her. Jean had come prepared for this confrontation, but not the magic that had passed between them on the bed. He looked back to her soft form on the bed, determined to have his way.

"Why can't you learn that you can trust me, Lisette?"

She picked up the goblet and threw it at him, but it missed him and hit the wall, clattering to the floor. "Get out of my chamber," she screamed.

Jean caught her wrists and pulled her to her feet. She wrapped the sheet around her in a furious sweep of her arms. Jean wrapped his arms around her angry, rigid form. He made one last, desperate try to convince her that she should come with him. "Do you know what you mean to me?" His voice gentled against her ear. "On my word of honor, I promise I will never touch Alexia as I have made love to you."

Lisette almost believed him. "I won't share you," she repeated, her face level to his chest. She pulled her bottom lip between her teeth, biting it so hard it burned. "Just get out and leave me alone, Jean."

"Is that all I mean to you, Lisette?" Jean shook her angrily. "I thought we were something special when we were together. That's all it takes for you, isn't it? Just 'Go away, Jean.' All our kisses are forgotten, aren't they?"

"Yes," she seethed. "I will never submit to being a concubine in your harem of women."

"There's that pride of yours again, Lisette. You amaze me! You really don't think much of me, do you? It doesn't matter to you that I have proclaimed my deep affection for you, does it? Or that you're the only woman I want in my bed? There is no harem. Alexia is very dear to me, and I won't cast her aside. As long as I live, she will have a home."

Her chin tilted in proud defiance. "Then I hope

you shall both enjoy it, because I won't go with you."

Jean cursed under his breath. "You leave me no alternative."

Lisette feared him when his eyes lit in vengeance. She had seen it before when he had abducted her, and it was there again. The gray of his eyes became dark as night. "What do you mean, 'no alternative'?"

Jean slung his coat over his shoulder. "Your father left Paris over a week ago, *ma chérie.*" The mordant tone of his voice was meant to scare her. There were other ways to get what he wanted, and at that moment, it was he who held power over her. "He is my prisoner until you agree to meet me in Normandy and leave for Spain at my command. If you refuse . . ." Jean walked to the door and opened it. He briefly turned back to her. "I will kill your father with my own hands before the week is finished. However, if you choose to join me I promise you will never regret it."

Lisette fell back on the pillows as he closed the door behind him. So, he thought to force her hand by taking her father hostage, did he? She would find Michel, and see if there was any way to stop Jean from killing her father. Lisette couldn't let the Duc de Meret die because of Jean's stubborn arrogance.

She woke Anna from a sound sleep. "Help me dress in my riding habit, Anna. I have to find the Marquis."

Lisette was buttoning her shoes when a knock came on her door. Thinking it was Jean returning to press his point, she threw the oak door open, and stood speechless to find the Countess in the hall.

Lisette's hand gripped the shoulder-high cold steel handle. "Where is the Marquis?"

Alexia pranced past her into the room. "Don't

you ever say *hola? Caramba,* but you French have such bad manners."

The Countess pointed to the rumpled bed. "I see you were entertaining the Baron again. Is he still here?"

"That is none of your business." Lisette couldn't hide the sarcastic tint to her voice. "Where is Michel?"

"Ah, you have finished with one *ami* and are ready for another? I didn't think you were capable. You won't find the Marquis at the palace. He's fighting a duel this morning on a field of honor. It seems that he has left his seed behind him, and a very proper young lady is now faced with an embarrassing situation. I refused to join him. If he's going to get himself killed because he doesn't know when to button up his breeches, then he shall get his reward."

"Alexia." Lisette had a barbed point to sink. "I thought you were loyal only to Jean."

"I had hoped to catch up to him before he left Paris." The Countess ignored the comment. Her gloves slapped onto the palm of her hand. The two women faced each other. "I see you decided not to be included in our journey to Spain. It's a pity you won't be there with us."

Lisette didn't know what else to do. She wouldn't be bested by the Spanish Countess. There was a strong sense of possessiveness that had harbored her doubts about Jean and Alexia, but now that she had time to think about what Jean had said, the doubts increased. Jean said he would never make love to Alexia. He would give her a home. That wasn't the picture she had in her mind about their relationship. Perhaps Jean was right, and all Alexia needed was a home to come back to? The Countess did seem overly concerned for Michel, Lisette mused. Jean had made her a promise, and she still naïvely believed in him.

"How wrong you are, Alexia. Why, I just woke my maid so that she can pack my trunks for the journey."

Anna's face was blank with shock. She covered her surprise with a wide smile. "Yes, my lady. I'll have you packed in a few minutes."

Lisette had to get a message to Michel. He was the only one who was in the King's confidence and knew about her efforts to free the Earl of Normandy from the charges against him. There was no time left. She couldn't wait for the orders herself. Michel would have to accept them on her behalf. Alexia was a bright pink, controlling her concern, and it was Lisette's turn to ignore her. She sat down at her writing desk.

"I have a message to leave for the Marquis. You don't mind delivering it, do you, Alexia?" Her voice purred with satisfaction as she scribbled the words on the parchment and sprinkled sand on the message. She held the candle over the envelope, and a drop of wax sealed the note. It was for his eyes only.

"He won't be able to read it if he's dead," Alexia bit in reply.

The Countess was genuinely worried about Michel. But Lisette had seen his skill with a rapier, and knew he faced any opponent with an advantage of speed and dexterity. Jean had taught him well.

"I wouldn't be so upset about Michel. He has been in more duels than I care to remember in the two months I have been at the palace. The Marquis can take care of himself. Please give him my note before he retires tonight."

Alexia tucked the note into her reticule. She still wore the gown from the ball, and suddenly had a pounding headache.

Lisette pulled her chapeau out of the wardrobe. There was a banging on her door that shook the room. Anna admitted Paul into the chamber, and he, too, noticed the disheveled bedding. Lisette was mortified. Outside, the sunrise was beginning to slice through the darkness, and yet no one would know it was so early by the crowd of people in her room.

"I beg your pardon, Lady Lisette. The palace is under siege by a band of vicious females."

"Good grief," Lisette gasped. "What is happening? Michel isn't the cause, is he?"

Paul grinned. "Not this time. The ladies outside the palace want an audience with the King. I think it is advisable that we depart before it turns into an ugly riot. It's luck that you are all here. I have a carriage ready that should transport us comfortably."

Alexia raised a hand to stop him. "I'm not leaving just yet. The Marquis will return if he lives, and I want to speak to him."

Paul left with Alexia. Lisette finally finished dressing. She took her mink-lined mantle out of the wardrobe. She managed to hide the sigh of relief that Alexia wouldn't be going with them. Within a quarter of an hour they were packed and ready to leave the palace.

"There's something you should know," Paul spoke up from the underside of a heavy trunk. "Your cousin Darias was here last night asking questions about you."

Lisette still cringed at the thought of Darias being in control of Meret. He had asked to see her many times, and she always refused him admittance to her chamber. "He won't find me, Paul."

The carriage bumped along the country roads leading to Normandy. Paul yelled above the

pounding hooves of the carriage team; they were
being followed by her cousin and a troop of men.

She knew they couldn't outrun the men on
horseback. Lisette gave the order to pull over. Darias was persistent, she had to admit. He climbed
into the carriage and seated himself opposite Lisette and Anna. Paul whipped the horses into
action again, and the carriage rocked over the pot-
shaped holes in the surface of the dirt road.

The Duchess extended her hand. "Why are you
following me, Darias?"

His lips touched the back of her gloved hand.
"Your father has been taken hostage by the ruthless Baron. I came to warn you of his antics, and to
persuade you to come to Meret for safekeeping."

Lisette wished she could wash her hand and burn
her glove where he had touched her. "I am well
aware of what has been happening to the Duc.
Monsieur Jolbert has already issued his demands
for the Duc's release. He wants me to go to Spain
with him, and as you can see, I am complying with
his order."

Darias's face became a bright red. "That miserable bastard thinks he can commit any tort he
wishes without fear of reprimand. How dare he try
to debauch a lady of the house of Meret!"

Lisette smiled to herself. If Darias knew she was
a willing partner to Jolbert's charms, he would
never leave her alone. "It is what he demanded of
me for the release of my father. I suggest you leave
this carriage."

"I have already decided to accompany you." Darias lay back on the sable-covered cushions. "Will
the Duc be released when you arrive in Normandy?"

"That is what the Baron has promised to do."

"Do you trust him?" Darias lit a small pipe and

deeply inhaled the opium paste mixed with to-bacco.

"What choice do I have? I will insist that you re-main in the carriage. Don't try to follow me." Li-sette didn't want to continue talking. The furrowed roads were making her nauseated. It wasn't long before Anna called out to stop the carriage. Lisette couldn't hold back the tremor in her stomach any longer. The dusty road and the smoke from the pipe made her dizzy. She walked into the brush and her stomach wrenched.

Paul noticed her pale face when she returned to the carriage. "I shall try to avoid any bumps," Paul quietly offered while helping her back into the car-riage.

Paul was too gentlemanly to question the reason for the stop. "Thank you," she said softly. Once in-side the carriage, Lisette closed her eyes for some much-needed rest.

Darias finished the contents of his pipe and tapped the small bowl against the side of the car-riage to clean it. He tucked the instrument back into his pocket, watching his young cousin out of the corner of his eye. She was *enceinte,* he ration-alized after her behavior this morning. His plans had all worked out to his benefit. He would make sure the Duc was killed during the attempt to free him from the Baron. It would look as though the Baron killed the Duc in anger, a murder the King wouldn't forgive. With the Duc and the Baron out of the way, he would control the heir to Normandy and all of Meret. It had turned out to be a pleasant day, after all.

"Very nice day," he said out loud, and noticed the flicker of response from his cousin. Soon he would have everything he had worked for. Their ti-tles and wealth would all be his, and the irony of it was, they didn't know that everything that had happened to them in the past five months was of his design. The Duc had stupidly followed his direction, and would have been king if the Baron hadn't intervened in their lives. Lisette had come home at precisely the right time. And all it had taken to accomplish that minute task was to deliver a letter to her with the Meret seal on it. Darias praised himself for the forgery of the Duc's handwriting.

Darias reclined lazily on the fur-covered seats. His mind drifted in an opium haze where he saw himself as the Emperor of France. Lady Lisette lay at his feet, broken and pleading for her life. He would kill her when the time came. With this thought, he drifted into his daydreams.

Chapter Twenty-seven

Exhausted from the night of love, Lisette dozed. As the carriage worked its way toward the west coast of France, the motion rocked her into a false sense of security. It was unusually hot for mid-October. She had spent over a month and a half at the palace and the seasons were changing. Though the nights cooled down to a chill, the sun made one last attempt to maintain the illusion of lazy summer afternoons. The crops were being harvested, leaving the fresh scent of newly mown hay to drift in the autumn air. Where tall fields of golden wheat had once stood, the stubble of gleaned grain remained. The farther they traveled out of Paris, the more she felt at peace with herself. Outside the noise and stench of the busy city, she relaxed and let her mind drift.

There were no more dreams for Lisette of the tall, handsome man who loved and adored her. Instead, her thoughts were filled with what Jean really meant to her. Lisette loved him—not in the schoolgirl way she had at first, but with a deep regard for the code of honor he lived by. He believed in freedom from the oppression of tyranny, yet behaved like a true gentleman born to the aristocracy. His sense of duty was as deeply ingrained in his upbringing as it was in hers. The nobility took responsibility for the education and welfare of the peasants. It had been that way since the beginning of time for Lisette.

She shifted uneasily on the carriage seat, troubled by the turn of her thoughts. She believed in the order of the aristocracy, but couldn't condone the actions of a cruel monarch. France needed a powerful ruler, not one who indulged his own pleasures and coddled the Queen. Forsaking the needs of the people had drawn an unfavorable reaction from the powerful Third Estate who represented the peasants in the *parlement*. A change was slowly spreading over the towns and villages of her country. It was an outcry of human misery that was soon to be heard throughout the kingdoms of the world. Lisette could see all the political ramifications of the statement scrawled in a pamphlet she had found on the street, "Civil war is imminent." There was going to be a power struggle of an incredible magnitude, and the peasants would win the battle simply because they outnumbered the nobility.

The carriage leaned heavily to one side as another passenger boarded. It jostled Lisette from her sleepy reverie. Paul hadn't slowed the carriage to accept the new arrival.

She smiled to herself as Paul's grumbling voice was overheard above the creaking of the carriage wheels. He was obviously displeased with the addition to his passengers. "You depraved cockroach! Go back to the palace."

Michel's answer was brief and to the point. "I don't give a damn what you say! I'm coming along."

Lisette was startled when the top half of his torso hung over the side of the carriage, presenting his upside-down smile in the window. "Good afternoon, darling." His greeting was meant for Lisette.

Her laughter was genuine. The Marquis was an irresistible rake who held a special place in her heart. "I see you survived the duel."

"Alas, my lady. Another one of *le bon Dieu*'s creatures has met his end."

"What of the young lady you left in a socially embarrassing situation?" Lisette forced a pout. She didn't like to think a young woman would be left with a child to raise without the protection of a father.

Michel's face was turning red from his upside-down position. He disappeared from view, and moments later swung feetfirst through the open window of the door. The Marquis gracefully landed in the center of the carriage, then seated himself next to Darias. "Do be a good sport and move over," Michel asked politely. Darias was mute with rage.

"The lady?" Lisette questioned again.

"Oh, yes, she had a change of heart. It seems the only thing she wanted from me was a financial settlement. The father of her child is a poor blacksmith by trade, and it seemed to her the only way to avoid poverty. Pity, because I do enjoy the patter of little feet."

Darias had regained his control. His lips curled in a half-smiling sneer. "It was so good of you to join us."

"Thank you," Michel quickly interrupted Darias. He ruffled Darias's wilted lace cravat with the tip of his finger. "I see you haven't changed your ways. Didn't we discuss the subject of your abhorrent dress earlier? It seems one can't put silk on a boar and expect it to withstand the odoriferous contact."

Anna giggled into her cupped hand. Lisette frowned at the young maid. She knew Darias was becoming agitated to the point of violence, and Lisette didn't want them wrestling inside the carriage. She decided on a change of subject to allow the air to thin of hostility. "Where is the Countess, Michel?"

Michel braced his elbow on his knees and took Lisette's hand into his. Turning her palm to his lips, he gently kissed her hand. "She had a terrible headache this morning. I had to leave her behind."

Lisette felt goose bumps prickling the skin of her arm at the soft contact of his lips. Her gaze filled with loving friendship for this tender man. She didn't know if the past few months of her life would have been bearable without his quick wit and companionship to diminish the brunt of the Baron's wrath.

He continued. "Alexia left the palace to reside at the Spanish Ambassador's apartments. The crowds outside the palace were shouting 'Bread, bread.' They threatened to cut the Queen's throat if the price of bread was not reduced from the inflated price of twelve *sous* to six or eight *sous*. They are a hungry lot, with more and more of their income going to feed their starving families. The mob murdered the baker and his son-in-law who tried to raise the price to eighteen *sous* and sell the stale loaves at a reduced cost. It is good that you left when you did, Lady Lisette."

"Then anarchy prevails," Lisette whispered, shaken by the turn of events at the palace.

Michel was oblivious to the other passengers. He dearly loved Lisette, and knew what awaited her at the end of her journey. Jean had come to his senses and wanted to marry her. It took very little persuasion to convince his old friend that if Jean didn't make her his bride, Michel would be happy to step in as the eager groom.

Her pale complexion worried him. Lisette's normally healthy glow was gone. Anna hadn't reported Lisette's illness to him and he mentally reminded himself to reprimand the maid for her lack of attention. Jean's scrutiny would instantly recognize the slight purple shadows under her eyes, and the lips that had once been a cherry red, paled by comparison. Michel was sure his friend would see that he had pushed her to the point of physical and mental exhaustion and take her to Spain where she could rest.

Darias watched the play of emotions on Lisette's countenance. Michel's affection for his cousin aroused his suspicions. What if Lisette had been unfaithful to the Baron and carried the child of this impudent rake? He didn't like changing his plans when he had worked so long to achieve the downfall of the Jolberts.

"Well, now. Isn't this interesting?" Darias broke the silence. "All the players are here. How do you think this drama will end?"

Lisette cloaked her emotions by remaining impassive. Everyone except Jean and the Earl of Normandy, she thought in the quiet of her own mind.

Michel leaned back on his seat and turned his head to Darias. "You're a dead man, Darias. Make your peace with God, because today the world will finally be rid of you."

Darias met his gaze evenly. "I believe it would take more than the likes of you to best me."

"It would be my pleasure. Unfortunately, Jean has a vested interest in killing you and I couldn't deny him the right. He alone will be the one to run you through. I'm just here to make sure you don't slither away before that happens."

Thankfully, the carriage began to slow down and soon stopped beside the chapel of Normandy. Lisette waited for Paul's helpful hand before emerging from the carriage door. The cool sea air was a pleasant change from the stifling heat of the carriage. It reminded her of the days she had spent at the château. She stretched her aching limbs, fully refreshed as the humidity washed over her skin. Paul put his hand at her elbow, guiding her into the chapel's private chambers, withdrawing once she was safely delivered.

Meanwhile, Michel detained Darias at the point of his pistol.

Anna didn't wait for orders to enter the chapel and prepare Lisette for the brief ceremony. She helped herself down and sought out the priest to give her directions to the room where Lisette would change her gown.

Jean was waiting for her to arrive. He rose to his feet as she was escorted into the room and straightened his suit coat. The chapel priest was an old friend of his and happily prepared the marriage document as the Baron requested.

He noticed her tired and worn appearance in one quick glance that swept her body from her nose to her toes. Jean walked to her. He was sure his feet never touched the ground. His gaze was focused on her deep blue eyes, and he was in awe of her beauty, which made his pulse quicken. She looked so young and vulnerable that he hated his actions, forcing her to come to him without resting before making the journey.

Lisette had to be worried that he would kill her father. The doubts of her loyalty surfaced to perplex him. Would she continue to justify her father's treason, or finally understand that it was a foolhardy dream to want the throne when civil war was threatening to crumble the Duc's empire? He wished with all of his soul that he knew the answer. Had he been duped by her love words? Was she in league with the Duc, and had she planned out his downfall in great detail even to the point of pretending to fall in love with him? Michel was his trusted friend, and the Marquis swore she was innocent of the Duc's plots. Could Jean dare believe that his old friend might have ulterior motives?

Jean realized he had lost control of the situation when Lisette first looked at him. He no longer had the ability to rely on his stringent sense of logic to untangle the web of deceit surrounding him.

Lisette saw the look of confusion that brought his eyebrows together in a worried frown. "Where is my father?"

"He is safe and at my command will be released. I should kill him just for pity's sake. He won't live long if he stays in France, and it is my opinion that he should retire to the island with us." Jean would be able to keep the Duc out of trouble on his island home in Las Palmas.

His concern for her father's life bewildered Lisette. Didn't he want to murder her father? It was a decision that wasn't hers to make.

"My father is capable of making his own choices." After the episode at the Duc's apartments in Paris, Lisette didn't care if she ever saw him again. Though, as much as she might detest her father, she couldn't be responsible for his death. "You have what you want. I am prepared to make the voyage to Spain with you." There was a bitter tone in her voice that she couldn't mask behind a pleasant exchange. Her future held nothing but heartbreak for her. The Baron had won by a show of force and she was a poor loser.

Chapter Twenty-eight

This wasn't the way Jean wanted their wedding day to begin. He raked his fingers through his hair, agitated at himself for his doubts. The Earl's disappearance continued to bother him, but Lisette couldn't be behind the vicious plot to destroy his family.

"I'm sorry for being a wretch," he hastily apologized. "Is it possible to put our differences behind us long enough to take our vows?"

She couldn't look at him and focused her gaze on the center of his chest. It was a relief to know she would be married to the Baron, but a disappointment that it wouldn't be the wedding she had envisioned for so long. At least their child would have a proper name and Darias couldn't hurt her anymore.

"I'm afraid the bride is in a disheveled state at the moment." It was true, she thought. The dusty ride in the carriage had rumpled her riding habit, and her hair had long since fallen out of the ribbon that had held the thick curls off her shoulders.

"The bride looks lovely," he said gently. Jean wanted to touch her. His arms circled her warm body, drawing her close to him. He could feel her shaking in his embrace. Was she nervous about the nuptials, too? It was a moment they had both dreamed about so often that it didn't seem right to elope. "If you want a big wedding with all the proper trimmings, it'll have to wait until we get to Spain."

"I-I want a big wedding," she stammered. *But I need you all to myself.* Her conscience warned her again that what she was about to do would end in a disaster with her heart broken. Was Jean really in love with her, or was this part of his design for revenge? He had promised she would come to him of her own free will and become his mistress. Lisette felt a twinge of shame grow warm on her cheeks. The Baron misunderstood her feelings for wedding jitters. It would be easy to feign indifference to sharing him with Alexia if she didn't love him so much. Jean was her life. It was he who gave her cause to live and the child they had created.

"It seems as if I've waited for an eternity to marry you." Jean pushed his doubts aside. The shadows of gloom would not ruin his wedding day. "I have thought of everything." He lovingly kissed the top of her head. "Your wedding gown was fitted while you were at the palace."

"Is there anyone you can't influence with your charm?" she pouted. "I didn't know about the gown."

"You weren't supposed to know. It was a conspiracy with your dressmaker, Madame Bertin. Anna will help you change . . . unless I could be of assistance?"

His smile was infectious. Lisette couldn't help but feel his excitement. It was her wedding day, at long last. Her chin tipped up, and the wonder of him filled her senses. "You'll have to wait until later."

Jean bent to kiss her lips. With one arm circling her back, his hand was freed to caress her cheeks with a tender touch. Lisette felt secure in his arms.

The burden of decision was past. Today she would marry her beloved Baron.

"Ma belle amie," he whispered huskily. "How could I ever live without you?"

Outside the chapel, Michel kept watch over Darias. But the Marquis made an error in thinking that Darias would wait patiently for the duel with the Baron. Darias had waited for just the right moment to take Michel by surprise and it only took a moment to subdue his opponent. He used the brass-plated head of his walking stick to knock the pistol out of Michel's hand and to inflict a stunning blow to his head, rendering him unconscious. There was a troop of the King's guard en route to the chapel, with orders from Darias to release the Duc de Meret from the Baron's forces.

Paul walked out of the chapel, not knowing the danger awaiting him inside the carriage. He believed the Marquis would keep Darias occupied until Jean completed the wedding ceremony. Then Michel would kill Lisette's obstinate cousin, Paul was sure.

Paul opened the carriage door, and felt the burning point of a rapier penetrate his broad chest. The deadly weapon withdrew into the shadows of the carriage covered with his blood. The action took him completely by surprise. His hand groped to the crimson stain on his chest. The weapon hadn't touched his heart, but succeeded in piercing his lung. Deep inside his chest, he could feel the white-hot pain spread through his arms as his lung filled with blood. Losing his balance, he stumbled backward several feet and fell to the ground. In his fight to breathe, his chest heaved in a heavy cough. Michel's body dropped beside him, and he noticed the flow of blood from Michel's temple.

The sky above him was a clear blue with an occasional snowy, castle-shaped cloud drifting by to contrast with the vivid color. All through his life Paul had protected the heir to Normandy. Now, when Jean needed him the most, Paul was unable to come to his aid.

Michel, his dearest friend, was beside him. Paul wondered for a moment if he, too, had been mortally wounded. It must be their fate to die together after spending a lifetime of quarreling. He could just see the Marquis getting to the pearly gates before him and then arguing about who would enter heaven first.

"Forgive me, Jean," gurgled from his mouth. It was the last thing he would ever say as he left the bounds of mortality.

Darias passed the window of the clerestory wall. He found the maid alone and made a noise to bring her to the window. When Anna investigated the sound, his hand clamped over her mouth and he pulled her through the opening into the garden, holding her bent arm behind her back, painfully jarring her shoulder until she didn't struggle. Anna blacked out from his hand over her nose and mouth blocking her breathing. Darias bound her hands and feet, securing her mouth with a silk gag knotted in the center, stuffed between her teeth, and tied behind her head. He carried her to the carriage and lifted her body onto the seat. The maid was special to Lisette. Darias knew his cousin wouldn't want her killed, and he could use that threat to get Lisette to do his bidding.

The final play of Darias's hand was to get Lisette to go willingly with him. She would never accompany him without coercion. Darias took a flask from his coat pocket and poured a measure of two fingers into a tin cup. The black tea was opiate-laced and would make the Duchess obey him.

Darias took a quick look around. "Where is that

guard I was promised?" He wouldn't wait for the King's men to kidnap Lisette. He made his way back to the window where he had found Anna. The room was still empty. Darias climbed in, tiptoeing to the door where he heard the voices in the hall-way.

The deep voice of the priest was overheard. "The lady needs time to change, my old friend. You may come with me to confess your sins before entering into the holy state of matrimony."

"I'll be along shortly," Lisette said in a soft voice.

Darias heard the footsteps echo down the hall. The door handle turned, and the door swung open as Lisette entered the room. She didn't see him hiding in the shadows. As soon as she turned to close the door, he slipped out of seclusion and had a hand at her throat with his fingers on either side of her windpipe. If she said a word he would tear her throat out.

Lisette gave a startled gasp as Darias tightened his hand on her throat. "Drink this, or I'll kill your maid. Do you understand me, cousin?"

Unable to nod her head, she whispered her defeat. "Please don't hurt Anna." Lisette knew the maid meant a great deal to Jean, and she couldn't allow someone to be hurt because of her insane cousin.

Darias held the cup to her lips, and she swallowed the thin liquid, gagged at the bitter taste, and pushed the cup away from her mouth. Darias forced her to consume another mouthful of the foul drink. He tightened his hold on her throat, threatening to cut Anna into little pieces if she didn't oblige him.

Lisette instantly felt the drug sink its talons into her stomach, nauseating her and making her breathing labored. It racked her nerves, leaving her anxious and despondent. *My baby will die,* her fears rushed on. Where is Jean? Michel, have you forsaken me? Her tears fell down her cheeks unchecked. Darias had backed up against the wall, maintaining the hold on her throat until the drug's initial effects gave way to the sense of detached tranquillity that followed.

The minutes passed, and soon Lisette was in a state of blissful unawareness. She followed Darias to the window and allowed him to lift her through the portal. Lisette couldn't feel her feet touch the ground. Darias followed her, guiding her with a hand across her shoulders.

Jean wondered at the length of time it was taking Paul to come back. His cousin was to stand beside him.

Lisette was taking an unusually long time to change, but Jean passed that off as bridal jitters. He was nervous and wanted the ceremony to start before Lisette changed her mind and refused to marry him.

His instincts warned him that something had gone wrong. Jean stalked out of the chapel, finding Lisette in the arms of her cousin as they made their escape.

"What in hell . . . ?" Was she crazy? He had given her the choice of joining him, or he'd kill her father. It didn't make sense that she'd come to him, then run away with her cousin. "Lisette!"

Darias had been caught. He had the door to the carriage open, and Lisette leaned heavily on him. Moving quickly, he lifted her onto the seat and closed the door before the Baron had crossed the distance between them. Darias had a pistol in one hand, concealed by his lace cuffs, and a rapier drawn and ready before the Baron closed in on him.

"She doesn't want to marry you, Monsieur Jol-

bert. I suggest you leave before the royal guard arrives and arrests you for kidnapping the Duc de
Meret." Darias had to buy some time. He didn't
want to duel the Baron, knowing his skill was no
match for the Baron Jolbert's.

Lisette was in an opiate haze. What Jean
couldn't see were the still forms of his cousin and
the Marquis behind the stone wall.

"Paul?" Her voice seemed to be coming from
someone else's lips. Hold on to that thought, her
mind raged against the drug. Tell Jean his cousin
is dead. Don't let Darias destroy the Baron. She
forced her body to sag against the side of the carriage so that she could see her Baron. The opium
that infiltrated her senses made her eyes close. She
couldn't cry anymore.

The Baron drew his rapier and stepped into a
fencing stance. *"En garde."* As the challenge was
issued he raised the tip of the deadly weapon in salute and tucked his left arm, bent at the elbow, behind his back for balance.

Darias needed an advantage. "I don't need to kill
you. Your own crimes are enough to send you to the
gallows. My cousin and I make a wonderful pair,
wouldn't you say? She has helped to outwit you in
every way. It was with her assistance that the Earl
of Normandy fell into our hands. Pity we had to kill
him, isn't it, Lisette?" Darias saw the flush of fury
on the Baron's face.

The Baron looked to Lisette. She was lounging
against the window ledge of the carriage as if she
didn't have a care in the world. "Is it true, Lisette?
Is my father really dead? Why won't you answer
me?" his voice thundered.

Lisette took several deep breaths before she
could force the words into an audible expression.
She didn't hear the Baron's accusation. All she

could see was the bright red stain on Paul's chest. "He's dead," she blurted out.

Jean couldn't move as the horror of what she had done to him sliced through his stunned faculties. His vehemence was uttered in a low tone. "If I ever lay eyes on you again, I'll slit your throat with my own hand."

Darias had what he wanted. The Baron charged on him. Darias raised his hand and pulled the trigger, wounding the Baron in the leg. With casual ease, Darias mounted the carriage. Grasping the reins, he fired another shot behind the horses' hooves, scaring the beasts into a full run.

Jean couldn't stop the moving carriage. "I'll kill you, Lisette," he called out, his shout choked with wrath.

As the Baron limped out of the gateway he found the bodies of Paul and Michel. The Marquis had lost a lot of blood and had a weak pulse. Paul was dead.

At the sound of a gunshot, the priest had come from the chapel. He went to the Baron, offering help for his cousin and friend. The priest stopped short when he saw the look of shock on the Baron's face. The old vicar reeled in anguish at the sight before him. The Baron held his cousin in his arms, mourning his death as tears fell down his tanned cheeks. Jean didn't hear the approaching royal guard. He was wounded, but alive. The priest got a bucket of water from the well and dumped the contents in Michel's face, rousing him from the fog of unconsciousness.

"Take the Marquis and leave this place," the priest ordered. Then, gently: "There is nothing you can do for Paul. You have to go before the guards arrive and arrest you. Your cousin gave me something he said you would want." He pulled the diamond ring out of his robe pocket and gave it to the

Baron. "Take it, and be gone before the King's guard arrives."

Jean's hand closed on the ring. She had betrayed him.

"I can't leave him here." Jean wiped the tears away with the back of his shirt sleeve. "Why did they have to kill him?" he sobbed in sorrow, trying to understand what had happened. "That vicious bitch will pay for this with her life. It doesn't matter that feudal laws have been abolished. I'll murder every de Meret on the face of the earth, starting with her father. Blood will pay with blood," he swore.

"Go, before the guards arrive and they take you to prison," the priest warned. He helped the Marquis to mount a horse. There wasn't time to take the saddle from the barn. They would have to ride bareback. The Baron groaned against the pain in his leg as he swung his body up behind Michel. Jean figured the Marquis's skull had to be cracked from the amount of blood he had lost.

Michel couldn't see straight and he clung to the horse's mane, his keen sense of survival keeping him from falling. He collapsed in the veil of darkness that engulfed him.

Jean moved by instinct through the wooded hillside. In the distance, a pillar of smoke curled and twisted in the breeze. The direction indicated that his château had been set to the torch. It would be burned to the ground before he could get help to fight the blaze. His hussars were camped in the hills and had orders to meet at the port before the sun set.

He tied a handkerchief around his leg to stop the bleeding and urged his horse forward. His world had come crashing down around him, taking the life of his cousin and leaving him empty inside. He would never forget what Lisette had done to him.

The de Merets would pay for this act of war. The Duc would be the first to be tortured. Since Jean sent him ahead to Spain, it would take longer to reach him. But when he did . . .

Chapter Twenty-nine

Darias drove the team of horses at breakneck speed. He passed the royal troop with hardly more than a shout that the Baron was wounded and waiting for them at the chapel.

Lisette was in a world of misery. She sobbed at the loss of Paul. Dear, sweet Paul had been killed because of her treacherous cousin. The guilt tore at her heart. If only she hadn't waited so long to join the Baron, Paul would be alive. It took all of her strength to untie Anna, and she gratefully fell into her maid's arms as the mourning continued to rack her body with lamentable sobs. All her hopes had been shattered when Jean threatened to kill her.

Her maid wept quietly. There was no way to escape Darias until they reached Meret and he allowed them some privacy. Anna's thoughts centered on rescue from the crazed man. Darias couldn't keep them locked up forever. Somehow, she would send word to the Baron and he would come and take them away. He wouldn't forsake his own child, even if he hated Lady Lisette. Anna had heard what had caused Jean to cast her aside. Darias wanted the Baron to believe that Lisette had something to do with the Earl's death. Lisette was innocent, Anna was sure.

"You've got to listen to me." Anna stroke Li-

sette's tear-soaked hair. With her lady's head resting on her lap, she made every effort to comfort her.
"You can't blame yourself," Anna said softly.

Darias put his arm around Lisette's waist, steer-
ing her into the parlor. The room was stripped of
all furnishings and wall hangings with the exception of a harpsichord and a straight-backed chair.
He seated Lisette on the chair and tied her arms
behind her back, securing them to the bottom rung.

The opium still had her will within its power.
Her insane cousin sat down on the harpsichord
bench, caressing the ivory keys with his fingers.

"I shall play for you, Lady Lisette." Darias
made the announcement that echoed through the
sparsely furnished room.

Her head fell back and she stared at the ceiling.
She refused to cry. Darias wanted her to react to
his cruelty, but Lisette held to her stubborn pride.
She found something to focus her gaze upon; it was
a dusty crystal chandelier, hung from a chain at-
tached to the ceiling, reflecting the late-afternoon
sun in rainbows dancing on the whitewashed
walls. A gentle breeze from the open windows
rocked the chandelier, and tiny sparks of brilliant
colors touched the doorframe, then bounced to the
other side of the room. The ornate fixture had cups
for twenty candles, and every one of the tallow
sticks had burned down to the brass holders, leaving wax icicles.

Darias played for hours while Lisette remained
in a dreamworld where pain didn't exist. She was
oblivious to everything but the loving memory of
Jean.

Upon their arrival Anna had been instructed to
prepare Lisette's chamber. She didn't waste any
time before writing a message to the Baron and securing the son of the gardener to run the errand for

her. Darias had ordered his men to prevent Lisette
or her maid from leaving the house. They were
trapped. Anna sealed the letter and gave it to the
boy.

"When you deliver this to the Baron, stay with
him. Don't return to this house lest the master
have you in his bed before dawn."

The boy was frightened of the new master. He
nodded his head and tucked the envelope inside his
shirt. His father stood behind him, agreeing with
Anna's wisdom. "Most of the men who were loyal
to the Duc have fled because of Darias and his
strange habits," the gardener explained. "I don't
want my son to become another one of his victims.
Stay with the Baron. He will protect you until we
can find some way to kill Darias."

Anna was scared. Darias had a small guard on
duty at all times, preventing her from moving
about the castle freely. Her authority reached only
within the realm of Lisette's chamber and the
kitchens.

The maid bent to kiss the boy's head. "Make sure
the message gets into the Baron's hands. He's our
only chance; Darias won't let us live past the spring
when Lady Lisette's child is born. Please, hurry,"
she pleaded.

The boy's father lowered him to the ground by a
rope around the lad's waist. The slim youth dodged
the guards, slipping behind the overgrown shrubs
until they passed, then darted out the open gates.

Anna had no way of knowing the letter would fall
into the hands of another female. Alexia met the
boy on the outskirts of the camp. Now that the Baron's château had been burned, they were rene-
gades. They couldn't return to Normandy Castle,
where a King's guard waited to arrest Jean for the
kidnapping of the Duc de Meret.

The Baron's act had brought about new suspicions concerning the charges against the Earl, thus delaying the necessary papers to clear the Earl of treason. The small doubt in the King's mind served Darias's purposes. When the Duc was kidnapped, Darias went to the King reminding him of the Jolberts' lack of consideration for his rule.

Alexia heard of the tragedy at the chapel and rushed to the Baron's side. He was in a state of intoxication when she arrived in the hills and his men escorted her to his camp. Jean was racked with fever, and through his delirious raving she learned the true extent of Lisette's treachery. She would never allow the Duchess to hurt him again. Alexia tucked the letter into her pocket.

The Countess tipped the boy's chin up with the palm of her hand. "You can see for yourself the Baron is wounded. He is in no condition to get on a horse, and I won't allow anyone to upset him. Paul Jolbert was killed recently, and the family is in mourning. I'll have to trust you to keep this a secret between us. Or I'll send you back to Castle Meret."

The boy shook with terror. "I won't go back there. The new master is wicked."

"They are well suited to one another," Alexia murmured.

"Pardon me, mademoiselle?" The boy was confused. He didn't understand the beautiful woman before him.

She's getting her just deserts, Alexia thought. "Go and get something to eat. Remember not to bring up your mistress's name, lest you be boiled in oil for mentioning the wench." Alexia tousled his hair. "Don't worry yourself over the matters of men. It will be taken care of." She sent him on his way.

There were two patients to take care of. Michel

was still unconscious. Jean had a hole torn into his leg, and it had taken five men to hold him down while she pried the shot from the fractured bone. A surgeon had been sent for and arrived as Alexia had completed the task. Jean had consumed a great deal of brandy before she arrived and, thankfully, passed out as soon as her ministrations started. She worried about infection most of all. Out in the wilds, there was no way to keep the wound clean. She had to keep him still and allow the medicine to work.

The Baron's men were fiercely loyal to their lord. Alexia was surprised to find Simon at the camp. The cousin to the Baron was Paul's brother. Simon had heard about the incident at the chapel and left his ships to the command of his first mate before the vessels went out to sea.

Simon Jolbert was lean, and when provoked he could be as wicked as Jean. The two men bore an amazing resemblance. Simon was younger than the Baron, but once seen together, they were easy to tell apart. Simon had a small scar on his forehead, a white line against his sun-bronzed face. It was Simon who could step in and command the respect of the Baron's troop. Most of the ranks were men who had also served on his ships while the Baron raised the bounty for his bride.

Alexia found Simon bending over the Baron. His mouth was set in a grim line as he surveyed the wounded men beside the campfire.

"It seems we have a new dilemma, Countess. Both Jean and Michel seem to be in love with Lady Lisette."

It was the last thing she wanted to hear. "What does it matter now that the wench has retreated to Castle Meret? Lady Lisette is under the protection of her uncle, the King, and there isn't anything you can do to get her back. I don't believe Jean wants her here except for the privilege of wringing her wretched neck. It is best that we leave France and give him"—Alexia paused, smoldering inside at what Simon had said—"give them time to recover."

Simon was puzzled at her reaction. "My cousin made me promise to protect the lady, also. If she is in some kind of danger, it is my duty to see to it that she is defended."

"Lady Lisette killed your brother, just as surely as if she had drawn the rapier herself. How can you continue to think she is innocent?"

"Jean said that she had agreed to marry him. It doesn't seem right that she would draw him into an ambush when she was in love with the Baron."

"Jean is delirious with fever. Wait until he recovers before you attack Castle Meret. Then you will understand why he hates her so much."

Simon was thoughtful for a moment. He had been part of the troop that had abducted Lisette in June, and he had heard her swear to have the King's wrath on the Jolbert family. Perhaps Alexia was right in proclaiming that Lisette had betrayed the Baron. Simon stood to his full height of six feet three inches and surveyed the young woman before him. Alexia was jealous of Lady Lisette. That was clear from her reactions.

"I'll wait until my cousin recovers before issuing my orders, Alexia." Simon had other problems to consider. The British fleet had been sighted off the coast of Brest, and he had to defend against the possible invasion of Normandy. The Baron was in a fever, and it would take him time to recover. Meanwhile, Simon had to put his thoughts of grief for Paul aside. There would be time for his reflections later, after Normandy was safe. Simon walked away, concerned with the command of the troop.

The Countess had no doubt that when Jean recovered he would renounce Lady Lisette. The letter in her pocket would never fall into the Baron's hands. Alone with the Baron and the Marquis, she dropped the envelope into the fire, watching the linen parchment turn black and shrivel up into ashes. She hadn't won the argument with Simon, but the Baron's hatred would prevent them from rescuing Lisette from Meret. Together, they would travel back to Spain where they had known some happiness. The sooner he forgot Lady Lisette the better off he'd be. Alexia would do everything in her power to make sure he wasn't hurt again.

Chapter Thirty

Lisette was ensnared by her cousin. He didn't allow her any more freedom than to pace the room. They had settled into a routine of Darias playing the harpsichord for her every afternoon, only because she promised not to try to escape when she was left untied. But each time she left her room there were several guards to escort her. The west wing of Castle Meret was blocked off, and Lisette and Anna were forbidden to go there. Since it housed Darias's men, they complied with the demand.

The weeks passed slowly for Lisette. Darias had called a surgeon to the castle to examine her, and the child she carried was no longer a secret. Her demented cousin laughed with boyish glee when the announcement came that her child would be born in late March or early April.

Lisette had used the opportunity to plant a seed of doubt in his mind. She leaned close to his ear at dinner and whispered. "Once before a man who controlled great power refused to beware the Ides of March."

She was learning. When help didn't come from the Baron, she had stayed in bed for two weeks, too depressed to move. Anna finally persuaded her to walk around the battlements every evening for the child's sake. On one of her evening constitutionals she discovered there was another prisoner at Meret. Darias had ten men to guard him, and yet eleven lights glowed from the west wing. It had vexed her at first, because Darias had taken over the Duc's chambers in the south wing next to Lisette's room and Anna slept in a cot that was brought into her room. There wasn't another person in the old castle that she knew of. It piqued her interest to a point where she sent Anna to the kitchens to glean what information she could about the prisoner.

Anna returned to Lisette's chamber with a glowing smile on her face. It was Christmas Eve, and the cook had been drinking since the stroke of noon. The brandy helped to unleash his tongue, and he poured out a wealth of information for Lisette. There was a man being held hostage in the west wing.

"Are you sure, Anna?" Lisette felt a surge of hope rush through her veins. The maid nodded. The Duchess knew who that prisoner was. "No wonder we couldn't find the Earl of Normandy. Who would have believed that Darias would take the Earl back to Castle Meret?"

"Darias is in the drawing room, floating on a cloud between earth and hell," Anna spat in anger. "If I could get my hands on a pistol, I'd kill him."

Lisette was astounded at her young companion. "Anna?"

"Why shouldn't I want to kill him? After what he's done to us? It's a matter of self-preservation. I'd kill him just like . . ."

"Like who?" Lisette questioned. She realized that she didn't know her maid very well. Seated in a rocking chair before the fireplace hearth, Lisette carefully looked at Anna. The maid fidgeted with the ends to her long braids.

"I might as well tell you. Darias is going to kill us in the spring after the child is born, anyway. Where do I begin?" Anna couldn't look Lisette in the eye. She stared at the frayed ends of the rugs. "My real name is Anastasia Yargovich. I killed my husband on my wedding night."

Lisette couldn't believe she was capable of murdering someone. Her gasp of surprise was muffled by Anna's soft sob. "Please continue," Lisette prodded. "It had to be for a good reason."

"He killed Anton, my twin brother, to inherit the Yargovich estates in Austria. On our wedding night, he got drunk and told me what he had done. I ran to my father's library and took out a gun to kill him. The Earl and the Baron were both there. They found me in my wedding gown with a smoking pistol in my hands and my husband dead on the floor."

"Who was he?" Lisette knew the memory was painful for Anna.

"I can't say his name, nor will I ever speak of what I did again. Believe me when I say I'd kill Darias if I had a pistol."

Lisette believed her. Jean had asked Lisette to be kind to Anna, and now she understood why. "I won't ever tell anyone." She felt so desolate that it was difficult to give comfort.

"What could have happened to the note you sent to the Baron?" She had asked herself the question so many times that the answer seemed an endless list of possibilities. The boy could have been waylaid or killed before delivering it to the Baron. Their worst fears came to light when the gardener mysteriously disappeared from the castle. Darias had probably killed him because of his loyalty to Lisette. Jean wanted to kill her, but she was sure he wouldn't leave her in the hands of her cousin if he received the note and knew about the child she carried.

"He must come," she said sadly. There was a slight thread of doubt that he wouldn't come to her aid. "We have to try again, Anna. If he knew his father was here . . . ?" It gave Lisette an idea.

"I've got to see him in person to know if he's alive and well, Anna. Will you help me?"

The maid quickly got up. "Of course I will. What do you want me to do?"

"Stay at the top of the stairs and tell me if the guards come back." Lisette's mind whirled into action. She couldn't send a note. Darias would find written evidence of their meeting. Anna couldn't pick a lock, but she could. The guard assigned to watch her room had left the door locked and joined his comrades in the library for a little holiday cheer. Lisette had to see the Earl before the men returned to the hall.

Before Anna's gaping eyes, Lisette opened the secured door. The Duchess smiled to Anna, pointing to a position at the staircase.

Lisette wasn't as agile as she used to be. With her belly growing a little more each day she lost all sense of balance. While she stole down the halls a sense of excitement surged through her. The west wing was unguarded, and finding a room with a light was an easy task. She immediately set about opening the door to the Earl's chamber.

A low growl issued from within the room. "Who's there?"

Lisette pressed her cheek against the keyhole. "It's Lisette," she whispered.

"Darias knows you can pick a lock. He had all the doors in this wing changed before you arrived," the Earl's voice said softly.

Lisette slumped against the doorframe. It was

true. She couldn't get the tumblers to move. "I must talk to you." Her voice was pitched low.

"You're alive, that's all that counts," the Earl replied.

Lisette felt tears sting her eyes. "I didn't know you were here. The King had promised to release you from the *lettre.* I almost had the papers in my hands, but Jean kidnapped my father and it made the King angry. Now he won't help me or listen to my plea."

"That bullheaded son of mine." The Earl swore quietly. "Are you unharmed?"

"Oui, I am fine, but there's something you should know. Your grandchild will be born in late March, and Darias will probably kill us both as soon as an heir is born. He has already killed Paul, your nephew, and has turned your son against me by telling him that I helped to kill you."

"A child in March? Paul is dead? Can you get a message to my son?"

"We tried. When we arrived, Anna sent a note with the gardener's son. The boy didn't come back."

"The gardener is dead, Lisette."

She fought the rising sense of panic. "Are you unhurt?"

There was a long pause before the Earl answered. "I am still alive, and I now have a reason to live. Darias told me my son was dead."

Lisette heard the question in his tone. "Jean was captured at Rouen, but he escaped."

"My son lives a charmed life." The Earl was greatly relieved.

Not lately, Lisette thought. "We can't get out of Meret."

"Have courage," the Earl spoke again. "My son will eventually see that Darias is at the bottom of this scheme. Jean will rescue us."

"I pray you're right." Lisette couldn't take the risk of being caught. "I have to leave now. I will come again when I can."

"Don't take any chances," the Earl warned. "My grandchild's life is at stake. Leave the rescue to my son. Promise me you won't do anything foolish, Lisette."

How could she promise not to try everything in her power to get out of the castle when she knew Darias would kill her as soon as the child was born? What if rescue didn't come from the Baron? Lisette didn't want to die. "I will promise to wait for now."

"I wish I could promise you everything will be all right."

"You have given me hope," Lisette whispered in return.

"My son loves you, Lady Lisette."

She couldn't answer that. He hates me, her mind raged. Lisette whispered, *"Adieu,"* and soundlessly tiptoed down the dimly lit hall.

Anna heaved a sigh of relief when she saw the Duchess. Without a word, they swept down the hall of the south wing. When the door was closed behind them, both Lisette and Anna stared at each other, then at the man seated in the rocking chair.

Darias was waiting for their return. "You didn't count on the back stairs, Lisette," he gloated.

Lisette's body sagged against the wall for support. "Don't ruin it for me, Darias. I was just to the point where I believed your designs were masterminded by my father. I see now that you are the genius behind the events of the last six months of my life." She knew better than to rile him. Once before she had vented her anger on her crazed cousin and found out for herself how far he would go. Darias had threatened to turn Anna over to his men. Lisette would get her back only after they raped the young girl. It was a threat, but one he would make good if Lisette threatened him again.

Darias liked to have his ego stroked by words of praise, however spiteful they might be. "You've been sneaking around the castle."

"Not sneaking, just investigating the eleventh light in the west wing. You were very clever to change the locks."

"I knew you would appreciate that small gesture." Darias rocked slowly. His face was alight with a dangerously curled smile. It conveyed his loathing for the lady and his firm belief that all the wealth and power he wanted would soon be at his fingertips. He couldn't beat Lisette as he did the Earl, or take any chances that she would lose the child she carried.

"I believe I warned you what would happen to Anna if you tried to escape the castle."

"There was no escape planned. We went looking around the castle to see your changes in the household. I give you my word I won't leave this room again."

"What makes you think I honor your word?"

"Because that is the difference between us. You don't have any honor to give." Lisette's maid recoiled against the bedpost, clutching the ornately carved wood post in terror. "A gentleman wouldn't consider taking a young girl and giving her to his men. Find someone else to fill their needs. She stays with me, or I will do everything in my power to kill my child before it's born."

"You're bluffing," Darias sneered.

"Am I?" Lisette had won. He believed she would do everything in her power to stop him. "I need Anna to help me deliver this child. She knows what to do when my time comes. I don't have the faintest idea how to birth a child."

Darias relented. "I will honor our truce as long

as you obey. A guard will be posted on your room night and day."

Lisette tipped her chin up in defiance. She couldn't say more lest she invoke his volatile temper and kill them both. Anna's face was a sun-bleached white as Darias paused beside her and touched her cheek with the tip of his finger.

"I'm sure you'll see to it that Lady Lisette does exactly what she has promised."

Chapter Thirty-one

In the Year of Grace 1790

The winter months were dreary for Lisette. Kept a prisoner in her room, she played backgammon with Anna and paced. Darias let her out of the chamber in the evening to stroll the battlements, and other than that small morsel of freedom, she didn't see another soul. The Earl had to be alive. Anna was in the kitchen every morning and checked the contents of the tray that was taken to his room. Occasionally, she persuaded the cook to include a newspaper from Paris and increase the rations to keep his health intact.

All too soon, a warm April sun released winter's frozen hold on the land. The snows melted, giving way to the fresh breath of spring. It was a time of anxious waiting within the castle. Lisette's belly had grown until her slippered feet were only a memory. She couldn't remember the last time she could get her shoes on without Anna's assistance.

For Lisette, it meant sleepless nights as the restlessness continued throughout her pregnancy. Lisette was given the fabric she requested to make the necessary clothing for the child. Darias was pleased the end was near. He sent one of his men to Paris to purchase a wardrobe for the child. He didn't want the heir to Normandy appearing in public for the first time in rags. Lisette and Anna spent a month sewing garments. The tiny gowns made tears wet Lisette's eyes when she thought about the baby she would never get to hold if Darias had his way.

She knew her time had come. The March winds ceased and the April sun warmed the cold stone castle, creating icicles of the melting snow hanging from the barren trees. The predawn light cast a gray shadow around her chamber when she woke to an unfamiliar cramping in her back. Lisette waited and soon another twinge of pain stabbed at her lower back. She was thrilled. Lisette slipped from her bed and walked slowly over to Anna's cot.

"Anna, wake up. I need you."

The maid's eyes clouded for a moment; then, as she realized what Lisette was saying, she bolted off the bed. "What did you say?"

Lisette laughed at the sight of Anna's eyes round in surprise. "My time has come. We can't wait for the Baron to come to our rescue. You have to go to him today."

"I can't leave you," Anna pleaded.

"You must get help, Anna. I have kept my promise to the Earl, but I can't wait any longer. Go downstairs with the pretext of getting my breakfast. Get a horse, and ride like the wind. Don't bother with a saddle. Can you ride bareback?"

"Of course. I can ride bareback and without reins. How can you be so calm?" Anna was so excited she put her dress on over her nightgown, then, realizing her mistake, dressed properly.

Lisette felt wonderful. There was a sense of peace that had come over her before she went to bed the previous night. It was nature's way of telling her to save her strength. She couldn't let Darias know of the pains. He would sit beside her with a pistol in his hand, waiting to kill her. Lisette had to behave as if her time wouldn't come for another week. She went back to bed, knowing Anna would risk her life to save the child. It fueled her feelings of guilt. Paul had been killed. Did Anna have to die to stop Darias?

Nervously, Lisette started pacing the floor again. Anna had been gone for over a quarter of an hour. Darias would be alerted the moment Anna got a horse, and when she made it out of the castle, Darias would come knocking on her door. He would be gloating if they had caught her, furious if they hadn't.

Darias barged into her room unannounced and unbidden, with a look of stormy anger reddening his face.

"That maid of yours has run off," Darias raged.

Lisette sat in her rocking chair, huddled in a blanket. She met the look of contempt from her cousin with nothing more than a shrug of her shoulder.

"Anna thought you would kill her. It doesn't surprise me that she's left me."

"I've sent my men out after her. If they find her, she won't live past sunset."

That was the risk they took, Lisette thought. Anna knew Darias would come after her. She knew where to find Jolbert's men; Darias didn't. Suddenly, she thought about what Darias had said. His men were all out chasing Anna. They were alone in the castle except for the Earl of Normandy, and he was locked in his room.

Lisette had little hope that Anna would find the Baron before her child was born. Normandy covered a vast area, and he could have left for Spain already. Her chance for survival seemed slim. Lisette had to take matters into her own hands. There was a poker next to her hearth that could serve as a weapon. The thought of killing him disgusted her, but it meant staying alive. The situation called for desperate action. She rose from her chair and dropped the quilt to the floor. Darias was raving like a madman. He wanted to see the little wench caught, and to witness her punishment. Lisette's full skirts hid the poker that was tightly clenched in her right hand.

"Darias!" Lisette screamed. She clenched at her belly as a new pain stretched its muscle-cramping fingers across her abdomen. Darias rushed to her side. Gathering her strength, Lisette brought the poker down on his temple.

Darias fell to the floor. There was a small cut on his skin where the poker had struck him. Lisette dropped down beside him, searching his pockets for the keys to the Earl's chamber. Darias didn't have them.

Her cousin was unconscious on the floor. Lisette felt the sharp stab of a pain. She had to get out of her room before Darias awoke. On her hands and knees, she crawled toward the door. Taking several deep breaths to stave off the hurting, Lisette reached for the door handle.

Darias grabbed her ankle. Lisette screamed, and kicked at him with her other foot. The cramping had ebbed, giving her a chance to collect her strength and give her cousin a sharp blow to his temple with a wooden heel of her shoe. He released her ankle, and Lisette scrambled to her feet. She took the poker with her just in case he managed to find her.

There wasn't a chance to save the Earl. Lisette was going to have her baby before Anna returned. She stumbled down the hall. *Where can I hide?* Her frightened mind thought of a thousand nooks and crannies in the old castle. With most of the furnishings gone, Darias would find her if she stayed in the house. In pain, she couldn't get to the stable. That left the battlements, and meant taking shelter behind a pile of forgotten shields and armaments and enduring the cold rain that had started to fall.

"I've got to live," she whispered to give herself courage. She found a warm cape in her cousin's chamber and tugged it over her shoulders. The stairs to the battlements were an excruciating climb. Her legs and back ached from the strain on her body.

She smudged her face as she brushed the raindrops out of her eyes. Cold, wet, and in agony, Lisette crawled into her hiding place, praying Anna would hurry. The peasants wouldn't help a member of the royalty. Her maid would have to find the Baron and bring him back before Darias killed her.

Chapter Thirty-two

Anna had the advantage of a ten-minute head start and knew the territory she was riding. The men behind her weren't familiar with the intricate paths and valleys in the hills of Normandy. The lush hills spread out before her were a mixture of colors, winter browns giving way to the rich hues of new green grass. Holding to the horse's mane, she leaned over the beast's neck to present a low profile to anyone who saw her pass. At a fast gallop, the horse's hooves dug into the wet earth, leaving a trail that was easily followed. Anna weighed less than the men who were following her and their horses would tire before her mount was too exhausted to maintain the headlong flight. With a willow branch for a whip, she kept the horse moving through the hills, stopping only to avoid a tree branch or a gully dropping fifty feet to a rocky valley floor.

Finding the Baron seemed an impossible task. But there was one way to find him that a lady like Lisette didn't think about. Anna hadn't mentioned the Rouen wench, Marie, who had kept Paul content over the past year. Marie had been able to give Paul assistance when the Baron was captured; perhaps she would help Anna now that she needed to find the Jolberts.

Her direction through the early hours of the morning had been a southern course. Anna backtracked her route and started heading north for Rouen.

Anna was soaking wet and miserable. She hadn't had a chance to grab a cape before she left Castle Meret and was now paying for her haste with a shivering chill racking her body. The men following her had picked up her trail again and weren't far behind when, long after the noon bells had rung at the Rouen chapel, Anna fell off her horse in front of the tavern where Marie worked as a barmaid. Exhausted and cold, Anna lay in a puddle of muddy water, too tired to move.

It was her horse that was first noticed.

The Marquis le Maire had won his hand of poker and, needing to stretch, walked out to the wooden porch. He saw the brown thoroughbred with foam dripping from his mouth.

"What do we have here?" the Marquis wondered. It irritated him to think someone would ride a horse that hard. The animal was skittish and shied away when he tried to touch it. Several Jolbert men came out of the tavern, watching the spectacle.

"There isn't a saddle or bridle on this horse," the Marquis commented to the men standing by.

Simon Jolbert stepped forward. "Someone was riding that poor creature?"

"There's another bum lying in the street," one of the Jolbert men spoke. "He probably took the horse for a ride, and fell off in a drunken stupor."

The Marquis slowly approached the still form in the middle of the muddy road. What he found both surprised and delighted him.

"It's Anna," he said softly, bending over the slight form of the young girl. "Get Alexia. She's fallen and looks chilled."

The Marquis scooped Anna into his arms. Her face and body were covered with mud, and as he suspected, she was shivering. Her lips were blue and her skin a deathly white. He carried her into the tavern, setting her down on a chair beside the speechless Countess Alexia Mariaga de Castellar.

"Where did you find Anna?" Alexia was astounded.

"Outside, in a puddle of water. She looks like she's been riding for hours."

"She wasn't alone." Simon made himself useful. "There's a small troop riding after her."

Michel's face was alight with mischief. "If they intend harm to Anna, don't you think we should stop them?"

"Absolutely," Simon agreed with a wide smile. "There's no telling what those rascals have in mind for our Anna. I believe we should take it upon ourselves to rid her of this problem."

"Capital idea," Michel agreed. Jean had gone to bed stone-drunk an hour before Anna's arrival. The Baron had been drinking heavily since Lisette had left him. Now he was a bona fide drunk, with hardly a sober moment. The Marquis had gone to the King and explained that the Baron had removed the Duc de Meret from France to protect him from the revolutionary factions threatening the Duc's life. The Baron was forgiven and the Earl of Normandy freed from the charges, but what good did it do them when the Earl was already dead? It sent Jean into a depression that was swallowed with each drop of brandy.

Michel knew he'd have to wake the Baron and tell him Anna had returned. Before he acted, he wanted to find out where Lisette had gone. He had an old score of his own to settle with her and her wretched cousin.

Alexia had taken charge of Anna and wrapped

her in a blanket. There was some hot tea brought to the table of the busy tavern, and all eyes and ears strained on the rumpled form picked up from the street.

The hot fluid brought life to Anna's bone-weary body. She shivered uncontrollably for a few minutes, attempting to speak. Every word she said was a stuttering failure at communication. They had to wait for her to warm up before getting the information out of her.

Jean woke to the sound of someone banging on his door. The booming noise echoed through his head, putting him in a murderous mood. He pulled on his breeches, thankful that he was alone and didn't have to make polite apologies to a woman. Mostly, the women were avoiding him. The Baron had vented his wrath on more than one wench, and his reputation was preceding him. The women that he took to his bed were all made to pay for the heartbreak caused by Lisette. His precious love had hurt him far more than anyone knew. In his soul he loved her, making the forgetting a daily battle that often ended in drunken stupor.

The ring he gave Lisette fell to the floor as he slid his arms into his jacket. The diamond sparkled in haunting memory of the Duchess. He picked it up and put it back in his pocket for safekeeping. Jean had tried to throw it away but couldn't bring himself to do it.

The Baron opened his door to find the Marquis. "What do you want?" All he needed to fuel his black mood was one more rioting village. He'd had his fill of sending hungry people home as he tried to maintain peace throughout the province. It had been a hard winter, and the peasants were suffering the most. They wanted food and shelter. Jean had done the best he could and opened the doors of Normandy Castle to those who truly needed assistance; to those who were found guilty of hoarding provisions, his justice had been swift. Jean tried to control the mob warfare. But the surly peasants had bludgeoned a man to death because he had a basket of grain when his neighbors had none. It was a miserable time to be alive.

Michel knew better than to disturb him for anything less than a crisis. "Anna has come back. She's in the tavern."

Jean staggered around the room, searching for his clothes and his boots. When he was dressed, he followed the Marquis down the stairs. His body ached and his head felt as if it had been used for a battering ram.

Anna broke into sobs when she saw the Baron. Jean took her in his arms, comforting her. "Don't cry, Anna. I won't make you go back to her."

She was so grateful to find him that she hung on for several more seconds before pulling back. Anna wiped the tears from her eyes with the back of her hand.

"Did they hurt you?" the Baron questioned. His muscles tensed as he remembered Lisette. Jean had warned her what he would do to her if she hurt Anna. He had tried to erase her soft, yielding body from his memory, but every day ended the same with him drowning his sorrows. When she rode away with her cousin, it left him a bitter shell of a man.

"I'll kill them both if they've hurt you."

"N-not me," Anna said. "It's D-Darias. He's going to kill her when the b-baby is born."

"Whose child?" Jean's fingers closed on Anna's shoulders, holding her at an arm's length. "Lisette is with child?"

Anna nodded. "Her time has come. It's your child he wants. Darias will kill her." The words came easier now that she had something hot to drink in her stomach. "Lisette couldn't get out of Meret. Her cousin has held her captive. Your father is there, and he has been beaten and locked up in the west wing. Lisette spoke to him on Christmas Eve, and he was still alive. We don't know how he's doing. Darias made her swear not to leave her room, or he'd kill me and the Earl."

"Did she betray me, Anna?" He didn't want to know, but had to find out.

"She was drugged the day we left the chapel. Darias used an opium-laced tea to keep her from crying out to you. She saw Paul and said, 'He's dead,' and Darias used that to convince you that she had killed your father. That day we came to you she was truly going to marry you, and her cousin knew that. We tried to get a message to you."

The Baron began to put the pieces together. Lisette was a prisoner, not a willing partner. His father was alive, and a child was soon to be born. *His child.*

"How could I not see what Darias was doing?" He swore softly.

"There are some men chasing m-me," Anna chattered.

"Not anymore," Simon Jolbert boasted. He shrugged to the Baron's questioning glare. "It seemed a minor problem and not worth disturbing you about."

"Saddle the horses," the Baron commanded. Throughout the tavern, men cheered, glad to finally be able to avenge the beautiful woman the Baron loved so much. The rooms at the top of the stairs emptied of their occupants as men dressed en route to the stable.

Alexia didn't know what to do or say. She hung her head, guilty of interfering in the Baron's life. Sooner or later, Anna would ask about the boy who had carried the message for the Baron. Later, she would have to answer to Jean for her meddling, but for now, she intended to accompany them to Castle Meret.

The Marquis bundled Anna in a blanket before him on his mount. "Rest now, *petite*. You'll need your strength to help Lisette."

"You loved her too, didn't you?" Anna had seen the look of jubilation on his face when she disclosed Lisette's captivity.

"She is a very special lady," the Marquis admitted. He spoke as they followed the troop. "If she didn't love the Baron so much, I would do everything in my power to make her happy. I thought there was something wrong with her throwing her lot in with Darias. Jean persuaded me to let it be. Simon and I were planning a secret attack on Meret."

"What happened to the boy? Did he reach your encampment?"

"What boy?" Michel was puzzled. There was a young lad taken in last fall, but he had never mentioned Meret.

"I wrote a message to the Baron and sent it with the gardener's son. He's an orphan now. Darias killed his father for being loyal to Lisette."

Alexia had fallen behind as the Baron led his men at a furious pace. She overheard what Anna said and nervously looked away.

"What do you know about this, Alexia? Did you get the message and keep it from Jean?"

Alexia's shoulders slumped in dejection. "And what was I supposed to do with it? Let him be hurt all over again? We all thought Lisette had betrayed him, didn't we?"

"That letter was from Anna." Michel's temper flared for the first time in his life. "What you did could have cost the life of Lady Lisette and her child."

"I know what I did was wrong." Alexia was repentant. She had only wanted to spare the Baron any further anguish. "I love him too much to see him scorned."

"He'll be in a wicked mood when he finds out," Michel warned.

Anna couldn't hide her anger. "You could have saved us months of worry." The maid sneezed and coughed against the chill in her body.

"We'll settle this later." Michel was in a hurry to reach the castle.

Jean Jolbert wouldn't wait for anyone. He urged his powerful horse into a gallop and maintained the grueling run for as long as his horse could hold out. The two-hour ride was a test of patience. He knew what danger Lisette was in and cursed himself for not listening to his better sense. His beloved Lisette had to be alive when he got there. Worry took over his reasoning, and suddenly he imagined all sorts of possible dangers. There could be complications with the birth. A child! It was amazing that she had been able to withhold that information from him. She had to be *enceinte* when he made love to her while she was staying at the palace. Why hadn't she told him about the glimmer of life she carried?

Slowing to a canter, the Baron ordered Simon to ride beside him. "Go into the village and find a midwife or a surgeon, if you can."

Simon separated from the troop with a small guard of his own. The towers of Meret were in sight, but still a few miles off.

Jean savagely reined in his black Arabian. They had to approach the castle slowly and secretly. If Darias saw them coming, he might kill Lisette before they got there.

It was the hardest thing he had ever done.

Knowing Lisette lay at the mercy of her opium-crazed cousin, he had to pick his way through the surrounding forest and silently overcome the castle. Darias was alone. His men were all dead, but he could have a pistol pointed at Lisette. The troop scattered to circle the old estate.

The Baron took a long drink from his liquor-filled flask. It steadied his nerves and helped him to relax. If he were lucky, he'd have Darias at the end of his rapier within an hour. If Lisette weren't alive, his retribution would include a long list of tortures for Darias.

Chapter Thirty-three

Lisette shifted into a dozen different positions. No matter what she did, the contractions continued to worsen, making the long morning and early afternoon seem like an eternity. She constantly defended her hiding place from the hairy, long-legged creatures that wanted to cuddle up to her warmth. The spring rain had stopped, leaving a bright afternoon sun to warm her cold body.

Darias was searching the house for her. From her hiding place on the battlements, she could hear the furniture being thrown around the rooms below. He was cursing, and from past experience she knew he was probably ingesting a dangerous amount of opium. Darias never confronted a situation until he was in a hazy state.

The noise inside the house fell to an unearthly quiet. Lisette leaned over, bracing her elbow on the stone and mortar to see if he had finally figured out she wasn't hiding in the house. The door to the stairs was open. Why hadn't she closed it? In the stairwell was the shadow of a man's form. It scared her more than if she had really seen her cousin, because she knew he would soon find her.

The pain started again. This time it ripped through her muscles, building to a burning fire that engulfed her back and abdomen, rendering her limbs numb from the excruciating pressure. Past caring if Darias found her, she had to lie down. The water from the morning shower formed puddles on the mortar between the stones of the battlement floor. It felt cool to the side of her head. Tears rolled down her cheeks, and she clamped her hand over her mouth to keep from crying out. As the pain ebbed, a warm sensation flowed down her thighs. Anna had warned her that after the water broke, the child would arrive shortly. It was a relief, and the saddest moment of her life. Lisette didn't want to have her baby while scrunched in a pile of litter. This child deserved to be born in her bed.

When she was able to look up again, she stared into the barrel of Darias's pistol. Unable to move, Lisette felt a wave of anger come over her. He was like a vulture waiting for her child to be born. His eyes were glistening and fringed in a brilliant red.

"Don't kill me yet, cousin." Lisette pushed herself to a sitting position as Darias crouched down on his haunches before her. Her hand was inches away from the poker that had inflicted the wound on his forehead. If he hadn't caught her in the middle of a contraction, she would have been prepared. As it was, all she could do was try to inch her way toward the weapon.

Darias saw her slight movement and lunged at the poker. He grabbed it before she did, stood, and threw it off the top of the battlement.

"You're going back to your chamber," Darias snickered. "I couldn't have the child catch a cold, now could I?"

"I can't move!" Lisette gasped in fright as Darias took out an arm's length of rope and bound her hands.

She took a deep breath and screamed, "Jean!"

* * *

They weren't alone in the house. The Baron had arrived to see the poker drop from the top of the wall. He directed his men with silent hand signals as they entered the castle. Half of his guard would find the Earl, the other half would remain with him. With their feet bound in rags, their steps were silent as a butterfly passing. They entered the stairway to the battlements, Jean at the lead. He couldn't put Lisette in any more danger. Darias would be armed and would kill her before he got within two feet of her. The element of surprise was all he needed. Darias had his back to the Baron.

The Baron's blood ran hot with revenge as he lunged out of the stairwell and caught Darias around the waist with one arm, flinging him aside. Darias dropped Lisette's hands as he toppled over. The gun went skittering across the stones, out of reach. Jolbert's man rushed from the stairs, circling the Duchess in a protective shield.

"I have waited a long time for this duel." Jean's voice was a deadly whisper. "Give the weasel a rapier. If you can wield it, Darias, you can defend your life."

"The odds aren't even," Darias whined.

"Did you ever give the lady a chance to defend herself?" Jean didn't dare look toward Lisette. His men were beside her, making her comfortable until the Baron finished with her cousin. The Baron needed to concentrate on the duel with Darias. Knowing his opponent was treacherous, the Baron prodded Darias away from Lisette with the point of his rapier.

Darias scrambled for the rapier that was tossed to him. He turned on the Baron, growling in anger. "If you hadn't come, I would have won."

"But you didn't," the Baron taunted. "Today you will die, and the lady and I shall retire to my villa in Spain, forgetting all about you."

"I don't think my cousin will ever forget the winter she spent here," Darias challenged. "I tormented her at every opportunity."

"Then I shall make sure you receive treatment in kind," Jean spat. He warded off the first blow Darias thrust at him with a flick of his strong arm.

Darias parried the Baron's thrust. He answered with a riposte, returning the blow so that tempered steel met tempered steel. His arm shook from the force of Jolbert's blows, and he knew he was weakening. Sweat poured from Darias's forehead as their rapiers crossed before him, and he had to keep the Baron's powerful right arm from moving an inch closer to him.

The razor-sharp point of the Baron's rapier was within a breath of Darias's cheek. "I think you need to spill some of your blood to know what it feels like," Jean commented casually. He nudged his arm closer to this opponent's pale skin and the blade left a red ribbon of blood against the smooth contours of his face.

Jean was angry at himself for allowing his reflexes to become sluggish. He had consumed too many bottles of brandy to maintain peak physical condition. Had he not been suffering from a wicked hangover, he would have killed Darias within a few quick thrusts of the blade. Because he had lost himself in liquor, trying to drown out the memory of Lisette, he wasted effort on his opponent. The Baron had him pinned against the battlement walls, but Darias leaped out of the way of the deadly swipe of his rapier. It was the mistake the Baron had hoped for. Darias underestimated the Baron's desire to make a quick end of the duel. Jean plunged a knife into his ribs as Darias tried to push past him.

The hilt of the knife was buried in Darias's torso. The Baron felt Darias sag as the knife was driven into his heart. Darias stumbled backward and finally fell to the floor.

The Marquis had arrived to witness the duel. "He's dead, Jean. Simon took Lisette to her chamber. She'd like to see you."

The Baron turned on his heel.

"Just a moment," the Marquis ordered, taking an authoritative tone of voice for the first time with his friend. "I will warn you that if this time you don't make her happy, I shall do everything in my power to make her forget you."

Jean didn't turn around. "I know you love her, Michel. But there is a bond between Lisette and me that you can't break, no matter how angry she is with me. I love her and will do everything I can to make her love me in return."

"You don't have to try too hard," the Marquis said with a sad tone to his voice. "She loves you more than life itself. Treat her well, my old friend."

"Will you go to Spain with us?" The Baron finally faced the Marquis. He knew they had to part.

"No, I'm staying in France. I will bid you *adieu.*"

"Don't leave yet. Stay to help her. She needs both of us at her side."

"If you insist." The Marquis smiled. "Your father is alive and well. He's waiting outside Lisette's chamber for the birth of his grandchild."

The reunion of father and son, the Earl of Normandy and the Baron Jolbert, was one of slapping, hugging, and good cheer.

"You're much too thin," the Baron said.

"You've been drunk for the last five months. How would you know what looks good?" his father teased. "I made her promise not to try anything foolish," he explained. "That promise almost cost her life."

"She's a headstrong young woman," the Baron agreed. Now that Darias was dead and his father was safe, his attention focused on the lady. "How is she doing?"

"Why don't you go in and see for yourself?" the Earl prompted.

The men in the hall all stood back as the Baron approached the chamber door. Jean was apprehensive about entering the room; birthing was a woman's domain. But he was concerned for Lisette. Would she be all right? It would be torture to wait for news, when what he really wanted was to be at her side through the greatest event in his life.

The door opened slowly and he walked in without hesitating.

Chapter Thirty-four

Through the fog of relentless pain, Lisette saw the face that had filled her dreams through the long winter. "Jean, is that really you?"

"I'm here, Lisette. Don't talk, save your strength." He knelt beside her bed, holding her hand in his. "I wish I could help you."

"I have to know." Her voice cracked in her parched throat. "Why didn't you come when Anna sent her letter begging you to help us?" Lisette took a drink of water that Anna held to her lips.

"What letter? I never got it, my darling. Don't tire yourself."

"Every night she asked herself that question. Why doesn't he come if he truly loves me?" Anna said softly.

Alexia was torn apart by guilt. The Countess stood at the end of the bed, knowing what she was about to tell the Baron could separate them forever. "She did send a letter to you, Jean. I couldn't let her hurt you again." Alexia sobbed into her hands. "I'm so ashamed of what I did. I didn't know he would hurt her. I thought she was in league with Darias."

Jean released Lisette's hand and stood up. "Did you read the letter, Alexia?"

"N-no, I didn't. I threw it into the fire the same

day it arrived. You can hate me if you want to, but I think Lisette will agree with me when I say that I love you, and truly didn't want you hurt again."

"You had no right to do that, Alexia!" Jean's fists clenched.

"She was protecting you out of love," Lisette intervened. "It won't be so bad to share you with her, knowing how she feels about you. Loving you can keep both of us busy."

"I think it's time you disclosed the nature of your relationship with the Countess." Anna wagged her index finger at the Baron. "You let Lisette go on believing there was a reason for her to be jealous of Alexia. Now tell her the truth."

"Anna?" the Baron questioned.

"If you won't tell her, I'm calling the men outside this room to take you away and hang you. She deserves to know."

Lisette was puzzled. "What are you talking about?"

The Baron knew Anna was upset, but Lisette was in no condition to be presented with a difficult explanation. "I couldn't tell you about my special relationship with Alexia to protect her. There were already too many unfounded charges against the Jolbert family, and I couldn't put her through any more turmoil."

"I'm glad that you care for her, Jean. Alexia is very young and brave." Lisette wanted to be a good sport, but the old doubts were hard to contain. Another contraction racked her body, and she squeezed Jean's hand until his fingers turned blue. When it passed, Lisette apologized for the death grip.

"Don't say you're sorry. If I could take the pain for you, I would. Forgive me, Lisette. You mean more to me than my own life. I didn't mean to hurt you or let you go on thinking Alexia was another lover of mine. If certain parties knew that she is my daughter, they would have put her into prison."

"Daughter?" Lisette was almost beyond thinking as exhaustion worked its way through her body. "That isn't possible, is it?"

"I was sixteen when she was born. Alexia just celebrated her sixteenth birthday. In fact, I didn't find out about her until just before you and I were betrothed. When her mother died, she sent a letter to the King requesting that he contact me and tell me about Alexia. That was what sent me to Spain after we became engaged."

Lisette put the thoughts aside as another searing pain tore through her belly. They were coming closer together so that she could hardly rest between them any longer. Jean eased his body behind her in a seated position as he cradled her in his arms. It was a relief to know he was there at the beginning and the end when the seed he planted was about to be born.

"Talk to me," she pleaded. "I want to hear your voice."

Jean looked at Alexia and Anna. "Isn't there something you can do to help her?"

Alexia didn't have to be told to know she was forgiven. "We can't give her any landanum or liquor. The pains are coming every five minutes and it will still be a while. Why don't you go boil water or something?"

"I'm not leaving. Have the men bring up what you need."

"You're being stubborn."

"Now I see where you get it from."

Alexia knelt on the floor beside Lisette's bed. "Will you ever forgive me, Lady Lisette?"

Though weakened, Lisette couldn't let her go on with the burden of guilt that she carried. "We'll be good friends."

Alexia sobbed with relief. "I acted like a child."

"You did what you thought you needed to," Lisette soothed. "Never once did it occur to me that you were his daughter."

"I don't think of Jean as my father. He's too young to represent a paternal image to me, so I think of him as my dearest friend."

Jean reached over and took Alexia's hand in his. "Later, we will discuss the letter. For now, help her if you can."

Alexia stood up, straightened her back, and smoothed the folds of her gown. She had an authoritarian flair for commanding the people around her. She crossed the room and opened the door to the hall.

"Gentlemen, I need linens, a sharp knife, and boiling water delivered to me in five minutes."

The Earl of Normandy paced outside the room. "Alexia!" He hugged his granddaughter with glee.

"Grandfather," Alexia purred softly. "How good it is to see you alive and well."

"What is the boiling water for?" Michel questioned.

"My tea." Alexia lowered her lashes and raised her piquant face to him. "They love each other very much. Do you care for me at all, Michel?"

"I adore you, Alexia. We all do." The Marquis's cheeks flushed for the first time in his life. Alexia was a jewel, ready to be buffed to the full luster of womanhood. Jean had warned him on several occasions what he would do to him if Michel forgot himself and made love to his daughter. There were detailed drawings of the torture Jean had devised for him, and the lengthy explanations of the time it took to complete each phase of the task. Alexia was far too beautiful for him to allow himself the luxury of touching her without wanting all of her.

It was best he stay away from the flirtatious young woman and stay healthy.

Alexia reentered the room, a pout drooping at the corners of her mouth. "I wonder what it will take to get him to notice me."

Anna understood why Alexia was flustered. She herself had fallen head over heels in love with Simon Jolbert, and he didn't know she was alive.

"Try a sledgehammer," she whispered to the Countess. They both broke out in giggles. Anna took a flask of brandy Michel had given her out of her shift pocket, took a long drink, and offered some to Alexia. It burned her nose and throat, causing her to choke.

"What are you doing?" Jean was frantic. He saw Anna and Alexia swallowing the liquor and couldn't believe they chose this time to get drunk. "That can wait until later."

"No, it can't," Anna said bravely. "You are in a woman's domain, and it will help relax her."

Lisette screamed in pain, and Alexia put the flask to her lips. "Where is the linen I requested?"

The Marquis was the only man who stood waiting in the hallway with enough courage to knock on the door and deliver the requested items. The door closed behind him, and when he handed the bundle over to Anna, he found the sight before him mesmerizing. They didn't seem to notice he was there, so he remained.

Jean helped Anna peel the gown off of Lisette's sweat-soaked body. They bathed Lisette and slid a warm nightgown over her head. Jean was scared because he didn't know what to expect. As he cradled his beloved in his arms he notice her pale cheeks and drawn lips.

"Don't let her die," he prayed quietly. He draped a woolen blanket over her to keep her warm. Jean sat with his back to the headboard, rocking her in his arms. Every once in a while her eyes would open and she would see him with her. She rested between the contractions, but each time the pain engulfed her body, she grew weaker. Jean's alarm mounted by the moment. He placed his hand on her engorged belly, feeling the muscles tearing inside her body. It filled him with a sense of awe. She was nearly delirious, and yet the pains continued. It suddenly dawned on him the sacrifice women made to bring a child into the world. This was a pain he had asked her to bear, and he felt a deep sense of fault.

Lisette slept through most of the afternoon hours. The fireplace was stoked, and water heated for the child's first bath. Anna and Alexia had everything laid out that they would need. They brought in every candelabrum they could find after the long shadows of daylight disappeared. The hours of labor ticked by slowly for them. Jean had his pocket watch out, counting the duration and frequency of the contractions. He tried to be helpful, and didn't know what else to do.

There was a knife lying beside Lisette's hip. Jean hadn't moved throughout the ordeal, preferring to give her what comfort he could by talking himself hoarse.

"What is that for?" He didn't like the looks of what was happening.

"There's a cord that has to be cut." Anna didn't tell him what she had been discussing with Alexia. If the child came too fast, they would use the knife to make a small incision in the birth canal so that Lisette wouldn't tear. If the child came too slow, they would have to sacrifice the mother and save the child. That was why they were drinking. Neither one of them could perform the second choice of cutting Lisette open. It didn't take much liquor to fuel their anxieties. Already, Anna was laughing hysterically.

Lisette woke with a start. As the pain mounted she began to scream. It was a different kind of hurting, and in a sense she knew the end of her labor had arrived. Her body wanted to push the child out of her belly of its own accord.

"No," Alexia coached. "Not so fast, Lisette. Slow it down. Don't push so hard. I can see a patch of black hair."

Michel got up from the rocking chair to see for himself and promptly fainted.

Anna stepped over the Marquis, taking the rocking chair for herself as the fits of hysteria continued. She couldn't help the Countess. All the worry and fear of the past six months were unraveled in the golden liquid of the brandy. Tears washed down her face as she joyfully watched Lisette's child being born.

Alexia's eyes were round with the wonder of it.

As the final cramp came, Jean and Alexia urged her to push in a slow rhythm, allowing her body to bring the child into the world.

"You've got to push now," Jean urged.

"I can't." Lisette was too weak to give the baby one final boost. She struggled to stay awake. The screams burned her throat and sent her into a black void where she couldn't feel the pain.

"Slap her," Alexia commanded.

"I can't hit her," Jean yelled in return.

"Do you want her to live?"

Jean lightly slapped Lisette's beautiful face.

"Damn it, Jean. Do it right."

He hit her again, this time a little harder.

"You wretched excuse for a father."

This time the slap was hard, bringing Lisette to consciousness. Jean's hand was shaking as he clenched her fingers over his. "Stay with me, love."

Anna finally recovered from her hysteria and joined the Countess.

Alexia squealed in delight as the newest member of the Jolbert family was delivered into her hands. "It's a son!" She started to cry at the sight of the perfect little male body in the palm of her hands. "He's so tiny."

"I wonder what he weighs," Jean spoke up. He was mystified by the small child Alexia held out to him. "He looks terrible. Do all children have that bright red skin? Where did the blood come from?"

"I had to make a small incision to keep your intended from tearing apart. I'll bet he weighs eight pounds or better." Alexia laid him down and briskly rubbed him with a warmed sheet, until he finally responded with a loud wail.

Lisette was too exhausted to stay awake. The moment she completed the birth, she fell into a deep sleep.

"She needs quiet now, Jean."

The Baron laid Lisette back against the pillows. Before parting, he kissed her pale lips, silently thanking her for the beautiful gift. Alexia passed the child to Anna, who bathed and dressed the infant.

Simon arrived too late. The child had already been born, and the surgeon Simon brought was sent on his way before Alexia knew he was there and could stop him from leaving.

Anna presented the baby to the Baron. Jean was nervous about holding his son until Anna showed him how to cradle the child in his arms. He liked the feel of holding something so delicate and precious.

Jean's dark hair fell over his forehead as he viewed the magnificent creation of a miniature human being. All his fingers and toes were accounted for, and beneath dark lashes were eyes as blue as the coral he had found in the sea.

"He's beautiful, like his mother."

"And handsome like his father," Anna noted.

"His hands are too small." The proud father beamed. "But I suppose I can't expect him to hold a rapier until he's at least a few months old."

"Why don't you show him to your men?" Alexia wanted to get the strutting papa out of the room to make Lisette comfortable.

Anna draped a clean sheet over Lisette while the men came in and dragged the Marquis out of the room. With Jean out of the way, they exchanged worried glances. Lisette had lost a lot of blood, and they didn't know where it was coming from.

"Do you think we should have told him about this?" Anna questioned.

"He's happy; let's not spoil it for him. Get some warm blankets for Lisette and we'll see what we can do to stop the bleeding."

Together, they stripped the bed and replaced the birthing sheets with clean bedding. Anna held the blankets to the fireplace to warm them, and Alexia worked for hours to stop the flow coming from Lisette. The Duchess was a sickly white, and they couldn't hide what was happening from Jean any longer.

Alexia found the Baron in the dining room at Castle Meret. Earl, Baron, and Marquis were all sitting at the table soberly considering the pros and cons of leaving France versus staying and riding out the revolution.

"How soon can we move her?" Jean had surrendered his son back into Anna's care. "I want to leave for Spain within the week."

"You want her to travel that soon?" Alexia was apprehensive about telling him the truth about Lisette's condition.

The Earl spoke up. "Darias has a family that went to the King and is screaming a murder has been committed. They are trying to incite a riot to hang my son. He must leave the country."

"How did they find out so soon?" Alexia was shocked. She had hoped all would be well for Jean now that he had been reunited with his love. A daring escape was the last thing Lisette needed.

The Earl explained. "The castle cook was sending word to the family. When no message was sent, they investigated to find the Baron's troop had arrived and Darias was dead. My son has nothing to hide. It was an honorable duel with plenty of witnesses. What worries me is that Darias's family might be able to raise a mob and come looking for him."

"We can't fend off the entire village." Jean was thoughtful. "While we were on horseback it was an easy task to elude them. Now, with a newborn child and a convalescing woman to care for, we can't outride them."

"You can't move Lady Lisette for at least three days." Alexia swallowed against a tight throat. Jean's gaze reflected his horror. "She is still bleeding in an unnatural way, and I don't know how to stop it. Every time we move her, it gets worse. You must give her time to recover."

The Earl leaned over to whisper to the Marquis. "Send someone for a priest immediately. I know that no matter what happens, my son wants to legally wed Lisette."

"I have an idea that might work," the Marquis said out loud to all present. "How about using the present I gave Lisette to get you both out of France?"

Simon agreed. "I can meet you on the coast. If you can maneuver the balloon to the port, I'll have my ships ready and waiting."

"In the Montgolfier!" Alexia clapped her hands

with joy. "It won't jostle her around the way a horse
or carriage would."

"I'm not going to kill us all in that contraption."
Jean glowered.

"You don't have any choice," Alexia proclaimed.

The Marquis rose from his chair to complete his
tasks. "I'll have the balloon here by tomorrow
night, and have it ready to go by the following day.
The hussars can keep the hounds at bay until
then."

The Baron didn't think it was a good plan. He
wasn't going to get into that death trap and kill his
heir or his lovely lady. Knowing it was futile to argue with them, he sighed heavily and threw up his
hands in defeat. He had two days to think of some
other way to get Lisette out of France without risking her life.

When he came to her bedside, Jean saw why
Alexia was so concerned. Lisette's face was a
transluscent white that showed the blue veins in
her face. Her auburn hair was brushed out and
gleaming in the firelight. Outside their room, it
was nearly dawn. They had spent the night rejoicing while she fought for her life.

He pulled up a wooden chair and took her hand
in his. He wouldn't leave her bedside until she was
well again.

"I love you, Lisette." He couldn't bear to live if
she left him again. Jean remembered the beautiful
young woman who raced him en route to Paris, and
the sensual woman who seduced him on a riverbank.

"She's got to live for all of us. What would we do
without her?"

Chapter Thirty-five

Lisette was cradled in the Baron's arms. He walked out of Castle Meret to the courtyard, and she lifted her hand to shade her eyes from the brilliant spring sun. Inside the quadrangle court was her balloon. She inhaled swiftly at the sight of the envelope bobbing up so high that it towered over the stone walls. Michel had instructed the seamstress who stitched the canvas together to incorporate the combined colors of the Jolbert red and gold with the de Meret white. On a golden background was a ruby fleury cross with a white dove set against the conjunction of the cross.

"It's marvelous." She sighed.

"You're feeling all right? Are you hungry yet?" Jean inched his way down the stairs, afraid that he would jostle the precious bundle of his woman and child.

"Has anyone ever told you that you're crazy?" Lisette teased him. For three days he had remained at her side, and the gaunt, tired lines around his eyes proved her accusation that he was too exhausted to carry her. Michel had offered his services, but Jean turned down the assistance.

The Earl of Normandy approached and held out a hand to touch his grandson's downy-soft cheek. "Have we decided on the name yet?"

"Jean-Michel Jolbert," Lisette answered proudly. "He is named after his handsome father and my dearest friend."

"My son will inherit more titles than he will know what to do with," Jean growled. He was still touchy on the subject of addressing his heir with the title of Your Grace.

"Only if I agree to marry you." Lisette looked up to his gray eyes and found his loving gaze on her again. "Thank you for my life," she whispered. "If you hadn't been there . . ." Tears filled her eyes. She was still feeling the moody changes in her body.

"Don't cry, sweetheart," Jean soothed. He bent his head and brushed his lips against hers. "I knew this would tire you out too much. We'll just have to wait and hold our position until you're well again."

"We can't wait any longer," the Earl cautioned. "You'll have to take her away from here as soon as the balloon is ready. Simon left for the port before the first light, and he'll be waiting for you off the coast. He took Anna with him to prepare your cabin on the ship. Michel made all the final arrangements with your pilot. It's time for you to leave."

Jean felt her stiffen in his arms. She still loved her country, even though she knew revolution would change her beloved France.

"I want you to do something for me, Monsieur Jolbert."

"By your leave, it would be good of you to call me Jules."

Lisette adored her soon-to-be father-in-law. "Jules, will you open the gates after we leave and ask the peasants to take Meret? Tell them I want them to have the castle, the grounds, oh, everything that made this my home. I'll never be back." Her voice trailed off as she silently said *adieu* to her life in France. "Tell them to guard their home."

"I'll do as you ask." Jules Jolbert, the Earl of Normandy, was proud of his soon-to-be daughter-in-law.

Lisette dabbed at the tears in her eyes. "It is still an *honor* to be French."

"We can't wait any longer for the priest to arrive." Jean slowly walked to the balloon.

"I didn't agree to become your wife yet," Lisette clarified for him.

He hadn't thought she was serious when she said those words a few minutes ago, but he now gave them his full attention. "What do you mean, you didn't agree?"

"You didn't ask."

"Should I?"

"Only if you want me for your bride."

"All right. Marry me, Lisette."

"Non, mon cher."

Jean was getting worried. "Why not?"

They reached the gondola and he gently hefted her over the side of the basket.

"Aren't you coming with us?" Lisette was prepared for this confrontation. Michel had warned her this would happen.

"I'll meet you at the port, Lisette."

"Then you give me no alternative. If you won't come with me, then I refuse to marry you."

"Be reasonable, Lisette."

"I have been reasonable. It's you that have been pigheaded. Get in, or I'll say *au revoir* now."

"You aren't joking, are you?"

"I tell you as surely as I just brought your son into the world that I won't marry you if you don't come with me."

A soft, mewing sound came from their son. He was waking and would be hungry. Lisette made herself comfortable on the floor of the gondola. There wasn't enough room to lie down.

How she wished she could be the pilot. They had
found a man who had managed to make several
successful flights and had every assurance that
they would make it to the port.

The winds were right, the time of day perfect. It
was time to depart. The basket bounced as Jean-
Charles Jolbert was added to the passenger list.

"Are you satisfied?" Jean pulled her to her feet
and wrapped his arms around her and his son.

From the battlements, Michel saluted her. Alexia was beside the Marquis, and Lisette was curious
if the Countess had ever gotten Michel's attention;
Alexia was infatuated with him. That was as clear
to her as was Anna's mad passion for Simon.

Lisette couldn't blame Alexia for what she had
done. If she had been in the same situation, she
might have been the one to drop the letter into the
fire. After she realized why Jean was so protective
of Alexia, she no longer worried that she had a rival in her stepdaughter. But it was strange to consider Alexia her daughter when the Countess was
almost as old as she.

Lisette knew Michel wouldn't come with them.
It was difficult to say good-bye to him when she
wasn't sure if they'd ever meet again. She worried
for his safety in a country torn apart by civil war.

"What will happen to them?"

Jean hugged her close to him. "They will stay
and continue what we started in working for a democracy."

She blew Michel a kiss, thankful he had been her
friend and confidant. Jean watched the exchange
between them, and a surge of jealousy went
through his senses. "Do you think you'll miss Michel?"

"Of course I will. But then, so will you. He was
always protecting you, my love. Never once would
he allow me to stop believing in you, even though

it was painful for him to see what was happening
between us."

There were six ropes holding the balloon down.
The moment the gondola left the ground, her stomach felt as if it had butterflies dancing around inside it. The ropes guided them past the walls, and
when they were high enough the balloon was released and they drifted off into the sky. They were
out of range of gunfire before the peasants knew
they had escaped.

Lisette leaned on the wicker railing with one
arm bracing herself against the dipping of the basket and the other holding her newborn son.

"Isn't it lovely!" She waved to the people who remained at the castle.

Jean didn't think so. He didn't want to look
down. In fact, if he did notice that they were now
six stories off the ground, he would probably faint.

"I want to know the truth, Jean. Are you guilty
of treason?" Lisette felt that she had waited a lifetime to ask that question.

"Will it make a difference if I am?"

"I want to know."

"Michel, Alexia, and I are all guilty. We could be
executed for the crimes we have committed against
the monarchy."

"You will explain the definition of 'crimes' when
we reach Spain. For now, believe I am certain you
would be forgiven by a power greater than the
King."

She had a sublime glow about her since the birth
of their son. Lisette was no longer a young child-
bride, but a woman who loved him deeply. It took
a moment of self-searching for Jean to admit how
much he needed her beside him. The long winter
had passed, and through a miracle they were together again—not just Jean and Lisette, but a son,

too. He was a little jealous of the tiny creature in her arms who snuggled so close to her.

A swift spring breeze picked up the strands of her hair and tossed them into a wickedly wanton halo about her head. Jean studied the pout of her mouth as they drifted away from her home. When she turned to him, her gaze filled him with love and a funny sort of happiness. He felt drunk on her attention, and wanted to bask in her loving arms again.

"I love you, Lisette."

She reached up and touched a hand to his cheek. His arms steadied her against the rocking of the wind. "I never stopping caring about you."

"I didn't deserve your loyalty."

Lisette turned with her back to him to watch the world below drift by. Jean was so close to her that she could feel his warm breath on her ear, and the contour of his body as he steadied her.

"I'll marry you on two conditions."

"Which are?" He kissed the top of her head and nuzzled her earlobe. It didn't matter what she asked for, because he could deny her nothing now.

"I want to be able to pilot my own balloon when I've recovered."

"Granted, as long as you stay within the limits of the island."

Lisette grinned. "The second demand is a proper wedding."

"How proper?"

"With all the trimmings. I want to be in a church, not a courtyard."

"So that's why the priest never arrived." Jean had suspected there was something more to this than divine intervention.

"I told your father you had to marry me properly, if you were going to at all."

"I'll give you the biggest wedding in the world,

if that's what you want from me. We'll invite at least a thousand guests." He was astounded at her requests and began to see how upset she had been when she first arrived at his château. "It really does mean something to you, doesn't it, Lisette?"

"It means many things to me, Jean. When you first kidnapped me, my dreams were all that I had. Now I want them to come true."

Jean stroked the downy head of his son. "You've given me everything I have ever wanted, Lisette. Do you still believe in the monarchy?" It was a question that had bothered him from the beginning.

Lisette raised her face to the wind. "No man has the right to oppress another because of his birthright. If you believe democracy will govern our country in a fair and just manner, then I give you my support. I welcome the new ways, but don't ever expect me to forget the old."

Their pilot, who had remained silent during the flight, spoke up in agreement. "Someday France will be free."

She felt released from all her commitments to the throne. "I think I shall plant a garden of my own that will be filled with white lilies."

Thinking about the last year of her life brought new tears to her eyes. Paul should have been with them. The burly captain would always be a part of her memories of France.

Jean sensed the direction of her thoughts. "Paul would have been very happy for us, Lisette. He saved this for you." Jean took the ring out of his pocket and slipped it back on her finger. "He will always be alive in our hearts."

"I miss him, and I think he would be proud of your son."

"When shall we set our wedding date?" Jean enclosed her in his arms. He would never leave her side again, not even for a day.

"Perhaps when we reach Spain."

"What do you mean, perhaps?"

"I think that I like being your lover, and I want you to be grateful to have me for a while."

"You wicked wench," he reprimanded lovingly. "It isn't going to be easy to resist me."

"You are charming. But you can be difficult."

"You'll get used to me. We did make a beautiful child."

"Will you get tired of being with me and want to leave me behind?"

"Where I go, so shall you."

"Promise?"

"My oath as a gentleman." The winds carried the balloon toward the coast and the journey that would take them to a new life. She saw only the love in his eyes as he steadfastly gazed into hers.

The Baron Jolbert never looked down.

Authors of
  exceptional promise

Historical novels
  of superior quality!

MIDNIGHT'S LADY   Sandra Langford
75018-X/$3.50US/$4.50Can

SAVAGE SURRENDER   Lindsey Hanks
75021-X/$3.50US/$4.50Can

THE HIDDEN HEART   Laura Kinsale
75008-3/$3.50US/$4.50Can

BRIANNA   Linda Lang Bartell
75096-1/$3.50US/$4.50Can

DESIRE AND SURRENDER   Katherine Sutcliffe
75067-8/$3.75US/$4.95Can

TENDER FORTUNE   Judith E. French
75034-1/$3.75US/$4.95Can

This is the special design logo
that will call your attention
to Avon authors who
show exceptional
promise in

THE AVON ROMANCE

the romance
area. Each
month a new novel
will be featured

SURRENDER THE HEART Jean Nash   89622-2/$2.95 US/$3.75 Can
Set in New York and Paris at the beginning of the twentieth century, beautiful
fashion designer Adrian Marlowe is threatened by bankruptcy and must turn
to the darkly handsome "Prince of Wall Street" for help.

Other Avon Romances by Jean Nash:
> FOREVER, MY LOVE   84780-9/$2.95

RIBBONS OF SILVER Katherine Myers   89602-8/$2.95 US/$3.75 Can
Kenna, a defiant young Scottish beauty, is married by proxy to a wealthy
American and is drawn into a plot of danger, jealousy and passion when the
stranger she married captures her heart.

PASSION'S TORMENT Virginia Pade   89681-8/$2.95 US/$3.75 Can
In order to escape prosecution for a crime she didn't commit, a young English
beauty deceives an American sea captain into marriage—only to find his
tormented past has made him vow never to love again.

Other Avon Romances by Virginia Pade:
> WHEN LOVE REMAINS   82610-0/$2.95

Buy these books at your local bookstore or use this coupon for ordering:
....
Avon Books, Dept BP, Box 767, Rte 2, Dresden, TN 38225
Please send me the book(s) I have checked above. I am enclosing $_____
(please add $1.00 to cover postage and handling for each book ordered to a maximum of
three dollars). *Send check or money order*—no cash or C.O.D.'s please. Prices and numbers
are subject to change without notice. Please allow six to eight weeks for delivery.

Name _____

Address _____

City _____ State/Zip _____

Avon Rom 8/86

Each month enjoy the best...

THE AVON ROMANCE

*in exceptional authors and
unforgettable novels!*

THE WILD ROSE René J. Garrod
89784-9/$3.50US/$4.50 Can
Alone amid the ruthlessness of the California Gold
Rush, a plucky English beauty is powerless to resist the
one love she dares not take.

HEART OF THE STORM Jillian Hunter
89956-6/$3.50US/$4.50 Can
This tempestuous saga charts the course of two lovers
who are forced to marry, but are consumed with conflict-
ing desires.

SHADOW OF DESIRE Fela Dawson Scott
89981-7/$3.50US/$4.50 Can
A beautiful renegade—driven by vengeance—vowed to
trust no man...until she met the one nobleman that
could tame her defiant heart.